Book 3:
The Sign of the Sengara

THE KINGBLADE CHRONICLES

Saga 1:
Tarnadins of the Elder Forest

Book 3:
The Sign of the Sengara

by Jarrett Skaddisson

Other Books by Jarrett Skaddisson:

The Kingblade Chronicles

Saga 1: Tarnadins of the Elder Forest
Book 1: Call of the Danna
Book 2: The Road to Anganor

This Work Is Dedicated
to
my dear son,
Fritz,
who was born while this book was being written,
and who has been and continues to be
an immeasurable blessing in my life

ACKNOWLEDGEMENTS

Here I wish to heartily thank those who have helped bring this book from my head to your hands with their various skills and talents: Max Garrison for editing and consulting, Ferdinand D. Ladera for cover art, Blaine Morehead for font and cover design, Cornelia Yoder for maps, Charlie Haas (CharlieHaas-Artwork.com) for the Questmongers symbol art and character and concept art for thekingbladechronicles.com, Dawn Allman for text layout and design, Shang Tea for countless cups of refreshing and inspirational tea and all my family and friends for inspiration and encouragement.

Table of Contents

Appendices

Maps

What Came Before

A Summary of Saga 1: *Book 1 – Call of the Danna*

ne fair spring evening in the village of Siloa, an unremarkable little hamlet in the hinterlands of the Kingdom of Velaris, nineteen-year-old Aradis Kingblade, a Manfellow, went to the village tavern to meet his dear friend, Girion Ringmark. There he encountered a mysterious stranger, who bade him follow him into nearby Rimwold Forest. Once they reached the woods, the stranger declared himself to be Nagello, one of the Hadathi, powerful beings of a realm known as the Haedra. To prove his identity, he unveiled his true, blindingly majestic form.

Nagello then informed Aradis that he had been chosen by a Haedran ruler, the Danna, also known as Telyon, to accomplish two great tasks. The first was to go to the distant Kingdom of Argonis and, with the aid of its monarch, King Thornoak, reunite the kingdom, which had become divided by many bitter quarrels. The second task was to go to Blackbough Woods, several hundred miles west of Argonis, and defeat the Witch Ravinia, who sought to destroy Thornoak and his kingdom.

Much to Aradis' dismay, Nagello insisted that he depart that very night for the port of Tarwyn, forbidding him to return until his mission was completed. He only granted him leave to bid his sorely ailing father, Darion, farewell. His mother, brother and sister were already asleep, and he was advised not to waken them. However, much to the lad's delight, Nagello also revealed that his friend Girion would be going with him on his adventure.

When Aradis arrived home, his father disclosed that he had actually met Nagello many years before and that the Hadathi had told him he would someday return to send his firstborn son upon a grand quest. After Aradis received his father's old sword, Brightbeam, he went to Girion's house and found his friend waiting outside, for Nagello had already apprised him of the matter. The two lads then set off across the Plains of Agleri, heading eastward to Tarwyn to get aboard a ship by the time Nagello had stipulated—the fourth twilight from that night.

Only a short distance from Girion's home, the two Siloans encountered a group of Elven riders, a dispatch of the Sardolia, the standing army of Velaris. Lying hidden in a wheat field, they overheard the dispatch's leader, Captain Fragezi, set forth a plot to kidnap young maidens of Siloa and, in the event of resistance, slay the villagers and burn Siloa to the ground.

Unfortunately, the lads' presence was discovered, and they were forced to flee eastward through the night. Thus they were unable to learn what transpired in Siloa. Over the next few days, with the help of a traveling healer named Harlin Halehand and a farming family, the Torfields, they made their way to Tarwyn, arriving just in time to catch their ship to a distant group of islands called the Fontskals. In those rocky isles they had been ordered by Nagello to seek out a sea captain named Felding Starwash, who would take them on to the port of Gorondil, from which they could reach Argonis.

After several weeks at sea, they came to the Fontskals. There, narrowly escaping a brawl with some drunk, angry sailors at a run-down inn, they met an old woman who offered to take them to Felding. This fellow, they soon found out, was actually her son, an infamous, daring smuggler and something of an oddball. Aradis and Girion then set sail with Felding and his first mate, Jiffaloo Timtale. Some days later, after barely surviving a battle with a sea monster known as an akwursa, they came to Gorondil, which was heavily guarded by Dwarves in the employ of the cruel Witch, Ravinia.

Disguised as Druids and carrying out an elaborate plan that Felding had concocted, Aradis, Girion and the captain made it only partway through the city before they were found out by the Dwarves. Following a harrowing rooftop chase, Captain Felding escaped back to his ship, and the Siloans managed to flee inland on horses stolen from the Gorondil stables across a plains region known as the Farren, which was strewn with large, bizarre rock formations.

For several days, Aradis and Girion were tracked by Druids from Gorondil all the way to the edge of a perilous place called Moonhound Moor. The Druids did not follow them on to the moor, but the lads were nearly caught and devoured by the moor's namesake, the dreaded moonhounds. In fact, they reached the safety of the nearly impenetrable undergrowth of a dark and forbidding wood named Thornberry Thicket with only moments to spare. As they struggled through the thicket toward Argonis, they began to hallucinate and fell unconscious, overcome by the poison of the thicket's thorns.

They awoke to find themselves in a wooden cage in the treetops of an enchanted forest clad in autumn foliage and learned they had been rescued by a people called the Fall-Elves. An Elf named Tandarron, along with a company of soldiers, escorted the Menfolk to the town of Fallbury to speak with Lodgemaster Goldquiver, the leader of the Fall-Elves. Goldquiver thought very little of the Siloans and their quest, but he agreed to let them go on into Argonis via the Briar Gate, which lay on the western edge of his lands. Captain Tandarron escorted the lads to the Briar Gate, and there the lads bade him farewell as they entered the kingdom they had come so far to save.

A Summary of Saga 1: *Book 2 – The Road to Anganor*

Aradis Kingblade and Girion Ringmark were traveling through the forests near the eastern border of Argonis, seeking to make their way to Anganor, from which they could set out to secure King Thornoak's aid in completing their quests of reuniting Argonis and defeating the Witch, Ravinia.

The lads, caught in a heavy thunderstorm, were forced to seek refuge on a wooded hilltop. However, in their haste to reach shelter, they fell into a crack in the ground and slid down a steep passage, landing in a subterranean lake. On the lake's shore, the Siloans encountered a Leprechaun named Rennig O'Balahan. Rennig informed the Siloans that they had fallen into the Emerald Run, a network of tunnels and caverns that was the primary residence of the Leprechauns of Argonis. He brought them up to a grotto, into a great celebration, complete with feasting, dancing and music, and introduced them to Shillelagh McDasher, the Leprechauns' leader, to see what he would have done with them. Shillelagh permitted the Menfolk to partake in the merriment, and they eventually passed out from exhaustion.

The next day, Aradis and Girion had an audience with Shillelagh and told him of their quest. He desired to help them and told them that the best way to reunify the kingdom was to persuade Thornoak to summon the Verdinnion, the council of the kingdom's leaders. However, as Shillelagh told the Menfolk, Thornoak was residing in a place called Paanu Assagwa and could not be accessed by anyone except his daughter, Princess Langwana. And in order to speak to her, the lads would likely first need to speak to Fergus O'Brannadon, the head of an organization of special agents in Thornoak's service known as the Questmongers, which was based in Anganor. Furthermore, if they wanted to ensure the Verdinnion would back them, they would need to gain support from more of its members, particularly Masterfarmer Mackle of the Wood-Gnomes and Boss Gronk of the Ogres.

After Shillelagh provided the Siloans a tour of the Emerald Run, as well as several meals and accommodation for the night, he sent them on their way. The Siloans journeyed southward toward the Wood-Gnomes' land and stumbled across an abandoned cabin, where they found a strange stone with swirling smoke inside, which they decided to take with them.

The lads slept in the cabin. However, during the night, they were awakened by distant screaming. They went to investigate and found a Leprechaun being tortured by a Druid and several Menfolk bandits. While eavesdropping, they learned that the Druid was called the Ravenstaff and that he worked for Ravinia, functioning as the secret leader of all the brigands that were terrorizing Argonis. Aradis sought to rescue the Leprechaun but was captured and interrogated by the Druid. Through Girion's intervention, both Aradis and the Leprechaun escaped, but the latter was killed by a blast of fire from the Druid's staff as he was running away. The Druid then set the forest on fire with his dark magic.

Aradis and Girion barely escaped from the fire, the Druid and his cohorts, and then hid themselves in a hollow log. The next day, they continued their southward journey and found a grassy lawn, adjacent to a pond, where they intended to spend the night. As evening drew on, beautiful lights appeared over the pond, and there was wondrous music in the air. But the music ceased and the lights went out at the approach of two flying Blackwing spies, Dolga and Charka, who stopped to rest on the greensward. From the cover of the woods, the Menfolk discovered that these Blackwings had killed the Fall-Elf Tandarron and had learned that Aradis and Girion had entered Argonis. The Blackwings also spoke of Ravinia's plan to use some additional forces from the south to attack Argonis at the end of the following month. Then they flew off, continuing their journey to bring word of these things to Ravinia.

The next morning, Aradis and Girion reached some fields and found a Wood-Gnome working there. They soon learned that he was Masterfarmer Mackle, of whom Shillelagh had spoken. Mackle agreed to give the lads food and lodging for the night in his cottage in the village of Harnabrig if they helped him work in the fields. They took him up on this deal, and that afternoon, back at his cottage, they explained their mission to him. He was sympathetic to their cause, but feared it was doomed to fail.

That night, the Siloans had dinner with the Wood-Gnome family. Due to a bitter quarrel between Mackle and one of his sons, Mackle left the cottage in anger, and his wife Lanny explained why he was so upset. The Wood-Gnomes had particularly drawn Ravinia's wrath by inflicting heavy losses on some of her forces in the Stony Wilds. As a result, she had commissioned the evil Dwarf, Bodvassar, to teach them a lesson. This he had done by coming to Harnabrig and beheading a number of the Wood-Gnomes' children, including two of Mackle's own. Subsequent retaliation by the Wood-Gnomes escalated Ravinia's vendetta, and she had cursed the Southern Meads, the Wood-Gnomes' farmland, so that it now only produced a crop called gren, which was almost unbearably disgusting. However, the Wood-Gnomes had taken an oath to eat gren until they had their revenge on Ravinia.

Aradis couldn't sleep that night, so, before dawn, he went outside, where he found Mackle sitting outside the cottage. Mackle had had time to think over what the Siloans had told him and had decided that Aradis and Girion just might succeed in their quest after all.

When morning came, the Menfolk continued their journey toward Anganor. Shortly after they crossed the Teraska River, they were attacked by two bandits. Aradis fought them off, but many more pursued the Siloans through the forest. However, the bandits were scattered by the approach of a huge creature known as a ketchiwah, which was being chased by a Shore-Elf named Peleus Chula. The Shore-Elf, who was rather batty, gave the lads a parchment with a symbol he said they could show to the Questmongers to gain their aid. He then wandered off into the forest.

The Siloans soon reached the Pastures of Seruga, and Girion managed to wrangle a ride to the town of Longarnu, where Boss Gronk lived, from a young Ogre fellow named Surg who was mounted on a creature called a jassa. When they came to Longarnu, they found Gronk in a rather foul mood. Aradis unwisely insulted him, and the infuriated Ogre challenged the lad to single combat on a rickety wooden structure, known as the Tower of Tangarosh, in the midst of a lake. Gronk would only agree to grant the Siloans an audience if Aradis won the contest.

After an intense battle, Gronk fell off the tower into the lake but survived. Aradis, though knocked unconscious, had not fallen and was thus declared the winner. In Gronk's hut, the Siloans told the Ogre of what they were seeking to accomplish, and, as he was quite impressed by Aradis' success in the battle on the tower, he offered them his support if the Verdinnion convened.

That evening, the Ogres of Longarnu were hosting a salnagok, a celebration with bonfires and feasting, and the Siloans were invited. While there, they noticed Gronk talking to an Ingan messenger. They learned from the Ogre that the messenger had come to spread the word that Thornoak would be addressing his people in Anganor the following morning. The lads set out that very evening to complete the remainder of their journey, elated that the next day they might get an opportunity to speak with Thornoak about their quest.

The Way of the Tarnadin is a road of woes,
A path that is harrowed by grievous foes;
E'er it is troubled by darkest night,
Yet he who would tread it must put fear to flight.

For the Tarnadin's task is clear and plain:
He must battle darkness for others' gain.
Indeed, for himself he must have no regard,
But passing through fire, he will emerge uncharred.
He takes up the cause of those who are weak,
Though he himself be the meekest of the meek.

When the powers of shadow upon flesh bear down,
And the cries of all mortals in anguish are drowned,
The Tarnadin stands in their stead to fight
As a bearer of hope, a bearer of light.

When the strength of the strong has at last come to naught,
It is clear that a Tarnadin must then be sought.
Indeed, all are in need of the Tarnadin.

The Way of the Tarnadin from mercy proceeds,
Then on through shadow and flame it leads,
Yet Death's Blade will be shattered and night be no more;
And the Tarnadin will stand in glory e'ermore.

Orona

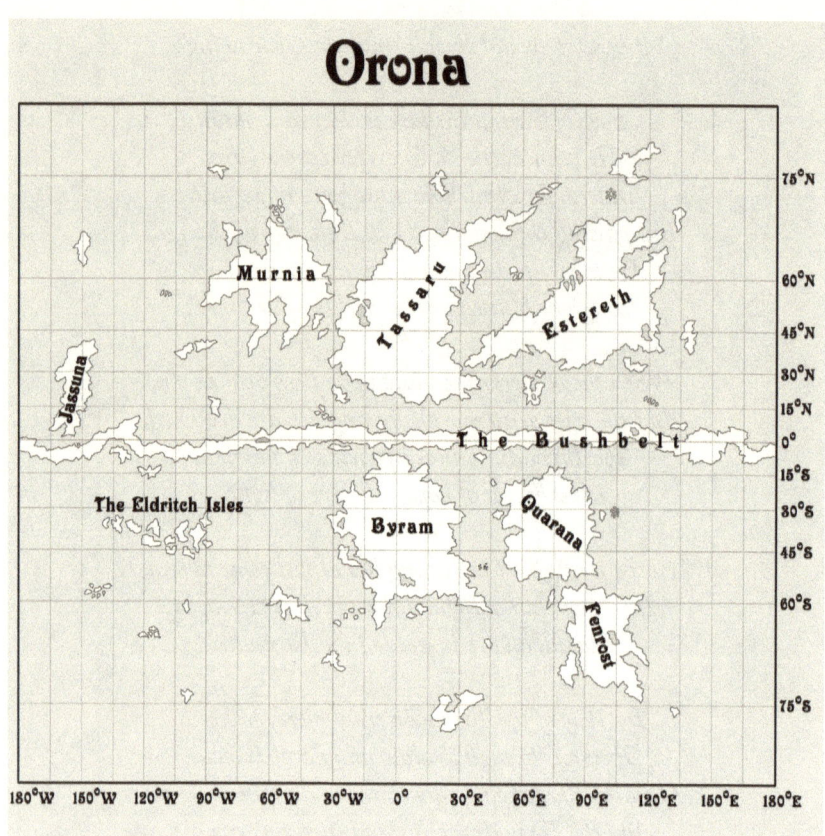

CHAPTER ONE

The Awakening of Anganor

n Mentasqua, the verdant heartland of the Kingdom of Argonis, a cool, cloudless night had turned into a gray, drizzly dawn. Within about an hour's time, the forests had transformed from dim caverns lit only by silver starlight into pale emerald labyrinths, as melancholy, brooding clouds blanketed the wide expanse of the heavens, obscuring the warmth and light that otherwise might have graced the land..

Driven on by the prospect of securing an audience with King Thornoak in Anganor, Aradis and Girion had traveled west by northwest from the Ogric settlement of Longarnu all through the night, all the while doing their best to ignore their bodies' repeated insistences for respite. Both of them had been on the move virtually the entire time since they had left Mackle's cottage in Harnabrig. Aradis, of course, had slept for several hours in the hammock in Gronk's hut, but Girion hadn't slept at all, and since the previous morning, they had traversed more than forty miles. This alone would customarily be more than enough to exhaust them, but on top of this, they had had to flee from a band of brigands, and Aradis had been obliged to battle Gronk on the Tower of Tangarosh. Yet Thornoak was so near, they could not tarry now, although each of them rather wished he had taken Gronk up on his kind offer to provide them with jassa as mounts. The kendarill they had first sighted near Paggawan Rise had flitted about some distance ahead of them much of the night, but it had departed a short while before dawn. While it remained as their guide, they felt invigorated, but now their weariness was catching up with them.

After a few minutes more of traveling through the dripping forest, the lads passed through what seemed almost to be a natural archway formed by the boughs of two large, strange trees. Just beyond it, they stopped

3

simultaneously and looked at what lay before them with both excitement and satisfaction.

"There it is." Girion smiled, tossing back his hood. (They had wrapped themselves in their cloaks when it began to rain.) "Anganor."

"And, just like when we entered Argonis itself, I can hardly believe we're both still alive and looking at the place with our very own eyes," Aradis delightedly declared, reflecting for a moment on all they had come through to reach it. "It's hard to fathom that we're actually here now, as we've been trying to get to Anganor for such a long time."

"All our travail, at least in that regard, is now ended," Girion said. "For here we are at last. So let's go find Thornoak and get on with this business, eh?"

And so the lads, freshly vitalized, began marching off down the road toward the city. Between the forest and Anganor, there was a tract of open land with high grasses that was crisscrossed by a network of pathways that appeared out of the surrounding woodlands.

From the spot where the path exited the forest, which was to the east and a bit south of Anganor, a considerable portion of the city was visible, for the road actually descended down a shallow slope to get to the city gate. Anganor stretched around two miles from its southern end to its northern boundary, and it was a little less than that from its eastern edge to its western border. The city, from what they could see, was guarded by a high stone wall, at least on the south and the east and, it seemed, the west. To the north there was a narrow river, and just beyond it stood mighty Malinoc Hill. The river split at the hill's western end and then converged again at its eastern foot, so that the hill itself was actually an island, one which could only be reached by a bridge that had been fashioned out of one of Strongbranch's enormous roots that ran south toward the city. The imposing, rounded rise was around four hundred feet in height, and atop its summit stood the towering Strongbranch Citadel, which shot up into the sky like some primeval remnant of a gargantuan forest. The citadel was, in fact, a single, massive tree with a trunk over four hundred feet in diameter at its base and a height that was more than thrice that. It looked positively unnatural, almost unreal in truth, and the lads' sheer wonder only increased as they continued to glance up at it.

Inside Anganor's walls, there were a number of structures, many of which were wooden, timber-framed buildings of several stories, such as could be found in many parts of Orona. But there were also a great many strangely shaped trees that looked to be serving as some kind of habitations. Also, high, green hedges appeared to divide the city into different sections. In the middle of Anganor, there was a tall, spreading tree that seemed to be the focal point of some sort of plaza. However, the city was still a way off, and the visibility wasn't the best, what with the weather and all, so the lads' curiosity was only piqued, not satiated, regarding these features. Thus, they were all the more eager to see the city's interior up close.

Before too long, the Menfolk noticed an Ingan, a lone Treefellow, plodding along a dirt track that connected with the one they were on. He had two large sacks, one resting on each of his shoulders, and his expression was markedly sullen. The Ingan was wearing no garments, save a sort of barkcloth kilt that had some simple geometric patterns sewn into it.

Neither of the lads had properly seen an Ingan before, except the one whose silhouette they had sighted by the bonfire at the Ogres' celebration the previous night, and so they regarded this one with great fascination. His skin was remarkably bark-like, but looked to be much suppler than tree bark, and his face had clearly distinguishable eyes, ears, a mouth and a nose. His head was crowned not with hair but with thin sticks that bristled when he walked and with what looked very much like stringy, dark green moss that hung down to his shoulders from the back of his head; the same mossy stuff served for his eyebrows. He had a sort of belly button in his broad bark breast, and his underlying musculature was evident throughout his body, faintly outlined on his bark skin, just as it would be in other Narthanna, other kinds of Barada. Also, like other Barada, his arms and legs divided from his torso, and he had a well-defined neck. His hands, fingers, feet and toes were not unlike those of Menfolk, except that his digits were somewhat twiggish, though not brittle, and his hands and feet were not quite as shapely as their Mannish counterparts.

When the Menfolk came to the spot where the Ingan's path intersected their own, they paused until he arrived, and Girion cordially called out, "Bright Marda, good sir!"

The Ingan looked over at them irritably. He was definitely not in a bright-Marda sort of mood this morning. "Hm," he muttered, then turned toward the city.

Aradis' eyes narrowed in considerable annoyance, as he stared at the back of the departing Ingan. Meanwhile, Girion started to jog after him, inquiring, "Are you going to Anganor?"

"No, I'm going to the Luminous Meridian," the Ingan sarcastically returned. "Where does it look like I'm going?"

Still, Girion would not be dissuaded from his pursuit of amiability. Panting slightly, he ran up alongside the Ingan and cheerfully declared, "I'm Girion Ringmark. And whom do I have the pleasure of addressing?"

The Ingan stopped and looked over at the smiling Manfellow, as he sighed and grudgingly said, "Kaslannaquet. Now what do you want, Manfellow? You want me to wish you a bright Marda? Very well, then. Bright Marda." And with that, he continued trudging on toward the city.

"Oh, I don't need a bright Marda or anything like that," Girion assured, as he tried to keep pace with the Ingan, who was over seven feet tall and, consequently, had a rather long stride. "My friend Aradis and I were just wondering if you knew where King Thornoak was going to be speaking this morning and if you could give us directions to get there."

Aradis, who was walking along at a somewhat slower pace behind them, shook his head, disgruntled at what he perceived to be the futility of Girion's efforts with this ill-tempered Ingan.

"Ha," Kaslannaquet snorted. "Another farmer came over last night and told me that Thornoak was supposedly coming to Anganor this morning to give a speech to everybody. I'm sure it will be grand, but whatever tripe he's going to come out and spout after nearly a decade of abandoning his kingdom, I can just as well hear it from somebody else after the fact. I'm already running late this morning, which is evident from the fact that – you probably haven't noticed it – there's nobody else out here going into the city because all the regulars got there about an hour ago. I've got fruit to sell, and if I spend half the morning standing around in the rain waiting for him to finish some sentimental soliloquy, I'll have a tough run making up for it in the afternoon. I've got a family to feed, and that means I haven't got time for the likes of Thornoak or for silly Menfolk asking silly questions."

"All right, then," Girion said, trying very hard to maintain a friendly demeanor. "If you would but tell us where we may find Thornoak, we'll not bother you with any more inquiries. I promise." With an expression both hopeful and persistent, he looked up at the Ingan, trying to catch his eye.

Kaslannaquet continued tramping down the road, his heavy sacks jostling about on his shoulders, and for a few moments, he said nothing. Then, somewhat abruptly, he grunted, "Go through this gate up ahead and follow Meskwasha Street to the Plaza of the Sagwan. After that, take Hoggawesh Road through the rest of the Sagwan. Now, Hoggawesh turns into Massanoc Street when you get to the Ikona-Sagwan Gate, and you'll need to head northwest through the Ikona on Massanoc Street until you get to the Plaza of the Ikona. Then take the Avenue of the Konaskwas up north to the Taskula. Thornoak's supposed to be delivering his address at the Possakwala, which is a big podium just west of the gate that leads to the Sentinels' Strand."

"Thank you very much, Kaslannaquet," Girion said politely, as he stopped to wait for Aradis. The Ingan, not hesitating for a moment, marched on, undoubtedly elated that this bothersome Manfellow would no longer be attempting to converse with him.

When the Ingan was out of earshot and Aradis was back by Girion's side, he caustically remarked, "Now that was supremely helpful, wasn't it? All we have to do is take Mesky Mammadasha Street through the Hoggibon and the Icklemop to get to the Porgikwammy. It's that simple."

"Actually, I think we'll only have to remember to ask how to get to the Sentinels' Strand," Girion said. "Besides, perhaps we'll get better help in the city."

"Yes, perhaps all Ingans are as chipper as that one," Aradis mumbled.

"Come now, Aradis," Girion chided. "You're apt to complain about others having prejudiced opinions about Menfolk. So don't let one cranky farmer who's probably just having a rough time in life right now color your opinion of all Ingans."

"Hm," Aradis sniffed, as he looked up at the slowly drifting gray clouds and let the cool drizzle moisten his face.

"Don't 'hm' me," Girion chastised, as they proceeded down the road. "You're just as bad as he is."

"Oh, fine," Aradis sighed. "But mark my words: that fellow's attitude doesn't bode well. Not one bit. If other folk in Anganor share his sentiments about Thornoak, then it seems we shall have just as difficult a time convincing them to follow him as we will in convincing him to lead them."

"If that becomes a matter of concern, then let us concern ourselves with the matter when it arises," Girion advised. "For now, let's focus on Thornoak himself. If we can persuade him to summon the Verdinnion, I have a feeling all the citizens in Argonis will be more inclined to rally behind him."

As the Menfolk walked along the slightly sodden road, they saw Kaslannaquet arrive at the gate, which consisted of a set of huge wooden double doors some twenty-five feet high. These doors were set into a stone wall around forty feet in height that was surmounted by stout ramparts. Atop the ramparts were two bright banners; one had a gray field centered on a white flower with eight rounded petals, and the other had a light-green field with a tree of much darker green in the middle. The tree was in the same shape as Strongbranch Citadel, having limbs and foliage beginning about halfway up, bursting out exuberantly and then tapering away toward the top.

At the gate, there were four Ingan guards who were armed with long iron spears and whips made out of thorny vines. However, they paid little heed to Kaslannaquet, and he gave even less to them, as he walked on into the city.

Encouraged that they apparently wouldn't have to undergo any kind of questioning from the guards, the Menfolk continued on until they were only a few yards from them. The guards did eye them with slight suspicion as they approached, likely because they had never seen them before. Still, their misgivings couldn't have been that substantial, since they didn't say so much as a single word to the Siloans. Girion nodded politely at them and wished them a bright Marda, but they did not return the gesture or the greeting, much to his disappointment.

"Must be an Ingan custom to be unsociable to strangers," Aradis muttered to his companion, as they walked past the sentries into the gateway.

"Oh, just give them a chance," Girion quietly reprimanded, hoping the fellows had not heard Aradis' remark. "Since they're guards, maybe they're not supposed to be sociable. Not talking to passersby might help them do their job better."

"There you go waving your optimism wand again," Aradis muttered.

"A little positive perspective might do you some good, you know," Girion countered, as they passed under a heavy iron portcullis and entered the great and ancient city of Anganor, the capital of the Kingdom of Argonis.

They now stood in a wide, crowded avenue that led north by northwest toward the heart of the city. On either side of the street, rising above galleries with arcades, there were timber-frame buildings of two, three, four or sometimes five stories. Occasionally, among these there could be seen large trees, often with doors at the bottom and windows set into the trunks. In most cases, the timber buildings were set up right against them. Everywhere the lads looked, they saw flowers, vines, shrubs, ferns and other types of greenery. They hung from windows and baskets of the buildings and were planted in the ground just outside the arcades. Also, nearly every door had a glass lantern of sorts next to it that was filled with large tufts of either purplish or bluish moss. This moss could also be seen hanging out of lanterns suspended next to windows on higher stories.

The street's occupants were primarily Ingans, many dressed, like Kaslannaquet, with simple kilts, although all of the females, the Treemaenas, were wearing garments that covered their torsos as well, whether they were knee-length dresses or blouses paired with skirts. Much of the Treemaenas' apparel was more elaborately decorated than that of the Treefellows, for it was garnished with more intense patterns and featured a good deal of beadwork and fringes. The females also had the mossy material that sufficed as Ingan hair done up in sophisticated braids with flowers woven into them. Aradis and Girion were both surprised at how remarkably the Treemaenas could appear both distinctly Treeish and feminine at the same time, as their waists and breasts were contoured rather like those of their own kind.

Among the many Ingans, there were scatterings of Leprechauns, Wood-Gnomes, Ogres and even Menfolk, much to Aradis and Girion's astonishment. There were also a few Dwarves and some dark-haired Timber-Elves. (At least the Siloans presumed them to be so based on their singular encounter with the Timber-Elf bandits just west of the Teraska.) And, in addition to all of these, there were individuals who seemed to be of a peculiar variety of Gnome. These were much slenderer and a bit smaller than Wood-Gnomes. Their arms and legs were rather spindly, their faces almost triangular, and they had ears that were shaped very much like conch shells. Many of them were wearing bright, gaudy clothes: jackets, tall stockings, short breeches and extremely pretentious, three-cornered hats.

After the lads had taken a minute or so to absorb all the exotic novelty with which they had just been confronted, they set off down the street in the mild summer rain, glancing at the dwellings and shops and looking through the windows at the wide array of wares displayed in them. There they saw merchandise of nearly every kind. There were foods aplenty: fruits, pastries, vegetables, breads, fish, wild game meats and even luxurious candies. There were the works of all kinds of craftsmen: weavers, woodcarvers, jewelers, chandlers, potters, leatherworkers, coopers, tailors, blacksmiths and many more besides. The assortment, of course, was not as varied as one might find in an even larger city like Aragest, where Girion had spent the majority of his younger years, but it was still quite impressive.

The streets were filled with the sound of a great many conversations, although most of them were at a lower volume, and there wasn't a great deal of laughter, even in groups of Barada who appeared to be well-acquainted. Indeed, there was a sort of brooding pessimism or gravity in the city that was certainly due to much more than the dreary weather that morning. However, there was music echoing out of a few alleyways, though it was rather lonely, and the melodies involved the frequent use of open intervals, which created an almost haunting atmosphere. The lads looked into a narrow, darkened lane and saw an elderly Ingan standing with his mouth open, emitting two high notes. Both were buzzing whistles; one pitch remained steady, and the other one moved about quite a bit. He had a little wooden bowl filled with coins at his feet, and an Ingan chap who was entering the main street tossed a little, rectangular piece of metal into the bowl as he passed, offering tribute to the singer's talents. A little farther on, they noticed an Ingan woman with extremely long, knotted moss-hair playing a low-pitched wooden flute, which she swayed rhythmically back and forth in front of her.

As the Siloans made their way through the crowd, Girion addressed a passing Treemaena. "Excuse me," he said. "How do we get to the Sentinels' Strand?"

"Ha," she laughed lightly. "That's easy enough. Just go toward Strongbranch. It's right before you get there." Then, cocking her head and looking intently at them and their sullied garments, she deduced, "You've come some distance, I see. But you do know what Strongbranch Citadel is, right?"

"Yes, it's that unbelievably huge tree fortress," Aradis replied, glancing up at it.

"Good, then," the Ingan maiden said, as she went on southward down the street.

Aradis and Girion, armed with their much simpler directions, set out again and followed the wide avenue until it came to an open square, the ground of which was covered with mulch. This area clearly functioned as a sort of market, but traffic from the street the Menfolk were on flowed right through it, so the lads crossed the plaza and continued down the street on the other side.

The Siloans walked on until they had gone a full mile since entering Anganor; it was only a ten-minute walk past the market square for them to reach that point. There they came to a high, green hedge, not unlike the Outhedge, the great wall of thorns that surrounded much of Argonis, although this hedge was somewhat shorter, a bit thinner and definitely less forbidding. A set of gates stood in it that led into another section of the city, and guards stood in rather uncommitted stances on either side of the portals. Their apparent lack of intensity seemed to be due to it not being necessary for them to halt, question or otherwise investigate Barada simply entering another portion of Anganor. After all, even the guards at the city gate had not questioned the Siloans. The Menfolk guessed the gate was just a convenient place to station guards in case trouble did arise. Grateful that they could avoid more prying into their business, they passed on through the gates without attracting even an ounce of discernible attention from the guards.

In the next district, nearly all the buildings were of a commercial nature, at least on the street they were on, whereas in the district they had just gone through, there were a fair number of residences as well. When the lads had gone about another third of a mile, the street fed into an enormous plaza, this one much larger and grander than the previous one. It was, in fact, the same plaza they had seen from their vantage point just beyond the forest that morning.

This plaza was, like the other, paved with mulch, but it also had several ponds, teeming with delicate lilies and brilliant red and yellow fish, as well as quite a few grassy areas, all of which were immaculately clipped and populated with magnificent wildflowers. In the midst of these grassy areas were hedges that grew primarily in a vertical direction, like great, green pillars some forty feet high. Bedecked with gorgeous flowers and vines of astounding shades, these living columns had been trimmed in all sorts of fantastic shapes, but the general patterns were those of fruits, flowers and an array of strange plants, each of which stood on top of the other. However, all of them were crowned by the same verdant sculpture of an unfolded, eight-petaled blossom.

All of this beautification surrounded a huge, spreading tree that stood at the very center of the plaza. The tree was around a hundred and twenty feet high, and it was draped with copious amounts of a light, golden moss similar to the stuff they had seen in all the city's lanterns. In its boughs, there were numerous species of birds, each with a different color of plumage. Many of them were similar in morphology to sparrows or finches. They were all twittering merrily, eating out of little feeders made of gourds attached to hanging vines.

In the green lawn around the base of the tree, there were four great stones shaped like big thumbs, seven feet high or so. There was one stone facing each cardinal direction, and all of them had different inscriptions, though each was engraved with the same Ingan script that Aradis and Girion had encountered in their travels through eastern Argonis. Around the base of the stones, the lads noticed some little creatures running about that looked rather like fat, brown mushrooms, except that these things had thin eyes and mouths and small, thick legs.

Also, throughout the plaza, there were vendors pushing carts with sundry commodities, many of which the Siloans surmised to be varieties of food and drink. There was a tremendous amount of activity here, with varied kinds of Narthanna, such as Ingans, Gnomes, Elves, Leprechauns and Ogres, transacting, trading and traversing the area. This would normally have been a rather comforting phenomenon, for it would indicate that Anganor was relatively at ease, but Aradis and Girion both realized that, in fact, this signified something rather disconcerting.

"None of these people seem to care that Thornoak is going to speak this morning," Aradis remarked to his companion, somewhat anxiously. "On the contrary, they just seem to be going about business as usual. You know, the Ingan maiden we talked to probably guessed we were asking about the Sentinels' Strand because we wanted to see Thornoak, but she didn't even mention the matter."

"Aye," Girion concurred, sighing. "It seems that most everyone in Anganor has adopted a view akin to that of our friend Kaslannaquet – namely, that Thornoak, for all practical purposes, has deserted his people. It's as if he's been gone for so long that now they don't much care what he has to say."

An exceedingly disheartening thought then struck both lads at the same time, but Aradis was the one who actually voiced it. "Perhaps trying to talk to Thornoak is a dead end, after all. Even if we can rouse him to action, would the people of Argonis respect him enough to listen to him? Indeed, it may be that our attempts to associate with him will completely discredit us."

Placing his hand on his friend's shoulder, Girion returned, "If so, it can't be helped now. Besides, we've come too far to not at least try working something out with Thornoak." Then, looking across the plaza, he suggested, "Let's take that street that goes north toward Strongbranch."

"Oh, all right," Aradis consented, as they headed off in that direction.

This new avenue was much like the one they had taken to the center of the city, although this one was a little wider and straighter and somehow felt more dignified. The gloomy, overcast heavens presided over this regal thoroughfare with due solemnity, as the lads approached another tall, green hedge that lay almost a quarter of a mile beyond the north end of the plaza. In this hedge stood a set of specially carved wooden gates. They were open at the moment, but together, these would have presented the image of several trees of immense height, all rather malevolent in appearance, except at their bases. The tree in the very middle had a chamber at the top where a young Ingan fellow with a vine whip was battling a staff-bearing Ingan in strange ceremonial garb.

When the lads went through this set of gates, the character of the city changed drastically. Here, the structures looked much more weathered and had a fair amount of stone in them, especially on their lower floors. As they proceeded through this new area, they also saw, to either side, that there were gigantic stumps, if they could be called that, rising above the Barada-made buildings. They were a hundred feet or more in diameter and stood between fifty and seventy-five feet high, featuring doors and windows that had been cut into their sides, of which many were accompanied by little flower boxes. If these stumps were indeed all that remained of humongous trees, then those trees must have been of a fantastic size indeed, though probably not as large as Strongbranch Citadel.

After the two Siloans, marveling at these new wonders, had gone a quarter of a mile through this district, the street they were on terminated at a high stone wall and yet another pair of gates. But these gates were shut tight and were attended by a squadron of sentinels. Both of the previous gateways that led from one district of Anganor to another had only boasted a handful of guards, none of whom looked too interested in keeping a close eye on things. But these Ingan guards were not only taller and stronger, they were standing at full attention. Furthermore, they were outfitted with heavy armor and formidable iron halberds, and all bore expressions indicating the utmost devotion to their duty.

The lads had now come to the very foot of Malinoc Hill, for beyond the gates, beyond the wall, the ground surged upward dramatically. There, the mighty roots of Strongbranch Citadel reached all the way to the bottom of the slope, perching upon the hill and gripping it like some monstrous bird. Among them, streams of clear, rushing water shot out of the hillside and tumbled down to the river at its base. The trunk of the tree had many openings of various sizes hewn into it for windows, and, in a few places, little wisps of smoke floated out of small, round holes in it. The great tree itself soared skyward, breaking through the low, brooding vapors that were still showering the fields and forests of Mentasqua. When Aradis and

Girion craned their necks from this spot, they couldn't even see the top of the citadel. In fact, they could hardly see its branches, which began some five hundred feet up, for the morning mists had descended even farther in the past half an hour and now veiled the upper portions of Strongbranch in an enigmatic haze. Consequently, the lads almost felt as if it could go on indefinitely, ascending beyond the clouds, beyond the sky, perhaps even all the way to the stars. They couldn't even imagine what Argonis must look like from the highest point of that fantastic, living tower.

As they were pondering the staggering majesty of Strongbranch Citadel, Aradis looked off to the left and saw that a substantial group of Barada had gathered in front of a wooden platform that was not far away from the spot where they were now standing. The Barada, who were mostly Ingans, were standing quietly, all looking in uneasy anticipation at the empty dais.

"That must be where Thornoak is going to speak!" Aradis exclaimed. "And all those people are waiting for him to show up."

Girion smiled a little, then commented, "Perhaps there are some people who really do want to hear what he has to say after all. It's a pity there aren't more."

"Let's go stand with them," Aradis suggested. "Hopefully we won't have to wait too long." He pulled his cloak a little tighter, and then the lads tramped across the muddy, open area and stationed themselves near the back of the crowd.

Before long, more Barada started showing up, and, within a quarter of an hour, the Menfolk found themselves right in the middle of a group of about two thousand Barada. Now, due to the presence of so many Ingans, the Siloans had to move to a spot where their view of the speaking platform was unimpeded. The lads didn't speak to each other much, as they were following the lead of the others, who were all standing in an uncomfortable silence, which was only occasionally broken by a slight murmur or a nervous cough or sniffle. The tension was growing minute by minute, to the point where it was almost palpable. And all the while, the rain grew steadily heavier, until it had moved from a light drizzle to a heavy shower.

Finally, Aradis felt so stifled and restless that he muttered to Girion, "I wish Thornoak would show up soon so that we could get out of this rain and sit down somewhere. My legs aren't exactly what one would call well-rested."

"Mine either," Girion reminded him.

Just then, there was a fair amount of movement over at the gates. Several soldiers called to each other loudly, and the massive portals began to swing open.

"It's him! It's Thornoak!" Aradis excitedly whispered, as did a great many others in the crowd. Almost all at once, everyone began murmuring and shifting around.

With keen expectancy, the Menfolk watched an old, distinguished Ingan in a long, hunter-green robe with gold embroidery step through the gateway. His moss-hair was grayish and glistening, and his features were a tad frail, almost as if his bark was a little soft. However, his expression was by no means dull; though his body may have paid a slight toll to the ravages of time, his mind had not. He had a longish, sharp nose and deep-set eyes, and he was carrying a long, wooden staff with a tree resembling Strongbranch Citadel carved on the top. It was the same design that Aradis and Girion had seen on the flag over the city gate, as well as on the staff of the Ingan messenger who had spoken with Gronk the previous night.

Aradis felt himself trembling slightly, not from fear, but from the exhilarating thought that there stood Thornoak, the Konaskwa of Argonis, the very Barada they'd been assigned to seek out around a month and a half ago.

Six guards who had emerged from the other side of the gate marched into a formation around this elderly Ingan and began escorting him toward the speaking platform. Everyone watched, many with bated breath, as the little procession ascended the old wooden staircase that led to the platform itself. When it reached the top, the Ingan in the robe stepped forward and pounded his staff on the dais four times, simultaneously lifting his right hand, his palm facing outward.

"Masku, Tagwan, Hanidosha, Yaggawat," the gathered assembly recited in unison.

"Pessanagwa," the old Ingan replied in a low, smooth voice that projected remarkably well, as he put his hand back down. After this invocation, each Barada in the crowd (except for Aradis and Girion) placed his hands together, palm to palm, finger to finger, raised them above his head, then lowered them.

"What's all that business about?" Aradis asked, leaning over to Girion's ear.

Girion shushed him, shaking his head. "Not now."

After a few moments, the elderly Ingan cleared his throat and, with considerable volume, announced, "Good Barada of Argonis, it gladdens me greatly to see you all gathered here this morning. There is much ill stalking abroad in our great kingdom these days, and it is a much easier course to fall into discouragement than to always look skyward, as our ancestors have. To always be looking at the sun and the moon, at golden Marda and silver Eoreth, is a strain on the neck. But it is a strain we must bear to gaze upon the light."

He paused, looked about at all the expectant faces staring back at him, then went on, "Hope is not lost for our land. I, as Thornoak's Ayonashka, his chief minister ..."

"You mean that isn't Thornoak?" Aradis blurted out loudly.

A number of Barada turned and directed censorious looks at the disruptive Manfellow, but the Ingan orating on the platform took no notice of him. He had continued, " ... have been in regular communication with Princess Langwana about matters related to affairs of state, and she has relayed the information discussed to her father in Paanu Assagwa. These discussions between the princess and myself are, of course, what led him to a decision that he should terminate his extended solitude in the burial place of his venerable ancestors and come speak with all of you in person. For the words of the Konaskwa, even if they should be few, would undoubtedly do much to infuse the downhearted and dispirited among you with fortitude and hope in your hour of need."

"However," he went on, his voice steady and confident, "today we must all come to terms with the fact that it is not always possible – for any one of us – to transform intentions into actions. Such is the case with our most esteemed Konaskwa. Though he had, of course, planned to address you in person here at this very spot on this very morning, he was unable to make the journey from Paanu Assagwa to Anganor last night, and so – "

A middle-aged, long-moss-haired Ingan fellow near the front of the crowd had had enough. "We didn't come here to listen to you blather on with excuses, Hoarstaff! We came here to see Thornoak!"

"Yeah!" an older Ingan woman yelled. "Get out of here, Kokyanu! Go sit back up in Strongbranch for a few more months, why don't you? And don't get our hopes up again unless Thornoak's already left that accursed Paanu Assagwa."

Hoarstaff remained poised, but it was obvious now that it simply wouldn't be feasible for him to finish his speech. He tried anyway, though.

"Thornoak, your beloved monarch, has been sorely afflicted with weariness and required additional – "

"That's dorganinka dung!" an adolescent Ingan lad shouted. "He's been 'resting' for seven years! He's a coward! That's why he didn't show up today!"

"Aye," a grumpy, old Dwarf fellow chimed in. "He's been stewing up there ever since Prince Makwaru ran off, and he hasn't come up with a single plan for how to get the kingdom to cooperate again, much less a plan to take on Ravinia. What a farce!"

"Thornoak is a rotting poltroon, and you're nothing but his stammering stooge, Kokyanu!" an Ogre brashly hollered.

This fellow's insult was apparently quite inspiring to all those who were already riled, for, at that very instant, complete pandemonium broke out. Everyone who had anything to say began saying it all at once, as the angry throng pushed toward the platform where Hoarstaff stood.

Quickly, the soldiers surrounded Hoarstaff and began ushering him back toward the safety of the gates. With long halberds, they managed to keep those at the front of the mob at bay, while the Ayonashka beat a hasty retreat. Then, as soon as he was safely on the other side of the gateway, the guards themselves backed up through the portals and pulled them shut behind them, leaving scores of angry Barada to hurl themselves against the impregnable gates in vain.

Meanwhile, Aradis and Girion, who were nearly as upset as those who had been bellowing out inflammatory remarks, were swept along with the vociferous mass of raging Barada. Because many of those next to them were large Ingans, they were actually in danger of being trampled. Neither of them could see very well over the tops of the heads of those around them, and the rough bark bodies of a great many stout Ingans were smashing up against them.

"Hey!" Aradis yelled. "Watch it, you Ingan louts! You're liable to crush us with all this shoving and smooshing!" But his yelling was completely useless. No one in the crowd cared much about anything at the moment except getting a chance to tear old Hoarstaff apart, limb from limb.

Fortunately for the lads, the crazed throng was moving up past the platform. Seizing this fortuitous circumstance, Aradis and Girion struggled for a moment with those pressing on them, then leapt up and grabbed the edge of the platform. They were nearly pulled back down into the maddened drove, which would almost certainly have resulted in them being trodden underfoot, but, just in time, they managed to drag themselves up onto the wooden dais.

Breathing hard, they stood up, went over and leapt off the north side of the platform, away from the crowd.

"I've half a mind to go give Hoarstaff a good knock on the noggin," Aradis panted hotly. "And the other half would like to do the same thing to Thornoak. For on his account, we tramped all the way through the night and exhausted ourselves for naught. I had so hoped we'd be able to see him this morning. Now I suppose we'll have to go back to our original plan of seeking out the Questmongers at the Gnarly Stump Tavern, for we can't very well go see Thornoak at Paanu Assagwa on our own, as that will only result in us getting executed."

"I know. It's terribly frustrating. But right now, we need to get out of here before this riot gets worse," Girion counseled.

"All right," Aradis puffed. "Why don't we go inside a building or something, at least until this rain stops?"

"Might as well go in that one," Girion suggested, pointing at a huge stump building that lay straight to the west.

"Might as well," Aradis agreed, and they ran over to it through the heavy rain, as the mob continued pressing in on the gates that led toward Strongbranch Citadel, shouting and screaming at the guards, who they knew were only a few feet away, just on the other side of the barrier.

There were three different doors into the stump building, but the Siloans elected to enter via the heavy, oaken door on its south side. The lads pushed on it, then stepped into an extremely large room, which, even with its great size, only took up about half of the bottom floor of the entire building. The room had a ceiling some twenty feet high and numerous high windows with yellowish glass panes set in crisscrossed ironwork. Also, it contained two enormous fireplaces, one on the west wall and one on the east. There were quite a few tables distributed throughout the room, all of them surrounded by carved stumps for seats. On all the tables, there were bowls with big clumps of some compact, blazing, red plant material that provided both heat and light and emitted a fragrant odor, like that of potpourri. In addition, there were several iron chandeliers hanging from the ceiling that provided illumination from more traditional wax candles. Nearly all the occupants of the place were Ingans, who were drinking translucent, sparkling yellow liquid out of big clay bowls, although there were some Wood-Gnomes, Timber-Elves, a few Dwarves and a Leprechaun or two sitting among them. They all seemed to be happily heedless of the racket going on a little less than a quarter of a mile away, though it was quite audible inside the stump building.

On the north wall of the room, there was an extremely long counter with a broad assortment of drinking vessels resting atop it. The counter was manned by a single Ingan, who was wearing a long, stained, barkcloth apron. He had olive-green eyes, looked to be somewhat young and fairly fit, and had dirty green moss-hair tied in a ponytail that hung down just a little below his shoulders.

"Hey, didn't Shillelagh say that the Gnarly Stump was up by Strongbranch Citadel?" Aradis asked, as he threw off his sopping hood.

"I believe that's exactly what he said," Girion replied, removing his own hood and briefly running his fingers through his curly, black hair. "It may be far simpler for us to move from one plan to the next than we might have guessed. Let's go ask the barkeep if this is the place because this certainly looks like a tavern to me, and we are right by Strongbranch."

So, much more at ease than they had been at the Draughtfish Inn in the Fontskals only three weeks previously, they wiped off their muddy boots on a woven mat by the door, then walked over to the counter, where Girion leaned across toward the barman and greeted him. "Good day, sir. We're looking for the Gnarly Stump Tavern, and we were wondering if this might not be it." He looked hopefully at the Ingan, who, at the moment, was busy cleaning a clay drinking bowl with a blue cloth.

The Ingan set the bowl and cloth down, scratched his cheek a bit with a long, barky finger, and chuckled, "No, Eskagwan, but you're close to it."

"Eskagwan?" Aradis repeated the word inquisitively and a bit testily.

"A foreigner. A person from beyond the Outhedge," the Ingan explained.

"How do you know we're from outside Argonis?" Aradis asked, mildly irritated.

"You are, aren't you?" the Ingan insisted.

"Yes," Aradis admitted, more irritated than before.

"Well, there you go," the Ingan smugly concluded. "Now, about the Gnarly Stump." He leaned earnestly toward Girion. "Do you have something to write with, by chance?" he asked. "Probably not, as not many folks carry around a quill and ink, or even parchment for that matter. Can't hurt to ask, though. You see, the place isn't far, but it's a bit complicated to get there. If you write the directions down, you can have them to refer to – just in case, you know."

"We're in luck," Girion replied. "Just a moment," he said, as he removed his pack, then fished through it until he found his notebook and tylon.

"Ah, here we go. I'm ready now," he declared, opening to a blank page and poising his tylon to inscribe the Ingan's directions.

"That's a fancy bit of apparatus!" the Ingan exclaimed, eyeing the tylon. "All right, here's what you're going to do," he explained. "You're going to go out the front door of this place and head straight south. There's a street that you can follow that runs in the same general direction. Now you're going to pass three streets on the right – actually they're more like lanes, I guess – and you're going to take the fourth one. You got all that so far?"

"Yep," Girion replied, while writing furiously.

"Okay, you're going to turn right onto that lane I told you about. The street you turn onto curves a bit, but just follow it. Now on this one, you'll pass two little alleyways, and at the lane after them, you want to turn right. Got that?"

"Mm hm." Girion nodded.

"You'll be pretty close at this point," the Ingan encouraged. "Not much left. Pass three lanes; turn east at the fourth. You'll see the Gnarly Stump Tavern right in front of you."

"I think we can manage that." Girion smiled, as he finished his notes. Then he extended his hand to the Ingan and said, "Thank you, sir. What's your name?"

"Osachi," the Ingan returned. "But most folk call me Brightbole." He winked merrily at the Menfolk.

"We're most grateful to you, Brightbole," Girion happily returned, as he looked at his page of directions one more time, then placed his notebook and tylon back in his pack.

"Let's go, Aradis," he said, as they set off toward the door and put their hoods back over their heads.

Very soon, they were out in the rain again and walking through Brightbole's directions out loud. They could still hear the sound of the mob at the gates off to the east, and the tumult seemed only to have grown more fervent. Strangely enough, just like those in the stump building, others who were walking around the district seemed merely to be going about their everyday affairs, as if the violent din did not concern them whatsoever. Perhaps, the Siloans surmised, those who were now so outraged at Thornoak and his minister were the only ones who had cared about him to begin with.

The lads easily spotted the three streets that Brightbole had mentioned and turned, just as he had directed, onto the fourth street. Exactly as he said, it curved a little bit, and they just kept on it. After the two alleyways, they turned on the third and headed north. After passing the next set of three streets that Brightbole had told them about, they turned east on the fourth, quite pleased with themselves; that is, until they looked straight ahead. They started to walk a little slower, then came to a complete stop. For there, directly in front of them, was the building they had just been in. It was then that they realized they'd been had for a couple of gullible nitwits.

For, of course, Brightbole's directions were leading them back to the very place they had started. He had intentionally made a big ordeal out of the directions and sent them out in the rain again just for a lark. Aradis and Girion were both furious.

"Brightbole won't be so bright by the time I'm done with him," Aradis growled through gritted teeth, as they started trudging through the mud back toward the Gnarly Stump Tavern.

"Aradis." Girion grew quite stern, though he shared Aradis' extreme annoyance with Brightbole. "Last time you lost your temper in a tavern, there were very unpleasant repercussions. We've already somehow avoided getting stampeded by a bunch of irate Ingans today. Let's not press our luck. Besides, the Questmongers are upstairs in this place. Undoubtedly, they'll overhear a ruckus if you decide to start one and might come down to investigate. Do you really want their first impression of us to be that we're a pair of immature brawlers? We gave Brightbole a good laugh, I'm sure. In fact, we probably made his day. When we get inside, let's just head straight upstairs and let him have his laugh. We have more important things to attend to."

Aradis set his expression, grunted and returned, "Oh, maybe we'll let it be for now, but if that underhanded Ingan ever comes to Siloa, I'll give him the runaround three times as bad as he gave it to us. I'll send him through Bernalla Elmensill's turnip patch. That'll fix him."

Fuming, Aradis shoved open the door to the Gnarly Stump and this time didn't pause to wipe off his boots. Girion followed right behind him, as they threw off their hoods once more. But they had only gone a few feet into the tavern when Brightbole yelled from behind the counter, "Well, boys, look who just blew in! I'll tell you what – if you were ever trying to find your way from the shore to the sea, these Menfolk could get you there with no trouble at all – so long as they had clear directions, that is!"

The whole tavern erupted into uproarious laughter, and both of the lads' faces turned bright red. Aradis glared with sheer contempt at the chortling Brightbole, but this only made the Ingan burst into full-on laughter.

Girion, after nudging Aradis lightly several times, grabbed him rather firmly by the shoulder and pulled him over toward a wooden archway in the northwest corner of the room. Beyond it, there was a well-swept, spiral staircase with rather tall steps, evidently designed for average Ingan statures. The lads, still smarting from the fact that they had been completely duped, began climbing it. Then, much to their indignation, they were ushered all the way to the second floor by the howls and unbridled guffawing of all the tavern's patrons.

The staircase opened into a long hallway that curved to the southeast, following the edge of the stump's structure. The hall was lined with pale-blue glass windows that cast a cool, calming light on the wooden floor, which was actually made not of planks, but of the remaining raw material of the stump out of which the hallway had been carved. There were two doors in this hallway. The first one was in the middle and the other at the far end; this second one was open and led to another spiral staircase that went on up to the third floor. Laughter from below echoed down the hallway, and the clamor of the mob to the east could still be heard as well, rising up to join it. But behind the door in the middle of the hallway was the sound of voices – low, lethargic voices.

"I suppose the Questmongers are in there," Girion inferred, nodding toward the oaken door.

Aradis took a deep breath and sighed, "Here we go, then." Boldly, he walked up to it.

"Remember, we have that symbol from Chula that we can show the Questmongers, so they'll help us," Girion mentioned, checking to make sure it was still in his jerkin. "And, though we haven't any idea how this meeting will go, even if they're quite unaccommodating, you must remember not to lose your temper. You know how you can get on occasion."

"Right. Of course," Aradis replied dismissively, as he knocked rapidly on the door three times.

The voices immediately stopped, and a few moments later, there was a raspy baritone voice with an unmistakably Leprechaunish brogue that said, "An' who be ye, that we should be invitin' ye in? An' who be we, that ye should be a-seekin' us out?"

"We be – " Aradis began, "or, er, I am Aradis Kingblade, a Manfellow from Velaris, and I am with my friend, Girion Ringmark, also a Manfellow from Velaris. And you're the Questmongers because this is the second floor of the Gnarly Stump Tavern."

There was a pause, then some hushed talking, and once more the voice called out, "An' what is it ye're a-wantin' to chit-chat about?"

"Thornoak and Ravinia. And summoning the Verdinnion."

More muted discussion followed. "That's big business, Manfellow," the voice stated. "Big business indeed."

A moment later, they heard a metal bolt being pulled. Then a little peep window slid open, and a pair of brownish eyes appeared, quickly assessing them. The peep window slammed shut, and there was the sound of a heavy wooden bar being lifted, the tinkling of keys and the click of a large lock. After that the door opened inward and revealed a tall, dark-haired Elf dressed in traditional adventuring garb.

"Come in, lads," he invited, and Aradis and Girion obliged. As soon as they had gone into the room, he closed, barred and locked the door. The Siloans both felt a certain sense of finality and total commitment the second the Elf had finished doing this. There would simply be no turning back now.

The room they had entered was only about two-thirds the size of the main hall of the Gnarly Stump Tavern, but it was still quite large, nonetheless. There were eighteen individuals in the room, and many different Narthanna were represented. There were six Ingans, three Wood-Gnomes, three Leprechauns, three Timber-Elves, a Manfellow, a Dwarf and a Gnome, who looked like the Gnomes with the shell-shaped ears they had seen earlier that morning. Most of them were lounging around, leaning back against comfortable, stuffed chairs or lolling on couches. A few were tossing darts at a large dartboard or playing a peculiar board game at a little table. One Elf was in the process of combing his long, glossy hair.

The room had a large fireplace on the north wall, toward its western end. There was also a table just to the east of it with a big, open ledger set out on it and a collection of maps pinned on the wall behind it. At the far east end of the north wall, there was a door that led off, apparently, to additional quarters. There was a counter in the southeastern area of the room with a cluster of big mugs on it, as well as a hodgepodge of bottles and jugs of spirits. Also, in front of the hearth, there was a thick black rug made from the hide of some large animal, and in various places around the room, there were racks of many different kinds of weapons. All along the west wall, there were bookshelves filled with old and fascinating tomes, pamphlets, scrolls, amulets, orbs and other strange artifacts. And next to the east wall, which was lined by big windows with light-yellow glass, there were open chests of clothing and coins.

In the middle of the room, on an old red couch, there sat the very definition of a veteran adventurer, a middle-aged Leprechaun who could be none other than Fergus O'Brannadon, Fergus the Fearless, the renowned leader of the Questmongers that Shillelagh had told them about. He was dressed in well-worn brown boots, rough tan breeches, a stained burgundy vest and a white button-up shirt, which was only done up about halfway, so that his hairy chest could be seen. He boasted scars all over his body, but his brownish hair was combed immaculately. The skin on his hands was leathery, but it was visibly apparent how much skill he had in his fingers; they practically radiated prowess.

"Are you Fergus the Fearless?" Aradis inquired, nodding toward the Leprechaun.

The Leprechaun nodded in reply, then said, "So we've got an Aradis an' we've got a Girion." It was, of course, he who had been speaking through the door. "An' they come a-callin' to the Questmongers on the very day Tornoak's supposed to be returnin' to Anganor. But Tornoak didna come. An' now they be wantin' to palaver abou' tree o' the biggest matters concernin' all Argonis: Tornoak, Ravinia an' the Verdinnion. Pity it be then that us a-speakin' about such tings canna be so loose, lad. For to go so deep, we'll be a-needin' very strong proof that ye be sound an' safe. 'Specially wit everyting 'at's a-goin' on outside right now. That mob is only the beginnin', I'm afraid. For we be a-witnessin' the very awakenin' of Anganor. An' it in't a good sort o' wakin'." With disquietude written all over his face, he looked toward the east windows.

Aradis looked around at the Questmongers, then asked, "So what you're saying is you don't have a good reason to trust us, right? And we can't really discuss much until you do have one? That's fair enough. But we come with a recommendation." He nodded at Girion.

"A high recommendation," Girion echoed, reaching into his pocket. A moment later, he drew out the parchment Chula had given them, the one with the symbol of the strange tree that he had instructed them to show to the Questmongers. Holding it aloft, he slowly waved it around so all of them could see it.

Fergus' eyes widened, as did those of the others. "How came ye by that?" he asked suspiciously.

"Peleus Chula," Aradis answered cheerfully, anticipating that any confusion would now be eradicated after the mention of the Shore Elf's name.

"Chula!" a few of the Questmongers moaned, shaking their heads.

"Hold on ye!" Fergus admonished. "The paper counts for summtin'. But it hain't a-gotten ye out o' the heat yet. What means the symbol? What's the story behind it? Can ye explain it?"

The Menfolk looked at each other, dumbfounded. "Why, it's a symbol of the Questmongers, I suppose," Girion said.

"Course 'tis," Fergus acknowledged. "But I asked ye afore, an' now I'll ask ye again. What's the story behind the tree?"

"I'm sorry, but that's all we know. We can't explain any further," Aradis insisted.

Fergus leaned forward on the couch anxiously, then popped up to his feet.

"Then ye didna get tha' paper from Peleus Chula," the Leprechaun bellowed. "Cuz if ye did, an' he really wanted ye to be received well here, he woulda told ye the secret. But he din't." The Leprechaun stared accusingly at Aradis, straight in the eyes. "So tha' means you're a liar," he charged, each word infused with scathing animosity.

Aradis could feel his rage rising. "I'm not a liar. We did meet Peleus Chula, and he did give us that paper."

"I know what ye are," Fergus stormed. "Spies! How'd ye get yer tricky little fingers on that paper?"

"I've had enough of this garbage!" Aradis exploded, as he kicked an empty brass pitcher across the floor.

"Aradis, your temper," Girion quietly reminded.

Aradis completely ignored him. "Girion and I have done nothing but try to help this stupid kingdom of Argonis! I mean, we walked all the way through the night to get to Anganor to see Thornoak, and then he decides to not show up like a miserable little milksop. Now, when we try to seek out help from the Questmongers – "

Right in the middle of Aradis' tirade, there was a loud knock on the door. Aradis cut off his diatribe just as abruptly as he had started it, though he was still breathing hard.

"Hullo," a familiar voice called. "Hullo, I do say, will you open up this door? It's Chula. I've returned, you see."

Fergus, who was also heaving and red-faced, nodded to a Timber-Elf. "How timely," Fergus remarked. "Let 'im in," he ordered the Elf.

The Elf checked through the peep window and then did as Fergus directed, and in walked – or, rather, stumbled – Chula.

"Gracious! I heard some dreadful shouting in here," Chula murmured. "I'm glad that's over with."

"Oh, 'tis just a-gettin' started," Fergus assured. "Say, Chula, do you know these blokes?" he inquired, motioning to the Menfolk.

Chula looked around the room, then stared at the Siloans as if he had just now noticed them. He squinted a bit, sniffed twice, then replied, "No, I can't say I've ever seen them before. Are they joining us?"

The Dwarf and an Ingan next to him both rolled their eyes, as Girion protested, "Oh, yes, you *have* seen us before – in the woods just west of the Teraska. You were chasing a ketchiwah because it took your wibblegop, and we – "

"You know, come to think of it, where is my wibblegop?" Chula wondered. "If I'm not quite mistaken, I never did find it."

"Do you remember, though?" Girion pressed, worriedly assessing Fergus' expression in response to the Elf's statement.

"No, I can't remember where it is at all," Chula lamented. "Unless that confounded ketchiwah still has it."

"Not the wibblegop!" Girion groaned. "Do you remember meeting us?"

A clear flash of recognition suddenly crossed Chula's face, and he abruptly laughed, "Of course! We met in the Tongapin Swath; that is, in the woods just west of the Teraska. You were being chased by bandits, and they got scared off by my ketchiwah mating horn. Then I drew you the secret symbol of the Questmongers so Fergus would provide you with aid. To be perfectly honest, I couldn't recommend lads any finer than the two of you to these good Questmongers. Certainly I remember."

One of the Wood-Gnomes, who was just then drinking out of a flagon, paused and nearly choked, as he snorted at the Shore Elf's absurdity.

Fergus could contain himself no longer. "Chula, you straw-brained milk-head!" he roared.

The Shore-Elf's mouth fell open rather stupidly, as if he had been quite caught off guard by this sudden invective.

Fergus continued, "I canna trust you wit anyting, apparently! If ya meet a pack o' wanderin' ninnies, ya canna jus' be a-givin' 'em our secret symbol as if ya were handin' out candy to a wee Gnomeling! Maybe they aren' the spyin' sort, but they could be up to no good, sure as rain. Dunce an' blunderbob that you are, don' be a-givin' any more secret symbols to any more strange folk. If I catch you a-doin' it again, I'll—"

Aradis now cut in with his own storm of contempt. "Oh, you've no one to blame for this but yourself, you pompous pinhead! You're the leader of this dumpy little group, so you should take responsibility for all this nonsense. And what good are all of you doing around here anyway? When we walked in, what were all of you up to? Sitting on your lazy behinds and playing games while the kingdom collapses all around you! For the sake of all that is sane and decent, there's a mob a few stone's throws from here trying to break into Strongbranch Citadel and attack Thornoak's chief minister, and you idiots are just sitting around like a pack of half-wit donkeys in their stable." Aradis concluded his verbal onslaught, staring viciously at Fergus.

Now Fergus was dangerously mad. "You've crossed the line, boy," he spat. "No one – an' I mean no one – talks like that an' lives around here. You've insulted me own honor an' the honor of ev'ry single livin' Questmonger, an' tha' witout a stray clue of all we've a-done an' all we're a-doin'. An' that's a ting I canna an' won' take lightly."

Girion felt completely powerless. It seemed a fight was now inevitable. He had often told Aradis that his temper would get him killed someday, and it looked like this was it. Somehow, the lad had survived the battle with Gronk, but he didn't stand a chance against nearly twenty armed Questmongers, for, even if he could beat Fergus, which seemed unlikely, the others certainly wouldn't let the matter rest at that. Girion had done nearly everything he could; he had even warned Aradis not to get carried away with his anger right before they entered the Questmongers' hall. But there was one thing left he could do. In sheer desperation, Girion threw himself between his friend and Fergus and exclaimed, "Aradis, apologize this very instant!"

But Aradis committed himself even further. "What are you going do, Leprechaun?" he taunted. "Dance a sparlag?"

Enraged, Fergus tore off his vest and then began unbuttoning his shirt.

"Oh, is it fisticuffs, then? Will you be sparring with my knees?" Aradis scoffed. Furiously, he threw off his pack and cloak, then pulled his shirt off over his head and flung it toward the door behind him. "Just keep out of this, Girion," he ordered, as he pushed his friend aside.

"You're done for, lad," one of the Wood-Gnomes mumbled, shaking his head. "Fergus will make faster than quick work of you."

"We shanna be a-boxin', lad," Fergus ominously announced, as he tossed his shirt onto a nearby chair. Grabbing a sheath from the couch he had been sitting on, he drew from it a hideously, sharp, curved blade and began taking slow, grim steps toward the now rather apprehensive Manfellow. "I jus' don' wanna get blood on me shirt."

Aradis, recognizing too late what a grave mistake he had made, quickly unsheathed his own sword and prepared to battle the formidable Leprechaun. Now that he thought about it, he realized that Fergus was likely a warrior of the first rank and that he had a single intention for this battle – to restore his honor by killing the one who had besmirched it.

All of a sudden, the Dwarf shouted out, grabbing Fergus by the arm. "Wait! Look at him, Fergus! Do you see it?"

Gasping in shock, Fergus halted and dropped his blade to the floor with a loud clang.

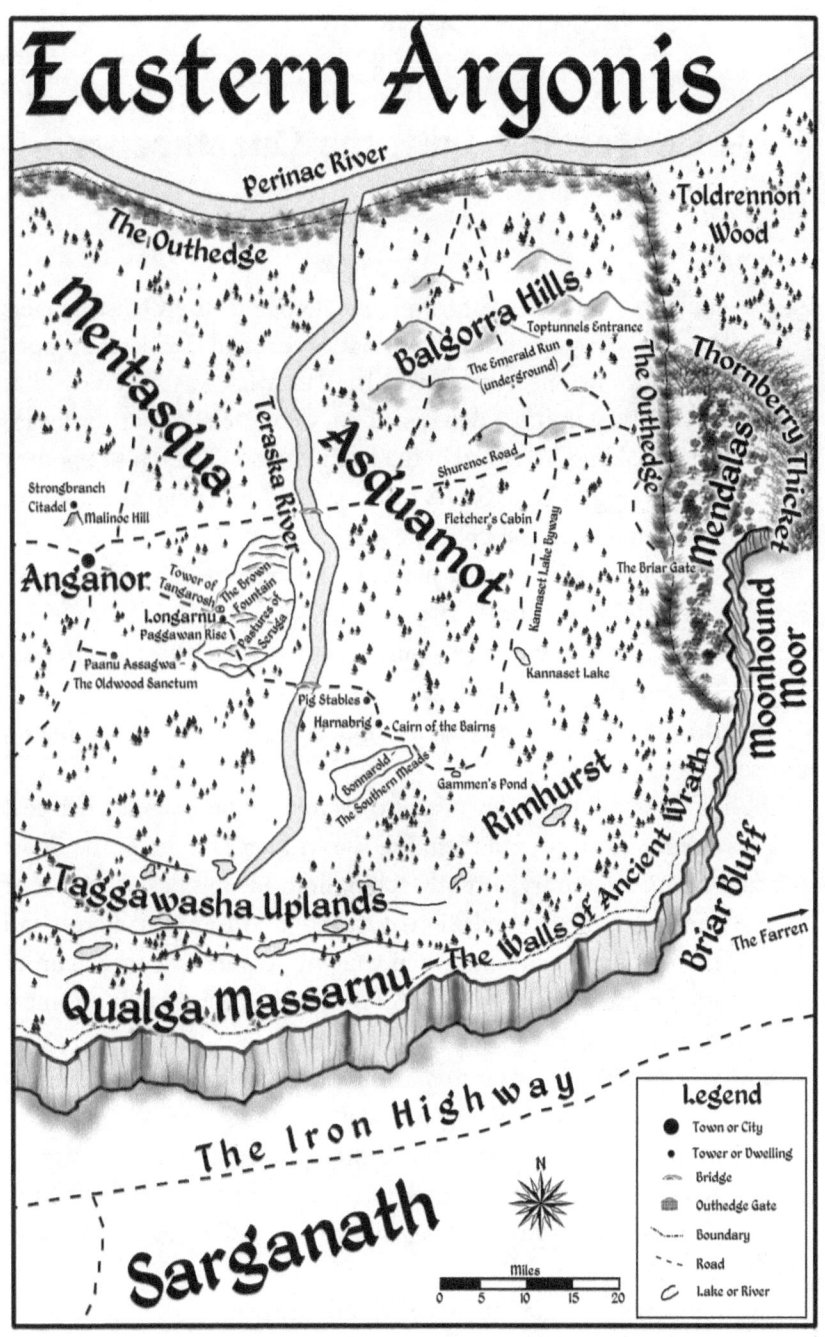

Eastern Argonis

Perinac River

Toldrennon Wood

The Outhedge

Mentasqua

Balgorra Hills

Toptunnels Entrance

The Emerald Run (underground)

The Outhedge

Thornberry Thicket

Terasha River

Asquamot

Shurenoc Road

Mendalas

Strongbranch Citadel
Malinoe Hill

Fletcher's Cabin

The Briar Gate

Anganor

Tower of Tangarosh
The Brown Fountain

Longarnu
Paggawan Rise

Pasture of Scrugla

Kannaset Lake Byway

Moonhound Moor

Paanu Assagwa –
The Oldwood Sanctum

Kannaset Lake

Pig Stables

Harnabrig
Cairn of the Bairns

Bonnarold
The Southern Meads

Gammen's Pond

Rimhurst

Briar Bluff

The Walls of Ancient Wrath

The Farren

Taggawasha Uplands

Qualga Massarnu

The Iron Highway

Sarganath

N

Miles

0   5   10   15   20

Legend

● Town or City
• Tower or Dwelling
⌒ Bridge
▥ Outhedge Gate
--- Boundary
- - - Road
⌒ Lake or River

CHAPTER TWO

A Conference with the Questkeeper

 moment later, every single one of the Questmongers began staring intently at Aradis, and their jaws dropped in one giant wave. The lad, who was now nearly as dumbfounded as they were, felt rather awkward crouching and holding his sword in the ready position when his opponent was simply gawking at him. So he relaxed, stood up straight and let his blade hang down toward the floor.

Then, ever so slowly, Fergus, his eyes still wide as could be, asked, "Boy ... where did ya get that?"

Aradis looked down at himself, quite confused, then back up at Fergus. "What? The sword?" he inquired, glancing at it.

"Not the sword," the Leprechaun emphatically returned. "Tha' ting on your neck."

The lad bent his head down again, examined the emerald half-leaf hanging around his neck, and then, like the striking of a fire in the midst of a dark night, a memory abruptly sprang into his mind. It was that of Nagello handing him the medallion at the edge of Rimwold Forest and saying, "There will come a time when you will require this medallion to win the aid of those who doubt you." All at once, he realized that this must be the very time of which Nagello had spoken.

Now in a vastly different frame of mind, Aradis looked up at Fergus and replied, "It was given to me by a Hadathi."

A few of the Questmongers sniffed contemptuously, but Fergus himself gave no signs of any clear reaction. "A Hadat'i ... " he repeated. "Where?"

"In a forest near my village, which is in eastern Quarana," Aradis answered.

"How much do ya know about it?" Fergus pressed.

Aradis met the Leprechaun's gaze firmly, as he boldly replied, "Practically nothing, to be perfectly honest. But the Hadathi who gave it to us is the one who sent us to see Thornoak, to deliver Argonis and to defeat Ravinia. And that, in truth, is why we have come. If you will not trust our word in this matter on its own merits, will you trust us on the basis of this medallion? For it seems to carry some great significance to you."

For a few moments, Fergus weighed this response. There was visible conflict in his eyes, as he evaluated the lad's statement. Then, after taking a deep breath, he made his verdict. "Fool though I may be for it, I do trust you. For tha' token you bear is unmistakable, an' if ya didna get it from a Hadat'i, then I'd guess it either fell to ya from the stars in the heavens or was tossed up to ya by the bowels o' the earth. For sure as Tyracus, I can't imagine where else you'd have come upon it." Then, turning to Chula, he demanded, "Did you spot the medallion when ya met 'em in the woods?"

"Of course. That's why I drew them the symbol and sent them to see you," Chula returned, blinking.

Fergus, thoroughly aggravated, growled, "You've got a way o' drivin' me up a wall, Peleus Chula. Do ya know tha'?"

The Shore-Elf swallowed sheepishly. "I actually thought I mentioned the medallion to you when I entered the den. Hence, I was quite confused when you grew displeased with me, as I was certain you'd be interested in it."

"You mos' certainly mentioned no such ting," responded Fergus, and several Questmongers clearly agreed, as they had shaken their heads in denial as soon as Chula had claimed he had previously spoken of the medallion.

Chula scratched his head a second, looked at Fergus with a deeply puzzled expression and then abashedly admitted, "Oh, now that I think about it, I did actually forget to mention the matter. You're quite right. Terribly sorry about that." Much chagrined, he went and stood as inconspicuously as possible up against the wall.

Fergus, still shaking his head at Chula's irritating lapses in memory, now turned to the Questmongers and said, "The door to the den is locked an' barred, an' it needs to stay that way, no matter what, unless, perchance, Tornoak or his daughter turn up here, which i'nt at all likely, mind ye. Me an' the lads shall be a-goin' atop to me quarters, and, unless I'm a turgid toadstool, I'll wager we'll be speakin' o' tings meant for the ears o' nary a soul but those who can be trusted more by Argonis 'an they can by themselves. Deep tidings these Menfolk bear for certain, an' when I spoke o' the awakenin' of Anganor, I hadna realized how awake everyting ha' jus' become."

Addressing the Menfolk, Fergus then inquired, "Have ye any suspicion that ye might have spies o' Ravinia a-followin' ye?"

Girion replied, "Our arrival in Anganor is, I think, unknown to both her and her agents."

"Good, good," Fergus said. "Ne'ertheless, we canna be too cautious in this case."

As he pulled back on his shirt and vest, he directed the Dwarf and the Timber-Elf who had first let the Siloans into the Questmongers' hall to stand by the door to the hallway. "Uldenrog an' Dirannion, I wan' ye to stay right by yon door until I come relieve ye in person. There shanna be no openin' of it till I've found out all I can from these folk, for we han't a clue whether they were tailed or not, an' Ravinia's lot are quite clever in that sort o' business. Got it, Questies?"

"Aye, Fergus," they affirmed, as they stationed themselves at their assigned post.

"Now, for the rest o' ye," Fergus instructed, "I wan' ye to be ready to aid them to the utmost, supposin' mischief arrives, an' keep an eye out the windows for all that's afoot, at least until I'm done upstairs. An' if ye tink it necessary, a few o' ye can go out there an' try to keep tings from escalatin' wit the rowdies, although I don' know if there's much to be done abou' the matter at this point. But Ashworthy an' Collic, the two o' ye guard down below just in case someone tries to get in tru the tunnel. O' course, as far as we know, no one's privy to that passage, but I still tink we ought to take all the precautions we can."

Without hesitation, an Ingan and a Leprechaun scuttled off through the door in the northeast corner of the room.

"An' Kelwyn an' Mordie," Fergus instructed, "guard up top near me own quarters. For all we know, someone might try to get in tru a window in one o' the upper stories. Not likely, o' course, but I don' intend on takin' any chances whatsoever, for this matter's much too importan' for tha'."

The single Mannish Questmonger present, along with one of the Wood-Gnomes, moved over by the northeast door to wait for their leader, who announced, "Tornoak's last quest for us is now complete; let's not have aught go awry wit it from silliness an' negligence. Hope has a-come to Anganor at last, and 'at not of our own doin'. But let's not let it be taken from us if our doin' can keep it from so bein'." With that, he stooped down, retrieved his blade and put it back in its sheath.

"Aye, sir." All the remaining Questmongers nodded in unison, as they dispersed throughout the room, with the greater part of them going over by the windows, where they began surveying the activities of the mob by the gates to Strongbranch.

Meanwhile, Aradis had sheathed Brightbeam, grabbed his shirt and pulled it back on over his head. As he retrieved his cloak and reshouldered his pack, he mumbled to Girion, "I'm sorry I spoke like that – to you and to Fergus. You even reminded me not to lose my temper, but I did anyway, just like a heedless child."

Girion, with a rather despondent sigh, replied, "Of course your intention is never to lose your temper. But you could have gotten yourself killed over it yet again and all because you can't control your blasted tongue. Do you realize how many times since we've left Siloa you've almost gotten one or both of us killed because of your mouth or simply from acting rashly? At least ten times. Probably more."

"Surely not ten," Aradis protested.

"At least," Girion retorted. "I'll name them. We weren't even two miles from my parents' house when – "

"Ye two yappers can yap all ye want after I've finished wit ye!" Fergus called sharply, motioning from the door on the other side of the room for them to follow him. "Come on, then!"

Dutifully, they joined him. With Kelwyn and Mordie following right behind, they passed into a hallway, lit by lamps of glowing, purple moss, that ran to the left, straight toward the center of the stump. At the end of the hall, there was a staircase that went up around fifteen feet. They carefully climbed this, for it was narrow and steep, and then emerged in the middle of a large, circular, windowless room, also lit by moss lamps. The room had a long, rectangular table in its eastern section, which had twenty or so drinking vessels, several of them half-filled, and a great many maps resting upon it. There were quite a few barrels stowed up against the south wall and some bookshelves to the north. Also, there were no less than eight doors leading out of this chamber. In the western part of the room, there was a sturdy ladder that ran up through a hole in the ceiling.

The lads watched Fergus, even with his meager stature, quickly and easily climb the ladder, and they followed suit. At the top of the ladder, there was a room with a tight, spiral staircase that ascended through the very heart of the stump; it too was illuminated by the lilac glow of the moss that was so prevalent in Anganor. They took these stairs up a single floor, then came out into a short hallway that ran to the east, terminating in a big, wooden door. Kelwyn and Mordie stopped just beyond the top of the stairs and leaned against the walls of the hallway.

Meanwhile, Fergus took a key out of his pocket, unlocked the door and then led the Siloans into a room with a large, east-facing, leaded-glass window with hexagonal ironwork. The chamber was furnished with four red armchairs of various sizes, which ranged from accommodating Gnome-sized Barada all the way up to those with the height of Ingans or Ogres. The chairs were set up facing each other next to the window, an arrangement decidedly ideal for intimate conversations. Set in the south wall, there was a small fireplace. Above its mantle, there was mounted a hefty spear, forged from some metal the lads didn't recognize and graven with curious markings. And against the north wall stood an antique writing desk made of cherry wood, above which hung a long, undulating, iridescent horn, evidently once belonging to some peculiar animal. Off to the left, the lads noticed a door that led to another room, which only contained a large featherbed and battered nightstand, upon which rested a leather drinking flask and a small tray with glowing, lavender moss.

Girion closed the door after he entered, and then he and Aradis, at Fergus' invitation, put their packs, cloaks and weapons on the floor. Gingerly, they sank down into plush armchairs opposite the Leprechaun, who had placed his curved blade, which he had carried with him upstairs, on the floor next to one of the chairs. The rain had died down a bit now, as had the fracas up by the gate, although the disturbance created by the angry Barada was not fizzling out altogether; it was simply taking another form.

As the lads glanced over toward the gates to Strongbranch, they saw that there were still a number of Barada pounding on the huge portals. Also, there were a handful of guards standing on top of the ramparts, and these were the target of a great deal of miscellaneous debris being hurled by the crowd below, which they were warding off with huge bark tower shields. However, a substantial portion of the enraged throng, realizing that it was futile to assault the gates, had begun to dissipate. But the rioting was far from over, for the Barada who had left the gate area were racing in groups of fifty or so around the district of the city in which the Gnarly Stump stood, shouting like madmen all the while. Many of them were headed off to the south, where, presumably, they were going to vent their frustrations in some destructive manner.

Fergus observed these roving rioters for a few moments, shaking his head. Sighing, he went over to the writing desk and pulled open one of the drawers. He drew out a little rectangular tin, closed the drawer and plopped back down in an armchair that was appropriately sized for his small frame. Then he opened the container, took out an amber-colored lozenge with glistening white crystals on it and tossed it into his mouth.

Noticing the lads' inquisitive expressions, he extended the tin toward them. "Rumbadinnies," he said.

Hesitantly, they each took one and placed it in their mouths. They found them to be mellow and sweet, faintly floral and soothing on the throat.

"Thank you," Girion said, as the Leprechaun placed the tin underneath his chair.

"'Tisn't any trouble at all, at all," Fergus assured, leaning back. Then, looking at Aradis' chest, he remarked, "But, ye know, that medallion ye've got han't giv'n anyting *but* trouble to the Questmongers. Ya see, we've been a-lookin' from the tops o' the towers to the dregs o' the sea for that ting for the pas' seven years. An' then two Menfolk jus' come a-strollin' in wit it one mornin'. Who'd e'er expec' such a ting?"

Now, folding his hands together, he leaned forward and said, "All right, then. Let's begin our wee conference. I'm Fergus O'Brannadon, as ye seem to know. I'm what's known as the Questkeeper, the leader o' the Questmongers. An' pardon me if I've forgotten the names on ye, but I've had a bit of a shock since me ears first heard 'em."

"I'm Aradis Kingblade," Aradis stated.

"And I'm Girion Ringmark," Girion declared.

"This time I'll hold on to 'em," Fergus promised. "Now, I'll be a-hearin' yer own tale before ye shall hear aught from me. For I'm the leader o' the Questmongers, sure enough, just as I said. An' though ye wouldn' be up here in me quarters unless I trusted ye to begin wit, I'd still have a fair bit out o' ye before I feel it wise for ye to hear a fair bit from me. The Questmongers ha' been some o' the folk most trusted by the Konaskwa for one tousan', one hundred an' seventy-nine years now. So I hope ye shall excuse me bein' a bit strong on the point, but I've got summtin of a tradition an' a reputation to uphold."

"We understand." Girion nodded, still savoring his rumbadinny.

"Yer story, then?" the Leprechaun prompted. "Tell me who ye are, how ye came by this medallion an' how ye came to seek out the Questmongers."

Aradis began, "Before I explain anything, I want to ask your forgiveness for the things I said downstairs. I don't always have the best control over what comes out of my mouth when I'm angry, and I freely confess that I was speaking out of rashness and folly. The truth is that I didn't mean any of that."

Quite gravely, Fergus returned, "At's fortunate, because if ya did, you an' I would have to fight it out yet. But I know ya didna mean anyting by it because I'm the same way. If a fella gets cheeky wit me, anyting's liable to come out o' me mout. But we've no score to settle, you an' I, Aradis, so ya needn' fret over it."

Much relieved, Aradis stated, "Then I shall begin our tale."

After a nod from the Leprechaun, he commenced, "Girion and I are simple folk from a village in a kingdom named Velaris, which is in eastern Quarana. Neither of us had any intention whatsoever of coming to Argonis. Neither of us knew about what was going on with Thornoak or Ravinia or, frankly, anything at all about this place. But one night we encountered a stranger who seemed to be merely a Manfellow, one of our own kind. Much to our surprise, he revealed himself with great power, then informed us he was a Hadathi named Nagello. Neither Girion nor I had ever had dealings with the Haedra, the realm of the Immaterial, before, so we were, as you can imagine, quite bewildered by all of this."

Fergus' expression revealed next to nothing about how he was taking this Haedran element of the narrative, so Aradis went on, a little more guardedly this time, fearful that the Leprechaun might be regarding them as mere tale-spinners. "This Hadathi relayed to us a series of orders from the Danna, orders that we were to come to Argonis and converse with

Thornoak, with the aim of bringing unity back to the kingdom. And then we were to go on to slay Ravinia."

"An' ye knew absolutely nuttin' o' Tornoak or Ravinia before this?" Fergus inquired.

"Nothing," Girion affirmed.

"An' ye've come from the east, then, have ye?" the Leprechaun queried.

"We have," Aradis replied.

For a moment, a curious look crossed the Leprechaun's face. "Have ye a token to show that ye are indeed from Velaris, this kingdom in Quarana?" he asked.

The lads looked at each other, and then Girion held up his index finger, as he often did when he had just struck upon an idea of considerable excellence. Within a few moments, he had retrieved his notebook from his pack. Opening it to the inside of the front cover, he pointed to an emblem there. "This is the Velarisian flag," he explained. "This crossed scythe and axe stand for the Plains of Agleri and Rimwold Forest, respectively, and the blue field behind them represents the Brines of Ferassi, which border the Marlassi Coast and Cape Loresso. Those are all regions in Velaris, by the way. My father got this journal at a stationary shop in Aragest, which is the capital of Velaris." Handing the notebook to Fergus, he urged him to examine it further. "Turn through it and you will see a careful record of our journey, which has taken us around a month and a half."

Fergus thumbed through its pages, examining Girion's numerous illustrations, maps and diagrams. After a few moments, he queried, with more than a hint of suspicion in his voice, "It only took ye a mont' an' a half to get here from eastern Quarana?"

Girion explained, "The ship we took from our homeland had an acrynon, an invention of the Field-Gnomes of Estereth that greatly increases the speed of a vessel, so it only took us nineteen days to sail from Velaris to the Fontskals in the Indurian Deeps."

"Ah, I see," Fergus said, handing the notebook to Girion, who put it back in his pack. "Now, let's speak o' the medallion. So the Hadat'i gave it to you?" the Leprechaun asked, turning to Aradis.

"Yes," the lad replied. "He didn't explain anything about its true significance to me, nor did he tell me where he got it. He only told me that it would play a substantial role in this quest and that I would need it to win the aid of those who would doubt me, even after someone they respect had … " Chasing a stray thought, he trailed off. Then, looking straight at Fergus, he asked, "Do you respect Peleus Chula?"

"O' course," Fergus answered, somewhat caught off guard by the query. "I know it may not a-seem that way, but all of us respect 'im, especially me. Remember what I said abou' tings comin' out o' me mout when I'm angry 'at I don' really mean? Well, I may have said some pretty bitter tings abou' Chula, but he's a warrior of incredible skill. A great healer an' tracker too. But that mem'ry o' his: it can be appallin'. Sometimes tha' bloke's as lucid as can be, but other times he'll forgot the simplest o' tings, though he's never let the finches fly amuck – he's never jeopardized our secrecy, that is. An' it din't used to be as bad as it is now, but it's gotten worse for sure. However, he's always been a wee bit eccentric. Actually, heaps of eccentric. He can't help it, ya see, comin' from the far side o' the Eldritch Isles an' all. They're all crazy there, jus' to varyin' degrees. But I wouldna let 'im in the Questmongers in the firs' place if his beneficial contributions din't outweigh his obnoxious oddities. Now, what was it you were a-sayin' abou' the medallion?"

"Oh yes," Aradis regained his trail of thought, as he swallowed the last fragment of his rumbadinny. "Well, when the Hadathi told me I would need to show the medallion as a sign in order to gain aid, I suppose this was the instance he spoke of."

"A sign indeed!" Fergus laughed. "A sign it truly is, to be sure, to be sure. The Sign o' the Sengara."

"Of the *what*?" Aradis asked.

"Don' ye mind for the moment. We'll get to tha' soon enough. I've got some more wee questions first. For instance, what brought ye here to the Questmongers' Den?" Fergus inquired, helping himself to another piece of candy from his tin. "Did the Hadat'i tell ye to seek us out?"

Girion now took up the tale. "No. We first heard of you only after we entered Argonis. You see, when we were in the Emerald Run, we had a rather lengthy conversation with Shillelagh McDasher."

"I'm sorry to hear that," Fergus stated rather brusquely. Shillelagh had, of course, warned the Siloans that he and Fergus were not presently on good terms, so neither of them was terribly taken aback by this remark.

At least Fergus didn't explode in rampant rage at the mere mention of the Forebounder's name, which is more than could be said for Boss Gronk.

"Well, um, yes," Girion went on, "but anyway, we told him of our plans to speak with Thornoak, and he explained that the only real hope of getting an audience with the Konaskwa lay in arranging it through his daughter, Langwana, but that the only feasible way of securing a meeting with her was by going through you and the Questmongers."

"'Ol' McDasher's not good for much of anyting, but at least he sen' ye to the right persons. Most folk would have advised ye to contac' Tornoak or the princess via Hoarstaff. But that wouldna gotten ye what ye needed."

"And why is that?" Girion asked.

"Hoarstaff, like as not, would have difficulty settin' up a chat wit the princess, not because she doesn' trust 'im, but because she doesn' necessarily trust everyone he trusts. But he canna be blamed for tha'. For he's only involved wit matters o' state, broadly speakin', not wit matters deep, heavy an' secret. For such matters, the princess consults wit me."

Fergus suddenly stood up, went into his bedroom and returned with a drinking flask, from which he gulped several times before sitting back down. Clearing his throat, he declared, "Now I've got another question for the two o' ye – how did ye get into Argonis in the firs' place?"

"The Hadathi instructed us to seek out a ship captain by the name of Felding Starwash," Aradis explained. "We found him in the Fontskals. By that time, we had heard from a great many people that it would be difficult to find anyone who would even consider taking us to the coast of Sarganath – anyone in his right mind, that is. But neither Felding nor his little, sausage-eating first mate, Jiffaloo Timtale, were entirely in their right minds, I guess you could say."

"Sausage-eatin'?" Fergus perked up. Then, scrunching up his face slightly, he asked, "Did this Felding, by chance, pull his ship in backwards in port?"

Both of the Menfolk, arrested by this uncanny inquiry, looked at each other, baffled. "Why, as a matter of fact, he did," Girion replied.

"I know the bugger," Fergus muttered rather irritably. "Sure as rain I know 'im, but I didna know his name."

"How is that?" Aradis asked, mystified that the leader of the Questmongers had previously made the acquaintance of the incomparable Captain Felding.

"Two years ago, meself an' a few o' the Questmongers had to tend to affairs abroad on behalf o' the princess, which was already a tricky business, on account o' how hard it is to be a-leavin' an' enterin' Argonis, what wit the Dwarves an' the Blackwings an' all. We were in a wee boat up in Azlangorash, a harbor in Hadarnagari – that's a land in southeastern Pollona – an' there comes a-blunderin' toward us a ship manned only by two Barada, this Felding an' his meat-chowin' chum. The boat was goin' all waggy-like, comin' in backwards. I han't e'er seen the like of it. Well, it so happened we needed to leave that harbor pretty fast, afore we were seen, as particular folk were a-comin' after us in order to execute us. But that ninny backed his ship right into ours an' smashed it up against the dock."

Aradis and Girion couldn't keep from laughing at this exemplary instance of Felding's antics; they could picture the entire episode quite vividly, and that only made the whole thing more hilarious.

"Oh, it weren't funny at all." Fergus scowled. "We nearly were captured an' killed on account o' those ding-dongs, since, after the captain wrecked our ship, we hadna proper way to leave the place. Let me tell ye: when that sausage-chewin' little minion came over to try to calm me down, I shoved 'im into the drink, an' then Captain Starwallow – or whatever ye called 'im – tried to assuage me wit twisty talk. But he an' his runt gave us the slip, an' we din't get a lick o' compensation for what 'e'd done wit his stupid steerin'. An', as I said, on top o' that, all of us were almos' put to death on tha' disastrous trip. We ended up havin' to hide in the Hadarnagari interior for a full week afore we could locate another vessel to come back to Argonis."

Fergus took another swig from his flask and then, still rather irked at the considerable unpleasantries precipitated by Felding on him and his colleagues, urged, "Go on wit yer tale, though. I'd wager if any bloke were mad enough to take ye straight to Sarganath, it'd be that maniac."

"All right, then," Aradis obliged. "Felding took us to Gorondil, and though he had come up with a brilliant scheme to get us through the place undetected, we were found out. He escaped back to sea, and the two of us went on across the Farren, trailed by Druids the whole way."

"Ravinia knows about ye, then," Fergus murmured. "Ah, that's bad. But carry on."

"Yes, we too rather wish she hadn't taken such an unhealthy interest in us," Girion remarked. "Having traversed the Farren, we fled into Thornberry Thicket and would have perished there had not the Fall-Elves rescued us. We were taken by Tandarron, who is the Master Warden of the Bounds –"

"I know 'im well," Fergus interrupted.

Aradis, his eyes wandering down to the floor, gloomily said, "Then you'll be sorry to hear that he is dead, and that on our account, I'm afraid."

"What?" Fergus started up.

"Several days after we left the Fall-Elves, we overheard some Blackwing messengers from Mardelac Forest gloating that they had found and interrogated him about us," Aradis glumly related. "He refused to reveal anything, so the Blackwings slew him. Unfortunately, another Fall-Elf told them that Goldquiver had permitted us to enter Argonis, but they killed him as well."

"All manner o' strange tings are afoot!" Fergus exclaimed. "I canna see Goldquiver allowin' ye to proceed into Argonis, but queerer tings have come to pass, I suppose. An' that really is poor news about ol' Tandarron. He was a good fellow. Loyal an' wise he was."

The Leprechaun paused, closing his eyes for a few moments, as he mourned the passing of Tandarron. Then he opened them, sighed softly and asked, "What else did ye hear from the Blackwings?"

Aradis replied, "Ravinia was apparently highly concerned that we were going to prove useful to Argonis in some capacity, but, from what we heard anyway, it doesn't sound like she knows about our involvement with the Danna or the Hadathi or that our whole purpose in coming here is to mend Argonis' disputes and then go to Blackbough Woods to slay her."

"Well, 'at's fortunate, cuz tha' rotten dame is madder than all the beasts o' the Bushbelt combined, an' if she had a notion o' what ye were on about, ye'd be dead afore ye could say, 'Whate'er ye do, don' give the bannymagracket a spoonful o' plum marmalade.'"

"The Blackwings also spoke of a plan to overrun Argonis by the end of next month, which, I suppose, would be Harasa, with some large, unexpected, additional forces from the south," Aradis recalled, as he puzzled over what a bannymagracket was and what it had to do with plum marmalade. "Of course, if she finds a way around the Greenwall before then, it will be a moot point."

Fergus leaned back, put his hands behind his head and twiddled his thumbs. "Ye lads have brought me bonnie much besides the medallion that is quite precious, not the least o' which is this heap of information. Indeed, 'tis mighty grand for the cause of Argonis that ye should be a-bringin' all this to me at such a time as this. Was there aught else ye learned from those Blackwing rascals?"

"Not really anything else of consequence," Girion said. "But we learned something the night before that, which you may find to be of interest."

"An' what is tha'?" Fergus eagerly asked.

Aradis explained, "When we spoke with Shillelagh, he told us the best course was to try to convince as many members of the Verdinnion as possible to support our quest if the council were summoned by Thornoak. Consequently, he encouraged us to go south to see Masterfarmer Mackle in Harnabrig. That route took us by an old cabin where we elected to spend the night."

"'Twas on Kannaset Lake Byway, was it?" the Leprechaun prompted, rubbing his thumbnail on one of his teeth.

"Aye," Girion replied, "only a few leagues south of the junction of the Byway and Redtimber Road. Anyway, around the Hour of Rayalta, in the very midst of the night, we heard screams of anguish. We went to investigate and found a Druid and six Mannish bandits torturing a poor Leprechaun."

Fergus swallowed hard at this revelation.

"Yes, what is it?" Girion inquired worriedly.

"Go on," Fergus returned. "What happen'd then, laddie?"

"We overheard the Druid, in essence, claiming to be a figure known as the Ravenstaff, an emissary of Ravinia, and he seemed to think the Leprechaun had been purposely hunting him down," Girion went on. "Aradis, I'm sorry to say, was captured."

"Did the Ravenstaff learn anyting about ye or yer quest?" Fergus asked.

"He did, unfortunately," Girion replied. "For, in the heat of the moment, Aradis declared that he intended to destroy Ravinia."

Fergus frowned. "I know you said tha' you didna tink the Witch or her folk knew ye were here in Anganor, but, what wit that accursed Druid a-bein' in league wit the Witch an' knowin' that yer aim is to kill her, ye can be right certain that he's a-puttin' forth all his best efforts to find ye. Now, how did ye escape from the Ravenstaff?"

"As it turned out, I was able to liberate both Aradis and the Leprechaun by throwing some well-aimed stones from the surrounding cover of the woods. Then all three of us fled. But the Ravenstaff used Daegar to set the forest ablaze and, with a bolt of fire from his staff, he struck down the Leprechaun."

Fergus sighed deeply, then hung his head. Looking up, his expression quite mournful, he revealed, "I'm afraid that was Landrig McOrrikin, one of our own Questmongers."

"How do you know?" Girion inquired.

"Because Landrig was in the very area ye're a-speakin' of, an' he was a-lookin' for the Ravenstaff."

"So the Ravenstaff *was* on to something!" Aradis gasped. "He suspected that the Leprechaun was doing the bidding of some other Barada, and he mentioned the princess or another nation as possibilities, though he did not mention the Questmongers. Was this Landrig on a mission for you, then?"

"He was," Fergus affirmed. "Ya see, we've been a-searchin' for the Ravenstaff for several years now, though we didna know 'im by tha' name until somewhat recently. We guessed a while ago that all the bandits were a-bein' directed by a single hand, ultimately itself directed by Ravinia, but we hadna got any proof o' the matter. Once we had verified the existence an' location o' this personage, we intended to strike at 'im an' render the huge snake o' the bandit operations headless. We commissioned a particular Questmonger, a Wood-Gnome named Ribble, who also happened to be an excellent fletcher an' bowyer, to scout around Argonis an' find 'im. Due to stray rumors tha' came to 'is ears, he guessed he might find the chap near the junction o' Redtimber Road an' Kannaset Lake Byway. So he took up residence in a cabin just a short ways from the Byway, which, unless I be greatly mistaken, is the very same cabin ye slept in. But, two years ago, we stopped receivin' communications from 'im, so we sen' Landrig to check out the matter, an' he foun' the place ransacked."

"Yes, I think it must be the same cabin, for everything in the hovel we stayed in looked as if it had been vandalized," Aradis confirmed.

"We suspected that the mysterious leader o' the bandits was behind all o' this, an' we presumed poor Ribble ha' been murdered by 'im, but we still hadna got an inklin' who or exac'ly where he was. Followin' that inciden', Landrig did a fair amount o' listenin' in the Naskanu, which is a rather seedy district of Anganor an' a place Landrig knew well, as he grew up there. After a great deal o' sleutin', he heard some o' the most indecen', insidious folk speakin' of a fella named the Ravenstaff. An', what's more, this fella was said to be operatin' out of a set o' caves under the Miccasaw Brakes, a densely wooded area a few miles west o' the cabin Ribble was a-stayin' in. So, a few mont's ago now, he wen' out a-lookin' for 'im in that region. But we hadna got a report from Landrig abou' the matter – not until now, that is, though it came from ye an' not from him."

Suddenly, in Aradis' mind, there loomed the image of Landrig's crumpled, burning body slamming into a tree trunk. Quite unsettled, the lad looked at Fergus and inquired, "Is Landrig survived by his mother and a sister? The Ravenstaff conjectured that it was so after looking at Landrig's locket. He actually threatened to kill them if the Leprechaun would not reveal his true identity."

Fergus' face was now lined with grave concern. "To be sure, bot his mother an' his sister live in the Quannamet, the Ward o' the Guilds, in Anganor. An' they are indeed in incredible danger if the Ravenstaff has it out for 'em, for a fella such as that most assuredly has ways of a-findin' out tings."

Rising, Fergus went over to the door, opened it and spoke to the Manfellow standing guard outside. "Kelwyn, I wan' you to go downstairs an' tell Limberleaf an' Stumpory to go to the Quannamet straightaway to get Rylish an' Breena NicOrrikin an' take 'em to Billowtwig at Strongbranch. On accoun' o' the hoo-ha up by the gate, they'll have to take our own special route, o' course. They're to stay there an' be cared for till other arrangements can be made by me personally. Have our boys only tell 'em what's needed at the moment, which is that there might be nasty folk a-lookin' for 'em an' that I shall tell them all abou' this business the day after tomorrow – or sooner if I can manage it. An' as soon as you've delivered your message, return here to guard wit Mordie."

Kelwyn nodded and went off to do Fergus' bidding. Then Mordie shut the door.

Strolling over to the window, Fergus surveyed the state of the ever-dwindling mob once more and then sat back in his chair.

"So ye've seen the Ravenstaff wit yer own eyes," he said, as he picked up his rumbadinny tin, opened it and tossed another candy into his mouth. "What did the chappie look like?"

Aradis thought hard about the point when he had been staring at the Druid as he approached him with the torch. "He was wearing a long brown robe and had a black staff with a raven carved on the top of it. His hair was brown and wavy and went to about his shoulders, I'd say, and his eyes were dark – very dark. He had a short, full beard too. And that's about all I can remember."

"An' did ye a-gather anyting about his usual haunts?" Fergus pressed.

"No," Girion replied, "except that he knew about the cabin because he sent one of his men to search it for others associated with Landrig. So, I would guess he knew that area somewhat well, which would make sense, since the caves you mentioned that he was using as a hideout were not far from there."

Then, reaching in his pocket, Aradis remarked, "Oh, that reminds me. We found this strange stone at the cabin underneath an overturned clay bowl." He opened his palm, and Fergus took the stone from him, holding it right in front of his eyes. The rain had faded even more by now, and there were a few sunbeams coming in through the window.

"Is it just a rock?" Girion inquired at length. "Or something more than that?"

The Leprechaun's brow furrowed noticeably, as he examined the stone from a number of different angles. At last, he announced, "This is a saranek, a sinister piece o' work indeed."

"And what is a saranek?" Aradis asked.

The Leprechaun looked at him, his face colored by a grim cognizance of just how dreadful the object he held was. "A saranek is an enchanted stone, an artifact o' Druidic Daegar, the evilest of all magics known to the Barada. In their dark rituals, the Druids invoke mighty Hadat'i to pour some o' their power into common objects – rocks an' pinecones an' the like – which can later be released by the pronouncement o' terrible, ancien' words. This stone is hard proof o' the trut' o' yer tale, an' pretty strong proof tha' the Ravenstaff is connected wit Ravinia. If we show this wee rock to the right people, we could accomplish what I've been tryin' to do wit the Questmongers all along. We can alert people to the fact – hopelessly horrid, but all too true – that Ravinia is already workin' among us, an' we've got to wake up all the good Barada of Argonis an' strike back against her afore 'tis too late. Yet we canna bring a large amount o' troops to attack the Ravenstaff an' his cohorts till we know precisely where his lair is. Unfortunately, it seems we'll have to send out another agent or two to finish tha' job."

Fergus got up again and anxiously began pacing his office. "So much. So much at once," he muttered. "Mercy, there's so much to be seen to."

"Is this saranek dangerous, then?" Girion wondered aloud, as he watched the Leprechaun briefly pause to drum his fingers on the windowsill. "Could it have drawn evil Hadathi to us?"

"It doesn' work like tha', laddie. 'Tis only dangerous in the hands o' the right – or, more properly – the wrong person. This particular type o' stone releases a cloud o' blindin', black smoke that terribly burns yer eyes an' skin when it's t'rown an' hits the ground. But it'll only do tha' if ye say the right words wit it an' link yerself to the evil Hadat'i who are providin' the power. I saw these beastly saraneks in action when I was a-spyin' on the Druids in Blackbough Woods a number o' years back – before the Greenwall came up, that is. Afore the Verdinnion disbanded. Afore Tornoak hid his-self away in Paanu Assagwa ..." he trailed off.

Suddenly turning to face the Menfolk, the Leprechaun declared, "I nearly forgot to ask ye whether yer aim to convince members o' the Verdinnion to support ye succeeded. I'm assumin' Goldquiver wanted no part o' the matter."

"Actually, we didn't directly ask him about it, as the idea was presented to us after we left Mendalas," Aradis said, "although he had nothing but nasty things to say about the Verdinnion. Shillelagh was, of course, the one who suggested that we speak to Thornoak about summoning the Verdinnion. He was eager for reconciliation with the other members who were holding on to grievances against him. Mackle came around after we conversed with him, as did Gronk, but it wasn't an easy task to persuade either of them."

"I can imagine. An' when we've more time to us, I should like to hear the full account o' how ye managed to convince 'em," Fergus said. His face now manifested the intense analysis that was going on inside of his head. The Questkeeper was undoubtedly pondering what to do next, as, just as he had stated, there was so much to be seen to, so much of great import.

For a few moments, Fergus looked out the window to check on the state of the riot, which had reached something of a lull. He then turned again to the Siloans, as he resolved, "I mus' go see Princess Langwana about all this witout delay. There's no time to lose, I'm afraid, as Ravinia an' her associates already have a fair amount of information that I rather a-wished they din't. But I must ask ye to trus' me, just as I've trusted ye. Aradis, will you grant me bot the medallion an' this saranek? For they shall be safer e'en wit the princess than wit me, an' they simply mustn' be lost to us now, especially the medallion."

"Of course," Aradis replied, as he reached up and began to lift the chain with the medallion over his head. Then he hesitated, as he asked, "What is this medallion? I know you may not be able to tell us everything, but I'd at least like to know something about it. You mentioned that it was the sign of something or other and that you'd explain the matter to us."

Fergus considered this, sighed heavily, then replied, "'Tis a deep matter, an' one I shanna be able to do justice to at the momen'. But I will tell you a little of it, just as I said I would. The sign I mentioned is the Sign o' the Sengara."

"Now, the Ingans around here who hold fast to the old ways have a language called Asla'gu. An' 'sengara' is a word in Asla'gu that refers to a particular sort o' bein' – a magical bein', if ye will, though often appearin' as a Barada an' nuttin' more. Only a few people ha' e'er seen 'em; they wander the woods and the wilds, it is said, an' they speak in riddles and prophecies. It is also said tha' all o' their words come to pass, unlike those o' the local Ingan oracles, so any time a sengara speaks, heed is taken."

"But how does all this relate to the medallion?" Aradis asked.

"Be patien', laddie," Fergus chided. "Now, ha' ye noticed that yer medallion looks to be only a half of a whole?"

"We have thought that to be the case from the beginning," Girion confirmed.

"Well, ye were correct. There *is* another half, an' it's been sittin' here in Argonis all by its lonesome for more than a hundred an' seventy years. An' at the time yer half disappeared from Argonis, a prophecy was given by a sengara to a soldier of Tengwaru – tha' was Tornoak's father – that when this half ye've got came back to us, a cascade of events would be set in motion that would lead to the fusin' o' the medallion an' the deliverance o' the kingdom from a time o' terrible trouble. However, that was merely a reiteration of a prophecy that was made by another sengara aroun' five tousan' years ago regardin' the exac' same matter. So that, laddies, is the Sign o' the Sengara – the return o' this half o' the medallion, which signals all the tings I jus' tol' ye about."

Aradis and Girion's mouths fell open in disbelief, and they could find no words to reply.

Fergus smiled knowingly, then declared, "I know. 'Tis madness. Yet here the sign is afore our very eyes. Now perhaps ye can see why I an' all the rest o' the Questies were so stricken when we firs' saw the medallion."

Clearing his throat, the Leprechaun then said, "An' now for your other question, the one about what the medallion actually is. This is all I will say at present; 'tis a very, very ancien' artifact called the Amulet o' the Akwarna, which has come down to us from the very beginnings of Argonis, from early in the Years o' Yore. An' 'tis directly linked to our only real hope against Ravinia, which is a bein' as powerful as herself, an Enchantress named Janura. She's the sengara from five tousand years ago tha' made the prophecy I mentioned. But Janura, unlike tha' fiend Ravinia, is good, exceedingly good, an' she will certainly help us. Yet only tru the medallion can we get to her."

"Do you know if this Janura is in league with the Danna?" Girion asked, at last recovering enough from his shock that he could think clearly and now wondering how all of this fit in with what Nagello had told them.

"I canna say for certain, the fact bein' that I'm not all that knowledgeable 'bout her meself, but my guess would be that she is. That's all I can say abou' the matter right now, as I'm pressed hard for time. Later we may speak more of it, but, in trut', Princess Langwana's far more qualified then meself to tell the full tale o' the medallion. For indeed, I'm privy to but a part of its deep history an' potency."

"With that being the case, the sooner this thing is out of my possession, the better," Aradis declared, as he took the medallion off and handed it to Fergus. "I've no wish to be the guardian of such an artifact as you have described, nor am I fit to be one." The lad's head was spinning wildly, as he contemplated the great significance and antiquity of this item he had been carrying, oblivious to all of it, for dozens of days and thousands of miles. Taking one last look at the medallion, which rested in Fergus' open palm, Aradis noticed that if the other piece of the medallion looked similar to this half, the whole thing would have presented a distinctly egg-shaped leaf, with the widest part near the stem.

After Fergus had examined the medallion fragment intently, rubbing his finger over its fine, silver filigree, he shoved both it and the saranek into a secret pouch just inside the left hip of his trousers.

Girion now asked, "Since there's another half of the medallion, and that's so pivotal to this Sign of the Sengara that you told us about, do you happen to know where the other half might be?"

Fergus grinned widely. "O' course I know where it is. That's why I was so delighted that ye brought this half. The Questmongers ha' been a-searchin' for this half for the pas' seven years, witout e'en a trace o' luck – until now. But the other half o' the medallion has been wit Tornoak till rather recen'ly; now 'tis in the keepin' o' Princess Langwana."

"Where is she, by the way?" Girion inquired. "At Strongbranch Citadel?"

"Not these days. At least not very often," Fergus returned. "She stays in a rather out-o'-the-way place called Iswa Hanahoma, the Groves of Silent Reverie. 'Tis a royal sanctuary, a series o' maginificen' gardens that's been aroun' since the close o' the Apex of Archaea. The princess has dwelt there e'er since her father wen' to Paanu Assagwa, for 'tis a few miles closer to that spot than Anganor is, a-makin' it easier for her to visit Tornoak. But also, there she can conduct affairs o' the kingdom witout ev'ry Barada an' all his relatives bein' in her business, if ya know what I mean."

Seeing the lads' uncertain expressions after this last statement, Fergus clarified, "If it weren' for the princess, Argonis'd surely be undone by now. For she has dealin's wit many more folk than the Questmongers, an' e'en I don' know all o' who she talks to. Also, much o' what she an' I speak of I don' share wit anyone – not e'en the Questmongers. That's prob'ly for the best, at any rate, for the fewer tha' know some o' these tings, the better. Hoarstaff, as I said, attends to matters o' state, bein' the Ayonashka an' all – the chief minister o' the kingdom, that is – but the princess attends to matters o' security. But her success in this depends on people not a-knowin' wha' she's up to. An' so, cuz she's far from pryin' eyes an' ears, she has twarted many a plot o' Ravinia's – bot inside an' outside of Argonis."

"Will we be going with you to see Princess Langwana?" Aradis asked, as he arose. "We want to try to convince her to let us see Thornoak, so we can persuade him to summon the Verdinnion."

"Regret is on me for it, lad, but ye canna see the princess yet," Fergus returned, though not in an unkindly manner. "It shall be tricky enough for me to get out o' the city alone wit this cargo, as Ravinia's spies know me face an' watch the gates of Anganor an' the area surroundin' the city at practically all times o' bot day an' night. I've got secret ways o' gettin' out, o' course, but I must go alone so as to not have to protect ye as well, for I may be spotted on the road sout to Iswa Hanahoma, an' then we should be in a pretty bind indeed. After I've gotten the saranek an' the medallion to the princess, I shall come back an' get ye, but I should like to have her approval o' meetin' ye first. For even I wouldn' presume upon one so high an' lofty in station as the princess. To be sure, she's the one that'll decide if she wishes to meet ye or not, and, if so, whether or not she will attemp' to bring ye to Tornoak."

"I suppose it will be better that way, anyhow," Girion said, "for I've not slept at all since yesterday morning, and Aradis has only slept a short while."

"In tha' case," Fergus remarked, "it certainly wouldn' be wise to take ye now, for e'en from the Quannamet Gate in the soutwest corner of Anganor, which is the nearest to Iswa Hanahoma, 'tis a journey o' more than tirteen miles. 'Tis best then, that ye stay here an' get plenty o' rest. Besides, supposin' Ravinia or the Ravenstaff have sen' folk after ye, here ye shall be well-protected by the Questmongers. I shanna return till shortly before dawn tomorrow, I expect. An' when I return, I like as not shall be takin' ye wit me back down to Iswa Hanahoma. At least so I hope."

Bending down, he retrieved the blade he had set on the floor when he had first entered and attached it to his girdle. Then he opened the door and addressed the Wood-Gnome on guard duty. "Mordie, take these lads back down to the Quest Hall. They're a-goin' to sleep for a while." Turning to the other Questmonger just outside the door, the Manfellow, he said, "Kelwyn, come in here a wee minute. I've got some tings to go over wit ye, tings ye shall need to do while I'm gone."

As Fergus and Kelwyn began their conference, Mordie waved to Aradis and Girion, who had by then gathered their belongings from the floor of Fergus' quarters. They followed him back down the spiral staircase and down the ladder to the room with the big table, where he showed them into a passageway that lay beyond one of the many doors. Just off this passageway, there was a small room with a chamber pot and a washbasin on a stand. He gave them a few minutes to freshen up and then took them back to the room with the long table, down the narrow staircase to the hall below it and finally back into the main hall of the Questmongers' Den. There they laid their accoutrements down and cast themselves onto two couches near the fireplace.

"I never would have guessed the medallion Nagello gave me had even half so much significance as all that business Fergus was talking about," Aradis said quietly, snuggling his head into a large pillow.

"Much of this adventure has been filled with things we could not or would not have guessed," Girion commented, also getting cozy. "The Danna, it seems, is full of surprises."

"Some of them good, and some of them not so good," Aradis remarked. "We've had some of both this morning."

Terribly exhausted as they were, they yawned widely, as they sunk into the soft fabric. There were so many matters of tremendous import bustling around in their heads, so many questions, but they could not entertain them presently. The persistent shouts of a few outraged Barada gathered around the gates to Strongbranch still reached their ears, though quite faintly now. These shouts were an embodiment of Argonis' unrest and peril to them, quite real and unsettling. However, their stamina and strength were too dim to do aught about the matter. While they had been talking to Fergus, they had remained reasonably alert, but now, their weariness swiftly overtook them. Within less than five minutes, they fell fast asleep, lulled to sweet slumber by the crackle of a low fire that had been kindled in the hearth.

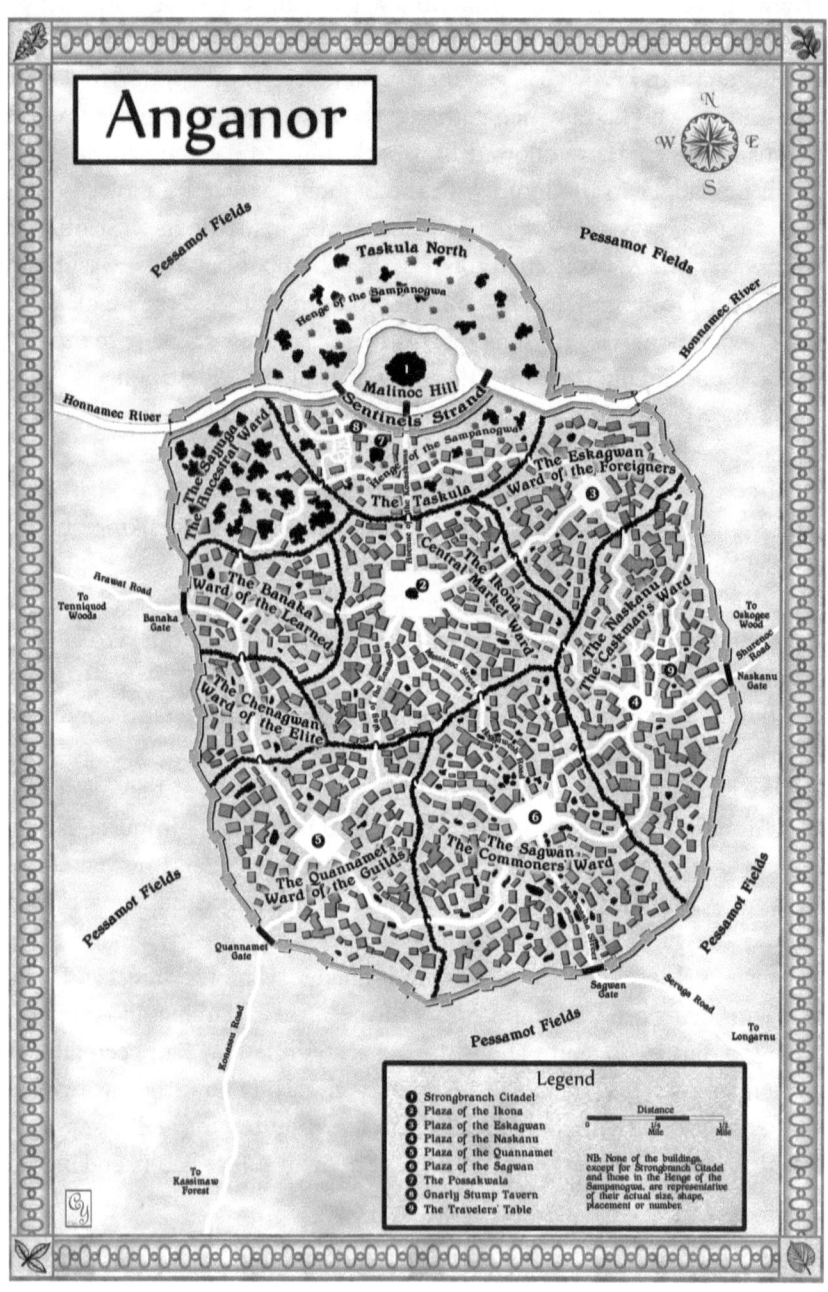

Anganor

CHAPTER THREE

The Company of Kelwyn Faircrest

number of hours later, Girion awoke and looked around. There were only a few Questmongers in the room, and two Ingans were guarding the door to the exterior hallway now, rather than the Dwarf and the Timber-Elf. A Leprechaun was sitting looking out one of the east windows, and Mordie and Kelwyn were sitting in chairs near the fireplace, talking quietly. Girion got up and walked over to the wide windows overlooking the area with the speaker's dais. He was rather pleased to discover that there was no longer any mob, as such, at least in the sense that there was nobody being raucous or rioting. However, there were about forty Barada, mostly Ingans, some sitting and others standing up by the gates, presumably keeping watch on them in case some guards from Strongbranch tried to sneak out.

Girion turned to the nearby Leprechaun and said, "Pardon me, but what time is it?"

"The Journey o' Marda," he answered, puffing on a little pipe. Girion had guessed as much, for from the sunlight, it looked as if the afternoon was well underway.

"What time did the mob finally calm down?"

"Quite a few hours ago now," came the reply.

"That's fortunate," Girion remarked. "I was worried that whole affair might end rather badly."

"Ah, the full repercussions o' the matter ha' not yet come to fruition," the Leprechaun asserted. "Many o' those folk were once some o' Tornoak's strongest supporters, but now they've been turned against 'im. 'Tis only a matter o' time before there'll be more trouble. In fact, there's already been a fair heap of it."

"What's been going on?" Girion asked.

"To start wit, folk went a-runnin' off to the Banaka, the Ward o' the Learned, an' the Chenagwan, the Ward o' the Elite, bot o' which are districts of Anganor. There they broke into the homes of a number o' government officials, where they wreaked heaps o' havoc. E'en worse, some upstart Ingan named Quagga is now fancyin' his-self the provisional governor of Anganor. Shortly after ye wen' to sleep, he got some folk gathered around 'im up by the gate, an' he told 'em that, seein' as how they couldn' get up into Strongbranch, they ought to take over the city. All they'd have to do is capture all the guards, who would be sorely outnumbered. Ya see, the folk he was a-stirrin' up have a good many ne'er-do-well friends who didna come to see Tornoak in the mornin'. An' those swinish vermin would take any chance to play a part in a storm o' mischief tha' they could get, e'en at the drop of a cake crumb. So it weren' difficult at all to get those grimy goons on board with Quagga's program."

"What exactly are Quagga's intentions? Or what do you suspect them to be?" Girion inquired.

"His plan is to keep folk from a-gettin' out o' Strongbranch, holdin' 'em hostage, as it were, till his demands are met. For he means to not relax his hold on the city till Tornoak comes to parley wit 'im. He shouted as much up to the guards on the wall an' told 'em to relay the message to Hoarstaff. Should Hoarstaff decide to do summtin' about it, he'll have to sen' down a messenger to the gates an' Quagga's folk will let 'im tru. O' course, all the soldiers in Strongbranch an' in Taskula Nort – which is the area just nort o' Strongbranch – could march out at any time an' knock this windbag Quagga an' his roustabout followers silly, but I rather suspect Hoarstaff doesn' wan' to stir tings up more than they already are, nor to bring about any bloodshed that isn't absolutely necessary. Quagga's such a pin-brain he likely doesn' realize the Strongbranch soldiers could beat him so badly, but e'en if he did, he'd prob'ly have started his ridiculous revolt anyhow. To be sure, folk like tha' let their fickle passions seize the rudder o' their minds while their better sense stays locked up in the hold. 'Tis really a pity, ya know."

"Do you think Thornoak will actually come speak with Quagga?" Girion asked, eyeing the ruffians up by the gate.

"Not at all, at all!" the Leprechaun laughed. "Tornoak hasn' cared enough to come out o' Paanu Assagwa for seven years, an' he certainly isn' a-goin' to be spurred out o' the place by some pompous bogtrotter like Quagga.

We can only hope that he doesn' cause too much trouble for the bonnie people of Anganor. His foul folk have already taken control of all the gates in the city, as well as all the guard posts right next to 'em. From what I've heard, no one's been killed on account of it, for they've only seized the guards an' tied 'em up, keepin''em in the cells o' their own posts. One might congratulate Quagga for havin' accomplished that feat wit an untrained group of underlings, but 'tis not really that impressive when you consider that there are only a handful o' guards at each gate, while there are prob'ly more than a tousan' Barada a-runnin' aroun' doin' Quagga's bidding. Also, the guards likely knew twould be pointless to fight back until everyone gets their heads on straight again, 'specially if Hoarstaff doesn' send 'em any sort of assistance. An' it seems likely he won't, at least not immediately – that bein' on accoun' o' the reasons I jus' mentioned."

"I'm glad that no one's been seriously hurt yet," Girion sighed. "Isn't there anything that can be done to stop this fellow, though?"

The Leprechaun shook his head. "Fergus went up to Strongbranch early this mornin' an' learned tha' Tornoak had sent word to Hoarstaff that he wasn' a-feelin' so grand an' simply wasn' up to makin' the journey to Anganor. Consequently, we were privy to the fact ahead o' time tha' Tornoak wouldn' be a-speakin' this mornin', an' all of us knew a riot was sure to result. But there was nuttin' to be done about it, considerin' how many folk would be involved, so we jus' had to let tings unfold. An' wit the way tings are now, we can do even less. For if the Questmongers were to go aroun' like vigilantes an' take out the ringleaders, people would jus' get more riled up. An', like I said, the folk at Strongbranch could come out an' clean tings up real quick if they wanted to. Besides, they've got plenty o' provisions to last 'em during this feeble excuse for a siege. This business could heat up like a tantrum o' Marda, though, if Quagga starts a-keepin' regular folk from leavin' an' enterin' the city, as there are a fair number o' Barada who live outside of Anganor but come in to the markets ev'ry day to sell their wares."

"Yes, we met a farmer this morning who is in precisely that situation," Girion said.

"Barrin' Tornoak' his-self actually a-comin' back, our next best hope to end all this tomfoolery would be that Quagga sets off a fair number o' the people who are currently apat'etic about this whole affair. If they get mad enough, they could subdue his silly revolt themselves, hopefully witout too much violence. To be sure, Hoarstaff would step in if tings got bad enough, but I tink he jus' wants to give the matter some time. But the problem is tha' so few care about anyting anymore. In fact, they're quite conten' to let Quagga imagine he's in charge for a while as long as he doesn' interfere too much wit their business. For, ya know, laziness is always an easier road in the momen', e'en if it comes back to sting ye like a nasty hornet later on. An' most folk fancy takin' an easier road – if they can get one, that is."

"In that, you speak the truth," Girion concurred.

He looked back over by the fire and saw that Aradis was stirring, so he thanked the Leprechaun for answering all his questions, then went and sat down on the couch next to Aradis. The younger Siloan yawned, stretched his tired limbs and sat up.

"Better?" Girion prompted.

"Much," Aradis sleepily returned.

Now Kelwyn and Mordie ceased their conversation and turned to their guests. Kelwyn was about the same height as the Siloans and had a very handsome face, a strong build, cool, amber eyes and a full head of lustrous blond hair that fell in gentle waves to the back of his neck. He was dressed in a simple gray shirt, trousers of a darker gray and high, black boots. Mordie was a young, stout Wood-Gnome with light-brown hair, a well-trimmed, brown beard and thoughtful, green eyes. He had on a pair of old, patched tan trousers, light-brown boots, a white shirt and a black leather jerkin.

Extending his hand toward the Siloans, Kelwyn smiled and declared in a cheerful, tenor voice, "I'm glad you've had a rest, dear friends. I'm sure it was severely needed if you slept so long in the middle of the day." Shaking their hands in turn, he introduced himself. "I'm Kelwyn Faircrest, a Questmason, and this is Mordie, a Questguard."

"Questmason? Questguard?" Girion repeated the terms inquiringly.

"Those are two different positions in the Questmongers," Kelwyn explained. "Each of us has to be quite versatile, and all of us are expected to be able to do anything that's needed, but we each have our specialties. Questmasons analyze intelligence and construct plans that will help us successfully carry out complicated missions. Questguards are the most gifted warriors and are consequently called upon most in situations requiring intense combat."

"Ah, I see," Girion returned. "And are there any other positions?"

"Aye," Kelwyn answered. "Questkeeper and Questseeker. Fergus is the one and only Questkeeper. He makes decisions about what missions must be attempted, how they must be conducted, who will conduct them and so forth. Questseekers are superb at disguises, blending in and collecting information, so many of them travel around quite a bit. That's actually – "

Suddenly, Mordie cut in, "Kelwyn, why the blazes are you telling them all this? There's really no call for you spilling all there is to know about the Questmongers to them."

Kelwyn shot a slightly perturbed glance at his companion, as he retorted, "I'm not telling them anywhere close to all there is to know about the Questmongers. Besides, the reason I'm in command when Fergus is gone is that he trusts my judgment. And if Fergus, who's rather hard-nosed about everything, as you know quite well, trusts my judgment, I don't see why you should doubt it. Besides, before he left, Fergus told me that we are to take these Menfolk into full confidence. He feels as if they've more than demonstrated that they are deserving of that. That's not to say that we shall tell them everything we know, but we needn't treat them with suspicion; that's all. But, if it makes you happy, I shall clam up about any more details regarding our organization."

"Oh, you needn't be so cross," Mordie protested. "I wasn't challenging your authority. I just would rather play things safe."

"These Menfolk *are* perfectly safe," Kelwyn rejoined.

Mordie ignored this last comment, as he requested, "Tell us your names again, lads, so that we may be better acquainted."

"I'm Aradis Kingblade," Aradis stated, as he nodded politely to Mordie.

"Girion Ringmark," the elder Siloan said.

"Fine," Kelwyn returned quite heartily. "Just fine." Roguishly, he continued, winking at Mordie, "Now, as Mordie may take offense if we speak any more about our own business, we should certainly be pleased to hear about yours instead. If you would, tell us all about yourselves and your story. For I recall you stating that you came all the way from eastern Quarana, for that is where you said you met the Hadathi. Eastern Quarana is so very far from here that the account of your journey alone must be remarkable."

The lads felt much more at ease talking to Kelwyn and Mordie than to Fergus, for a lot had been at stake in their interview with the Questkeeper, which naturally added a great deal of tension. So together, over the next few hours, they gave an account of their lives in Siloa, as well as the principal events that had transpired on their adventures since the night they had met Nagello. The two Questmongers were excellent conversationalists, especially Kelwyn, and thus the time passed swiftly.

A little before sunset, the foursome were discussing Aradis' battle with Gronk on the Tower of Tangarosh, when they were interrupted by the sound of a single, tinkling chime. Startled, the Siloans looked off to the right and spotted what had produced it, a small, polished bell hanging next to the table on the north wall of the room. The bell was attached to a thin cord that ran down through a tiny hole in the floorboards.

"What's the bell for?" Girion asked, as he glanced over at the windows and noticed how late it had become.

"It's a warning system," Kelwyn replied. "Brightbole, who runs the counter down in the Gnarly Stump and is a good friend of ours, rings it whenever somebody goes up the stairs, unless it's a Questmonger, that is. If he's not around, one of his helpers rings it; they're our friends too. Lots of times people are just going up to the third floor, so we don't need to do anything. The bell rings once if it's someone who looks harmless, twice if it's somebody that could be potentially troublesome and three times if it's someone known to be dangerous."

"Did it ring when we came up here?" Aradis inquired.

"Yep," Mordie answered. "You got one ring."

"I'm glad we didn't get two or three," Girion laughed. Then, after looking around the room, he said, "I don't mean to further interrupt the story of Aradis' fight with Gronk, but I've been wondering about something ever since we arrived here. Are we currently inside of a huge stump?"

"That we are," Mordie returned. "This stump is all that's left of what was once a huge tree."

"But there are quite a few buildings like this up near Strongbranch," Aradis said. "Why were all of those trees cut down to stumps?"

"No one knows for sure, historically speaking," Kelwyn replied, "but there's an old Ingan legend that explains why, and many Barada in Argonis are content to accept the story as true."

"What is it?" Girion asked.

Repositioning himself in his chair, Kelwyn explained, "Nearly two thousand years ago, early in the Bridging of the Tides, all of these structures that are now just stumps were the bottom portions of huge trees,

trees which stood in a grove encircling the entirety of Malinoc Hill and Strongbranch Citadel. Each of them was around five hundred feet high, they say. Well anyway, at the time, there were twenty-five chalgunas, or priests or shamans or whatever you want to call them, living in twenty-five temples built into the trunks near the tops of these trees, with the most eminent chalguna living in the tree that was straight north of the hill. These chalgunas were extremely powerful and had even learned to control the weather – so it is claimed, anyway. With that being the case, they felt they could subdue the Konaskwa so that he might do their bidding. Thus, the chalgunas, being well-supplied with stores of food and drink, threatened to spoil the crops of the whole land with lightning and hail if the Konaskwa and his people did not cooperate with their every whim."

"The Konaskwa and his subjects were greatly terrified by this, so they granted the chalgunas their tyrannical terms. Thus, in short order, the chalgunas were able to subject Argonis to bitter enslavement, for that was what they had wanted all along: a great force of chattels who would do their every bidding. But there was a brave Ingan warrior named Hakwandasha who, having just returned from fighting as a mercenary in a foreign land, resolved to overthrow them. After a few weeks of recruiting, he had gathered a force of five hundred courageous Ingans around him. Hakwandasha delivered a fiery, bold speech to the people, beseeching them to cry to the powers of heaven and earth for victory, and then he lead his followers in an assault on the twenty-five trees. The chief chalguna, Kamonasoc, who was highly learned in powerful enchantments, responded by animating the trees from their crowns downward with his magic. Soon the trees begin to hurl down great pinecones the size of boulders upon the invaders, and it became exceedingly difficult for those already inside the trees to advance, for at Kamonasoc's command the passageways squeezed many of them to death, as the trees themselves were coming alive, as it were."

"However, Hakwandasha, with the aid of a strong rope, scaled the exterior of the chief chalguna's fortress and vanquished him atop his tower, hurling him to his death and thus ending his charm. When the chief chalguna perished, the portions of the trees that he had brought to life became blackened and twisted, as they perished along with him. The other chalgunas were soon defeated, for their powers were significantly inferior to those of their leader. Subsequently, Hakwandasha ordered that the cursed portions of the trees be removed, for they were unsightly and only served to remind the people of the chalgunas' wickedness. Thus, as the chief chalguna perished when the spell had animated all but the bottom sixty or seventy feet of the trees, that is all that remains today of that once mighty grove, which was known as the Henge of the Sampanogwa; its remnants are still called by that name. For that variety of tree, which has now quite vanished from Orona, save for these stumps, was known as a sampanog."

"Ah, that legend you've just related must be what the gates that led into this area up by Strongbranch were depicting!" Girion suddenly realized, recalling the image of the wicked-looking trees with the two Ingans battling atop the center one.

"That's it exactly,' Kelwyn affirmed. "But," he dolefully announced, "I'm afraid my telling the tale of the Felling of the Sacred Sampanogwa has deprived Aradis of the opportunity to finish his own tale of the battle on the Tower of Tangarosh, at least for the moment. For now, we must make our way out of the city to meet Fergus."

"What?" Aradis exclaimed. "Isn't he coming back here to get us?"

"That was his original plan," Kelwyn returned, "but, as we were discussing the matter, he decided that even the Questmongers' Den was not a safe enough place for you to spend the night, though you should have many strong warriors defending you."

"Does he really think there are people who might come here to kill us tonight?" Aradis asked, rather alarmed, glancing out at the dimming daylight.

"He thinks it's quite possible. But if they can't find you, they can't kill you, now can they? So, if there is an attack tonight, the Questmongers will be ready, but they shan't have to worry about protecting you, for we're meeting Fergus at a place called Duskdarrow, which is a small Questmongers hideaway in the forests to the east of Anganor. From there, if the princess has given her consent, he will take you on to Iswa Hanahoma to meet with her."

"Why are we meeting Fergus to the east of the city?" Girion asked, scratching his head. "I thought he said something about the southwest gate being the closest to Iswa Hanahoma when he was talking about going to see the princess."

Kelwyn replied, "That's a bit complicated to explain. Spies and all that, you know. Iswa Hanahoma, where the princess is staying, *is* to the southwest of Anganor – although it's a great deal more to the south than to the west – but it's not a good idea for us to be seen exiting the city through the gate he was talking about. You see, there are four gates out of Anganor: the Sagwan Gate, where, presumably, you entered the city since you were coming from Longarnu, the Quannamet Gate, which is in the southwest, the Banaka Gate, which leads to the west and the Naskanu Gate, which leads to the east. All four gates are watched, some more closely and more often than others, but the Quannamet Gate is watched most closely of all."

"The Questmongers have one secret tunnel that leads out of the city, which comes out in the forests to the west of Anganor. But we can't use the tunnel because Fergus said it would be much too dangerous. When he used it several days ago, he spotted some of Ravinia's spies near the exit, and it seems they may be lurking near there now. He doesn't think they know about the tunnel, but, nonetheless, it was difficult even for him to use it and remain undetected. That would make it ever so much more difficult with four of us. And, if Ravinia does have spies that know about you, it'd be much safer for us to meet Fergus to the east of the city, rather than to the south, which would be the direction they'd most expect us to go if we were going to see Thornoak or Princess Langwana. And it would be reasonable for them to suspect that if they know who you are and what your mission is."

"But if we can't use any of the gates and we can't use the tunnel, then how are we going to leave the city?" Aradis inquired.

"Ah, you're forgetting that I'm a Questmason." Kelwyn winked. "Earlier today, I went over to an eatery called The Traveler's Table; it's in the Naskanu, the Caskman's Ward, the district where the eastern gate of the city lies. One of the Questmongers' trusted contacts works there, and I spoke with him about whether or not anyone had been asking about you over there. As of when I talked with him, no one had been. But I requested that he keep his ears open for inquiries of that sort."

"Also, we hatched a plan to get you out of the city without being detected by Ravinia's spies at the Naskanu Gate. He's got a wagon with a hidden compartment that could fit the four of us, though it'd be a bit cramped. If we meet him at The Traveler's Table, he can take us to the gate in his wagon under the pretense that he's going to visit a friend who lives outside the city. Oh, and while we're at the eatery, we all can have some dinner. I'm sure you're famished after not having eaten all day."

"Now that you mention it," Aradis said, "I am terribly hungry, and I'm sure Girion is as well." His companion nodded.

"Splendid. You will be able to utterly vanquish your hunger at this place." Kelwyn smiled. Then, after pausing to clear his throat, he stated, "Now, I must inform you that there could potentially be a snag in the plan I just told you about. The rowdies taking orders from Quagga have taken control of all the gates of Anganor, including those leading between districts, and they may be restricting passage out of the city or even from one district to another. They weren't earlier this afternoon, but they may be by now. It depends on how seriously Quagga decides to take the security of his new little regime."

"Wait – what's all this about a new regime?" Aradis asked, alarmed. "And who's this Quagga fellow?"

Kelwyn, with assistance from Mordie and Girion, explained to Aradis all about the business with Quagga that had unfolded earlier that day. In response, Aradis shook his head exasperatedly, commenting, "As if Argonis didn't have enough problems already ... "

When they had finished discussing Quagga's insurrection, Girion returned the conversation to the plan for their escape from the city. "Now, how many sets of gates would we have to go through to get to the Naskanu?" he asked.

"Two," Kelwyn replied, "as we'll have to pass through the Eskagwan to get to the Naskanu."

"Pass through the what?" Aradis asked a bit peevishly, feeling as if he must have missed a great deal while he was sleeping, especially since Girion seemed to already know all about Quagga.

"The Eskagwan. It's one of the city's districts," Kelwyn explained. "There are nine districts in Anganor, and most of the time people call them by their old Ingan names, but occasionally they'll use the Daigan terms. We're currently in the Taskula, a word which is rather difficult to translate, but it roughly means 'the significant place of the remnant.' That, I believe, is a reference to the stumps of the sampanog trees. To get to the Naskanu, we'll have to go through the Eskagwan, the Ward of the Foreigners, which is where my house is – the house I live in when I'm not at the Questmongers' Den, that is. Eskagwan means 'foreigner', though the literal sense is 'person from beyond the hedge.'"

"Brightbole applied that word to us, I believe," Girion recalled.

"Brightbole's a good-natured, jolly fellow at heart and didn't mean any offense by it, I'm quite certain," Mordie assured, grabbing a tattered cloak from an arm of the sofa where it had been draped. "Now, shouldn't we be going, Kelwyn?" he prompted.

"Indeed," the Manfellow returned, "for Marda's Farewell is nearly upon us."

Now turning to the Leprechaun who was sitting on the windowsill, he said, "Drisham, after we've safely delivered these lads to Fergus at Duskdarrow, Mordie and I will return, likely an hour or two after midnight. If there's an attack, you know what to do."

Then, clapping the two Ingans standing guard at the door on the back, he encouraged, "Fear not, dear Morningstem and most excellent Redgarth; if there is an assault, you shall repel it brilliantly, I'm quite sure. But keep watch on the door well tonight and heed Brightbole's bells, so that no needless ill shall befall any Questmonger."

Grabbing a dark cloak from underneath his chair, Kelwyn put it on and stated, "The four of us shall be leaving here through a secret underground passage, as it would be preferable for us not to be seen leaving the Gnarly Stump. When we get to the Taskula-Eskagwan Gate, I will assess the situation and decide our best course of action if Quagga's sentries are regulating travel between districts. There's no need to worry about the matter until then, though."

After the Siloans had collected their effects, folded up their cloaks and put them in their packs, Kelwyn took them and Mordie back through the northeast door into the hallway that led to the staircase in the middle of the stump building. But, instead of going up the stairs, Kelwyn opened a door on the right-hand side of the hallway that was cleverly designed to look like part of the wall. Beyond it, there was a narrow passage that stopped only a few feet farther on. Kelwyn led the company into this, shut the door to the previous hallway and then lifted up a trapdoor in the floor that led to a stout ladder. They all climbed about forty feet down the ladder and into a tunnel that was only barely visible. It would have been utterly indiscernible were it not for the presence of a few purple moss lamps.

An Ingan and a Wood-Gnome, who had evidently been sent to replace Collic and Ashworthy in guarding the tunnel, cordially greeted the foursome and then bid them the best of luck in their journey to Duskdarrow after Kelwyn briefly explained where they were off to.

As Kelwyn and the others went down the tunnel, he called back to the Ingan, "Tortrunk, you must tell me more about that askaleeka soup recipe that we were discussing earlier when I get back later tonight. It sounds delicious."

"Certainly," the Ingan heartily replied.

The tunnel ran off to the west and got narrower and lower as they went along. After they had followed it for a short distance, another tunnel branched off to the northeast, but they continued straight ahead. After about five minutes, they came to an old wooden ladder that led up to another trapdoor. Kelwyn climbed the ladder, heaved the trapdoor up and then helped all the others into a small dark, room before he shut it again. Taking out a little key, he inserted it into a tiny lock in the wall, then pushed on that same section of the wall, opening another secret door. Mordie and the Siloans followed him into the room beyond it, which was filled with large, bulging sacks. Kelwyn shut and locked the door behind him, and the lads thought to themselves that they would have tremendous difficulty finding the portal at that very moment, even though they had just seen where it was, for it blended so perfectly with the wall.

Kelwyn then opened yet another door, this one not secret at all, that led to a small courtyard. At the south end of this courtyard, there was a wooden gate with a peephole in it. Cautiously, he opened the peephole and peered into a narrow alleyway.

"Excellent," he muttered. "There's no one about. Quickly, let us go!"

Drawing out a small iron key, he unlocked the gate, then ushered his charges out into the alley and locked the gate behind himself. Casually, they strolled out into the lane at the end of the alley and began making their way through the streets of Anganor. The sun was getting lower and lower in the sky, but there was still a fair amount of bustle, as people were going about their evening affairs. One would hardly have guessed that the city had been seized by a revolt of some of its more disorderly commoners.

After a little more than a quarter of an hour, they came to a gate at the eastern edge of the Taskula, the district with all the stump buildings. Sure enough, some of Quagga's hooligans were standing by the gate, armed with cudgels and spears (which they had presumably taken from the guards). They were stopping anyone who approached from either direction, briefly interrogating them and then letting them pass.

The foursome watched this procedure be executed repeatedly until Kelwyn was certain that Quagga's men were merely ascertaining whether or not anyone was openly opposing the uprising. It seemed that the rebels, as might be expected, had very little finesse in their questioning and were primarily concerned with making sure everyone understood and at least verbally assented to Quagga's recently acquired leadership.

At length, Mordie commented, "Perhaps we won't have to worry about this trouble developing further, after all. For as long as Quagga isn't greatly disrupting things, his cronies watching the gates isn't much different than official guards of the kingdom doing so, at least as far as the citizens of Anganor are concerned. Furthermore, I suspect we needn't anticipate that fighting will break out between regular folk – those not taking part in the rebellion, that is – and Quagga's men. I mean, none of these people seem to be taking the questioning very seriously, likely because they're playing along just so they can go on with their business."

"And that is precisely what we must do," Kelwyn advised, as he led the company up to the gate.

It was not terribly difficult for Kelwyn to persuade Quagga's stooges that their group was fully supportive of the new self-styled governor of the city or that they were no advocates of Thornoak or Hoarstaff. After the sentries had been properly convinced that Kelwyn and his companions were merely going about their daily affairs, they let them pass into the adjacent district, the Eskagwan, the Ward of the Foreigners.

This district certainly lacked the sense of great age and venerability that was present in the Taskula, but it had its own unique and rather eclectic architecture. The streets were a little narrower, and there were merchants underneath awnings here and there, calling out to each other and to passersby in the growing twilight. Some of the buildings were like those they had seen in the central and southern districts of the city, simple timber-frame houses. Others had a more rustic, Wood-Gnomish feeling to them, resembling the structures of Harnabrig. Still others had

odd projections jutting out on their upper stories and quirky designs for
their doorways and windows. A wide variety of Narthanna were ambling
about here. Aradis and Girion spotted all of the types of Barada that they
had seen in Anganor that morning, but here they were present in greater
abundance. However, there were far fewer Ingans in the Eskagwan than
there were elsewhere in the city.

As Marda had now retired for the night, the streets of the Eskagwan
were covered by long evening shadows. But little islands of light floated in
the darkness. These were primarily the soothing glow of all the blue and
lilac moss-lamps that were affixed to nearly every building, but there were
also a few small fires that gave off thick, aromatic smoke, crackling away in
burnished metal pans hanging from beams near doorways.

As they continued down the street, Girion noticed that each building
had only one color of light associated with it, so he inquired, "Why do
some of the buildings have only blue moss and others only purple?"

"The moss you're referring to is called pachacuri," Kelwyn replied.
"It's a light-emitting plant that the Ingans have used for thousands of
years. The purple pachacuri is hung on dwellings, and the blue is used
on everything else. And the red plant material that you see burning in
braziers here and there is called kuringa. The Ingans use it if they want
heat or even if they simply desire brighter light than that which is given
off by the pachacuri, though many of them also burn it simply because
they are so fond of its odor."

After that brief conversation, the foursome walked in silence, keeping
a keen eye on their surroundings. When they had gone nearly a half-mile
from the eastern gate of the Taskula, having passed through a plaza in
the Eskagwan, they reached the gate into the Naskanu, the Caskman's
Ward, the district where they were to meet the contact Kelwyn had spoken
of. Again, they were obliged to undergo a brief questioning by Quagga's
followers. These fellows were a bit more aggressive than the previous ones,
and they informed the company that they had best be certain they were all
right with being stuck in the Naskanu until the morning.

"And why is that?" Kelwyn politely asked the scuzzy Ingan conducting
the interrogation.

"Because," the Ingan brusquely returned, "Quagga doesn't want folk
running around Anganor after twilight."

"But it's Marda's Passing right now!" Kelwyn protested.

"Exactly," the Ingan snapped. "I said *after* twilight. So wherever you happen to be at the Dawn of Eoreth, that's where you'll be until the Call of Marda. Now, if you're going into the Naskanu and you've no problem with being there overnight, then move along."

"I'm just curious ... is Quagga letting anyone leave the city, then?" Mordie casually queried.

"Not anymore," the Ingan declared. "We just received word a few minutes ago that no one's to come in, and no one's to go out. Not without special permission from Quagga. Folk have got to realize that everyday routines simply must be put on hold until this issue with Thornoak and Strongbranch is resolved."

"Of course," Kelwyn affirmed. "And if Quagga thinks barring passage in and out of the city is the best way to finally get something done around here, then I'm all for it."

Clapping Aradis and Girion on the back, he encouraged, "Now, let's be going, my friends." He nodded at Mordie, then bowed his head respectfully to the Ingan, who waved them on with his spear.

When Kelwyn and his company were a number of paces from the Ingans, Girion remarked, "This doesn't bode well at all. The Leprechaun that I was talking to back in the Questmongers' hall said that things could get rather ugly if Quagga kept people from passing in or out of the city."

"In the morning they will, I'll wager," Mordie said. "But I think there may not be much strife over it tonight because, as we've seen, people don't seem to be giving Quagga's doings a great deal of notice. Besides, since the order reached his gatekeepers only a short while ago, many of those who live outside the city probably haven't heard about it, as most of them would have gone home by now. And they're the ones who would be most likely to be upset about the matter. Folk in Anganor don't leave the city much. Not these days, anyway. But I wouldn't be a bit surprised if farmers and craftsmen from the surrounding area assaulted one or even all of the gates when they learned that Quagga was keeping the city shut up tight. And, come to think of it, it may be that folk on the inside will fight Quagga's minions as well, not so they can leave the city, but so that merchants from outside it can continue to provide them with their commodities. Folk won't take kindly to these sorts of intrusions on daily life. I just hope that, if a counter-rebellion arises, there won't be bloodshed over it. But, if it gets bad enough, it will be unavoidable."

Aradis' concerns were more immediate. "And what exactly are *we* going to do now that Quagga isn't letting anyone out of the city?" he anxiously inquired.

Kelwyn quietly returned, "I'm going to have to talk to Limbluck, our friend at The Traveler's Table, and revise our plan, obviously. But again, you're forgetting that I'm a Questmason. Revising plans and finding schemes to accomplish difficult objectives is what I do for the Questmongers on a regular basis. We'll get you safely to Fergus tonight. I promise."

"Oh, all right, then," Aradis sighed.

Looking about, the lad began to notice how much darker, dingier and more run-down the Naskanu was than any other district of Anganor. Paint was peeling off the majority of the buildings, many of which were in moderate disrepair, and the streets were littered with all kinds of refuse. Also, mangy animals of various kinds loped along the margins of the muddy thoroughfare. Most of them were dogs or rodents of some kind. Running off the main street, there were a great many narrow, forbidding alleyways, and there Aradis spotted poorly clad, stooped Ingan beggars stumbling along in the shadows. Though there were a fair number of pachacuri and kuringa lamps about, most of these were tucked under low-hanging arcades, so that the streets themselves were still in comparative gloom. There was a fairly even mixture of blue and purple lamps, signifying that both dwellings and other structures were present, but the windows of all these were smeared with mud and soot, though red fires blazed away behind many of them.

The farther the company traveled into the Naskanu, the more unsavory it became, until Aradis found himself imagining that spies of Ravinia were lurking in practically every shadow. He wasn't altogether certain of how her agents could actually discover his or Girion's whereabouts, but the concern Fergus had shown that the Ravenstaff might well be able to find Landrig's mother and sister had prompted him to suspect that the same ability could certainly be used to find him and Girion.

"Are we nearly there?" he asked at length, desperately hoping the answer would be in the affirmative, for the sinister and unsettling atmosphere of the Naskanu was making him more jittery by the second.

"As a matter of fact, we're quite close now," Kelwyn replied, as he directed them onto a side street that led straight east.

They followed this for a short way and at last came to The Traveler's Table, the eatery Kelwyn had told them about, which was on the south side of the street, just a short way east of where a broad lane ran north and south. Once more checking to make sure they weren't being followed (as he had been doing rather frequently since they left the courtyard in the Taskula), Kelwyn nodded to Mordie, who took the lads into the building. He entered right behind them after taking one more look around the darkened street.

The interior of the eatery was much as one might expect for any establishment in the Naskanu. It was dingy and ill-kept, though the air was filled with a number of appetizing odors, unfortunately mixed with ones that were less so. Presumably, the latter originated predominantly from the customers of the place or even from the building itself. The main room was rather smoky, due to the high number of bowls of blazing kuringa set on the tables, and, though there were quite a few patrons, there was little in the way of merriment among them. Over on the west wall, there was a door from which cooks were issuing with trays of food, which they were setting upon three long tables near that same wall, all containing various types of edibles sorted by categories. Aradis and Girion thought they recognized some Leprechaun dishes in the assortment farthest from them (although, to their great disappointment, there were no jewelcakes present) and some Ogre meats and sauces in the collection two piles closer to them than the Leprechaun heap.

Aradis glanced about to see if there were any individuals who seemed likely to be henchmen of Ravinia, but this proved to be an unwise decision as far as his peace of mind was concerned, for nearly every individual there could have passed for a highly disreputable character. The patrons of The Traveler's Table were, for the most part, wretched-looking Barada with shabby attire and ill-favored expressions. Many were hunched over tables and speaking in low voices, with their eyes darting suspiciously around the room.

Aradis nudged Girion, who gave him an uneasy look.

Kelwyn looked at the lads with a slight, reassuring smile, then confidently took his party to a table in the northeast corner of the room. There they all sat on benches placed against the walls in the corner.

"I know this place looks rather, ah …" Kelwyn hesitated, as he addressed the Menfolk. "Well, I know it probably isn't the sort of place you'd want to frequent, but it's actually one of the nicest establishments in the Naskanu. And the food is decent, even if the same can't be said of the clientele."

Then, his countenance brightening a little, he said, "But never you mind that. None of these folk will do any harm to us, so long as we mind our own business. Now, this place is rather unique, for it offers foods from a number of different Narthanna of Argonis. Each pile on the tables has food from a different cuisine. From left to right, you'll see food of the Leprechauns, Wood-Gnomes – or, at least, the kinds of things the Wood-Gnomes used to eat – Ogres, Ingans, Sky-Gnomes and Timber-Elves."

"Sky-Gnomes?" Aradis asked. "And who are they?"

"A sort of Gnome that lives to the west of Anganor in Argonis," answered Kelwyn. "Well, they live in other parts of Orona too. They've got rather distinctive spirally ears."

"Oh, we saw some of them earlier today," Girion recollected.

"Yes, there are many of them in Anganor," Kelwyn said.

"Now, I'll be paying for your meals tonight, so eat as much as you desire," he urged, nodding over toward the tables. "You pay for whatever you take from the tables over there, so just show one of the three Ingans on the other side of the tables what you've got. It's pay as you go, so I'll go up there with you. Right now, let's go get our food, and then I've got to go have a chat with our friend Limbluck, who is presently behind the drink counter. We need to figure out if there's any way we can still use his wagon to get out of the city. He might know more about Quagga's policies than we do, as Quagga is actually from the Naskanu, and the sort of folk that consort with him come in here often. Perhaps Limbluck can get special permission from Quagga for us to leave the city."

"You don't see any spies of Ravinia here, do you?" Aradis asked, as Kelwyn was standing up.

The Manfellow looked around the dim, hazy hall of The Traveler's Table, examining the many grimy, disagreeable faces there. He shook his head. "None here that I can see. This is just the usual lot."

Coolly motioning for the others to follow him, he said, "Come on."

The three Menfolk and the Wood-Gnome went up to the tables and took large tin plates upon which to place their food. As they were doing so,

Girion remarked to Aradis, "Neldon Broadbuckle would absolutely love this place."

"If they ever open up a place like this in Siloa," Aradis said, "they'd have to designate an area with food just for him; otherwise, there wouldn't be anything left for anybody else. They could call it 'Neldon's Corner.'"

"Indeed," Girion chuckled. "With him, the limiting factor would definitely be his purse, not his stomach."

Shortly, they had all constructed mounds of a variety of victuals, with Aradis and Girion primarily opting for the Leprechaunish and Ogric items, as they already knew them to be delicious. However, the food here looked and smelled to be of greatly inferior quality to that which they had consumed at the McDasher's Mirth and the salnagok, and the lads rather suspected that there may have been some elasticity in Kelwyn's use of the word 'decent' to describe this eatery's fare.

When each of them had finished making their selections, Kelwyn handed over to the Ingans on duty a number of rectangular coins (which, as he explained to Girion, who inquired about them, were bannagums, the base coinage of the currency of Argonis). Then they all returned to their table. After they had been eating for less than half a minute, an Ingan fellow came by and gave them all bowls of a sparkling yellow beverage, which Kelwyn identified as an Ingan sap mead called tapusa.

While Mordie and the Siloans had their supper and carried on a quiet conversation, Kelwyn went up to the drink counter on the south wall of the room and found the Questmongers' contact, a young, handsome Ingan, though every bit as soiled as his place of employment and most of his patrons. As inconspicuously as possible, Kelwyn went with him through a door behind the counter.

Although Aradis was glad to be able to satisfy his ravenous appetite (despite the poor quality of the food) and also quite grateful that Mordie had remained with him and Girion, he found himself constantly looking around the eatery for signs of trouble. As he drew near to concluding his meal, he grew increasingly apprehensive, for Kelwyn had been gone for a good third of an hour. In fact, he actually began to entertain the possibility that both their new friend Kelwyn and his contact, Limbluck, had been killed by some of Ravinia's thugs and were now lying dead somewhere in the back rooms of The Traveler's Table.

Then, just when Aradis was considering asking Mordie if the Wood-Gnome could go back and find Kelwyn to make sure things were all right, the door behind the counter swung open, and Kelwyn and Limbluck reappeared. The Manfellow quickly came out from behind the counter, then nonchalantly made his way back over to his company's table. Meanwhile, the Ingan exited out the front door of the eatery.

As Kelwyn sat down, he looked at Mordie and the Siloans and related, "I've got some unpleasant news and some encouraging news, but the latter far outweighs the former."

"Do tell," Mordie prompted, finishing his last bite of nippi-nappa meat.

Kelwyn subtly checked to make sure no one nearby was listening too closely, then explained, "I confirmed what that fellow at the Eskagwan-Naskanu Gate told us. Quagga's got all the gates out of the city shut down. The good news is that we've still got a plan to get out of Anganor, but the bad news is that it's going to be more complicated and perhaps a little trickier than the one we had before."

Aradis frowned, then took a drink from his bowl of tapusa. "How so?" he asked.

"We're still going to hide in Limbluck's wagon until we get to the Naskanu Gate," Kelwyn said. "Then, when we arrive, Limbluck is going to start dramatically arguing with whoever's in charge down there, demanding that he be allowed through so he can go see his friend outside the city. While all the sentries are distracted by that, we're going to slip out of the wagon and make our way into the gatehouse."

"Is your plan to open the gate and then make a run for it?" Girion inquired.

Kelwyn shook his head. "Much too conspicuous. If Ravinia has any spies skulking about, any opening of the gates surely won't escape their attention. Hence, we're going to have to take a less direct approach. I'm guessing there will be a few of Quagga's folk in the gatehouse, but Mordie and I can render them unconscious quite easily. Once we have done so, we will be able to take some stairs inside the gatehouse that lead up to the ramparts. From there, we're going to climb down the outside of the city wall."

"We're going to do what?" Aradis asked, incredulous.

"Climb down the city wall," Kelwyn repeated. "Well, Mordie and I will be climbing, but we'll likely lower you and Girion with a rope."

"Have you or Limbluck figured out where we're going to get one of those?" Mordie asked, as he wiped some drops of tapusa out of his beard with his sleeve.

"Limbluck's gone to get one, so all we have to do is sit tight here until he gets back," Kelwyn said. "Then we'll all load up in the wagon. In the meantime, it'd be best for all of us to be on the lookout for Ravinia's agents. The longer we're here, the more likely it is that the wrong sort of person will come in and spot us."

Girion, who was just finishing a bite of rashty pie (which suffered from a lack of both authentic ingredients and skillful preparation), commented, "I, of course, believe we should be as cautious as possible, but I've been thinking on it and realized that the last time that any of her emissaries knew where we were was a spot some miles south of where Redtimber Road meets Kannaset Lake Byway, and that was four days ago now. Besides, when we did have that run-in with some of her agents, they didn't find out exactly who we were or that we were the same two Menfolk who had fled westward from Gorondil. I guess what I'm trying to say is that I find it hard to believe that Ravinia or any of her spies really know that we're in Anganor."

"Perhaps you aren't giving Ravinia enough credit," Kelwyn warned. "She is exceedingly cunning, and her spies are all over the place, even in this city, as I've told you. You may well be in a great deal more danger than you think, but with Mordie and I here to protect you, you needn't fret."

Just then, Kelwyn's face was seized with a look of tremendous concern. His eyes locked with Mordie's, and he whispered, "We may have to do a bit of protecting rather soon. Two of those blighters just walked in."

Aradis immediately felt his heart start beating faster, and his hands began to sweat. A single glance at Girion told him that his companion was probably having a similar reaction, at least judging by the look on his face.

"Do we stay or go?" Mordie whispered back.

"We'll go," Kelwyn said decisively. "They've just entered the place, and thus they haven't spotted us yet – at least I think they haven't – but it won't take them long. If we go into the storerooms behind the counter, we can go out through a back window."

Looking gravely at the lads, he instructed, "You must do exactly as Mordie and I tell you. We're obviously going to be making up our escape plan on the run, and I don't know what's going to happen or what we'll have to do. But trust this – I know the Naskanu well, and if something dreadful happens, stay with me, and no ill will befall you."

Swiftly rising from the bench, he said, "Now, follow me."

Kelwyn began striding toward the counter, and Mordie, Aradis and Girion, after gathering their accoutrements, followed him, quietly excusing themselves past the eatery's patrons. As they navigated the room, Aradis could not help noticing two individuals in ratty-looking, black cloaks standing near the front door of The Traveler's Table, their faces concealed by dark hoods. These were, he thought, most assuredly the two spies Kelwyn had sighted.

Kelwyn muttered something about Limbluck to an Ingan behind the counter, and the fellow waved them back. A few moments later, the two Siloans and the two Questmongers slipped through the door behind the counter into a room with a number of crates and barrels that was only illuminated by a few expiring kuringa lanterns.

"They may well have seen us coming back here, I'm afraid," Kelwyn said, "so we've got to get out of here immediately. I hadn't the presence of mind to specifically tell the Ingan at the counter to waylay them, but I seriously doubt he'll just let them come behind the counter without intervening. Standard protocol and all that, you know."

He now led the company through a door on the left into another room, this one filled with kegs and sacks. There was a window in the back wall through which the lads could see a shadowy alleyway. Kelwyn hastened over to the window and tried to force it open, but it wouldn't budge.

"Blast it!" he cursed. "They've got it locked."

Just then, they heard a door open in the room they had just come from.

"Quickly! Down to the cellar," Kelwyn whispered, as he flung open a large trapdoor and urged his companions down a set of darkened stairs. When they were all near the bottom of the stairs, he pulled the trapdoor shut behind them. Above them, they heard the sound of a heavy door opening, and the Siloans' breath caught in their throats.

Kelwyn looked rapidly around the room, then exclaimed, "Ah, of course! What a ninny I've been. We can use the crawlspace!"

Racing over to a large crate, he pushed it to the side just enough to reveal a small hole, only big enough to crawl through, though a larger passage opened up a few feet into the hole. They scurried into the tunnel, and Kelwyn pulled the crate back in front of the hole from the inside. No sooner had he done so than they heard the creak of the trapdoor to the cellar being pulled up.

All four of them froze, awkwardly scrunched up on their hands and knees as they were, and held their breath. After a few moments, there were heavy footsteps on the stairs. Then there was the sound of booted feet shuffling on the dirt floor of the cellar. The four fugitives sat tensely in the darkness, as silent as could be, until, after a good half-minute, a harsh, hushed voice said, "They must have opened and shut the trapdoor to lead us down here. They probably have gone back and snuck out the main door of the place by now."

"Aye," another low voice concurred. "Then we'd best go catch them before they slink off into the Naskanu."

After this brief conversation and to the hidden company's great relief, there was the tramp of boots up the stairs, the thud of the trapdoor and the creaking of the door that led back to the room behind the counter.

"Where does this tunnel go?" Girion asked, as Kelwyn shifted the crate out of the way so they could crawl back into the main room of the cellar.

"Nowhere," Kelwyn said. "It's just a secret crawlspace that Limbluck told me about some months ago. He and some others here at The Traveler's Table made it; though, out of respect for him, I shan't divulge the reason why. Let's just say that nearly everyone in the Naskanu has a bit of a shady side. And in Limbluck's case, that is part of what makes him so useful to the Questmongers. Now, let's get out of here."

Once the company had exited the crawlspace, Kelwyn carefully positioned the crate in front of the tunnel and then made his way up the stairs. Ever so quietly, he lifted the trapdoor and peered around the low-lit room above. No one was present, so he waved the company upward and shut the trapdoor after they had all climbed to the top of the stairs.

"If we go out through the main hall of The Traveler's Table, we'll be quite easy to spot," Kelwyn said, "and I'd like to avoid that if at all possible, just in case one or both of them come back or one of them has stayed behind. We've no guarantee that won't be the case. So, I suggest we try to get out through one of the windows upstairs, as they'll be less likely to be locked."

Once more leading the way, Kelwyn took the company through a door on the opposite side of the room from that through which they had first entered. Beyond this door was a set of stairs leading up to a hallway where wan beams of Eoreth fell in diamond-shaped patterns on the floor through the latticework in the south-facing windows.

Kelwyn crept up to one of these windows and pushed it open. It led onto a sloped, shingled roof. "All right, now we just need to find a good place to jump or climb down to the ground," he declared.

All of a sudden, out of the darkness farther down the hallway, two cloaked figures strode into the moonlight. "So there you are!" a voice hissed.

Instantly, Kelwyn leapt toward the figures, shouting to his companions, "Run! Run! I'll catch up!"

As Kelwyn and the two cloaked agents were tussling, Aradis, Girion and Mordie didn't hesitate to follow their leader's instructions, as they clambered out the window and then leapt from the roof down into an alleyway. They heard shouts and scuffling from behind and then the breaking of glass. Not even pausing to catch their breath, the two Siloans and the Wood-Gnome began racing down the alleyway toward a lane at the end of it, panting furiously.

Aradis glanced over his shoulder and saw Kelwyn appear on the roof and then spring down into the alleyway. Moments later, Aradis and Girion reached the lane, and Mordie told them to turn right. Mordie then glanced back, waved to Kelwyn and took off after the Siloans. Kelwyn was sprinting desperately behind them, and when he reached the intersection of the alleyway with the lane, he shouted to them, "Not that way! It dead-ends in that direction."

"I thought it would lead us back to the main street!" Mordie yelled.

"No, we'll be trapped if we go down that way," Kelwyn called out, dashing off to the east. "Come on!"

The other three raced after him, and as they were passing the alleyway, they saw the two cloaked agents leap off the rooftop down into the alley.

"Hurry!" Kelwyn hollered at his companions, as he rounded a sharp corner to the right.

The next few minutes were a blur of adrenaline and terror for the Siloans. Heaving and gasping, they darted through a labyrinth of crooked, narrow lanes swathed in shadows, moonlight and the pale blue glow of a few scattered pachacuri lamps. They seemed to be going deeper and deeper into the dark heart of the Naskanu, for they saw nary another Barada, and the buildings were increasingly dilapidated with each new turn they took. All the while, they heard the pounding feet of their pursuers some distance behind them.

Finally, they came to a spot where the alleyway in which they were running narrowed to only a few feet, and up ahead, they could see five or six dark figures sitting hunched in the shadows. One of them rose and unsheathed a blade, which glinted ominously in the moonlight. "Three Menfolk and a Wood-Gnome," he laughed maliciously. "They're the ones, all right!" A moment later, the metallic ring of more blades being drawn sounded in the lane.

Kelwyn 's whole company immediately halted, aghast. "Mordie, hold them off!" Kelwyn shouted, bounding off back down the lane toward the direction from which their pursuers would be coming, which now seemed to be their only route if they wished to avoid confronting the cluster of thugs before them. "Follow me, lads!" he yelled.

The Siloans lost no time in obeying him, their hearts racing like mad. Meanwhile, Mordie pulled out a stout hatchet from his jerkin and growled at the cutthroats confronting him. "Come here, you dogs! Let me see your ugly faces before I make them even uglier!" he snarled, as he stepped toward them, his hatchet poised for an attack.

"Quickly, down this way!" Kelwyn urged, as he paused at the entrance to an alleyway on the right and waited for Aradis and Girion to catch up. The lads could hear weapons clashing and voices crying out behind them from where Mordie was battling the ruffians. They feared for their friend, but they feared more for themselves. Ravinia's two spies would round the corner before them in a matter of seconds. So, desperately, they plunged right into the opening Kelwyn had indicated and found themselves in a narrow lane that quickly dead-ended.

"This doesn't go anywhere!" Aradis exclaimed, dismayed.

The lads turned to see Kelwyn standing, blocking their exit from the alleyway. "Of course not," he replied, a cruel grin forming on his face. "And neither are you."

A moment later, particular spots on his forehead began to glow with a sickly, bluish tint. Most prominently, there were three dots that formed a downward-facing triangle. These were bounded by two lines that were vertical in their upper portions but turned at a moderate angle inward halfway down. Before their very eyes, Kelwyn Faircrest was enveloped by a brief, bluish mist, and, a moment later, where he stood, there was no Kelwyn to be seen. Instead, there was a huge, snarling dark-gray wolf.

CHAPTER FOUR

Ṙamtari, Ṙavoc and Ṙooligans

efore Aradis had a chance to draw his sword or even properly register what had just occurred, the wolf ran down the alleyway and sprang toward him with terrible ferocity, its long claws aimed directly at his throat. The lad raised his hands to grapple with the beast, but just before it landed on him, Girion swung mightily with his staff and knocked the creature aside.

In the brief window where the wolf was readying itself for another attack, Aradis unsheathed Brightbeam and held it steadily in front of him. The wolf growled viciously, then lunged at Girion's leg, just barely managing to dodge his staff and sink its teeth into his thigh. Girion yelled wildly, trying to clobber the creature with his staff, while Aradis attempted to cut open its right side. But before either Manfellow could strike successfully, the wolf, which had pulled back from Aradis' attack, darted between Girion's legs, knocking him to the ground.

The wolf then sought to slice open the fallen Girion's throat with its claws, but it was forced to leap back again to avoid a wide sweep of Brightbeam. Aradis, now on the offensive, jumped forward, flashing his sword left and right to keep his opponent at bay. The wolf began retreating to escape the sword's reach but then abruptly jumped toward Aradis, scratching his right hand and causing him to drop his blade with a shout of pain.

"Curse you, Kelwyn Faircrest – or whoever you are!" Aradis hollered, as he kicked angrily at the wolf, which was now trying to bite his leg.

Girion had risen to his feet and picked up his staff by this point, so he attempted to strike the wolf in the head. When the beast jumped back to avoid this, Aradis was able to grab his sword. Both of the lads now brandished their weapons menacingly in front of them, trying to get the wolf to move toward the mouth of the alleyway.

But just then, the two agents whom they had first encountered in The Traveler's Table ran around the corner, carrying long, wicked daggers that gleamed banefully in the blue lamplight. Their hoods had been cast off, and they looked to be fair-haired Manfellows. Also, oddly enough, they had just come from the direction where Mordie was facing off with the ruffians who had waylaid them in the narrow neck of the alley.

"They givin' you a bit of trouble, are they, mate?" one of them asked the wolf. "We'll put a stop to that right quick."

While Aradis and Girion were momentarily distracted by the arrival of the two agents, the wolf jumped at Aradis, causing him to stumble backward and slam his head against the side of the alleyway. Instantly, Girion let go of his staff and sprang with his entire body upon the wolf, trying to pin it to the ground. Then he and the wolf rolled over and over, back and forth on the floor of the alleyway, while the beast scratched and clawed frantically at his chest. Meanwhile, the thugs were stepping forward, preparing to finish off the Siloans. Aradis, still dazed from the blow to his head, was trying to think of a way he and Girion could make it out of this fight alive, when he noticed that one of their Mannish attackers was just about to hurl a dagger right at his heart.

But at that very instant, there was a loud, horrific squishing sound, and the Manfellow with the dagger gasped in agony. As he fell forward, Aradis saw the hilt of a blade sticking out of his back. His partner, startled, turned around and saw a tall, cloaked and hooded figure stalk out of the darkness, wielding a strange weapon, which consisted of two long blades joined at a handle in the middle.

At that particular moment, the wolf was still on top of Girion and tearing into him mercilessly, though it could not get at his throat, either with its paws or its jaws, because Girion was clutching and pushing its upper forelegs backwards with tremendous force. Aradis, shouting in rage, seized this opportunity to slice open the wolf's flank, spilling its blood all over Girion. The beast howled madly, then jumped backward, whirled around and darted toward the entrance of the alleyway.

The mysterious Barada who had come to their rescue was now battling the other Manfellow, but, as the wolf passed him, he struck out at it with his blade. He missed, however, and the creature swerved to the right, sprinting desperately down the dark lane and out of sight.

Aradis was now intending to attack the second thug from behind, but this act would prove to be unnecessary, for a few moments later, their unexpected ally deftly kicked the thug's hand, causing him to cry out and drop his dagger. Quick as lightning, his foe struck him hard in the face with his fist, knocking him against the wall of the alleyway. Then, with a swift knee to the stomach, his assailant drove him against the wall once more. The thug tried to punch back, but the hooded Barada seized his fist and kneed him in the belly again. Coughing, the thug collapsed to the ground, and his opponent held his blade to his throat.

"I don't believe we've met before," the cloaked Barada calmly addressed his vanquished foe. "I'm Peleus Chula. And who are you?" Abruptly, he threw off his hood to reveal a familiar olive-skinned face topped by dark, curly hair.

Aradis and Girion could hardly believe either their eyes or their ears, for the Barada was indeed none other than the zany Shore-Elf Questmonger.

Surmising that the immediate danger was now past and overcome with great concern for his companion, Aradis dropped his sword and bent down to see how severely Girion had been hurt. With warm blood dripping from his own wound, he quickly examined Girion's chest and saw that his jerkin had done a great deal to protect him, although it was now shredded rather badly, and there were spots where he was bleeding. Also, vicious bite marks could be seen in Girion's thigh, and blood was trickling from these as well.

The thug, still coughing, said nothing in response to Chula's query, so the Shore-Elf kicked him hard in the head, as he inquired, "Have I damaged your ears so badly that you can't properly hear me? I did ask you a question, you know, and it wasn't a difficult one. Most people know their own names. Although, come to think of it, I only know part of mine."

The Manfellow, with blood streaming down his bruised face, looked up at him with utter contempt. "Cut my throat and be done with it!" he spat.

"That would be preferable to you, I'm sure," Chula replied, "but, at the moment, you're not exactly in a position to be ordering me about. Now, let's try this again. Who are you? And, for that matter, who is Kelwyn

Faircrest, in truth? If you tell me what I wish to know, I shall spare your life."

"If you really think I fear death so much that I would betray any useful information to you, you're quite mistaken," the thug grunted.

"Very well, then," Chula calmly returned. "I wanted to offer you the choice of life or death, but you've clearly already made your decision. I haven't a great need of you, anyhow. It's obvious that Kelwyn is no Manfellow; he's a Druid, and one with more than meager acquaintance in Daegar for that matter, as he was able to turn into a wolf. And there's no doubt that he is a spy for Ravinia. In addition, you and your chum aren't Manfellows either, though I must say that you've done a pretty fair job of disguising yourselves as such. You're Druids as well, as is evident from the few spots where the dye has faded at the base of your fingernails. I'm sorry to say it, dear chap, but you're merely one of the Witch's thousands of disposable dupes. Unfortunately for you, your glorious career is now at an end."

As soon as Chula had made this last remark, he forcefully jabbed his blade into the thug's throat, and the fellow perished with a ghastly gargle. Aradis and Girion felt their stomachs flip and instinctively turned away from the grisly sight, as Chula pulled this blade out, retrieved his other blade from the other thug's back and then quickly wiped the blood off of both of them. When he had finished, he turned over the thug he had killed first to get a look at his face.

"Dear Chula!" Aradis gushed, helping his gasping companion to his feet. "Had you not arrived when you did, we both would certainly have been slain."

"Most certainly indeed," Chula confirmed, as he walked over to the lads. "Three against two wasn't a very sporting arrangement, especially when one of the three was a wolf, so I'm glad I could even things out a bit."

"What are you doing here in the Naskanu?" Girion asked, holding his shredded jerkin against his bleeding chest.

"I followed you all the way from the Questmongers' Den," the Shore-Elf explained. "You see, I came down to the Quest Hall a few minutes after you left and was startled to discover that you weren't there. Drisham O'Davin the Leprechaun was there, and apparently he'd been there when you left. He told me where you'd gone off to, and my suspicions were aroused, as I found it odd that Fergus wasn't going to be escorting you out of the city himself, considering how high the stakes are in your particular case. As Drisham said you were going to be meeting up with Limbluck at The Traveler's Table, I raced to the eastern gate of the Taskula and arrived there just as you did. Then I kept my distance as I trailed you to your destination. I stayed close by for quite some time, hidden across the street, waiting for you to emerge. Then, when Limbluck exited the place, I saw these two odious chaps that are now lying dead in this alleyway slink across to the entrance of The Traveler's Table. They were very careful about making sure that Limbluck didn't see them, so I feared the worst. I actually entered the eatery just as you went through the door behind the counter, and I saw these blokes slip back there right behind you. I must say, they did a splendid job of doing so without being seen by the Ingans back there pouring out drinks. But such abilities must be requisite for agents of Ravinia."

"Did you continue following them, then?" Aradis inquired.

"I did try, but the Ingans wouldn't permit me to do so, as I wasn't quite so stealthy as Ravinia's agents. Since I was thus obstructed, I ran outside and tried to find an alleyway that would lead me to the back of the building. Just when I found a lane I thought would do the trick, I heard Kelwyn's voice crying out that you all were going the wrong direction and Mordie replying that he was trying to get back to the main street. As it turned out, Mordie seemed to have been on the right track, as you and he were evidently running toward the very alleyway I was coming from. For I then raced toward the voices and pursued you all the way here."

"Mordie!" Aradis suddenly gasped, remembering that they had left the poor Wood-Gnome back in the lane all by himself to ward off the band of ruffians. "Did you see what happened to Mordie? Oh, how could we have forgotten about him? What careless idiots we've been! Is he all right?"

"Not at all." Chula grimaced. "He's quite dead, I'm afraid. Knife in the back, courtesy of one of these rank scumbags here. However, Mordie did manage to kill every last one of the scoundrels in that alley before he died. These rapscallions saw that Mordie was triumphing, so they jogged past you and Kelwyn, stabbed Mordie in the back as he was slaying his last opponent, then came back to help Kelwyn finish you off. You likely didn't notice them running by you, though, since you were busy battling Kelwyn."

Aradis and Girion both sighed heavily. Neither of them had been prepared for anything of this sort to transpire tonight. It was, in fact, almost too much for them to absorb.

"Oh, Mordie," Girion breathed. "I'm so sorry we abandoned you."

"There wasn't anything you could have done, I'm afraid." Chula shook his head. "You were fully occupied with Kelwyn, and I was a little too late to save him. But he died bravely and valiantly as a loyal Questmonger in the line of duty. We shall all mourn him more when great danger presses not so imminently upon us."

"Speaking of Kelwyn, what are we going to do about him?" Girion asked, wincing as he leaned over to retrieve his staff. Meanwhile, Aradis started cleaning the wolf's blood off of his sword.

Chula began searching the bodies of the dead thugs, as he responded, "I think it very likely that he will flee Anganor tonight and hide somewhere in the forests of Mentasqua until he has recovered from his wounds, though it may be a bit tricky for him to leave the city. Of course, he won't be able to go out through any of the gates, so he'll have to go over the city wall. Nonetheless, I would imagine he can figure out a way to accomplish that objective. He is an excellent Questmason, after all. Since he obviously knew that he was going to attempt to kill you tonight, I doubt he intended to return either to the Questmongers' Den or his house in the Eskagwan. I may be incorrect in that reckoning, but I rather guess that I am not. The only alternative he would have other than outright leaving Anganor would be trying to fool Fergus with a contrived explanation of how things went awry, but that would be a terribly risky business, for if there were the slightest chink in Kelwyn's story, Fergus would most assuredly be all over it."

Still rummaging through the thugs' garments, Chula went on, "Kelwyn is, undoubtedly, a villain of the most contemptible variety, but, for now at least, we must trust that judgment will fall on him from some other hands than our own, for we've presently got far more important business than revenge. The greatest damage resulting from his undercover work for Ravinia has already been done, I would suspect, and all the information he acquired about you and the medallion has indubitably been relayed to other spies of the Witch by now. However, as soon as we bring word of

Kelwyn's treachery to the Questmongers – and we'll be seeing to that quite shortly – he will no longer be able to show his face anywhere in Anganor, so his utility as a spy will be utterly negated. Thus, it is of little consequence to us right now what he's up to, though I do hope that, whatever it is, he's having a dreadful time of it."

"Aha!" the Shore-Elf exclaimed, as he extracted a crumpled parchment from the pockets of one of the thug's trousers. Shaking his head, he muttered, "Tsk, tsk. When is Ravinia going to institute a better training program for her agents?" Quickly, he scanned the note, which had writing on both sides, then held it up so the lads could see it. "Any spy worth his salt should know better than to carry papers on his person unless he has a very good reason to do so, which I doubt this fellow does," he said. "Ah, well. His folly. Our gain."

"What does it say?" Aradis asked.

Chula read through the note once again, then shoved it into his pocket. "I'll tell you as we go. Right now, we've got to get back to the Questmongers' Den and tend to your wounds."

"But how are we going to get through the garrisons that Quagga has left at the gates between districts?" Girion inquired.

"Oh, that shouldn't present too great of a difficulty. Leave that to me," Chula confidently assured him.

Now, aided by Chula, the lads embarked into the shadowy network of alleys and lanes of the Naskanu. Before they left the area, the Shore-Elf examined the corpses of the six ruffians that Mordie had killed, four of whom were Timber-Elves and two of whom were Menfolk, 'hmm'ing and 'o-ho'ing frequently to himself as he did so. Then he and the Siloans carried Mordie's body into a nearby alleyway and hid it behind some crates. Chula insisted that it would be inexpedient for them to attempt to cart the body back to the Questmongers' Den now, but he intended to send a few Questmongers to come back and pick it up later that night.

Having finished with concealing Mordie's body, they passed into a larger street, one which was mostly devoid of Barada, and shortly thereafter, Chula began relating what he had discovered from reading the note. "It seems our friend Kelwyn was just as incautious in putting so much information in that note as that fellow was in holding on to it. And that perplexes me because for him to have been in the Questmongers for nine years while working as a spy for Ravinia and yet have remained undetected, he must possess tremendous acumen. Very smart lad. Very smart indeed. But even very intelligent people make mistakes – sometimes very bad ones. Still, the only reason I can deduce that he was so careless is that he thought no one in Anganor could decipher this script."

"Was it merely written in a code? Or was it not written in Daiga at all?" Girion inquired, limping along, trying to go easy on his left thigh.

"It was composed in neither Daiga nor a code," Chula replied. "It's in a special script used for Hamtaric, a language which is only spoken by a few tens of thousands of Druids in a colony in southern Tassaru called Iyontarka. So, I suppose it would be reasonable for them to assume that hardly anyone this side of the Bushbelt would be able to read or even recognize it."

"You know how to read Hamtaric, I'm presuming," Girion surmised. "How did you come to learn it?"

Chula stopped and looked around the street for a few seconds. Then, blinking a few times, he asked, "Come to learn what?"

"Hamtaric," Girion said.

"You know Hamtaric?" Chula inquired excitedly, his eyes widening with glee.

"Not remotely," Girion returned, suspecting that Chula might be having one of his fits of amnesia.

"That's a pity," the Shore-Elf moped. "It's such a lovely language."

"Yes, about the note ..." Aradis cut in.

Chula looked quite perplexed. Then, abruptly, he exclaimed, "The note! Oh yes, the note." This thought seemed to have ignited Chula into motion. He began walking again, as did the Siloans. "So, it seems to have been penned by Kelwyn, who signed it as Gornok. I would guess that he didn't give the note to them directly because if you're a double agent in the spy business, you never want to be seen communicating with your contacts if you can help it. Therefore, he probably left the note in some predesignated place for his two accomplices to come by later and pick it up. I suspect he did so when he left the Questmongers' Den with the pretense of conversing with Limbluck at The Traveler's Table, a bit that Drisham O'Davin filled me in on, by the way. We'll have to check into that with Limbluck later. I do hope he's not a spy for Ravinia as well, although I highly doubt that he is, since Ravinia's two agents purposely concealed themselves from him when they snuck into the eatery. Most likely, Kelwyn had simply told them that Limbluck's departure would be their signal to enter."

"But in any event, the note contained the entirety of the plan to murder you that Kelwyn just tried to carry out. It mentioned a portion of the plan that I cannot attest to – though you could – wherein you were supposed to hide in a crawlspace in the cellar, and they were to say aloud that they thought you had tricked them and were leaving out the front door of the eatery. Then they were to go wait in the upstairs hall for you."

"That's exactly what happened!" Aradis exclaimed, as he felt his stomach churn with nausea. Shaking his head, he declared, "So all that while, Kelwyn knew precisely what was going to happen. He was just trying to get us to trust him more and be caught that much more unawares when he led us into that alleyway to kill us."

"Precisely so," Chula affirmed. "He had every single detail planned out and every possibility thought through, I assure you. The knave even mentioned that he thought it would be too risky to try to kill you in the crawlspace because Mordie might prove to be troublesome; that's why he instructed those two blackguards that pursued you to get six other persons of nefarious character – hooligans for hire, if you will – to set an ambush in the narrow section of that particular alley, with the aim of occupying and ultimately murdering Mordie. Dear me, that Kelwyn Faircrest is utterly ghastly. And to think that he could so callously ordain the slaughter of one with whom he had feigned friendship for so long …"

"I hate to even *think* of it," Girion sighed.

"It's revolting, really," Chula concurred. "But there was even more mischief in the note than that. It unfortunately had a fair amount of information, relatively speaking, about the two of you and your quest, as well as statements revealing that you had brought the medallion fragment and that Fergus was taking it to Langwana at Iswa Hanahoma. Oh, yes, and it demanded that those two scoundrels I dispatched back there, Bezgaron and Tijkarot, pass on all the information in the note to a Druid named Agzareeb. What's so fascinating about all this is that Gornok, Bezgaron and Tijkarot are all Hamtaric names, although Agzareeb is a regular Druidic name. The Hamtari, the Druids of Iyontarka, are some of the few in all Orona who are actually fair of hair, and it very much seems that Ravinia has taken advantage of this fact in finding excellent spies for her operations, as few Barada even know that fair-haired Druids exist."

"I certainly didn't," Aradis admitted.

"Yes, all of this is quite devilishly calculated on Ravinia's part," Chula said, musing on the matter. "Of course, there are Menfolk who are dark of hair and a great many who are dark of skin, but there are very few fair-haired Druids; thus, they could easily be mistaken for Menfolk. But I really am convinced my conjecture is correct for another reason: there is a renowned cadre of Daegar instructors in Iyontarka, which explains why Kelwyn knew how to turn into a wolf, for that feat requires much study of dark magic. I wouldn't be a bit surprised if the other two chaps could change into animals, just like Kelwyn, and furthermore, I would suspect the reason they didn't change into their animal forms is that they weren't suitable for combat, but for secrecy. They probably could only transform into creatures like birds or rats. And –"

"I'm sorry," Aradis interrupted, as they turned onto a main thoroughfare, where a number of Barada were still traipsing about, late as it was. "I'm a bit jarred by all of this still. I didn't even know it was possible for Barada to change into animals. It shall likely take me far longer to recover from that shock than it will to recover from the injuries I received tonight."

"Oh, I thought it was common knowledge," Chula said rather apologetically. "Yes, Barada can change into animals. But only Druids can do it – only those who have trained extensively in Daegar. And even then, each one can only change into a particular animal, which is signified by the Druid's takhma, the glowing markings that appear on his forehead right before his transformation. It is rumored that a few exceedingly powerful Druids of antiquity could change into multiple kinds of animals, but –"

"How did you know the other two were Druids also?" Girion interrupted. "I remember you mentioning something about their fingernails."

"Oh, yes. Druids have rather dark lunulas; that's the area at the base of their fingernails. But they can put dye there to hide the fact if they want to appear as Menfolk. However, those chaps had missed a few spots. Hardly noticeable, but enough to give them away if you were examining them closely, as I was."

"Do you have any idea what Fergus will propose we do when he finds out what's happened?" Girion now inquired, as he narrowly avoided stumbling over a rough spot in the street.

Chula scratched his head. Then, in a rather muddled manner, he asked, "And what, may I ask, has happened?"

At first the Menfolk thought that Chula was merely jesting with them, but from the expression on his face they deduced that his inquiry really was in earnest.

"Never mind," Aradis muttered, shaking his head. Chula had saved his and Girion's lives on two occasions now, but he was really getting rather tired of his sporadic lapses in recollection.

"Right, then," Chula mumbled contentedly, as he picked up his pace. For this, the lads were quite grateful, for they were eager to depart from the sinister Naskanu and return to the safety of the Questmongers' Den.

After this, Chula and the Siloans made their way through the Naskanu until they came near to the gate that led back into the Eskagwan. Suddenly, the lads became aware that a wagon was rolling along behind them. Chula looked over his shoulder, peering into the night.

"Keep walking and don't alter your gait," he said to the lads.

They did as he ordered, though they were somewhat perplexed by this odd command and feared that some new mischief was nigh upon them. The wagon drew closer and closer, yet Chula divulged no further information about what was afoot.

Then, all of a sudden, when the wagon was only a few feet behind them, Chula turned and hailed the driver of the cart, which was drawn by two haggard horses.

"I say there, chap! What is your name?" he asked quite courteously.

The driver, a slovenly old Ingan gentleman, pulled back on the reins, halting his horses, and returned, "Bricklebick. Who wants to know?"

Without warning, Chula sprang up into the wagon and shoved poor Bricklebick off the other side.

"Get up here!" the Shore-Elf beckoned to Aradis and Girion.

Though quite stunned by what Chula had just done, the lads hurriedly complied. They had barely dragged themselves up onto the front seat board of the cart before Chula slapped the reins and the horses lurched forward. Meanwhile, Bricklebick picked himself up off the ground, cursing, and tried to lay hold of the wagon. But he was too late.

As the wagon rolled down the street, with Bricklebick running after it and shouting all kinds of violent denunciations at Chula and the Siloans, Girion inquired, "And what exactly was that all about?"

"We needed a wagon," Chula explained quite nonchalantly, digging around under his cloak for something. "I asked the fellow his name so that I can return his wagon after we're done with it. Also, now that I know who we've inconvenienced, I can reimburse him with Questmonger funds to repair or replace his property – that is, supposing it gets damaged while we're using it."

"Why do we need a wagon?" Aradis inquired, glancing back at the raving Bricklebick, who was attracting a great deal of undesirable attention from the few Barada who were yet in the street.

"To get through the gate, of course," Chula replied. Then, quite delightedly, he pulled from the folds of his garments an object that Aradis and Girion recognized almost instantly. It was Chula's ketchiwah mating horn.

Before the lads could even do such much as protest, the Shore-Elf placed the instrument on his lips and blew heartily. A great, terrifying growling sound blasted out of the bell and echoed through the Naskanu. The second the horses heard it, they started to gallop in wild alarm.

"Mad ketchiwah!" Chula shouted in a panicked voice, fighting to keep the wagon from careening out of control or crashing into fleeing pedestrians. "There's a mad ketchiwah on the loose! Run for your lives!"

He slapped the reins furiously, and the horses ran even faster. Bricklebick was now left quite far behind. Up ahead, the gate that led into the Eskagwan loomed rapidly out of the darkness. The portals were shut, and the silhouettes of a number of Ingans and a few Wood-Gnomes, Timber-Elves and Ogres could be seen just in front of them. Presumably, these Barada were Quagga's nocturnal garrison.

"Flee to the Eskagwan!" Chula yelled. "It's our only chance!"

One of the Ingans by the gate hollered, "Hey, open up, you louts! Open up!"

The drawing of a huge metal bolt and the lifting of a great wooden bar could be heard from the other side of the portals, although just barely, as there was a great deal of shouting, neighing and general mayhem going on. Just as the wagon was reaching the members of the garrison, who were scattering to make way for the oncoming catastrophe of Chula on wheels, the gates were pushed open from the other side. The crazed horses and the wagon narrowly passed through the gap between the portals, and several Ingans and a Wood-Gnome who were on the Eskagwan side frantically dove out of the way, only just in time.

Aradis and Girion were both gripping the wagon, white-knuckled, desperately hoping that they wouldn't be flung from it. They were feeling sick to their stomachs and rather wished that Chula had warned them beforehand of what he was going to do. It was almost like being with Felding again.

"Why didn't you tell us you were going to do this?" Girion, who was looking queasier by the second, demanded from the Shore-Elf.

"I didn't know myself until moments before," Chula shouted over the rattle of the wheels and the snorting of the horses.

"You can slow down now, you know," Aradis yelled, closing his eyes for a moment as they just barely missed running over an elderly Leprechaun lady.

"No, indeed," Chula yelled back. "We've still got one more gate to get through."

As soon as he had said this, he let go of the reins with one hand in order to take out his ketchiwah mating horn again. Girion, dismayed, saw the reins beginning to slip out of Chula's other hand and reached out to grab them. Fortunately, he caught them in the nick of time and then strove mightily to steer the horses away from a vendor's stall on the side of the street. Meanwhile, Chula blew on his preposterous horn, and the Eskagwan was filled with an almost perfectly accurate imitation of a ketchiwah's growl.

"Mad ketchiwah!" Chula raved again. "Beware of the mad ketchiwah! Everyone flee!" Then, quite startled, he looked at Girion and saw that he was driving the wagon.

"Have you been driving the wagon this whole time?" he asked, blinking. "Or did I just give you the reins a moment ago?"

Girion, exasperated, replied, "You almost lost them, and I grabbed them to keep us from crashing into a market stand."

"Ah, I see," Chula said quite calmly. "Carry on."

"What?" Girion exclaimed. "I'd rather not."

"Very well, then," the Shore-Elf conceded, snatching back the reins.

As he did so, the wagon bounced over a rather rutted patch in the street, and the threesome heard the sound of shattering glass behind them. To the Siloans' great consternation, they realized that a lantern in the wagon bed had just broken, and now several items stowed there were on fire.

"No matter," Chula sang, upon witnessing the rising flames. "It will only add dramatic flair to our departure from the Eskagwan."

The lads both thought again how very much this whole affair was like being with Felding. They could only imagine what nonsense would transpire if Peleus Chula and Captain Starwash were working together.

The Barada in the Eskagwan were even more distraught than those in the Naskanu, and it wasn't long before people began sticking their heads out of upper-story windows to see what all the commotion was about. Those in the street screamed at the approach of the flaming wagon and the impending destruction that would almost certainly result from this rampant ketchiwah that everyone was yelling about. This effect was only increased after Chula blew his maddening horn yet again.

Fortunately for Chula and the Siloans, they soon sighted the garrison at the gate that led to the Taskula. Fire had not completely engulfed the wagon, but they were starting to get uncomfortably warm.

Chula shrieked at the garrison, "Open the gate! Get to safety in the Taskula before it's too late! The ketchiwah is coming!"

Nearly hysterical, Quagga's minions begged their companions on the other side to open the gate and let them through. Again, just in time, the gates swung open and the wagon made it through without hurtling into the huge wooden portals. Barada were running to and fro, uncertain of what to do or where to go to keep from being stampeded.

As soon as they entered the Taskula, Chula began pulling back firmly on the reins, but it was to no avail. The steeds were far too agitated to care or even notice. They continued barreling down the street, whinnying wildly all the while.

Chula, who seemed to find the situation only mildly disconcerting, remarked, "It would appear that we are in a predicament that can only be resolved by doing something a bit drastic – namely, jumping out of the wagon. But don't do it until I say so. And when you leap, tuck your chin and try to land on your back."

Glancing up ahead and seeing an area he thought suitable for the maneuver, he cried out, "One! Two! Um … jump!"

Aradis and Girion, neither of whom had time to properly consider how perilous this stunt might prove to be, threw themselves out of the burning, speeding wagon on Chula's command. They landed on the ground more clumsily than they had hoped for, rolling away and scraping up their elbows. When they stopped, they moaned much as old Bricklebick had done. Yet they were fortunate, for neither of them had broken any bones or cracked their heads open, though their clothes were now covered in dust from the street and Girion's leg was throbbing with pain.

Chula had performed the leap with much greater finesse, springing down to the street and rolling gracefully away from the flaming conveyance, as it sped on to the west, then veered off to the south. The Shore-Elf stood up, brushed himself off, then went and assisted the lads in getting back on their feet.

"That was really quite a jolly time, wasn't it?" Chula cheerfully prompted.

"I don't think it was jolly at all," Aradis sullenly returned. "Stealing someone's wagon, almost running a fair number of folk over with it, catching it on fire and almost dying at least a score of times in the process doesn't really fall under my conception of a jolly time; I'm sorry to say."

"Oh dear," Chula sighed, looking rather crestfallen. "You make it sound as if we were regular hooligans. Well, I suppose it can't be helped now. If we are hooligans, at least we're the sort that has a sense of decency, unlike those chaps we left deceased in the alleyways of the Naskanu. Now, shall we sojourn to the Gnarly Stump? We've still got to see to those wounds of yours, you know. Also, I'm afraid we'll have to leave extinguishing the wagon and calming down the horses to others, for we cannot afford to be detained. Indeed, there is much we must see to."

"Lead on," Girion groaned, wincing at a sharp sting of pain in his thigh.

"Very well," Chula agreed, as he marched off down the street.

For the next quarter of an hour, Chula and the Siloans made their way back west through the Taskula toward the Gnarly Stump, though they took a somewhat circuitous route. The lads were uncertain of whether this was to throw off any pursuers, whoever they might be, or simply because Chula was having one of his bouts of forgetfulness.

Regardless, they came to their destination, although this time, they didn't bother with the secret tunnel. They just went straight into the tavern, which was still occupied by a number of customers, all of whom were murmuring anxiously. As the lads walked through the main hall of the Gnarly Stump, they caught snatches of conversation heavily peppered with the words "monster," "terrible growling" and "curse from Thornoak." They chuckled to themselves, as they surmised that, even here in the Taskula, folk must have been able to hear the bombastic blasts of Chula's horn. It seemed that some of them were convinced that whatever had produced the horrifying sounds must have been sent by Thornoak as a curse or punishment, probably for Quagga's revolt.

The threesome passed through the tavern proper largely unnoticed, though they caught Brightbole's eye, and he nodded congenially. Although the Siloans had not forgotten the Ingan barkeep's bamboozling of them that morning, the fact that he was a close friend of the Questmongers had redeemed him somewhat in their eyes. So, they returned the gesture and then followed their Shore-Elf companion up the staircase to the second floor.

They promptly arrived at the entrance to the Questmongers' Den, and, after Chula had knocked and announced himself, the door was opened by a husky Wood-Gnome, whose eyes immediately filled with dismay when he saw the Siloans' condition. Alarmed, he hurried them into the Quest Hall and shut, barred and locked the door.

The room was quite dark now, save for the fire in the hearth and a few purple pachacuri lamps that had been placed around the room. The Wood-Gnome, along with a lean Timber-Elf, were the only ones still guarding the main hall.

"Chula, what happened?" the Gnome asked. "Where are Kelwyn and Mordie?"

"Is everything all right?" the Timber-Elf pressed.

"I'll tell you all about it in a minute," Chula promised. "Fergus isn't back yet, is he?"

"No," the Wood-Gnome answered.

"Well, hopefully he will return soon. Boffin and Hundareth, will you please get these Menfolk something to drink and help them find good, soft couches to lie down on? I've got to run upstairs and get some medical supplies."

"Of course," the Questmongers responded, as they took the Siloans back over to the spot where they had spent most of the afternoon slumbering away. There the Menfolk wearily put their packs and weapons next to the couches. Meanwhile, Chula darted off through the door that led to the upper quarters of the Questmongers.

As the Siloans were examining their injuries more fully in the firelight, Boffin and Hundareth went over to the counter with all the mugs in the southeastern part of the hall and filled two tankards with some tapusa. They then rushed back to the Menfolk and handed them the tankards. The lads thanked them, sat upon the couches and took several swigs of the draught.

"I'm really fine, except for my hand," Aradis assured his caretakers, as they positioned pillows for him to rest his head on. "But Girion's been torn up rather badly. He got scratched up by a wolf. Well, by Kelwyn Faircrest, who turned into a wolf."

"A wolf? Is Kelwyn a Druid, then?" the Timber-Elf exclaimed.

"Apparently so," Girion replied, as he placed his hand on a tender spot on his chest. "And he's a spy for Ravinia."

"What?" the Wood-Gnome roared. "That's – that's – how could that be?" he stammered. "Surely some mistake has been made!"

Just then, Chula rushed back into the room with a glass bottle filled with orange liquid. He hastily pulled the cork out of the top, then told Girion, who was now reclining on the couch, to just relax. Holding the Manfellow's nose, Chula poured a fair amount of liquid into Girion's throat.

"Had to protect your nose from the smell, you know. All right, now swallow it. That's a good chap," he said.

Girion did so, and he immediately felt as if it would be impossible to keep his eyes open. A few moments later, his vision became fuzzy, and he passed out.

"What did you just do to Girion?" Aradis crossly demanded, as he sat up on the couch.

"Here now, you've got to relax as well," Chula insisted. Grabbing the squirming Aradis, he similarly held his nose and tipped the bottle, and some of the orange solution tumbled into the Manfellow's mouth.

"You – you screwy ... " Aradis spluttered, as his head begin to feel outrageously light. It was only a moment more before he too fell unconscious.

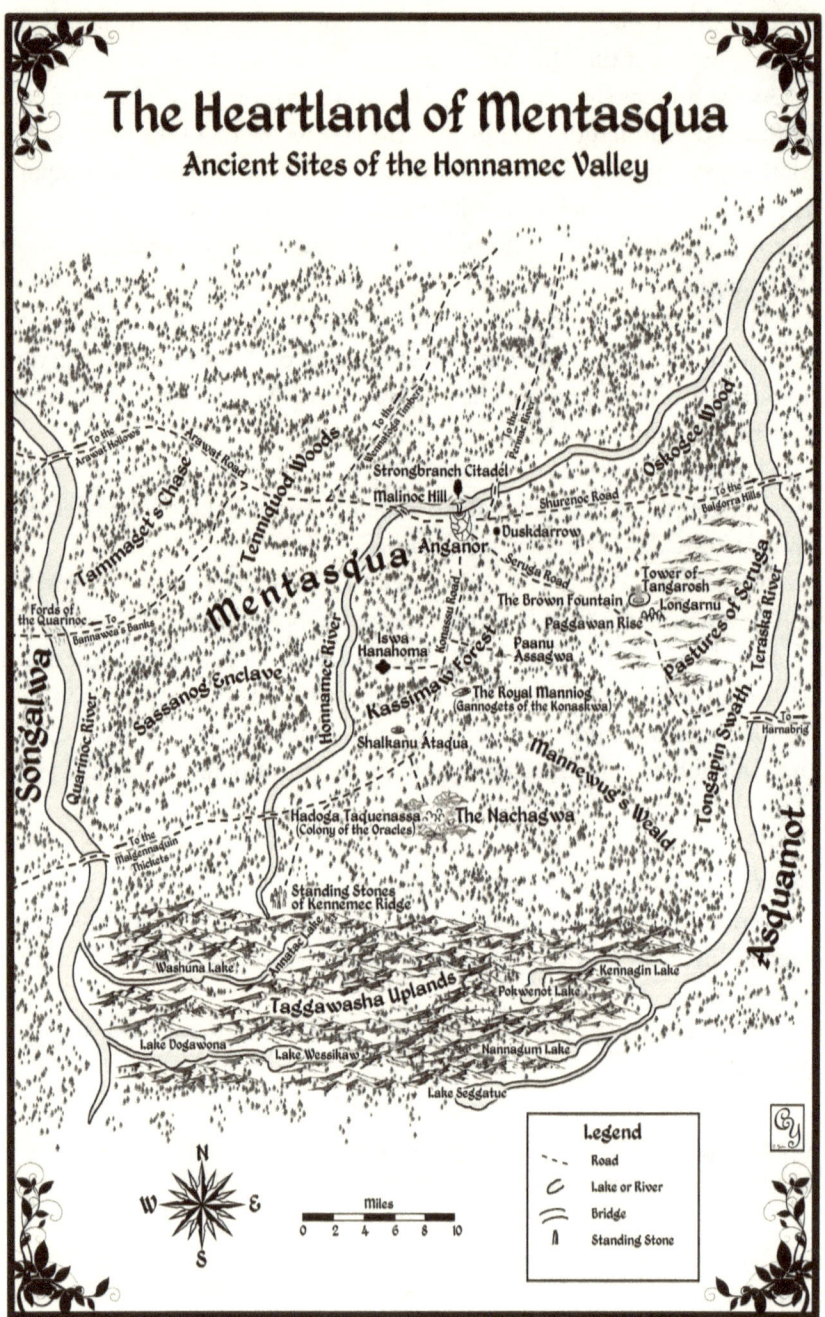

The Heartland of Mentasqua
Ancient Sites of the Honnamec Valley

To the Arawat Hollows
Arawat Road
To the Honnamec Tirhelp
To the Forest Reaches

Tenniduod Woods
Oskodee Wood
To the Baldorra Hills

Strongbranch Citadel
Malinoc Hill
Shurenoc Road

Duskdarrow

Anganor

Seruda Road

Mentasqua

Tower of Tangarosh
The Brown Fountain
Longarnu
Tammaset's Chase
Pastures of Seruda

Iswa
Hanahoma
Paggawan Rise

Paanu
Assagwa

Fords of
the Quarinoc
To
Bannawee's Banks

Sassanos Enclave

Honnamec River

Kennasol Road

Kassimaw Forest

The Royal Manniog
(Gannogets of the Konaskwa)

Terasha River

Songaliva

Shalkanu Ataqua

Quarinoc River

Mannewug's Weald

To
Harnabrig

Hadoga Taquenassa
(Colony of the Oracles)

The Nachagwa

Tongapin Swath

Asquamot

To the
Malgennandin
Thickets

Standing Stones
of Kennemec Ridge

Amathec Creek

Washuna Lake

Kennagin Lake

Pokwenot Lake

Taggawasha Uplands

Lake Dogawona

Lake Wessikaw

Nannagum Lake

Lake Seggatuc

Legend

- - - Road

C Lake or River

Bridge

Standing Stone

N
W E
S

Miles
0 2 4 6 8 10

CHAPTER FIVE

A Quarrel with Quagga

hen Aradis awakened, he was in the middle of mumbling, "You screwy Shore-Elf. Just who do you think you are?" He still felt a bit lightheaded, and his right hand was slightly numb. His eyes fluttered, and he opened them to stare up at the dark, raftered ceiling of the Quest Hall. The fire was still burning in the hearth, and he could clearly distinguish the voices of Chula and Fergus, along with a few others, discussing the medallion.

Fergus' voice hurriedly whispered, "The princess has it now, an' we canna afford to wait any longer, just in case Gornok tries to go after it. Get the lads up, Padarellig. We're a-goin' to leave as soon as they're on their feet."

A Gnome with spirally ears came over to Girion and began shaking him. "Hoy, Manfellow! It's time to get up. You've got a far journey to make."

Girion groggily lifted his head, coughed a few times and sat up. Satisfied, the Gnome went to Aradis and, seeing that he was already awake, instructed him to get ready to depart.

"Ah, me heart gladdens much to see ye alive!" Fergus exclaimed, as he went over to the lads. "I canna tell ye how sorry I am about wha' has happened, but at least we've got that scurrilous weasel Gornok out of our midst."

"Where are we going?" Aradis asked, as he buckled on his sword. "To see the princess?"

"Indeed, ya guessed it. We haven' any time to lose. I lef' the medallion wit her, so we've got to get back and warn her tha' Ravinia's lot might be a-comin' after her to get it. But also, she agreed to meet wit ye, that bein' on accoun' o' ye bringin' the medallion as a token. She believes, as I do, tha' ye have fulfilled the Sign o' the Sengara. Plus, there's the fact that ye did come halfway across Orona to save Argonis. Tha', too, counts for summtin, she said. Besides all that, tings are gettin' quite bad here in Argonis, as ye know. The noose is a-tightenin', an' if summtin's a-goin' to be done, it's got to be done soon. An' curse me cousin's cap – this whole business wit Quagga is only makin' tings worse."

By this time, both lads had gotten their packs and weapons and were ready to go.

Aradis, staring somewhat peevishly at the Shore-Elf, now said, "Chula, may I ask what you did to us?"

Gently clearing his throat, Chula replied, "I gave you a drink called onohalga, which is a powerful concoction to put you to sleep. Your slumber gave me an opportunity to work on your wounds, which probably feel rather deadened at the moment, as I put several different solutions on them which should speed up the healing process."

"Oh, well, thank you," Girion said, with genuine gratitude, as he looked down at his chest and saw only a faint amount of blood through several bandages applied there, evidently by Chula.

"Yes, thank you indeed," Aradis echoed.

"Certainly, if ye've got wounds, Chula's the one ye ought to go to," Fergus asserted. "But we've got to get a move on. Ashworthy, call the others who are a-goin' wit us down here from the Parley Attic."

An Ingan went to do as Fergus asked. Meanwhile, Girion walked over to the window to look out into the street below, half-expecting to see Gornok in wolf form prowling at the base of the Gnarly Stump. To his relief, there was only the empty lane, bathed in the hushed, purple glow of the moss-lamps. After a few moments, he turned and asked the Questkeeper, "How did you get back into the Taskula, what with all of Quagga's people guarding all the gates?"

"To be sure, 'twas right difficult enough," Fergus replied wearily. "I used a tunnel to get back into the city an' had then but two gates to pass. Now, it so happen'd tha' Quagga was headed from the Banaka, where I was, up to the Taskula, where I a-wanted to go. So I jus' snuck behind him an' his lousy bodyguard tru the gate into the Sayuga, which is the district between the two, an' after that, tru the gate into the Taskula. But now we've got to go back by that same route, an' we shanna have such a luxury available to us."

"Tankfully, Chula's foolhardy blowin' o' that bedeviled horn o' his has got a fair number o' folk in Anganor a-believin' tha' Tornoak sen' the spirit of a ketchiwah, a huge, truly terrifyin' animal that lives in out-o'-the-way parts of Argonis, to haunt the city an' teach Quagga a jolly lesson. Many folk in Anganor, especially the Ingans, don' ya know, are o' the superstitious sort; in this case, we can use tha' to our bonnie advantage. Now, me an' the Questies ha' come up wit a ruse to persuade the garrisons to let us tru, at least back to the Banaka, where the openin' o' the tunnel lies. Some o' the Questies ha' tried this trick out already, an' it worked marvelously. But there isn't time to speak o' that now. As I said, though, the trick should get us tru to the tunnel. An', though Ravinia's folk ha' been a-lyin' in the forest near the tunnel's exit, they shanna be able to vanquish so many Questmongers as there shall be wit us tonight. Besides, I'd wager me mother an' me own bonnie teacup tha' Kelwyn tol' them about the tunnel a long time ago, so I care not if they see us a-comin' out of it. For their own sake, they'd best not tangle wit Fergus O'Brannadon tonight. If they do, they'll wish they had a ghost ketchiwah a-comin' after 'em instead o' me."

Looking exceedingly pleased with himself, Chula asked, "Since my horn worked so splendidly earlier, do you think I should blow it again when we're close to the gate into the Sayuga, just for good measure?"

"I tink not. Anganor has had quite enough o' tha' nonsense for tonight," Fergus sternly replied.

Chula, quite deflated, now began wandering morosely around the Quest Hall. Meanwhile, Fergus spoke with the Siloans briefly about their afternoon and evening with Kelwyn and Mordie. As might be expected, his face grew red, and his speech became filled with invective when they spoke of the masquerading Druid's betrayal of them and Mordie, even though he had already heard most of the tale from Chula.

A few minutes later, Ashworthy returned with five additional Questmongers. Of the total of thirteen Questmongers that were now in the room, eight stood clustered together just behind Fergus.

"Aradis an' Girion," the Questkeeper announced, "we shall be a-travelin' wit an escort to Iswa Hanahoma, so if we be attacked on the way, we shall have a good lot to fight back wit. These Ingans are Ashworthy, Redgarth and Stumpory. The Timber-Elf is Sarranil, and the Leprechaun is Collic McGarrus. Then we've got Logar Mannerus Uldenrog – or just

Uldenrog – the Dwarf. Chula ye know. An' the Wood-Gnome is Jecko. The rest – Padarellig an' Drisham an' Limberleaf an' so forth – they'll be a-stayin' here to guard the Den."

Fergus now gave the Menfolk one final word of instruction. "Don' take me amiss in this, laddies, but I'm a-orderin' ye here an' now for yer own good to let me Questies do the fightin', for yer lives are wort' much to this kingdom, ya know, an''tis me own folk's duty to protect ye. I'm not implyin' ye lack the skill to fight or anyting o' that sort; 'tis merely that, if some trouble arises, 'twill be better if ye let us contend wit it as best we may, an' ye only get entangled in combat if need drives ye. Understood?"

The Siloans nodded respectfully to the Questkeeper, promising they would assent to his request. Then they went and stood among their guardians.

The Questmongers who were traveling to Iswa Hanahoma quickly bade farewell to their comrades who were staying behind. Then Fergus led the party out the door into the second-floor hallway. An Ingan closed the door and locked it behind them.

The troop now marched down the stairs and into the tavern proper, which was quite deserted by this time. All the bowls of kuringa, the burning red plant material, had been snuffed out, and the fires in the two great hearths had turned to smoldering ashes. Fergus unlocked the door of the place, then locked it back up after all had passed outside. Evidently, he didn't think it necessary to take everyone out through the secret tunnel at this hour of the night, or else he figured that if Ravinia's agents were trying to spy on their movements, they would know about the tunnel anyway (thanks to Gornok), so it wouldn't make a difference whether they used it or not.

It was now around an hour and a half before dawn, and the sky was pensive and still quite dark, but clear. The streets of Anganor were hushed and empty, but the pachacuri lamps glowed steadily on. Moving in silent formation, the party went west down the street a little way, then turned south. A few minutes later, they arrived at a gate into another district, which Fergus said was the Sayuga, the Ancestral Ward. There was, to none of their surprise, a garrison of Quagga's folk standing by the gate, a group of ten Barada armed with clubs and spears.

"Keep silent an' stay in formation," Fergus ordered. "This shanna take long, I expect. Stumpory, remember wha' we talked about." A short, stocky, somewhat elderly Ingan striding along next to the Leprechaun nodded.

The guards grew nervous upon seeing the crew of Barada, and a tall, lanky Ingan, called out, "Just what do you all think you're doing? This gate's closed until first light."

"We're on our way to see Quagga," Fergus coolly replied, still walking forward. "He summoned us, ya know. Wants to talk to us abou' the ketchiwah situation."

The Ingan shifted uncomfortably, as the Questmongers and the Siloans drew nigh. "What about it?" he pressed.

"We've seen it. Over in the Eskagwan. We sent a message to Quagga, an' he sent one back, a-sayin' he wants to interview us abou' the matter. The fella said Quagga was in a right hurry about it too. Now he's escortin' us to go see him." Fergus lightly gestured to Stumpory.

"Quagga told me, he did, that I'd best bring them straightaway," Stumpory confirmed in a high, excitable voice that was as comical as it was sincere.

"Where is Quagga right now, incidentally?" the guard inquired.

"In the Banaka," Stumpory said.

"Huh, that's odd," the sentry remarked. "Last we heard, he was in the Sagwan."

"He's been moving around quite a bit tonight, as a matter of fact, making the rounds and whatnot," Stumpory explained, "and that's why we've got to hurry back to him before he moves on to somewhere else."

"Very well, very well," the Ingan on duty conceded. "The sooner this whole ketchiwah matter is sorted out, the better. We can't have Anganor thinking that Quagga doesn't have things under control because he certainly does. I'm confident that when you tell him just what it is that you saw, he'll know exactly what to do."

He ordered his comrades to open the gate, and the Questmongers marched onward into the Ancestral Ward. The gates thudded shut behind them.

"Just like before, laddie. Worked like a charm," Fergus congratulated Stumpory.

Now the troop began heading southwest through the Sayuga. Here and there, this area had timber-frame buildings like those in all the other districts, but most of its structures used large, peculiar trees for their frameworks. These extraordinary trees had not one trunk, but five or six at their bases, all of which curved toward each other, then joined into one massive bole some twenty or thirty feet up. In-between the multiple trunks, there were wattle-and-daub walls, so that these constructions gave the appearance of large domes with fat, gray trees growing out of their tops. Many of them had either chimneys or holes in their ceilings, and presently, ghostly streams of smoke were rising from them up into the night air.

The Siloans kept looking up at these bizarre structures, and Fergus, noticing the lads' fascination with them, pointed to them and explained, "Those are osguna trees; they only grow in Argonis an' a few spots in the Stony Wilds, an' the Ingans have traditionally used 'em for this sort o' dwellings tha' ye see, which are called kahonasi. Anganor, for most of its history, was filled wit kahonasi, but as the Latter Epoch progressed, many o' them were a-cut down an' replaced wit reg'lar wood buildings. Most o' the Ingans tha' live in this district are very tied to the old ways, so they've insisted on keepin' their kahonasi. A lot o' the forest villages o' the Ingans, especially in western Argonis, have kahonasi as well."

The party kept on through this district for almost ten minutes, cutting through the rows of kahonasi, and then they reached yet another gate, which, as expected, hosted one of Quagga's garrisons. Fergus told the lads that they were now going into the Banaka, the Ward of the Learned, and from there, they would be leaving the city through the tunnel he had mentioned.

The conversation at this gate went much like that at the previous one, although the Ingan in charge here was a little more skeptical. Nonetheless, Stumpory's assertion that Quagga would be sure to grow outraged if there was much more delay proved to be sufficient motivation for him to let them pass. So, they went on into the Banaka, delighted that they would at last be rid of dealing with Quagga's troublesome minions.

The Banaka had its own distinct ambience, featuring a number of stone buildings with pillars wreathed in blue pachacuri. The streets seemed to be extremely well-kept in this area, and some of the timber-frame buildings had abstract, stylized murals on them. Fergus quickly led the group off the main road and then took them on a zig-zagging path to the southwest. It was another seven or eight minutes before they reached an area among some three-story buildings near the western wall of the city. Here there was a small alley that ran off to the south, and Fergus halted the group shortly before they reached it, for there were a number of gruff voices echoing out of it.

"I'm telling you, old Elmsprig's holed up in the Banaka somewhere, along with a bunch of other Strongbranch sympathizers," a rough voice proclaimed. "He's not at his house, though, nor at the Ministry of Correspondence. We've checked both those places."

"Maybe he slipped through one of the gates," another voice offered. "I'd say we've searched nearly everywhere in the vicinity."

"Don't be silly," yet another voice retorted. "Our folk have been watching all of them since this morning, and besides, Dinny the Wood-Gnome spotted him here in the Banaka this afternoon."

"Everyone knows Wood-Gnomes can't be trusted in this affair," still another voice called out scornfully.

"You watch your mouth, you moldy barkface!" a voice, evidently that of a Wood-Gnome, reprimanded. "I'll have you know that we Wood-Gnomes have been every bit as loyal to Argonis as you Ingans, if not more so, for the past – "

"Oh, cut this jabber," demanded the voice that had first spoken of Elmsprig. "Right now we've got to figure out where Elmsprig is. We can't very well have a government official on the loose inciting a counter-rebellion; it's very important that he be found and taken into custody. Now, let's talk through this again. You know, we all would be a lot more efficient if you would just listen to me. I've done quite a bit of investigation into this matter in the past few hours and have narrowed down his potential hiding spots considerably. We've got exactly four buildings near here that ..."

The voice blustered on, but Fergus had heard more than enough. "Uldenrog, go an' have a look at these seditious scoundrels," he directed the lone Dwarf who was with them.

Uldenrog crept up to the corner and peeped around it. He then scurried back and reported, "There are nearly thirty-five Barada down there, and some of them have plopped their fat behinds on the very cellar door that leads to our tunnel. I think we could frighten them all off, though, if we attack them unawares."

Fergus looked extremely annoyed. "We could indeed, but ye know as well as I do tha' we'll wake folk for sure if it comes to fightin'. But I don' wan' to risk any o' these brickbrains or someone livin' in the buildings nearby a-spottin' where the entrance to our tunnel is. For e'en if only one Barada should see it, that would be enough to spoil the matter. We shanna risk it, an' I haven' the patience for these ding-dongs to finish their palaverin'. We've been a-sneakin' around all night on accoun' o' this steamin' pile o' stupid they call Quagga, an' I've had quite enough of it. It's time for Action Step Fergus, as all o' ye like to say. No more dallyin'. We're just a-goin' to break out tru the Banaka Gate, for time is short an' so is me temper."

As the voice in the alley went on haranguing, the Questmongers and the Siloans made their way back east a few streets, then southward until they passed onto a main street that ran to the west. A short way down this road, there was a huge set of gates that were just like the ones that Aradis and Girion had come through when they had entered Anganor from the southeast. In front of the gates, there were around thirty Barada of various kinds, though mostly Ingans, gathered around a particularly vulgar-looking fellow who, from his demeanor, conduct and appearance, the lads guessed to be none other than Quagga himself.

This fellow, who was in the middle of leveling a series of exceedingly demeaning insults at the Barada standing in front of him, had an air about him that was unmistakably charismatic, but in an obnoxious sort of way; that is, his personal magnetism, though powerful, would only be likely to attract persons who were somewhere on the spectrum from questionable to altogether foul. His eyes were narrow and dark, and his face exuded sneering and hostility. Presently, he was chewing a clump of small, dark leaves, which had stained his teeth a very unattractive brown. His bark-skin looked almost oily, and he had scraggly, tangled, dark moss-hair that hung down to his shoulders. Covering his chest was a breastplate that he had obviously purloined from one of Thornoak's guards, and he had on a heavy leather kilt, to which there were several daggers and swords attached. In his hand was a long spear, which he was waving about angrily, as he spouted off at the guards of the Banaka Gate, cursing them, apparently, for having mentioned something or other about the ghost ketchiwah.

Fergus paused and held his hand up, signaling for the rest of the company to hold back.

"Well, well, 'twould be our luck, wouldn' it?" he sighed. "To begin wit, 'tis a bitter irony that, of all the districts of Anganor, the Banaka's the one Quagga happens to be in. At least we weren't a-lyin', it seems, when we told his guards that's where he was. But of all the spots that miserable sass-mouth mopface could be, he would be a-standin' at the Banaka Gate right when we're a-tryin' to leave the city. Curs'd be the cur! Well, there's nuttin' for it but to trounce 'im good an' proper, for, sure as rain, I shanna be a-waitin' for 'im to move on. We've too great a need o' time for tha'. Action Step Fergus is really a-hankerin' for haste now."

"Stay in the shadows till the tusslin' begins," he ordered, as he turned to face his band, "as I'm bonnie certain it will. Then subdue however many ye must, but there's to be no killin', mind ye. An' don' hurt 'em much – no more than necessary, that is. Fools they may be, but e'en fools ought to be spared extra harm if it can be helped, for they do plenty o' harm to themselves, ya know."

Then, motioning to a large door, just south of the gate, that led into a chamber in the city wall, Fergus instructed, "As quick as ye can after the fight's begun, some o' ye get into the gatehouse an' open the gates an' the portcullis; then we'll be on our merry way. I don' tink they'll be inclined to follow us, but supposin' they are, we'll merely drub 'em as needed an' sally on."

Finally, turning to the Menfolk, Fergus said, "Aradis an' Girion, the two o' ye jus' stay back out o' the way until the gates are open, an' then run up an' join us. Remember, yer safety is of the utmost importance on this mission."

The lads nodded, though Aradis half-considered disregarding this directive. Girion, who could predict Aradis' trail of thought almost before Aradis himself could embark upon it, gave his friend a reproachful glance. Accordingly, Aradis abandoned the idea of hurtling himself into combat with Quagga and his followers, though begrudgingly so.

Fergus now looked back at those gathered by the gate, shook his head in disgust at Quagga, then marched directly toward him, as the Siloans and the Questmongers moved into deeper shadows on the side of the street.

"If I hear one more word about this stupid ghost ketchiwah, I'll have the lot of you fed to a *real* ketchiwah!" Quagga threatened, fuming. "I've been over to the Naskanu and the Eskagwan in person, and there's naught to indicate that any ketchiwah, ghost or otherwise, has been there tonight, but for the fact that folk said they heard a deafening roar or two. There was a burning wagon causing some havoc, apparently, but if that's enough to frighten you out of your wits, then why don't you all crawl back in your cradles and remove your feeble selves from my service? I simply won't have my followers shivering in their skins over ridiculous things like that in the midst of us trying to make demands of Thornoak and Strongbranch. Do you want people to think we're a bunch of bippledrops from a Sky-Gnome candy parlor?"

"Well, that's exac'ly what ye are – especially you, Quagga!" shouted a voice out of the darkness. It was Fergus.

Quagga whirled around, bristling, and, to his astonishment, saw the Leprechaun step boldly out of the shadows.

"How dare you!" he roared. "And who are you, filthy runt?"

"None o' your bonnie business, ya wimpy, windbaggin', weak-minded excuse for a Barada," Fergus sharply returned. "Now, you and your pathetic, jughead Quaggies best open up the gates before I'm obliged to give the lot o' ye a sound drubbin' – one ye shanna soon forget."

Quagga's followers were so utterly stunned that anyone would dare speak in that manner to their leader that they all stared at the approaching Leprechaun with their mouths agape.

Meanwhile, Quagga's face drew into a grotesque configuration that was a mixture of absolute shock and uncontainable rage. He was, in fact, so thoroughly seized by his ire that he could barely sputter a reply. "You – you miserable little pipsqueak!" he puffed. "If you had even a drop of sense in that tiny head of yours, you'd never dare to – "

"Oh, shut your fat, ugly mouth, ya lumpish, dizzy-eyed jackanapes," Fergus snapped, as he stopped about ten feet from the recipient of his invective. "I didna come here to listen to you showcase your stupidity by a-waggin' your tongue about like some pompous oaf."

"Have a care, wretch!" growled Quagga, raising his spear menacingly, "For at any moment, I could skewer you like the worthless riffraff you are. Indeed, I ought to have done so already! You should be grateful I've got more dignity and courtesy than you seem to have."

"You're a fine one to talk abou' such tings," Fergus retorted, "seein' as common dung rats ha' got a hundred times more courtesy an' dignity than you've ever had in your whole life, I'd guess."

Quagga drew himself up to his full height and stamped his foot. "Enough of this! I'm the governor of this city, and I simply will not – "

"Governor indeed!" Fergus snorted. "You're nuttin' but a common scoundrel an' a measly coward, an' ya ought to be hung from Strongbranch's highest bough for your sedition."

"Oho!" Quagga bellowed. "So you're one of those poor fools who still holds loyal to Hoarstaff and Thornoak and their sorry lot. Ha! Simpleton! No doubt you're planning to go scurry down to Paanu Assagwa and bring the oh-so-mighty Thornoak back here to set me straight. That's why you want to be allowed through the gate, isn't it? You're just – "

"You'll get no accountin' from me of any o' me affairs, treasonous mongrel," Fergus spat. "Now, listen here, Quagga McQuaggerson, I already tol' you once to get those gates open right quick, an', sure as rain, I meant it. So get a move on, ya blunderin' baggage, or I'll turn you an' your slobberin', slavish stooges upside down afore ye can – "

Now it was Quagga's turn to interrupt. "You stupid sop!" he roared. "Do you really think you can – "

The enraged Ingan's diatribe was cut short quite abruptly, for Fergus pulled a stone from his vest and flung it lightning quick at Quagga's right knee. The rock struck hard and true. Quagga buckled and hollered at the top of lungs. Then, before any of his followers could come to his aid, Fergus darted forward and shoved the Ingan forcefully, so that he tumbled backward onto the ground.

Immediately, the Questmongers sprang into action, racing to the cluster of Quagga's followers, which was mobilizing to apprehend Fergus. The eight of them, with extraordinary rapidity, knocked quite a few of Quagga's cronies flat on their backs. Then Redgarth and Ashworthy, two Ingan Questmongers, sprinted up to the door to the gatehouse. It was unlocked, so they flung it open and darted inside. Moments later, there were shouts from Quagga's soldiers within the gatehouse, as they were knocked to the ground or against the walls by the Questmongers. A few moments after that, the iron portcullis began to rise.

Meanwhile, Quagga had managed to stand up and was attempting to find Fergus amidst all the fray. Cursing the Leprechaun, he began thrashing about, even striking some of his own men with his fists in the process. Suddenly, he was bowled over by Jecko the Wood-Gnome, one of the Questmongers. This only caused him to curse all the more, as he landed smack on his face.

Just then, Aradis and Girion, who were still lingering some way back from the gate, heard shouts behind them. They turned and saw a group of Barada consisting of several Ingans and Timber-Elves running toward them. "We've got to stop all those lunatics attacking Quagga!" one of them shouted. Evidently, they were a group of Quagga's minions simply marching about on patrol in the Banaka. However, their spotting abilities left something to be desired, as they had not sighted the Siloans.

Aradis, now too eager for combat to resist, swiftly drew out his sword, as Girion objected, "Fergus said for us not to fight unless it was absolutely necessary."

"Well, it is," Aradis replied, as he waited for the approaching Barada.

"Why don't we just stay in hiding? Or even run up to the gates?" Girion suggested. "I really don't think it's a good idea to upset Fergus."

"He won't get mad about this. And if he does, then that's his problem. Besides, there are far more guards up by the gate than there are right here."

As soon as Aradis had finished saying this, he stepped out of the darkness to where the running Barada could see him. "Hey, you lunkheads! Over here!"

A Timber-Elf let out a sharp cry, then swerved toward them. Three Ingans and another Timber-Elf followed him, and the rest continued racing toward the gates.

The Ingans threw spears toward the lads, which they just barely managed to dodge, and then the Timber-Elves drew swords as they charged. Aradis sparred with the first one that reached him, swinging his blade aggressively toward him, causing him to stumble and fall backward. Two of the Ingans were gathering their spears, while the third came rushing at Girion, who frantically batted at him with his staff. The second Timber-Elf tried to attack Aradis from the side, but the lad deftly blocked him, then leapt up onto a pile of sacks set against the wall of the nearby building.

Meanwhile, the Questmongers had incapacitated a fair number of Quagga's fighters, so they ran to the gates, flung off the bar that held them together and pulled them open. No sooner had they done this than Ashworthy and Redgarth emerged from the gatehouse and rejoined them. Fergus looked back down the street to where they had left the Siloans, and, seeing that they were engaged in combat, whistled and motioned to them to break it off.

Girion was now backed up against the wall by the Ingan he had been fighting, so Aradis sprang from the sacks toward the Ingan, who turned to confront him. Girion took his chance to flee, though an Ingan spear whizzed by quite close to his head and stuck into the thick-planked wall. Aradis swung at the Ingan, who stepped back, and the lad skirted around him, taking off after Girion. However, he looked back over his shoulder to dodge any weapons that might be hurled after them. This proved to be prudent because he had to evade two spears that sought to pierce him only a few seconds later.

The lads quickly reached the area where the Questmongers were battling Quagga and his sentinels, and they navigated through the fighting to Fergus, with their Ingan and Timber-Elf assailants close behind them. However, the Questmongers engaged these pursuers in swift and decisive combat, disarming them and knocking them sprawling.

Now the Siloans and the Questmongers gathered by the gate, holding their enemies at bay, and Fergus saucily sang, "I tol' ya, Quagga, that I meant business, an' business I meant." Grabbing his vest and straightening it, he led his company out onto the grassy plain that lay in-between the city and the woods of Mentasqua.

"Shut that portcullis, you idiots!" Quagga stormed. "And the gates too." Several of his men began to do so.

As the portcullis was being lowered, Quagga yelled at the departing Questmongers, "You may have gotten out of the city, but you'll not find it so simple a matter to get back in. Now, be off with you, you filthy, no-account scum!"

"Why, tank you, Quagga. I believe we *shall* be off now," Fergus called.

Then, so that only his company could hear him, he sighed, "What a sorry fella that Quagga is. Tankfully none of us is any the worse off for a-dealin' wit the likes o' him, save for a brief delay. Now, laddies, we've got to hop an' trot an' make as good a pace as can be made, for the princess may be in danger."

"Aradis. Girion." Fergus gestured to the Menfolk. "What happened to ye back there? Where'd those other hooligans come from?"

"Behind us," Aradis replied. "That was one of Quagga's patrol squads, I think."

"Ye didn' get hurt at all, did ye?"

"No," Girion answered. "We're all right."

"Grand. Now, get ye in the middle o' the group, so as to be better protected. For if Ravinia's maggots are a-goin' to strike at us this mornin', 'twill be between here and Iswa Hanahoma. An', mind ye well, they're a far more formidable lot than Quagga's goons back there."

The lads dutifully marched to the center of the pack of Questmongers, as Aradis whispered, "I told you he wouldn't mind."

"That's because he didn't know that you let them see you on purpose," Girion returned, a bit peeved. "I'm adding that one to our list."

"What list?" Aradis asked.

"You know exactly what list I'm talking about."

Aradis gave Girion a puzzled look, and the latter clarified, "The 'Times Aradis Has Almost Gotten Us Killed for No Good Reason' list."

"Oh, that one."

The lads concluded their conversation, as Fergus saluted the still-raving Quagga, who was now glowering at them from the ramparts. "Best o' luck to you!" the Leprechaun cheerfully called. "An' a very merry rebellion to you an' all o' your cronies! After all, treason is in season!"

After this last parting statement, which Quagga did not find even remotely amusing, the Questmongers and their charges, led by the inimitable Fergus the Fearless, set off on their journey.

Moving at a rather vigorous speed, the troop headed south, following the wall of the city, until they came to another gate. A wide dirt road ran out of this gate, then headed off into the forest to the south. As they joined this road, Fergus instructed Collic and Sarranil to scout ahead of the group all the way to Iswa Hanahoma, as he didn't want to be caught off guard by any ambushes. So, the Leprechaun and the Timber-Elf jogged on ahead, promising to stay just in sight so Fergus would know immediately if something were amiss.

After they had been traveling south on this road for about twenty minutes, the first rays of dawn gently colored the landscape, as Marda crawled up over the horizon, driving back the darkness in the east. All the grass glistened with morning dew, and cheerful, little woodland birds warbled from their perches and nests in the dense foliage overhead.

The road ran straight southward for four miles, shaded much of the way by long, arching boughs. Then it began turning slightly, so that it ran south by southwest. This section traversed a few streams via old, wooden bridges and passed through several bright meadows overspread by delightful summer blossoms. At a point a little more than eight miles from Anganor, they encountered a sign with the same curving script that the Siloans had noted on signs in the east of Argonis. However, this sign had no kendarill on it; instead, it featured the distinct outline of Strongbranch Citadel. Here the road branched off into two routes, one running to the east and the other continuing on south by southwest. They took the latter and followed it another two miles, at which point it forked again, accompanied by another sign in Asla'gu. This time, one of the roads went off to the west and the other continued on a southwesterly course. In this instance, they took the road leading west, which entered a thicker section of the woods.

When the party had gone a little over three miles down this route, the road surged up out of a little hollow, and the forest abruptly came to an end. There before them stood a grassy expanse, on the other side of which was a high, moss-covered, stone wall of considerable height. This wall was fitted with a great set of black wooden gates. Above the gates there was an impressive barbican, a wide guard tower, rising up some thirty additional feet. The wall curved gently away to the west on either side of the gates – that is, as it ran to the north and the south. On the wall's ramparts, Ingans in shining armor were looking out to the east, with the points of their tall spears gleaming in the late-morning sunshine.

They had come at last to Iswa Hanahoma, the magnificent abode of Princess Langwana, she who was the Siloans' sole key to an audience with King Thornoak.

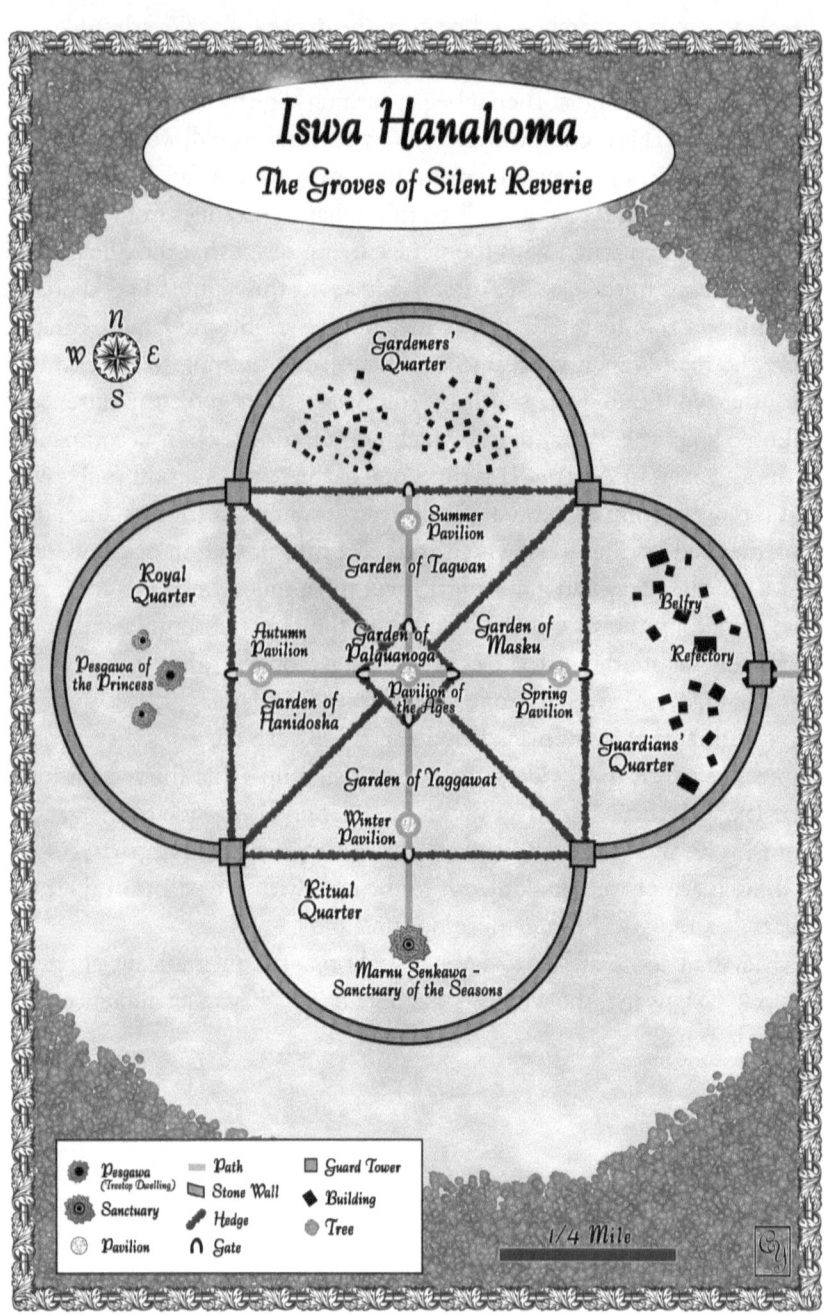

Iswa Hanahoma
The Groves of Silent Reverie

Gardeners'
Quarter

Summer
Pavilion

Garden of Tagwan

Royal
Quarter

Belfry

Refectory

Autumn
Pavilion

Garden of
Palquanoga

Garden of
Masku

Pesgawa of
the Princess

Pavilion of
the Ages

Garden of
Hanidosha

Spring
Pavilion

Guardians'
Quarter

Garden of Yaggawat

Winter
Pavilion

Ritual
Quarter

Marnu Senkawa –
Sanctuary of the Seasons

Pesgawa (Treetop Dwelling)	Path	Guard Tower	
Sanctuary	Stone Wall	Building	
Pavilion	Hedge	Tree	
	Gate		

1/4 Mile

CHAPTER SIX

The Sanctuary of the Sacred Quinary

striding swiftly, Fergus led his troop toward the gates of Iswa Hanahoma, hailing the sentinels as he did so. These guards signaled their fellows below and inside the barbican, and as the party drew nigh, the gates slowly, ponderously swung outward. A few moments later, a tall, muscular Ingan of noble bearing strode into the gateway and nodded at Fergus. He was clad in a breastplate of polished silver and a brown leather kilt, which was held around his waist by a girdle embellished with stones of green, yellow, red, blue and white.

When they reached the Ingan, Fergus respectfully greeted him, as the gates closed behind them. "Hail, good Paskasha! Would ya happen to know which garden the princess is in at the momen'? We've got summtin' terribly urgent to discuss wit her."

"I believe she's presently in the Garden of Hanidosha," Paskasha replied. "You'll most likely find her in the Autumn Pavilion. At least that's what I was told by some of her maidservants, whom she sent here to await your coming," he added, as he beckoned to two young Treemaenas; the taller of the two had finely braided, dark-green moss-hair and was garbed in a long, white gown.

"Hello, Fergus," the taller Ingan maiden said, as she approached. "Would I be correct to assume these are the Menfolk you spoke of?"

"Ya would." Fergus nodded.

Then, turning to the Siloans, the maiden declared, "I am Na'ikeyana, Princess Langwana's chief lady-in-waiting. She has been eagerly anticipating your arrival, Menfolk from across the sea. Now, if the two of you and Fergus will follow me, I will take you to see her."

"Positively grand, m'lady," Fergus said. "We'll be right along. Gran' me just a wee moment."

Now addressing the Menfolk, the Leprechaun explained, "On accoun' o' the fact that this is a sacred site an' we're a-goin' to see the princess, we've got to be leavin' our weapons here. Ye can leave yer packs here too, if ye wish. May as well, ye know, so ye won' have to haul 'em around wit ye."

"Oh, of course," Aradis replied, as he took off his pack and began to unbuckle his sword and dagger. Meanwhile, Girion pulled his notebook and tylon out of his pack and placed them in his jerkin.

Paskasha signaled to a nearby soldier to come over and tend to the Siloans' items. The fellow jogged up and took both the lads' packs, as well as Girion's knife and staff and Aradis' sword and dagger. He also took Fergus' weapons, most of which had been hidden under his clothing. The soldier then went to stow these items inside the gatehouse, and Paskasha promised the lads that their things would be brought back to them when they returned to the gate.

As all this was transpiring, Fergus turned to the Questmongers and directed, "As for ye, Questies, stay here in the Guardians' Quarter, an' I'll come get ye when we're finished."

Then he inquired of the armored Ingan who had greeted them, "Paskasha, would your folk be able to get 'em summtin' to eat in the refectory?"

The solider nodded, and the Questmongers went off after Paskasha, who was walking over to a large wooden building inside the compound, half a furlong to the northwest.

Meanwhile, Na'ikeyana had spoken to her companion in a strange tongue, and the latter had hastened off to the west, heading toward an opening in the high, green hedge at the western edge of this portion of the enclosure. Now Fergus, Aradis and Girion walked just behind Na'ikeyana, as she led them toward this verdant barrier, which lay about a quarter of a mile away. The Siloans soon noticed that a few hundred feet beyond the hedge and soaring above it, there was a dark-green marble dome, bathed in rich sunlight.

The compound which they were presently traversing was in the shape of a half-oval, formed by the curving wall and the straight hedge. There was hardly any grass in this area, as the ground was mostly covered by dirt and gravel, but there were a number of timber structures to the north and the south, a few of which were two or three stories high. Many stately Ingan men, all outfitted in armor, were going in and out of these buildings.

When the Treemaena, the Leprechaun and the two Menfolk came to the hedge, they passed through an arch in which stood two large, open gates made of a luxurious, black wood. Just beyond them was a green marble path leading straight to the west.

The lads were hardly prepared for the stunning magnificence that lay beyond the arch. They were now in a large area that was shaped, from what they could discern, rather like a huge triangle, with one point being approximately a quarter-mile in front of them and the other two, also a quarter-mile distant, lying straight to the north and south of the gates. However, it was difficult for them to verify the exact shape of the area for certain, as the dome they had seen was resting atop a large structure that was less than a hundred and fifty yards directly in front of them, somewhat blocking their view of the western terminus of the enclosure. The dome was actually the crown of a massive, green marble pavilion, around a hundred feet in diameter, and from the floor of the pavilion to the top of the dome was a distance only slightly less than that. The pavilion was supported by gigantic green marble pillars, all wrapped in flowering vines, and, in its dim interior, they could make out the back of a large statue of some long-haired Ingan figure rising from extraordinarily carven froth and foam. Surrounding the statue were pedestals, also of green marble, with green crystal vases upon them.

Throughout the triangular enclosure in which the pavilion stood could be seen drooping trees that looked rather like willows, as well as green marble fountains of various sizes, all gurgling with shimmering cataracts and sprays of clear water. Also, there was at least a score of tranquil ponds, many edged by cattails and arched over by simple, wooden bridges. On the surface of these ponds were splendid lilies of a great many hues, around which small amphibians frolicked. The Siloans caught occasional glimpses of brightly-colored fish just below the surface of the waters. The portions of the ground not taken up by the little ponds were covered with lush, neatly trimmed grass, through which ran a network of green marble pathways. A few Ingans clad in long, barkcloth robes could be spotted throughout the area, tending to gardening pursuits.

As the Menfolk were taking all this in, the foursome were continuing on the particularly wide path that ran from the gates to the pavilion. Upon reaching that structure, the path split and ran along its circumference. Soon, the party arrived at a set of four steps leading up into the pavilion.

Na'ikeyana turned right, and the rest followed her. When they reached the far side, the paths joined up again, and they followed the marble walkway on to the west toward another high hedge, also set with black wooden gates. Beyond this hedge, the lads spotted another dome, just as large as the one behind them, but this one had been constructed with white marble. Also, they noticed that this area was not quite triangular because, in fact, the hedge in front of them ran off straight to the northwest for several hundred feet to the north of the gates and straight to the southwest for the same distance to the south of them. Thus, the area was more like a triangle with its third point slightly inverted.

When they had gone only a short way past the pavilion through this section of the gardens, Girion walked up beside Na'ikeyana and asked, "What is that big marble building back there? Some sort of temple?"

"You could say that," Na'ikeyana replied. "It is the Spring Pavilion, the shrine to Masku, the River Princess. At certain times, sacred water is poured upon her altar there, for she is the guardian of all waters in this world. This is her garden, and that is why you see all these ponds and fountains here; they are emblematic of her domain."

"How many gardens are there in Iswa Hanahoma?" Girion inquired, trying to keep stride with the Ingan maiden.

"Five," she answered, "for this is the Sanctuary of the Sacred Quinary, the five ontara, or mighty beings of the Haedra, most revered by our people. Each garden is situated in the position appropriate to its ontara. Also, each is filled with symbols of its ontara's dominion and is accented by aspects of his or her respective color and season. The Garden of Masku, the River Princess, through which we are now passing, lies here on the east. It is the place of childhood, of water and of the spring, and the paths and the pavilion here are green. To the north lies the Garden of Tagwan, the Sun Prince. To him belongs adolescence, and he is the possessor of light. His is the Summer Pavilion, made of yellow stone. In the west, where the princess awaits us, there is the Garden of Hanidosha, the Forest Queen, the matron of all living things and of maturity. The Autumn Pavilion is there, erected from red marble. Then, to the south, there is the Garden of Yaggawat, the Hill King, the ruler of stone and old age. To him is dedicated the Winter Pavilion, which is dark blue. Finally, in the center, there is the Garden of Palquanoga. He is the Sky Lord, the master of birth and death, dwelling in timelessness. His realm is energy of all kinds, and his pavilion, the Pavilion of the Ages, is white."

"That's a lot to keep track of," Girion chuckled. "You may have to remind me of some of that as we go through the gardens."

"To you, it may be perplexing," Na'ikeyana said, "but to those of us who are faithful to the veneration of the Sacred Quinary, it is unavoidable, for there is nothing in the fabric of Orona which does not fall under the dominion of those I have just named. If we displease them, there is no end to the misery which may befall us. In fact, that is why Argonis is presently in such a dreadful state."

"You believe you've angered the Sacred Quinary? Those five beings you just mentioned?"

"Yes: Masku, Tagwan, Hanidosha, Yaggawat and Palquanoga. Their wrath has burned against us since the Sundering of the Erynos."

"That's the battle where Thornoak spoke the word that collapsed the Erynos Divide into a huge chasm, isn't it? The same word that brought the Greenwall into being, which now keeps Ravinia and her forces at bay?"

A dark melancholy fell across Na'ikeyana's face, and she did not answer immediately. Eventually, however, she said, "That's correct. But it is not my place to speak more of it. If the princess so desires, she may elaborate on the matter."

Girion nodded, and noting the maiden's brooding solemnity, he inquired no further.

By this point, the group had reached the set of gates in the hedge and entered a square area, much smaller than the one they had just left behind. The whole place was walled by hedges, its corners were oriented in each of the cardinal directions and it was only an eighth of a mile from its eastern corner to its western one. This garden was covered with grass as well, but among these luxurious lawns, there blossomed thousands of little, white, eight-petaled flowers.

"These flowers are a-called sigwalus," Fergus explained, waving his hand at them. "The sigwalu is the city flower of Anganor and o' the Haedran bein' to whom this bonnie buildin' is dedicated."

"Palquanoga," Na'ikeyana said, almost inaudibly, as she glanced up at the white marble pavilion. This structure, unlike the Spring Pavilion, had walls between the pillars, and its only points of access were four archways, one facing each cardinal direction. From these four openings, white marble paths ran toward the four gates that led out of the Garden of Palquanoga. The lads could not espy anything of note inside the pavilion except for a tall, white pillar, around which a narrow marble staircase wound to reach a majestic flame burning in a large brazier at the top.

Na'ikeyana, as in the case of the previous pavilion, led the party around it rather than through it, and shortly, they came to the western gate of the Garden of Palquanoga. Beyond this was the Garden of Hanidosha, at the far end of which stood a red marble pavilion, nearly identical to the Spring Pavilion in the Garden of Masku. The pathways here were of red marble as well, and a single, broad path ran from the gates of the garden all the way to the steps of the Autumn Pavilion. On either side of this path, there were alternating rows of trees and flowers, all aligned to run in a north-south orientation.

The rows of flowers were positively wondrous. The blossoms were all greatly varied in shape, size and color, but there was not a single white flower to be found among their ranks. The trees were all fruit trees, and the lads marveled at the different varieties that grew in their stout boughs. One of the rows had trees with pink and purple bell-shaped fruits. Another had whitish potato-sized fruits that were shaped like upside-down strawberries; these fruits were colored here and there by streaks of dark red. Yet another row had long, thin fruits of a deep bluish hue. Around the bases of the trees grew mushrooms of many curious colors, some of which seemed almost to be faintly glowing. And up above them, sitting or hopping on the trees' branches, were myriads of birds quietly cooing. The lads guessed that they represented twenty or more varieties.

As the party approached the Autumn Pavilion, a solitary Ingan maiden stepped out from the shadow of a pillar and stood at the top of the steps, watching their approach. She was attired in a floor-length, yellow silk dress with small jewels sewn into it that glittered in the sunshine. Her moss-hair was a resplendent light green, with shocks of a darker emerald, and it was done in many separate braids. These were joined into a ponytail, which was also braided. As the group came closer to her, the Siloans studied her face. All of her features were remarkably elegant and soft, and her eyes were the color of a flourishing spring meadow basking in the morning light.

"Bow yer heads when we get right in fron' of her," Fergus whispered, and the lads nodded in acknowledgment.

When the four Barada reached the foot of the steps, the maiden raised her right hand, and all of them bowed their heads, while Na'ikeyana and Fergus intoned, "Masku, Tagwan, Hanidosha, Yaggawat."

"Pessanagwa," the Ingan maiden at the top of the steps solemnly pronounced, as she lowered her hand. The four now raised their heads, and Fergus and Na'ikeyana put their hands together as the crowd before Hoarstaff had done, lifted them above their heads and then brought them back down.

Now that the lads were closer, they noticed that there were four rings on the maiden's right hand, one on each finger, each having a different colored stone: green, yellow, red and blue. The ring finger of her left hand was graced by a single silver band, which appeared to be a signet ring, for it featured the same likeness of Strongbranch that rested atop the Staff of the Konaskwa, which was borne by all those who spoke on Thornoak's behalf. The lads had seen the emblem before on the staves of Hoarstaff and the Ingan messenger who had spoken with Gronk in Longarnu.

Turning to the Menfolk, the maiden in the yellow dress spoke in a flowing voice that dripped with honey, sweet and golden. "That means 'blessings' in Asla'gu, the ancient tongue of my people. And may the Sacred Quinary bless you greatly, for you have done much for Argonis already."

Coming slowly, gracefully, down one step, she said, "I am Princess Langwana. Akantasakwe, one of my ladies-in-waiting, just came from the front gates and informed me that you had arrived at Iswa Hanahoma and were on your way to speak with me. I presume you are the Menfolk from across the sea that Fergus told me about."

The lads, quite uncertain about how to properly comport themselves in the presence of Ingan royalty, or any royalty for that matter, nervously cleared their throats.

"Yes," Aradis replied, his voice faltering slightly. "I – I'm Aradis Kingblade, and this is my companion from the Kingdom of Velaris, Girion Ringmark. We are honored to stand before you, Princess."

"Nay, Manfellow," the princess returned, "it is I who am honored to stand before the two of you. If all that Fergus has told me is true, you have come leagues practically unnumbered and that to save a land in which you had no vested interest. And in so doing, you thrust yourselves into unimaginable peril. It is indeed a great wonder that you did not join the hordes of hapless victims of Ravinia. Yet you have not escaped wholly unscathed, it seems."

Looking at Fergus, she said, "You told me the lads were weary from their trials, but you did not forewarn me that wounds such as I see, especially on the dark-haired one, had marred them."

Fergus looked back at the princess, his countenance dim. "Since we last spoke, fair Princess, a terrible ting has a-happen'd. A ting which has put ev'ry single one of us, includin' you, in awful danger."

A shadow fell over Langwana's visage, as she spoke to Na'ikeyana. "Tasoygashemeku, ko Na'ikeyana. Pa'olgakamyasa panoskatiganase."

After the princess had said this, Na'ikeyana curtsied to her mistress, then went off to the north, circling around toward the far side of the pavilion. As she was departing, Langwana addressed Fergus again. "You must tell me all," she said. "But let us walk through the gardens as you do so. If we must speak of grave tidings, let us at least do so where we may drink of Orona's beauty. Perhaps it will ease the sting of the matter."

The princess came down the steps to join them, then embarked toward a marble path that led to the south along a row of trees.

No sooner had they commenced their walk, than Fergus began to relay his dreadful news. With much heaviness of heart, he told of Kelwyn Faircrest's multiple treacheries, his attempt to kill the Siloans and his part in the murder of Mordie, as well as his functioning as an agent for Ravinia. Princess Langwana was, quite understandably, aghast at this and wondered how Kelwyn had been able to enact his plans without the Questmongers suspecting that mischief was afoot.

Fergus explained that he had given instructions to Kelwyn to have the Siloans remain at the Questmongers' Den until he returned. Indeed, that was what he had told the princess he had done when he had come to see her the day before. However, Kelwyn had lied to the Siloans, Mordie and the other Questmongers about what Fergus had actually said. Deflecting any and all questioning from other Questmongers with shrewd alibis, he had claimed that Fergus' orders were for him to take the Siloans to the forest hideout of Duskdarrow to the east of the city. The reason this deceit had prevailed was that Fergus had given his instructions to Kelwyn and no one else; they had met alone up in Fergus' quarters. That was because Fergus had fully trusted him to follow his directives down to the letter, as he had for years. Now, of course, he thoroughly regretted doing so.

Never in his wildest dreams did he suspect that Kelwyn, or more properly Gornok, would lie to the Siloans about his own orders and take them out into the city to try to murder them.

As Fergus filled in details of the previous night's events for the princess, the lads even learned of some things they themselves had not been privy to, as these had occurred while they were passed out on the couches. For instance, a few of the Questmongers had gone to Kelwyn's house to search for any items that might further illuminate his duplicitous activities but had discovered nothing of significance. They had also retrieved Mordie's body and brought it back to the Questmongers' Den. The Siloans wondered how the Questmongers had been able to accomplish these tasks, since Quagga had shut down travel between districts, but an answer was shortly provided to this query. Indeed, the lads now discovered what Fergus had been referring to when he said that the Questmongers had already tested the stratagem that they used to get over to the Banaka. Apparently, Stumpory and some others had told the guards at the Taskula-Eskagwan Gate and the Eskagwan-Naskanu Gate that Quagga was sending them to look into the ghost ketchiwah situation. The guards, who had been quite rattled by that whole affair, had completely fallen for this fib and eagerly let them through. It was then a simple matter for the Questmongers, on their return trip, to convince the guards that they had collected a number of reports and a victim of the ghost ketchiwah (the deceased Mordie) that they needed to take back through the gates in order to bring them to Quagga. And thus they returned to the Taskula.

In addition, while these Questmongers were over in the Naskanu, they had intently questioned Limbluck. From him they learned that Kelwyn had indeed come to converse with him earlier that afternoon, and the two of them had actually come up with the plan to help the Siloans escape in the wagon at that time. Furthermore, in the evening, when Kelwyn had returned with Aradis, Girion and Mordie, his discourse with Limbluck had gone precisely as Kelwyn had reported. The Questmongers who conducted the interrogation were quite skilled in that sort of matter and detected no falsehood in Limbluck's statements. Thus, his reputation was cleared of any misconduct. Kelwyn had feigned virtue and loyalty to the Questmongers and their affiliates to the very end, it seemed.

All of these items were of great interest to the princess, as she wanted to know the precise extent of Kelwyn's treachery and whether there were others associated with the Questmongers who could potentially be involved in his deceits. Also, the particular concern she showed regarding whether or not Mordie's body had been tended to indicated that she was more than casually acquainted with or invested in the lives and well-being of the Questmongers.

Having finished their discussion of Kelwyn's traitorous deeds, Fergus and the princess then spoke of Quagga's rebellion. Apparently, Langwana was already apprised of much that had transpired in that affair. However, she had, of course, not yet received news of the Questmongers' confrontation with Quagga himself and was delighted to hear how they had humiliated him in front of his men. Nonetheless, though Fergus and the princess concurred that Quagga was both cowardly and foolish, they agreed that he could not simply be ignored, at least not for very long. He was, after all, the primary agitator of the current unrest in Anganor.

Both Langwana and Fergus were rather concerned about the possibility of a counter-rebellion leading to an escalation in violence, and they bandied back and forth a few ideas about what might be done to guard against such a possibility. There were only two viable courses, as they saw it. The first would be to let Quagga continue running amok, just for the time being, and hope that folk didn't get too riled about his restrictions. The second would be to have Hoarstaff issue soldiers from Strongbranch Citadel and Taskula North, the area just north of the Citadel, to take all the rebels captive, but this might cause more trouble in the long run by mobilizing anti-Strongbranch sentiment. Either way, there were risks to be taken.

However, there was, as Fergus reminded the princess, a third option – Thornoak returning to squelch the uprising himself. Langwana agreed that this would be the optimal course of events and said there was an item of considerable importance that she needed to relay to the Questkeeper regarding that subject. However, there were other things they had to discuss first, not the least of which was the medallion and its relation to the quest of the Siloans, so she decided to put the matter aside for the moment.

"Have you any more ill tidings?" she asked.

"Tankfully, me store is emptied," the Leprechaun answered.

"Good. What we already have is plenty."

After the princess had said this, she seemed to be wrestling for several moments with all she had just heard. Then, solemnly, she declared, "All this is grave indeed, Fergus – especially this business about Kelwyn. For, as you said, Ravinia almost certainly knows nearly all that we know, save for the most recent news, for there has not been time enough for it to reach her. Alas! This detestable Gornok has been harvesting information from us for almost ten years – provided he was acting as a double agent that entire time, that is. And, all the while, he had us believing he was a valiant, orphaned Manfellow from Pollona, fully resolved to do all he could to protect Argonis and defeat Ravinia. We have been utterly deceived, and I'm sure the Witch has relished that thought every day for years. But we cannot let that trouble us now, for time is short presently, and we must act more quickly and decisively than even I had anticipated."

Suddenly, Langwana stopped, bowed her head and sighed deeply. She was silent for some time; then she raised her head, looked at the Menfolk, and said, "I apologize that Fergus and I have taken so long to discuss these recent events, but those were matters that needed to be addressed. However, now we shall speak of the reason why I summoned you."

Her face lined with grim concern, she continued, "If you wished to be free of your quest, having now come more fully to realize what it entails, I'm afraid you are quite irrevocably entangled in it. Gornok, if nothing else, has made sure of that. Undoubtedly, all the information that he gathered about you will soon be on its way to Ravinia, if it isn't already. When it reaches her, she will know you by name, and she will know everything about your quest here in Argonis, along with your ultimate intention to destroy her."

The lads felt cold shudders run through them at this thought. Ravinia was not someone whose attention any decent person would want to draw.

"But," Langwana went on, "for this very reason – that is, your complete involvement in the very heart of Argonis' fate – I feel that it is only right that I should inform you of the full significance of the token you bore with you to our land."

"Are you referring to the medallion?" Aradis inquired.

"Indeed, I am," Langwana replied. After looking around the garden for a few moments, the princess set out again, and the others followed just behind her.

Striding across the green grass under the shade of the orchards of Hanidosha, Langwana quietly, but ever so earnestly, asked, "Menfolk from across the sea, did you really receive your half of the medallion from a Hadathi, just as you reported to Fergus?"

"We did," Aradis affirmed.

"And all you know about it is the little that Fergus told you yesterday morning?"

"That's correct," Girion replied.

"Then I shall explain everything from the beginning," the princess said. "First, you must understand that the medallion you bore here is an item that is bound up with the very fate of Argonis. Aradis Kingblade, whether you knew it or not, you had the destiny of this kingdom hanging around your neck."

Aradis swallowed uncomfortably as the impact of this sank in.

"You see, the shard of the medallion that you brought with you from afar is half of a terribly ancient artifact known as the Amulet of the Akwarna, an object about which there are several highly significant prophecies, of which I will speak shortly. 'Akwarna' is a very old Asla'gu word meaning 'powerful magic user.' In this case, it is a reference to the Enchantress, Janura. Fergus told me he mentioned her to you."

"Yes," Girion confirmed. "He said that she was really our only hope of defeating Ravinia."

"And I'm afraid he's right," Langwana replied. "Ravinia is too powerful a foe for any mere Barada to vanquish. But Janura is no mere Barada."

"Then what precisely is she, and what has this medallion to do with her?" Aradis inquired.

Langwana continued strolling onward, as she began an explanation of these deep matters. "Janura is what is known as a walemmu, a handmaiden of the Sky Lord, Palquanoga. Have you heard of him before?"

"Only just a short while ago," Girion said. "Na'ikeyana mentioned him as we were passing through the gardens to see you. He is one of the Sacred Quinary, is he not? The one whose pavilion is in the central garden of Iswa Hanahoma?"

"That is correct," the princess confirmed.

"What exactly is he?" Girion asked. "A Hadathi or something of that sort?"

Langwana pondered this inquiry and wrinkled her face slightly, as if she were thinking deeply. "No, not if you mean Hadathi in the sense that most people use the term. The Ingans of Argonis don't really use either that term or that exact concept in their reckoning of beings of the Haedra anyhow. Regardless, Palquanoga is quite unlike the Hadathi, at least in certain respects. Like them, he is a being of the Haedra, yes, but he is – well, it's difficult to explain. I'm not sure how to summarize all that our people believe about him. You might think of him as the Danna, depending on how you regard that title."

"Ah, I see," Girion said. "But Palquanoga is simply the personal name by which you call him."

"It is," Langwana affirmed. "Palquanoga is the name by which the Ingans of old spoke of him. But I have been diverted from answering Aradis' questions. Let us return to them."

"As I said, Janura is a walemmu, a maidservant of Palquanoga. The walemmu are a subclass of the beings known as the sengara. Fergus said he discussed them briefly with you, but I will explain them again and perhaps more fully. The sengara are not Barada; they are, rather, creatures of the Haedra who, on rare occasions, take the form of Barada and walk thus clad in Orona. Yet they do this not for trite pursuits or caprice, but to deliver oracles or to provide much-needed counsel or aid to mortals. The sengara are beings from the dawn of the world, wrought of primordial wind by Palquanoga for his direct service."

"There are many strange creatures of the Haedra found in the tales of the Elder Forest, but the sengara appear in the very oldest of them, and their description and role in the world have never been altered, even as the ages have rolled by. They are always mighty, even terrifyingly so, yet they are never capricious, unlike so many of the creatures in the lore of our land. Also, their deeds seem to be directed toward a particular purpose, which is the honor of Palquanoga. They appear at hours of great need or trial and are known as bearers of grave oracles of things to come – oracles which are often strange, but always sure. Consequently, they are held in great veneration. In fact, it is even claimed by the loremasters of Argonis that every proclamation of a true sengara is as certain as the rising of the sun. Also, the sengara are possessors of a pure and bright magic, which they may yield to oppose the evil that is diffused throughout Orona. Now, since Janura is a walemmu – that is, a specific kind of sengara – all of these things I have said apply to her. That is why we seek her aid in combating Ravinia, so that she may set her wholesome magic against the corrupt, defiled magic of the Witch."

"But why are you seeking Janura specifically?" Aradis wondered. "Are there not other sengara who might serve the purpose just as well?"

"Perhaps, but Janura is connected with the fate of Argonis in a special way," Langwana said, "and thus it is she whom we seek. You see, long ago, back in the Years of Yore, when the dew lay fresh on this land and the Elder Forest was still waking, my people, the Wennatoga, were threatened by enemies from the north. There is a great deal of variance in the old legends regarding why these invaders came, as well as who or what they were, but all the stories agree that they were formidable and ruthless and that, had not some form of intervention come, the Wennatoga would have been exterminated by them."

"Fortunately, though, intervention did arrive in the form of the Enchantress Janura, who was sent, it is said, by Palquanoga himself. With Janura's help, the Wennatoga were able to destroy their enemies. The means by which that was accomplished is a tale all its own, but it does not concern us directly at the moment."

Taking a substantial breath, she went on, "As a token to remind my people of what Palquanoga had done for them, Janura imparted to them the Amulet of the Akwarna. And, when she left this world, she said that, someday, aid would come from Palquanoga again, at a time known as the Sannadosh."

"And what is that?" Girion asked.

"'Sannadosh' is an Asla'gu word meaning 'The Great Adversity.' Before her departure, Janura prophesied that the time would come when Argonis would be brought to the utter edge of ruin. It is this period that is referred to as the Sannadosh. And Janura gave particular signs that would mark this period."

"In fact," the princess went on, "there is a poem about the Sannadosh that my people have long recited to help them remember such things. It was translated into Daiga around a hundred and fifty years ago by a scholar at Strongbranch, since the use of Asla'gu had severely waned among the Wennatoga. Unfortunately, even the Daigan version is not widely known among many of the Wennatoga these days. The majority of the Ingans of Argonis have retained knowledge of what may be called Mahgataquenna or Lower Lore – that is, traditions and practices which affect their daily lives and involve veneration of their ancestors, as well as of the Sacred Quinary. This lore also includes tales about lesser creatures of the Haedra – spirits of the woods and so forth. But they have forgotten the Shonataquenna, the Higher Lore, the ancient stories and older, deeper teachings and customs. Certainly, they are familiar, for the most part, with the most important tales but lack much context for them. That is why today, especially among the Ingans of Anganor, one can witness a certain amount of apathy toward the Taquenar, which is the entire corpus of traditions, lore, beliefs and practices of the devout Wennatoga. Regrettably, their general lack of knowledge has spawned indifference to those things which are most vital."

The princess sighed and shook her head dolefully, looking far ahead down the row of trees along which they were walking, as she contemplated this state of affairs. Then she glanced up at a little green bird singing in one of the boughs above them and recommenced, "However, I digress; we were speaking of that poem I mentioned, which is called 'The Signs of the Sannadosh.' The Asla'gu version is fairer and subtler, in my opinion, but it wouldn't do to recite that one to you, of course. In any event, in Daiga it is rendered thus:

> *Someday will come the Sannadosh, when sorrows shall prevail;*
> *Foes without and strife within Argonis shall assail.*
> *Barada and beasts of evil stock will lurk throughout the land,*
> *And murd'rous hosts on ev'ry side against the kingdom stand.*
>
> *There will arise an enemy in the woods of the darkling west,*
> *A wielder of a black and deadly rain, by evil utterly possessed.*
> *Against this foe not a single soul of Argonis can succeed,*
> *But help will come from lands beyond at the hour of greatest need.*
>
> *Fear not, O Children of Argonis! For Palquanoga will verily lift you up.*
> *As the Sannadosh comes crashing down, you will rise bright and free.*
> *The foe will meet a sudden end; look for a hand from across the sea.*
> *As the shadows lengthen in the west and doom comes tumbling down,*
> *Look to the east for this hand to come and bring back the absent crown.*
> *Aye, look to the east for this hand to come and bring back the absent crown.*

When the princess finished, the lads looked at each other, utterly astonished. The words of Langwana's recitation had smitten them with their beauty, their embodiment of hope in the midst of blackest night and, most importantly, the realization that they delineated quite well the current state of affairs in Argonis.

"How long ago was this prophecy made?" Aradis inquired.

"Around five thousand years ago," the princess answered.

The Siloans' astonishment had now turned into complete stupefaction.

"Tha' about describes Argonis now, doesn' it?" Fergus remarked wryly, as he nudged Aradis.

"Did Janura really say all those things five thousand years ago?" Aradis asked, finding Langwana's claims almost too incredible to accept.

"Do you not believe in prophecy?" the princess gently queried, halting and turning to face the lad.

"I don't know that I have a fully formed opinion on the subject," Aradis admitted. "I mean, I – well – I guess I can either choose to take your word on the matter or not. I haven't anything else to go off of, though."

"I would not consider you foolish if you did not accept my word for its own sake," Langwana returned, as she resumed walking through the orchards, with the others following. "After all, you've only just met me, and princesses are just as capable of fabricating tales as anyone else. Therefore, I can be content for now with your doubt. However, you should know that many scholars at Strongbranch Citadel could verify that these prophecies about the Sannadosh have been around for ages. Indeed, even common folk among the Wennatoga who are exceptionally ardent in their devotion to the Taquenar know the foundational elements of all the matters we have just discussed. They know that, near the very inception of this kingdom, enemies from the north came to destroy us, and Palquanoga sent Janura to deliver us. They know that she gave us the Amulet of the Akwarna as a gift and spoke of a time of great darkness known as the Sannadosh, even if they do not remember the specific signs that would mark it. But they would also know that the amulet was not merely a reminder of Palquanoga's benevolence, but also a sign of future deliverance."

"For Janura said that, eventually, the medallion would be sundered, and part of it would vanish. However, she also declared that the pieces of the medallion would someday be reunited, as the missing portion would return from across the sea, though it was not made explicit whether this would be by the hand from across the sea mentioned in the poem I recited or by some other agent. In any event, when the other piece returned, the amulet would be remade, and its power would be awakened. Also, the return of the other half of the amulet would be the sign that Argonis would be rescued from the doom of the Sannadosh. This sign is known as the Sign of the Sengara, the sengara in question being Janura, for it was she who gave it. And it is you who have fulfilled it. Not only that, you are seeking to bring my father back to Anganor."

Once more she recited the last words of the poem, "Aye, look to the east for this hand to come and bring back the absent crown."

"Now, ye did come from the east, ye know," said Fergus.

The lads suddenly understood why the Questkeeper had specifically confirmed that they came from the east during his interview with them at the Questmongers' Den. Also, it now made perfect sense why Langwana and Na'ikeyana had addressed them with the peculiar moniker "Menfolk from across the sea."

Aradis halted abruptly under a large tree with round, deep-purple fruit. Almost frantically, he exclaimed, "You can't be serious about all this. Do you really believe that the hand from across the sea in the poem is a reference to us? And do you really think that us bringing the shard of the medallion is the fulfillment of this five-thousand-year-old prophecy of Janura?"

Langwana again turned to face him and adamantly inquired, "What else *could* it be? The prophecy said that the missing piece of the medallion would be returned from across the sea at the time of the Sannadosh. And such is currently upon us. You *have* come from across the sea, and you *did* bring the other piece of the medallion with you. I don't see what other conclusion you could reach than what I have proposed. Also, you are seeking to do that which the prophecy specifies the hand from across the sea will accomplish – bringing about the return of the absent crown. And again, you have come from the east, across the sea; that much is undeniable. I will admit, however, that your full identification with the hand from across the sea is dependent on whether you actually bring my father back to Anganor or not. But the matter of the medallion has already been accomplished and is thus indisputable."

Aradis couldn't think of any way to refute this logic, so he stood there rather awkwardly and said nothing.

Girion was nearly as overwhelmed as Aradis by all that the princess had been saying, although he hadn't manifested this nearly as overtly as Aradis had. Now, seeing that Langwana was as sincere as could be regarding her belief that they were the ones who had brought about the advent of Janura's oracle, he slowly said, "If these ancient prophecies really are genuine, then I agree that Aradis and I have fulfilled them – at least a part of them, anyway – the part about bringing the piece of the amulet back to Argonis. But the amulet has not yet been remade. Yet, even if it were, would that only serve as a sign, or is there something we could actually do with the amulet?"

"The amulet is both a sign and an object of power," the princess replied, setting off again through the trees. "But its powers are mysterious and are a great matter of speculation among the learned. Nonetheless, it is clear that the amulet itself is connected to the promised deliverance of Argonis during the Sannadosh. All the tales agree on what Janura said, just not what she meant. She stated that during the Sannadosh, the power of the amulet would be awakened. It's a vague description, I know. It could mean almost anything, really. But Janura was very explicit on this point; the amulet must be taken to the place of her departure before help would come. That way, when aid did arrive, Palquanoga's involvement in the matter would be confirmed, for things would have to unfold exactly as he foretold."

"What do you mean by Janura's 'departure'?" Girion asked. "Are you referring to her death? Can sengara even die? From your description of them, I got the impression that they were immortal."

Langwana explained, "Immortal they are. Thus, in speaking of Janura's departure, I am merely referring to the fact that she has left Orona, as such. But to say that she left the world is not to say that she is no more, nor that she perished, but rather that she has gone elsewhere; she has gone to a realm veiled from our sight. That is all. But, regardless, we needn't journey to that realm to make use of the medallion, merely to the place of her departure from *this* world."

"And where is that?" Girion inquired.

"As far as I am aware, no living Barada knows that except my father. I suspect my brother, Makwaru, may have known it before he was lost to us, though I do not know for certain."

Aradis, pondering all this, asked, "Did Janura say what form the promised aid would take?"

"Not exactly," Langwana returned hesitantly, "but we have always assumed that Janura herself would return to help us, as she was the one who had left the amulet in question."

"Hm," Girion mused, briefly looking up at a little, scarlet songbird that was sitting on a branch just above his head. "So, if we can find out where Janura left Orona, it sounds like we might be able to use the medallion to call her back."

"That is our hope," Langwana returned, "but we can attempt no such feat until two conditions are in place: first, we must learn the place of her departure, and secondly, the two pieces of the medallion must be joined together again."

"How did the medallion come to be broken in the first place, and how were the two pieces so widely separated from each other?" Aradis asked.

Turning onto another red marble pathway that led through the rows of trees and flowers, Langwana replied, "This amulet has a long and incredibly complex road through history. I wish I could simplify matters by saying it was passed down from Konaskwa to Konaskwa until the present, but that would not be the truth, or even near it. Suffice it to say that the Amulet of the Akwarna did descend through the ages of Orona, sometimes nearly vanishing from all knowledge, even for centuries, but never completely, until it at last came to my great-grandfather, Margwalu."

"Now, Margwalu had a brother named Agwassu, who aspired to seize the throne of Argonis, though it belonged rightfully to Margwalu himself. Agwassu, to attain this nefarious end, hired a Druid named Malatar, who was well-versed in Daegar, to assassinate Margwalu and his family. This is the very same Malatar who is now in the employ of Ravinia and leads the Druids of Knobstaff Village in Blackbough Woods. Unfortunately, Malatar succeeded in murdering Ganassa, Margwalu's wife, before this plot was found out. Knowing it was too dangerous for him to stay in Anganor, Margwalu took the Amulet of the Akwarna, a much-valued heirloom, along with his only child, his son Tengwaru, and fled into the Stony Wilds."

Langwana paused briefly before continuing, "Malatar followed them into the wilderness and caught up with them in a glade deep in the forest. Using Daegar, he flung a bolt of fire from his staff at Margwalu, killing him and sundering Janura's medallion into two pieces. Young Tengwaru grabbed these fragments, knowing how precious they were, but he nearly lost his life in doing so. Had it not been for the timely intervention of mighty spirits of the forest, the Druid would have killed him as well. Shielding him from the Druid's fire, these spirits, which we call hala-hanarwa, drove Malatar away, then sent Tengwaru into hiding in a land far to the north, known as Orowan. There he was instructed to remain until he had increased in years and gathered sufficient strength to retake Argonis."

"Before he left for Orowan, Tengwaru inquired if he might use the pieces of the medallion to summon Janura, for his father had informed him of the place she had departed from Orona. However, the hala-hanarwa told him that the medallion's powers were broken and would thus remain until the amulet was made whole again. They also stated that the pieces could not be fused back together until the proper time, the time of the Sannadosh, just as Janura had foretold thousands of years before. In fact, they chided Tengwaru for not knowing her ancient prophecies better."

Now beginning to walk southward along a row of bright-blue flowers, Langwana said, "It was there in Orowan that Tengwaru met my grandmother, Naskwanoc. Also, in that distant land, he grew into adulthood and became a warrior of great valor and skill. Over a period of some years, loyal Barada of Argonis sought him out and joined his cause, and many became excellent fighters under his leadership and instruction."

"Finally, in the year 546, Tengwaru was ready to take his forces to reclaim his kingdom, for in addition to his own soldiers, he had just enlisted a host of Ogric mercenaries from the kingdom of Nagota. He surmised that if he could only vanquish the armies of Agwassu, the common people would turn wholeheartedly to his cause because, for the most part, they only served his uncle out of fear. Agwassu had greatly oppressed them, and even slight disapproval of him or his policies was treated as if it were treason. Indeed, he had massacred and exiled many of the Wood-Gnomes, who had lived in Argonis for ages and were even more ardent than many of the native Ingans in their opposition to him."

"However," the princess went on, "Agwassu learned of Tengwaru's whereabouts before he commenced his march and tried to forestall his campaign by stealing the medallion. You see, he mistakenly believed that Tengwaru would try to summon Janura using the medallion, for he knew not that it was yet sundered. He assumed it had been recently remade, and this was what had emboldened Tengwaru to prepare to assault him. Thus, he determined to retrieve the amulet, so that this outcome might be prevented. However, if Agwassu had paid greater attention to the prophecies of Janura, he would not have made this error, for the signs of the Sannadosh she had given had not yet been fulfilled, and, according to her, the amulet was not to be remade until that time."

Turning onto yet another marble pathway, Langwana explained, "When Agwassu seized the throne several decades before that time, the Questmongers had split, with the majority siding with the true Konaskwa and joining him in the wild. Some of the Questmongers were executed by Agwassu before they could escape from Argonis, but others violated their oaths to the true Konaskwa and began working for Agwassu as his own clandestine agents. These traitorous agents were the ones in charge of stealing the medallion, which they were shocked to discover was yet in two pieces. They nearly succeeded in absconding with both halves of it, but they were apprehended by the true Questmongers before they could get very far. A battle ensued in the forest where they were intercepted, at a spot many miles to the north of Argonis, and one of Agwassu's Ingan agents fled with one of the two pieces. An Ingan Questmonger chased him down and slew him, but not before he himself was mortally wounded."

"Meanwhile, back at the battle, all of Agwassu's agents were defeated, and thus the other half of the medallion was kept safe. This was accomplished with the help of Tengwaru himself, who, after the battle, ran to find the Questmonger who had chased down Agwassu's agent. Some ways off in the woods, he found him. As the Ingan Questmonger, Makassaget, lay there dying, he told my grandfather a remarkable story. He said that he had been lying there, unable to move, with the medallion fragment only a few feet away, when he saw what appeared to be a cloaked Barada, a Manfellow, approaching him."

"A Manfellow?" said Aradis, who was rather startled by this.

"Aren't they rather uncommon in the Elder Forest?" Girion asked.

"They are indeed, and that was the case to a much greater degree in those days," Langwana replied.

"Sorry we interrupted you. Please continue your story," Girion urged.

"Certainly," Langwana said. "When the Manfellow came nigh, Makassaget asked him whether he was a supporter of Tengwaru or of Agwassu, and he replied that he was neither. He said that he was actually a sengara sent by Palquanoga, the Sky-Lord. The sengara then told the stricken Makassaget this: 'You have fought valiantly, son of Argonis.

Undoubtedly, you will think what I am about to do is in opposition to your kingdom, but it is not. It is quite the opposite. I must take this piece of the medallion now and bear it far away, that the ancient words of Palquanoga might be fulfilled. But fear not, for it will return from across the sea at the appointed time, at the Sannadosh. When it does, the Amulet of the Akwarna will be remade, just as Janura so long ago said it would.' When he had finished saying this, the sengara took the medallion fragment and disappeared into the forest. And when Makassaget had ended this tale, he died. Since that time, the remaining fragment of the medallion has been in the keeping of Tengwaru and then that of my father after Tengwaru's death, as they awaited the return of the other half."

The lads were completely stunned at this revelation. They both stopped in their tracks, and the princess and Fergus turned to look at them.

"Do you think that sengara could have been one and the same as Nagello?" Aradis asked, looking at his fellow Siloan. "I mean, the sengara do seem to be rather similar to the Hadathi – at least to the sort of Hadathi that Nagello is. That's my perception of the matter, anyhow. And I do find a rather compelling connection between the two to be the fact that this particular sengara appeared as a Manfellow."

"So do I," Girion affirmed. Then, turning to the princess, he asked, "Do the sengara often appear as Menfolk in your tales of them?"

"This is the only instance I am aware of in which one did," Langwana answered. "It is actually considered by loremasters of Argonis to be one of the strangest parts about Makassaget's story."

"I think it almost certain that Nagello and this sengara are one and the same," Girion declared to his Siloan companion.

"Is Nagello the Hadathi who gave you the medallion fragment?" Langwana asked.

"He is," Aradis answered. Then, shaking his head, he muttered, "Nagello really got us deep in this business, didn't he? Well, I suppose we've gotten ourselves into it by following his instructions."

"So it would seem," Langwana replied, smiling sympathetically at the lads. "But it is noble that you have done so, for our own efforts to reunite the pieces of the medallion have utterly failed."

"Seven years ago," she said, "right before my father entered Paanu Assagwa, he gave one final task to the Questmongers: to find the missing half of the medallion. He thought to have them bring the prophecy to fulfillment through their search. Our dear Fergus, even knowing that the task was all but hopeless, has had Questmongers looking for it ever since. His loyalty to Thornoak is magnificent and commendable, but it seems the prophecy was not to be brought to fruition through our own efforts, but by two unlikely Menfolk of Velaris, sent to us, as it would seem, by the Haedra itself."

"But what about the fusing of the medallion?" Girion inquired. "Did not the prophecy say that it would be remade? Have we only to take it to a metalworker to accomplish that?"

"Ha!" Fergus laughed. "A smit'y canna do anyting wit it, laddie. Tornoak's father tried to have it put back together years ago a-usin' natural means, for he had initially ignored the message o' the hala-hanarwa – early during his exile in Orowan, that is. He soon gave up on a-fixin' it, though, an' on summonin' Janura for that matter, for all his attempts wit the smit'ys were o' no avail. The amulet's a magical artifact, ya see, an' no bellows or furnace or tongs or hammer can join the two parts. Only magic can do that. An' if we canna make tha' happen, the medallion's useless to us. Only once the ting is whole again can we use it to summon Janura."

"Can *you* fuse it?" Girion eagerly asked the princess.

Langwana shook her head. "I have absolutely no skill or even ability in magic."

"But Tornoak does," Fergus asserted.

Langwana looked sternly at the Leprechaun. "You know as well as I do that he hasn't used even a speck of magic since the Sundering of the Erynos. Nor will he."

"Why is that?" Aradis asked, confused by the princess' severe countenance.

This query seemed to have made both Fergus and Langwana tremendously uncomfortable. They looked at each other quite awkwardly for a few moments, but Langwana finally responded. "Because his magic killed his wife, my mother, on that grievous day."

"What?" the Siloans exclaimed in unison, aghast.

"My mother, Sanagwa, unbeknownst to my father, was up on the ridge of the Erynos Divide, making her way through Ravinia's forces in an attempt to get to the Witch and kill her. When he uttered the word that collapsed the mountains and brought forth the Greenwall, she tumbled down into the chasm to her death. My father soon learned from his army that she had gone up onto the ridge, though many had tried to convince her to turn back. Then he realized that the magic he wielded had not only killed many of his own soldiers along with Ravinia's and taken its toll upon his body, as he had suffered the effects of many years of aging in that instant, he had also lost his beloved Sanagwa. He was no longer willing to run the risk of destroying himself or others with his magic, so he took a vow that very day to never use it again as long as he lived."

The lads were all but speechless. Finally, Girion managed to utter some condolences. "We're terribly sorry to hear that, Princess. And we are exceedingly grieved that you have suffered the loss of your mother."

Fergus bowed his head and sighed. He stared at the ground for a few moments, then looked up and said, "I know, sure as rain, tha' day still fills Tornoak wit awful pain, but do you tink if he saw bot pieces o' the medallion tha' his hope might be rekindled? Then, perchance, he could use his magic one last time, jus' for the sake of a-savin' the kingdom, an' fuse the medallion back together again."

Langwana looked deeply troubled, as she replied, "In order for him to do that, someone would have to go into Paanu Assagwa and bring the fragments of the amulet to him."

"O' course," Fergus returned. "That's plain as can be. To be sure, there's a taboo on the place because yer people hold it to be sacred, an' any who enter witout Tornoak's permission will be put to death. But you're his daughter, an' you have the right to go see him whenever you wish witout incurrin' the death penalty for a-violatin' the taboo, or the ashaska, as ye Ingans call it."

"Not anymore," Langwana quietly declared.

"Now, what do you mean by tha'?" Fergus returned, shocked.

"Only a few hours ago, some of my father's messengers came to me and said that he had come to the entrance of Paanu Assagwa early this morning to speak with them. He commanded them to deliver word to me that he had extended the ashaska to include me as well. If I try to enter Paanu Assagwa, the guards have instructions to kill me. Also, he issued a directive for me to burn five sigwalu blossoms in the flame of the Pavilion of the Ages at sunset tonight."

The Siloans and Fergus were completely stricken by this dreadful news.

"Blazin' bannocks! Why would Tornoak forbid you, his only link wit the outside world, from enterin'?" Fergus demanded.

"And what is the meaning of the ritual with the flowers?" Girion asked.

Langwana's face now became terribly grim, almost ashen, as she replied, "The burning of five sigwalus is what was prescribed in ancient times as an offering for safe passage into death. My father intends to kill himself tonight."

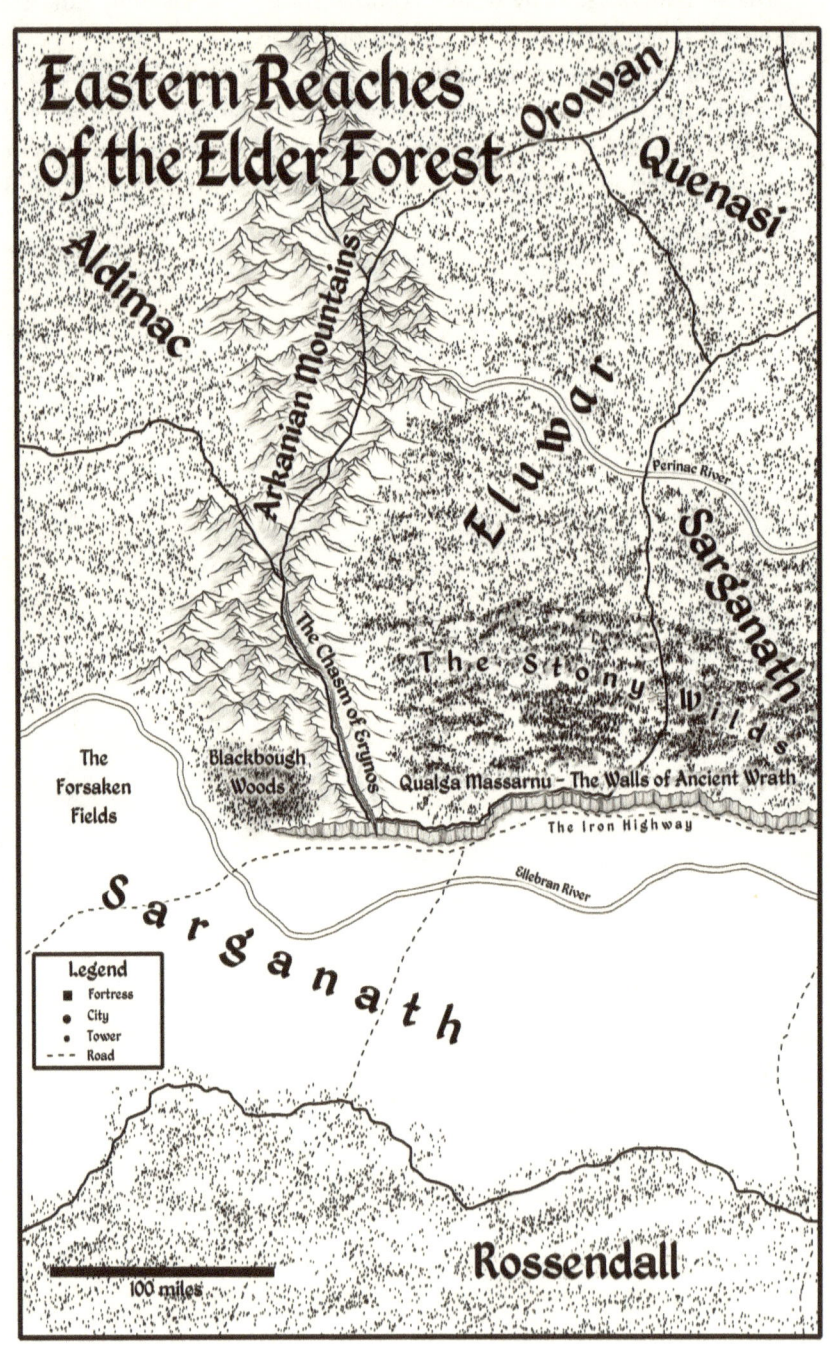

Eastern Reaches of the Elder Forest

Orowan

Quenasi

Aldimac

Arkanian Mountains

Eluwar

Perinac River

Sarganath

The Chasm of Erunos

The Stony Wilds

The Forsaken Fields

Blackbough Woods

Qualga Massarnu – The Walls of Ancient Wrath

The Iron Highway

Ellebran River

Sarganath

Legend
- ■ Fortress
- ● City
- • Tower
- – – Road

Rossendall

100 miles

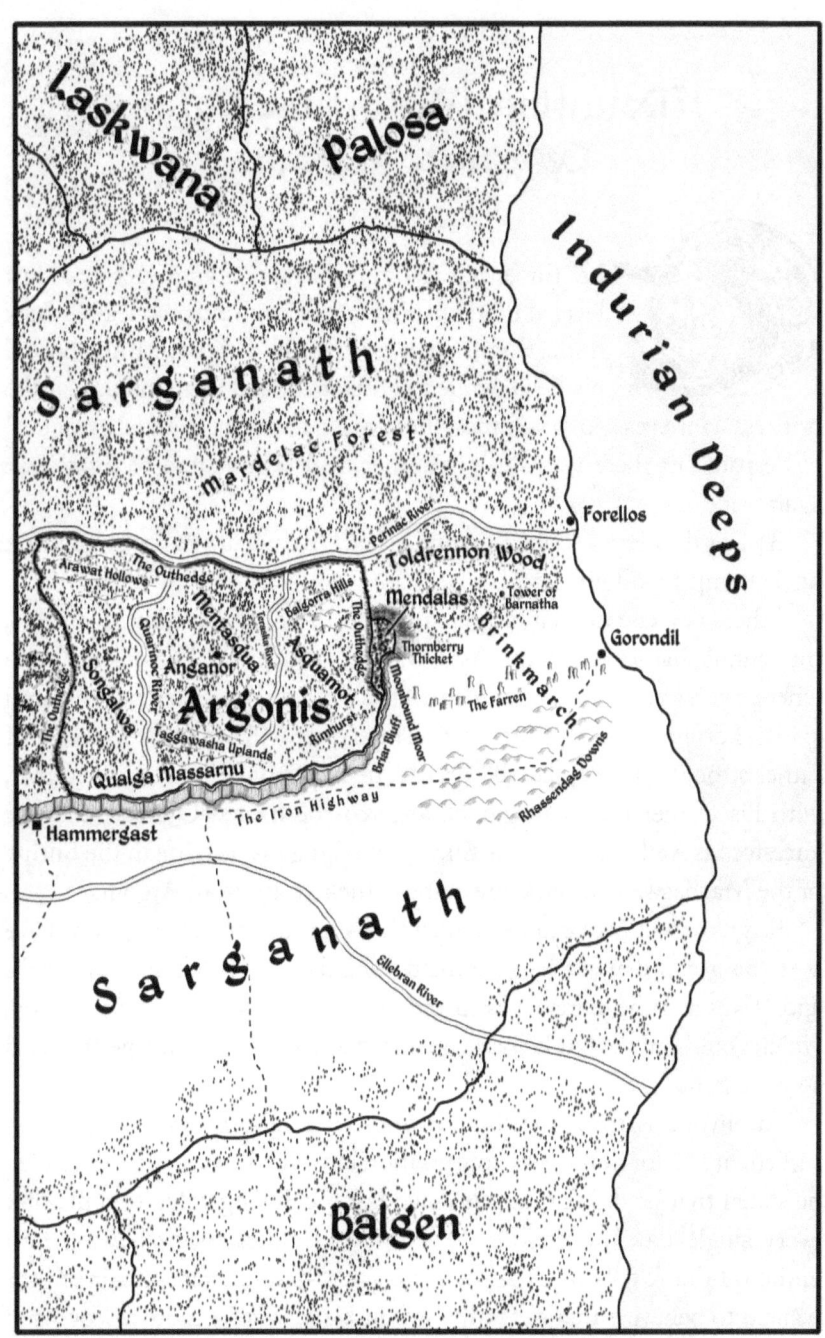

CHAPTER SEVEN

Mounting Misfortunes and
Desperate Designs

he three Barada upon whom Langwana had just leveled this appalling revelation were practically struck mute. Fergus put a fist in front of his mouth and bowed his head, while the Siloans stared incredulously at the princess. Her eyes spoke volumes; there was sadness there and a great deal of despair, but there was also a glimmer of determination to fight back against it.

At length, Fergus looked up and asked, "By what means do you tink he'll attemp' to kill himself?"

"There is a ceremonial dagger stored in the Shrine of the Machaswa, the central chamber of Paanu Assagwa," Langwana said. "That is the place where, twice a year, five fawns are sacrificed for the appeasement of ancestral spirits. I do not know for certain that my father will use that dagger, but I rather strongly suspect he will. Of late, he has frequently mentioned that, with his former use of magic, he angered the Sacred Quinary and our ancestors as well. Thus, he may think that taking his own life in the Shrine of the Machaswa will somehow remove their wrath from Argonis."

Fergus shook his head despondently, as he lamented, "I ought to have seen this a-comin' when he gave you the shard o' the medallion a few weeks ago. 'Twas as if he were a-passin' the kingdom on to you after a fashion, which could only mean he was convinced as a contrary cabbage that he'd soon be gone."

"If anyone is to blame for not foreseeing this sooner," the princess sighed, "it is I, for in the very conversation in which he gave me the amulet, he stated that he didn't think he could last much longer. He told me that every single day, the darkness was drawing closer to swallowing him entirely. I didn't tell you or anyone else about that because I believed – or wanted to believe – that my father was just temporarily more discouraged than normal."

"Well, it shanna do a bit o' good to quibble over it, for 'tis now the Crown of Marda; see, the sun is straight o'erhead. Really, the importan' ting at the momen' is to come up wit a plan."

"I've already got one," Langwana confidently returned, as she began walking north toward the main path that led back to the Autumn Pavilion.

Fergus and the Siloans started after her, as Girion inquired, "What, then, are we going to do?"

Still striding briskly northward, the princess answered, "As soon as I received my father's message, I sent soldiers to Shalkanu Ataqua, which is a place about seven miles to the southwest of the turnoff to get here from Konassu Road, the main thoroughfare that runs down this way from Anganor. These soldiers were instructed to retrieve forty tonquit, which are mounts rather like large, antlered deer, and bring them back here. They should be returning soon, and when they do, we, along with a fair number of my finest guards, shall all ride over to Paanu Assagwa. The reason I decided to have the tonquit brought here is that I wanted to wait until after I had spoken with you to depart. I knew that we might be pressed for time, for Paanu Assagwa lies three leagues from here, and the journey there takes several hours by foot. Also, since Fergus brought me the other piece of the medallion yesterday, I didn't want to take any risks with it, what with all the bandit activity in these parts, so I decided to travel with a large company."

Fergus jogged up beside the princess and congratulated her. "That was a marvelous bit o' tinkin' on your part to already make such preparations, but what intend you to do when the bonnie lot of us get to Paanu Assagwa?"

"I'm going to go in and speak with my father, of course," the princess flatly replied.

Fergus immediately halted and stamped his foot. "Owl scales and lizard feathers! That's madness!" he roared. "Sure as rain, your father's guards will put you to death the very instan' ya set foot in the sanctum! Ya simply canna be trowin' your life away like tha'. Argonis needs you now more than ever. The last ting we need is the only remainin' members o' the royal family committin' suicide on the same day. There's got to be another way."

Langwana calmly turned around to address the furious Questkeeper. "What do you propose we do, Fergus? Just let my father kill himself? If no one goes in to stop him, I assure you by the sweat of the sun and the tears of the moon that he will be dead by nightfall. You know as well as I do that none of his guards would dare break the ashaska themselves, for fear of incurring the wrath of the spirits of the ancestors, which haunt that place. And rightly so, for if a living Barada doesn't kill one who trespasses unlawfully into Paanu Assagwa, a dead one almost certainly will."

"Ha!" Fergus snorted. "Come now, Princess. You know quite well that I don't a-put any stock in those Ingan superstitions. Some o' the Taquenar, yer beloved hoard o' traditions, is fine as far as it goes, an' I'm e'en inclined to believe some o' your legends, like those surroundin' the sengara an' the Amulet o' the Akwarna, for instance. Anyway, the proof o' that business has been fortcomin'. Of the Haedra's existence, I haven' a doubt, but I tink this whole insistence on taboos involvin' ancestral spirits is pure poppyrot. So, believe it or not, these silly spooks you speak of aren't in Paanu Assagwa; they're in the minds o' your people."

"This is no time for airing your disdain of certain elements of the Taquenar, Fergus," Langwana reprimanded. "Even if you don't believe in the machaswa, I and my people do. Therefore, the fear of the soldiers to violate the ashaska is quite justifiable and real to them, even if, as you suppose, its object is not. Besides, you should know better than to be so crass as to refer to the machaswa as 'spooks.' You are well aware, I am certain, that that is not how I and my people conceive of them. We believe they are the spirits of our forebears and should thus be held in high regard. Obviously, that's why we present them offerings and frequently seek their advice. And the fact that the machaswa at Paanu Assagwa would be inclined to defend the sanctity of that place and uphold a hallowed taboo cannot rightly be used as a reason to artlessly classify them as 'spooks.'"

"O' course I know 'at's what ye tink about the machaswa, but me point is tha' I tink you're wrong," Fergus returned.

"And I suppose I and all the rest of the Ingans of Argonis are simply to take the word of Fergus O'Brannadon that we're utterly mistaken and that our people have been deluded about this matter for the past several thousand years?" Langwana shot back.

"Me argument is not that you're wrong merely because the likes o' me bonnie self says so. It's that I don' tink ye've got any solid evidence for these bein's. For instance, have you e'er seen one o' the machaswa?" Fergus demanded, somewhat sharply.

"No, but others have," Langwana replied, with equal intensity. "And besides, just because I personally haven't seen any machaswa doesn't prove that they don't exist."

"Fair enough, but it also doesn' prove tha' they do."

"I never said it did. But if they do exist, they are indeed to be feared, for they are said to show themselves to be both hideous and merciless to those who hold them in contempt."

Fergus, still glaring at the princess, rejoined, "Well, if you believe these miserable machaswa will be sure to slay any who enter Paanu Assagwa unlawfully, then why are you a-goin' in anyhow? An' supposin' you do, wouldn' you be a-goin' against your own beloved traditions, behavin' like a regular heathen, as some o' your folk are wont to put it? Why in the name of all tha' is sane an' decent are you insistin' on doin' this?"

Langwana, her expression firm, even defiant, replied, "Because the ultimate cause to which I am committed in this – namely, the deliverance of the kingdom – is, I believe, even more sacred than the taboos which forbid me to enter the sanctum. Also, Thornoak is my father, and I must try to stop him from killing himself, no matter what the cost may be to me personally. Besides, I did not say that the machaswa would certainly slay any who enter but that they would *almost* certainly do so; there is a slight margin of doubt, since they might behave unexpectedly. There's a difference, you know – between certain death and almost certain death."

"Is there now?" Fergus hotly returned.

"Indeed. But even if death were the certain outcome of this, I would not reconsider my course. For if my life is taken from me, either by Ingan sentinels or spirit guardians while I am attempting to save my father, then I do not scorn such a fate. For truly, death in valor is far more preferable to me than a life preserved by gutless passivity."

"B-b-but … " Fergus sputtered. He sighed, then paused to gather his thoughts. A few moments later, he said, "You may very well prefer such an end, but if you be slain, then who shall lead the kingdom?"

"Hoarstaff," Langwana returned. "He has a good heart and a strong mind, and with your help, he may yet succeed in leading Argonis to brighter days, days without the accursed shadow of Ravinia the Heartless."

Fergus shook his head in exasperation. "How can you do this to your bonnie people, Princess? I canna le' this happen. I could ne'er live wit meself."

"Quite respectfully, Fergus O'Brannadon," Langwana said, "I must remind you that this is not your decision to make. If I wish to take my life into my own hands, then I shall do exactly that. You, after all, are a counselor of mine, not a minder."

The Leprechaun sighed heavily, then huffed, "I don' presume to be your minder, but I fear tha' great evil will come of all this. If you trust me judgment in this case, as ya have many times before, I tink Argonis shanna suffer so deep a loss. O' course, you can do as ya please in the end, but if there's any other way to save Tornoak besides endangerin' your life, I'd rather take tha' way."

Langwana, her face riddled with a gray fatalism, replied, "So would I. But I've been thinking on the matter for hours and have come up with no alternative. I'm afraid, terrible as it is, there is no other way."

"Very well, then," Fergus concluded, as he nodded decorously to the princess. "I shall be a-goin' now. If you should have need o' me, I'll be up by the gates in the Guardians' Quarter, awaitin' the arrival o' the tonquit from Shalkanu Ataqua." And, with that, he walked off toward the eastern portal of the Garden of Hanidosha.

During this entire segment of the conversation, Aradis and Girion had been reluctant to say anything, as they were so flabbergasted by everything they had just learned, and they dared not intrude into the dispute between the princess and the Questkeeper. It seemed strange to them that Fergus had not invited them to come with him when he departed, but they guessed that he was so upset he just didn't have the presence of mind to do so.

Noting the befuddled state of the Manfellows, Langwana gently prompted, "Aradis and Girion, would you join me for lunch in the Royal Quarter? My apartments are there, inside of a pesgawa – that is, a traditional treetop dwelling. You can rest there until word reaches us that the tonquit have arrived."

"Why, yes, of course," Girion replied, bowing his head slightly to the Ingan maiden. "So long as that wouldn't be any trouble, that is."

"Not at all," Langwana assured, as she began leading them back toward the Autumn Pavilion.

Soon they arrived at the eastern side of the huge marble structure, and the lads, gazing into the interior, saw a statue of an Ingan woman dressed in a robe made of leaves and crowned with a wreath of flowers. Sculptured birds were perched on her shoulders, and a stone fawn was lying down at her feet. In her left hand was a large, round fruit, and in her right was a sheaf of grain. Just to the east of the statue, there was a red marble altar, upon which a bronze tray of vegetables had been laid. Throughout the pavilion, there were large ferns, all some shade of red, resting upon red marble pedestals.

The Siloans desired to examine the interior of the pavilion more closely, but Langwana bade them follow her around it to the right. When they came to the far side, she took them down a marble pathway to a set of gates that led through the hedge that formed the western bound of the Garden of Hanidosha. Beyond it, there was an area shaped exactly like the area with the guards through which they had entered Iswa Hanahoma that morning, except that it was a mirror image of it. This area was covered with grass, instead of gravel and dirt, and its curved wall lay to the west, while its straight hedge boundary was on the east.

In the midst of this area, the Royal Quarter, there were three large treehouses. Langwana took the Menfolk to the central one, which was a bit larger than the other two, and they began ascending a spiral staircase with an ornate railing that wound around the trunk. This took them seventy feet above the ground before it passed through a trapdoor into a rustic, yet splendid, fully furnished sitting room, which was centered around the great tree's bole. Langwana guided the lads up another spiral staircase inside of this room, and when they reached the top, they were standing in a large dining room, also centered on the trunk, with a long, oaken table and ten chairs. To the east, just past the table, there were two large openings in the wooden walls, huge windows that overlooked the gardens of Iswa Hanahoma.

"Odawu, Na'ikeyana!" Langwana called. "Pasokawe'et. Asantwayashme pasnako taya'iguraeku hanog tenaswasaku."

Moments later, Na'ikeyana appeared at the top of a spiral staircase that led up yet another floor.

"Taʔa me hasha hanadwa, ga?" she asked.

Langwana nodded, and Na'ikeyana hurried back up to the floor above. The princess then sat down upon a long divan by the room's western windows as she notified the Menfolk that their luncheon would be ready in a few minutes.

While they waited for the food to arrive, Aradis and Girion stared out the dining room's eastern windows, taking in the fantastic lay of Iswa Hanahoma. Over the tall hedges, the lads espied the areas through which they had come, the gardens of Hanidosha, Palquanoga and Masku, as well as the Guardians' Quarter beyond that. To the north of the Garden of Palquanoga, there was a garden with many large, tall rocks, all of which were draped with luminous moss and sparkling with quartz crystals. In other areas of this garden, the Garden of Tagwan, there were trees, not unlike golden rain trees, with boughs clad in thick, green foliage and vivid yellow inflorescences. Hanging from the limbs of these trees were strands of brightly-colored moss, but also many crystal mirrors, which gleamed brilliantly in the afternoon sun. At the garden's northern edge, there was a pavilion of yellow marble. Beyond the northern hedge of the Garden of Tagwan lay an area shaped like a half-oval that was enclosed by a hedge on the south and a curving stone wall on the north. Many wooden cottages were in this ward, and the lads spied a number of Ingans, many of whom were carrying gardening implements, walking about on the green grass.

To the south of the garden of Palquanoga, there was an area predominantly occupied by carefully raked gravel. Throughout this space, which was the Garden of Yaggawat, there were sizeable, strangely shaped rocks, all hosting peculiar blue lichen. At the garden's southern end, a pavilion made of magnificent, dark-blue marble could be seen. Just to the south of the pavilion, there was a hedge, and beyond it was yet another ward in the shape of a half-oval. It, like the other wards outlying the five gardens dedicated to the Sacred Quinary, had a curving stone wall separating it from the grassy area that lay between the complex of Iswa Hanahoma and the surrounding forests. This final ward housed a single, massive tree, which had a large rectangular opening, some twenty feet high, in the northern side of its trunk. Leading up to this entryway was a series of ancient, moss-covered stones, shaped to look like large thumbs, standing on either side of a stone pathway that led from the gate of the ward to the entrance into the tree.

The lads were about to ask Langwana about this tree when Na'ikeyana and two other Ingan maidens came down the stairs with golden trays filled with many different types of fruits, vegetables and fish, as well as bowls of tapusa, Ingan sap-mead. Eager for what looked to be an excellent meal, the Siloans joined the princess at the table. She thanked her ladies-in-waiting, then dismissed them. As they were going back upstairs, Langwana placed her hand upon her tray of victuals and uttered something in Asla'gu, after which she put her wooden drinking bowl to her lips and downed a wash of tapusa.

Aradis and Girion enjoyed their meal tremendously, especially the fish, which were quite warm and buttery. Langwana identified the two kinds present as sakwessa and munnateg. The lads found the fruits to be marvelous as well; there were so many different varieties, and they all had distinct, exotic flavors. There were deep-blue, pulpy hakonas, bright-yellow shonnagwets, of which they ate the seeds, spiky, vivid orange chennaselgas with a considerable bite and many more kinds besides. As the Siloans consumed their traditional Ingan fare, Langwana asked them a little bit more about themselves, but it seemed her mind was rather far from their conversation, which was just as well, for their thoughts were also occupied elsewhere. Just for the lads to process where they stood in relation to current events was a monumental task. Indeed, the past few days were a tangle of intrigue, danger and weariness, and the future was a looming wall of intimidating uncertainties.

When they finished lunch, the Menfolk went and lay upon couches near the eastern windows, while Langwana started pacing back and forth in the western part of the room. The lads felt themselves getting drowsy, and before too long, they fell into a welcome slumber, thoroughly sedated by rays of the warm afternoon sun.

Suddenly, they awoke to the sound of swift feet on the stairs leading up from the sitting room. Moments later, Fergus emerged in the dining room and put his hands on his knees, as he tried to catch his breath.

Langwana, who was still pacing, stopped abruptly and asked, "Fergus, what is it?"

"Bandits," he panted. "A whole slew o' bandits! They attacked the folk that were a-bringin' the tonquit back here from Shalkanu Ataqua. Almost half o' your folk were killed or wounded, an' only four o' the tonquit made it here to Iswa Hanahoma. The rest were killed or scattered."

For a while after this, there was only the sound of Fergus' rapid, frantic breathing. The Menfolk slowly sat upright, while Langwana turned away to face the western windows. The princess sighed profoundly, and then her shoulders fell, as if she had just assumed the weight of these awful tidings.

"Do you think Gornok was behind the attack?" Aradis asked, after he had finally sorted through some of the implications of Fergus' news.

"If it a-turns out he wasn', then I'll be a cross-eyed cuckoo bird," the Leprechaun swore. "He knew, o' course, that I intended to take ye lads to see the princess here at Iswa Hanahoma. I'll wager ye ten hundred tankards o' tapusa that he spoke wit his foul consorts an' told 'em to keep this place under watch. Then, when they saw that Langwana's messengers were a-goin' down the road to Shalkanu Ataqua, they laid brigands in the brush to attack 'em when they came back. For certainly they would tink tha' a large company o' soldiers would only be a-travelin' tha' way if they were goin' to be a-bringin' mounts back. An' they didna even need to know what the mounts were for to know it wouldn' be summtin tha' would work in their favor. Hence, they reckoned it to be wort' the risk o' givin' themselves away if some o' the soldiers escaped."

"If there were enough of Ravinia's lot to spare for watching this place, why didn't Gornok send bandits to try to attack us on our way down here?" Aradis inquired.

"Because," Fergus explained, "Gornok knows me an' the Questmongers too well to attemp' summtin like tha'. He would guess, an' quite correctly so, that it'd be very difficult to catch us off guard, especially considerin' the circumstances. Besides, he'd know I'd choose some of our best and bonniest fighters to come wit us, an' one Questmonger is wort' ten common brigands in a tussle. Furthermore, ye must remember tha' Gornok himself hasn' had much time to trow a plan together. The survivors o' the attack said that only abou' twenty bandits were involved. Perhaps Gornok only had time to gather twenty ruffians; otherwise, I would tink he'd use more. Whatever the case, the main reasons the bandits succeeded in overcomin' a greater force was tha' they took your folk completely by surprise an' that they spooked the tonquit, a-hollerin' like bogies an' a-blowin' on wild horns or summtin' o' tha' sort. Also, they were hidden quite well in the trees wit bows an' arrows – an' they knew how to use 'em pretty well, it seems."

"But now we're in a terrible bind," the Questkeeper went on. "For, witout mounts, we'll have to go to Paanu Assagwa on foot, which is fine, as far as tha' goes, if we've only got twenty bandits to worry about. An' o' course, we can send scouts ahead this time so we shanna be caught off guard. But there may be more than twenty, an' it will take much longer to go on foot. 'Tis a shamefully bad predicament, to be sure. Already, the Dance o' Marda is well underway, an' it shall take us a good t'ree hours or more to get to Paanu Assagwa on foot – walkin', that is, not runnin'."

All of a sudden, Princess Langwana turned around and announced, "I must go to the sanctuary and meditate."

"Aren't we already in a sanctuary?" Aradis asked.

"Yes, but that is not what I'm referring to. I'm talking about Marnu Senkawa, the Sanctuary of the Seasons. It is a shrine inside of a very ancient tree in the Ritual Quarter, which is just south of the Garden of Yaggawat."

"Oh, we saw that place from this window," Girion remarked, glancing out at it.

Fergus shook his head disapprovingly, as he declared, "Princess, wit all due respect, this is hardly the time for tha' sort o' ting. At the momen', we've got to come up wit a plan."

"What do you think I shall be meditating about?" Langwana returned rather bitingly, as she began to descend the spiral staircase that led down to the sitting room.

"Princess, please," Fergus protested. "Take counsel wit me an' Paskasha, an' let's come up wit a solution together."

"You take counsel with Paskasha and whoever else you like," Langwana urged, as she continued down the stairs. "I shall be taking counsel with the Sacred Quinary."

Fergus threw his hands up in the air, then slapped his leg in sheer exasperation, as he yelled down after the departing princess, "Well, I hope the Sacred Quinary doesn' take the whole afternoon to give ya an answer, for we've only got a few hours, at most, to decide our course! As for me, I'll be in the Guardians' Quarter, so whene'er ya be ready, you can join me there an' tell me wha' they told you."

The princess did not reply to these final remarks. As her soft footsteps receded down the spiral staircase that led all the way to the ground, Fergus looked at the Menfolk and sighed, "Likely as not, she'll be in the sanctuary for several hours at least, so ye can stay here, walk around the gardens or do whate'er ye like in the meantime. However, it's prob'ly best if ye stay out of the Gardeners' Quarter an' the Ritual Quarter, which are the areas to the nort an' the sout o' the gardens, seein' as those areas are private. But if ye hear a big bell a-ringin' in the Guardian's Quarter, then come runnin' immediately, for that will mean the princess has a-come to us. We'll be a-usin' the bell to assemble the guards anyhow, I expect, for there's no sense a-worryin' about any o' Ravinia's lot hearin' it. After all, they can guess good an' well we'll be leavin' here at some point this afternoon. But supposin' ye don' hear the bell any time soon, I'd just as soon ye came up to the Guardians' Quarter in an hour or so; just in case, ya know, so we won' have to wait for ye."

"All right," Girion replied, as Fergus started off down the stairs.

For a little while, the lads sat there on the couches, talking over all that had transpired that morning. Then, inspired by a few glances out the window, they decided to go explore the two gardens they had not yet visited. So, they went down from the treehouse and returned to the Garden of Hanidosha.

Since they were passing by the Autumn Pavilion anyway, they went into it for a few minutes and looked around. First browsing around its perimeter, they eventually made their way to its center and got a much closer look at the statue of Hanidosha, the Forest Queen, and the offerings that had been set upon her altar.

As Aradis stared at the stone Treemaena, he felt as if there was an odd tingling in the air, and he could not shake the sense that unfriendly eyes were watching him. In fact, the more he looked at the statue, the more his skin began to crawl. When he mentioned his sentiments to Girion, the latter said that he felt a little strange as well, but couldn't put his finger on why.

"This place is really quite fascinating," he said, "but you're right. There's just something off about it. Perhaps we should move on."

Aradis quickly agreed to this, and the lads exited the pavilion, taking the red marble pathway back to the Garden of Palquanoga. After that, they headed out the north gate of that garden and entered the resplendent

Garden of Tagwan. There, they wandered around for a while before making their way to the Summer Pavilion, where they found a statue of a fine-looking Ingan lad bearing a golden scepter set with hundreds of tiny, clear crystals.

Aradis found, much to his dismay, that he experienced the same measure of disquiet in this pavilion as he had in the other, and he voiced this to his companion.

"I'm telling you, Girion, there's something going on in these pavilions," Aradis insisted. "I just feel prickly all over, like there's some sinister power in the air itself. I feel as if we shouldn't be here."

"I don't know that I would go that far," Girion remarked. "Like I said, I do feel like something's off, but, at the very least, the architecture, décor and so forth in these places are worth taking a look at."

"Yes, all that stuff is really quite splendid," Aradis agreed, "but I'd rather not linger in these pavilions, nonetheless."

Having completed their investigation of the Garden of Tagwan, the lads headed back through the Garden of Palquanoga and went down into the Garden of Yaggawat. This garden, in addition to all of its patterned gravel, had a great many stone sculptures, none of which were of anything recognizable, as they were all of raw shapes and curious symbols. There were only a few trees in this garden, and most of them were relatively short evergreens.

After a brief debate, Girion convinced Aradis to go into the Winter Pavilion, which had a statue of a hale, greatly aged Ingan holding a large stone.

"How do you feel about the Winter Pavilion?" Girion asked. "Cold?"

Aradis did not laugh. "It's just like the others," he mumbled. "Creepy air and creepy eyes watching."

"Is it the statues that are disturbing you so much?" Girion asked, as he stepped up to the statue before them.

"Mainly," Aradis said. "Statues for decoration are one thing, and I don't mind those at all – not that I've seen that many statues in my day. I guess I've really only seen that gallery of statues down near the waterfront in Gessel. But these statues don't seem to be merely for show. I get the impression that they're supposed to *do* something. Otherwise, why would the Ingans put offerings on the altars? Thus, they're not merely stone, if you know what I mean. Well – in one sense, they are, but there's more going on here."

Looking up at the statue's face, Girion then laid his hand on its foot. It was cold and hard, just as he had expected.

"It's stone and nothing more," he declared, withdrawing his hand. "Were you worried it'd come to life or something?" he inquired.

"No," Aradis replied uneasily and somewhat unconvincingly. "Can we just go now?"

"All right, all right. We'll go," Girion said, as he led the way out of the pavilion.

Now the Siloans went back into the Garden of Palquanoga one last time, as they would have to pass through it in order to reach the Guardians' Quarter. Here, they debated once more, as Girion wished to go inside the Pavilion of the Ages, but Aradis was against it.

"When's the next time we'll be in Iswa Hanahoma?" Girion pressed. "Don't you want to be able to tell the fellows at the Ploughman's Shanty that you, Aradis Kingblade, went into the Pavilion of the Ages in some gardens in the Kingdom of Argonis that hardly anybody's allowed to enter? At least, it doesn't seem like this is the sort of place that regular denizens of the kingdom could just waltz into. I mean, you're standing right here. Come on; they'll all be incredibly jealous."

Aradis rolled his eyes, as he conceded, "Fine. I'll go in because if I don't, I'll never hear the end of it."

So, together the lads entered the elegant, white Pavilion of the Ages. Almost immediately after they had passed through its southern portal, they felt a strange sense of awe come over them, and both felt it with equal acuity. This pavilion, utterly unadorned except for a tall, white pillar, wrapped in a narrow stair and with a strange, solitary flame atop it, had an unmistakable ambience of reverence that was quite unlike that in the other pavilions. There was a definitive presence in the air, but it was neither friendly nor unfriendly, as it was beyond such things. It was, rather, majestic, ancient and brimming over with vitality. Also, the very fact that there was so little here – no carvings, no altars, no statues, no ritual ornaments – made it seem that much more sacred.

"What do you think of this place?" Girion whispered.

Aradis looked up at the roof of the dome and quietly returned, "This one's different."

"Very much so," Girion agreed.

"I still feel as if we ought not to be here," Aradis said ever so softly, as if he didn't want anyone to overhear him, "but not for the same reason."

Girion looked at his friend inquiringly, and Aradis attempted to clarify, "There's a strong sense of – what shall I call it?" He paused. "There's a strong sense of *otherness* in here – of otherness and something else. Purity perhaps. I simply don't know how else to put it. And we've intruded on that with our lack of those things, I think."

Girion nodded knowingly, and the two lads departed out the east door of the pavilion. Taking one last glance over their shoulders into the pavilion's dark interior, they found that they were filled with a longing for something they could not name and also with a fear of that very same thing. They shook their heads, as if to dispel these puzzling sensations and then passed into the Garden of Masku with its bubbling fountains and serene ponds.

They were now somewhat weary from their exploration of Iswa Hanahoma, so finding a long, green marble bench in the pleasant shade of a blossoming tree, they sat down on it. However, as soon as they had done so, Girion realized that they had not yet gone inside the Spring Pavilion. He knew that Aradis was quite done with pavilions for the time being, so he simply informed him that he would be going to take a look around in the Spring Pavilion and then would come right back. Aradis, of course, had no problem with this as long as he didn't have to go himself, so Girion went off to the Spring Pavilion, surveyed it to his satisfaction and came back not long afterward, rejoining Aradis on the bench.

Then Girion took out his tylon and notebook and began to write, while Aradis mused on the peculiar impressions he had experienced in the pavilions, as well as all that had befallen him and Girion since they had come to Anganor. They occupied themselves with these respective activities for quite some time, but as the sun proceeded lower and lower in the sky, they grew rather concerned, for there had been no sign of the princess nor any sound of the bell Fergus had mentioned. They knew that Fergus was probably on the verge of having a tantrum by now and thus decided to remain where they were instead of going back to the Guardians'

Quarter, for it would only put them more on edge to be waiting with the irate Questkeeper.

Finally, when it was rather late in the afternoon, Aradis decided to ask his friend about something he had been pondering on and off since that morning. If nothing else, it would take their minds off the anxiety of the present situation. "You know how Princess Langwana said that Palquanoga was analogous to the Danna?" he softly inquired.

"Hm?" Girion said, setting down his tylon and looking over at Aradis. "What did you say?"

"You remember how Langwana said that Palquanoga was similar to the Danna?" he repeated.

"Oh, yes," Girion replied, blinking.

"Well, do you think Palquanoga and Telyon are one and the same?"

Girion thought about this for a few moments, then answered, "I suppose that would be roughly correct, and by that I don't mean to say that I think it to be a simple matter of equating one to the other. That's why I said *roughly* correct. I'm no expert on the Danna, but based on what my father has said and on what we learned from Nagello, the Danna is who he is, regardless of what people may think about him, just as you are who you are and I am who I am, regardless of what people may think about us. So Telyon is Telyon, and if Palquanoga, as described by the Ingans of Argonis, is just like Telyon, then Palquanoga and Telyon are one and the same. However, if he differs in some respects, then Palquanoga may simply be the Asla'gu name for the being who is most *like* Telyon in these Ingans' lore."

"Of course, neither one of us knows a great deal about the Ingans' beliefs or legends," Girion went on, "but, as we saw in our examination of the pavilions, Palquanoga seems to differ in some peculiar way from the rest of the members of the Sacred Quinary. The very fact that his pavilion was so barren of any suggestion of who he was, save for the mysterious fire burning there, leads me to believe that he is unique in some regard. I can't say that I think much of the other four in the Sacred Quinary, the ones representing the seasons, nor do I think those machaswa Langwana spoke of are anything more than Fergus suggested, but I – I really do think the connection between Palquanoga and Janura is a connection between Telyon and something that happened at the founding of Argonis. And, the more I've thought about Langwana's story about the sengara who took the medallion fragment nearly two hundred years ago, the more I'm convinced of my previous assessment of the matter. That is to say, I really do believe he was one and the same as Nagello."

Girion sighed, then looked up at the sky. "But what do I know? I'm afraid we may be out of our depth in this whole affair, Aradis. And I know – you're the one who's supposed to make the pessimistic comments around here," he laughed, "but I'll admit that I'm feeling outmatched at the moment."

"You're in good company." Aradis smiled, as he patted his friend on the back.

Aradis sat and thought for a few moments and then said, "I wish that our families were sharing this adventure with us, though. It's rather difficult to bear all the weight of it with just the two of us."

Sighing, he declared, "Actually, I wish that they could share only the good parts of it and leave out the bad ones. I wouldn't want them to experience all the unpleasant things, like encountering the Ravenstaff or fleeing from the moonhounds into Thornberry Thicket. But I know they would love the more beautiful parts, like these gardens, for instance. Mellora would especially like the one we're one in now. And both your mother and mine would very much fancy the Garden of Hanidosha."

"Maybe we can plant gardens like this back in Siloa someday for them to enjoy," Girion said. "That might be easier than bringing them all the way back over here to Byram."

"If their journey turned out to be half as harrowing as ours, then it might indeed," Aradis concurred, laughing. "But there'll be no pavilions in our replica, or at least no statues, if I have anything to say about it."

Just then, he looked up and noticed Princess Langwana quickly striding out of the gateway that led into the Garden of Masku from the Garden of Palquanoga. She was wearing a simple, brown barkcloth dress, an outfit much less magnificent than her attire from earlier that day but much more suitable for travel.

"Look, Girion!" he exclaimed. "Langwana's coming."

"So she is," Girion said, as he placed his notebook and tylon back in his jerkin and the lads rose to go meet Langwana. "And now, I fear, we haven't much time. Look at the sun."

Aradis didn't need to; he had been glancing at Marda every ten minutes or so during the last few hours. "Fergus the Fearless is going to be Fergus the Furious," he muttered.

When the lads reached the princess, Girion asked, "Have you a plan now? Did you find what you were looking for in your meditations?"

"I did," she returned. "But I will share it with everyone when we speak with Fergus and Paskasha."

Walking swiftly, the threesome soon came to the Guardians' Quarter, where the Questkeeper and Paskasha were intently conversing up by the gate. As soon as they spotted the princess and the Siloans, they jogged over to them, and Fergus somewhat impatiently said, "Well? I hope your meditations ha' proved wort'while, for you've nearly whiled the whole afternoon away wit them."

"My meditations were somewhat clouded," the princess confessed, ignoring Fergus' barb, "but I do have a plan."

"What is it?" Paskasha asked expectantly.

Langwana took a deep breath, then said, "We have four tonquit, and tonquit can run quite fast, as you know. I propose that you, myself and the Menfolk take the Amulet of the Akwarna and ride with as great a speed as the beasts will give us to Paanu Assagwa, for time is now very much against us. The only reason I would leave you behind, Fergus, is that it would be difficult for you to ride on a tonquit, considering its large size. Of course, if we are attacked by bandits, we shall have less protection by far than I had originally intended, but I think we shan't be easily assailed by them, on account of our being mounted on swift steeds."

After Langwana finished, everyone stood there in silence for a few moments. Then Paskasha quietly stated, "Princess, I believe this plan is very unwise."

Fergus, with considerably greater vehemence, declared, "It's bad enough already what you're a-plannin' to do when ya get to Paanu Assagwa, but this scheme is sure to keep you from a-gettin' there in the first place. If ya ride wit all haste, e'en at the greatest speed wit which the tonquit can bear you, I guarantee ya shanna make it there alive. It's far too risky. Who knows how many or wha' sort o' folk they may have a-lyin' in wait by now? Besides, tonquit may be fast, but they canna outrun well-aimed arrows."

"What would you have us do, then?" the princess asked, somewhat defensively. "Our misfortunes have mounted to such a degree that they call for desperate designs to combat them. Besides, can I in good conscience ignore the counsel given to me by the Sacred Quinary?" she solemnly inquired.

"You yourself said that your meditations were clouded," Paskasha pointed out. "Besides, there is still enough time, though barely, for the four of us to ride upon the four tonquit while a company of soldiers walks with us. I think, if we leave immediately, we can arrive at Paanu Assagwa before sunset, though we shall have to push our pace quite a bit."

Langwana considered this for a moment, then returned, "If we arrive too late, all shall have been in vain. Either way, we will be taking terrible risks. For my part, I would rather trust to the strength and speed of the tonquit than to the pity of Marda. For the sun will not halt for us if we have not yet reached Paanu Assagwa. Verily, whether the fate of Argonis shall be freedom or desolation, it concerns him not. Even Tagwan himself could not persuade him to alter his relentless course. How much less, then, could we?"

"Well," Fergus said, biting his lip, "you are the princess, after all, so choose as ya will, an' we shall be obliged to accommodate you. But I'd sooner trow the amulet in the sea than let it fall into the hands o' Ravinia. An' that's exac'ly what will happen, I'm afraid, if ye don' take sufficient protection wit ye."

"I completely agree with Fergus," Paskasha said. "We will all almost certainly perish if we simply try to dash over there without soldiers to protect us. But, as he said, the prerogative to select our course is yours. Whatever you choose, I will defer to your judgment."

Langwana shook her head, replying, "The decision cannot lie with me. I was resolved to heed the fruit of my meditations, but now I am torn, for to completely disregard the counsel of you and Fergus would be, I think, imprudent." Then, turning to the Siloans, she proposed, "Let us have the Menfolk decide, for their part in this is perhaps greater even than our own."

Paskasha frowned, and Fergus' expression was immediately seized by both shock and alarm.

"Us?" Aradis, who was quite flustered by this, exclaimed. "How can we make such a decision when you cannot?"

"If you would have us choose, then choose we shall," Girion asserted, much to the surprise of the others, especially Aradis, "for we know that time is fast escaping. But can we have a moment to discuss the matter alone?"

"Of course," Langwana returned.

Hastily, Girion drew Aradis aside toward a spot some distance away in the ward. As they were walking there, they heard intense, yet hushed, dialogue erupt among the three Barada they had left behind.

When the lads were standing an appreciable distance from the others, Girion prompted, "Well, what do you think?"

"You were just saying you felt outmatched, and now you're volunteering for us to make a decision of really tremendous magnitude. What happened?" Aradis asked.

"I don't really know, but I just felt that because the decision was thrust upon us, there was no choice but to rise to it."

"We didn't *have* to accept that responsibility," Aradis peevishly replied. "*You're* the one who said *we* would make the decision. I don't want to make this choice. You do realize that this decision could affect the survival of the entire kingdom of Argonis, right?"

"Certainly," Girion acknowledged. "But it's a decision that has to be made, and we've been asked to make it by no less a person than the princess of Argonis. Personally, I think Fergus and Paskasha are right. It's too dangerous for us to go without proper protection. So, I say we take a company of soldiers with us."

"Let's do that then," Aradis sighed, "because your judgment is often better than mine, and I think we should make a dash for it."

"Ha," Girion laughed. "It doesn't surprise me that you would have chosen that course. But this isn't my decision. It's ours."

"We'll do it your way," Aradis insisted. "Paskasha thought there would be enough time for us to still make it, even with all the soldiers on foot, so why would we not elect the safer course?"

"Very well." Girion nodded. "But we have one more thing to discuss before we give them our answer."

"And what is that?" Aradis asked.

"Well," Girion said, "the princess plans to sacrifice her life, if necessary, to save her father. She's intending to march right into Paanu Assagwa and defy the taboo – or the ashaska, to use the proper Ingan term. All the while, the rest of us are apparently just supposed to wait outside and hope that she brings Thornoak out alive so we can speak with him. I don't know about you, but I won't be doing any such thing. We were sent by the Danna himself to speak with Thornoak and rescue Argonis. With both being in such a precarious position at present, how can we stand idly by while Langwana risks her very life? If we're going to Paanu Assagwa, I think we must go *inside* Paanu Assagwa, taboo or no taboo. We cannot allow the princess to face death alone. Besides, those lines from the poem she recited seemed to indicate that the Konaskwa would only be brought back by someone from the east, across the sea. Don't you remember? 'Look for a hand from across the sea.' There's a line I don't remember, and then it says, 'Look to the east for this hand to come and bring back the absent crown.' We're the only ones around here who fit that description. Thus, we've no choice but to join her."

Aradis opened his mouth to rebut Girion, but then closed it, for he was too addled to come up with anything to say. His mind reeled as he desperately sought for a robust rejoinder or even a threadbare excuse that would release him from the onerous sense of duty and honor that now pressed upon him. Fear clenched his gut with a terrible barbarity, screaming at him to reject Girion's proposal. But there was also a bold, red fire within him, one that yearned to march confidently into Paanu Assagwa alongside the princess, disdaining both peril and death. In this manner, the ancient rhyme would be fulfilled, and he and Girion would play a pivotal role in it, which would be extraordinary indeed. Though part of him still vehemently wanted to fight back, in an instant, this fire roared up, consuming his fears, as he quietly replied, "You're right, Girion. We cannot let her face death alone. We shall face it with her. But we'll have to convince Fergus and Paskasha to let us do so, which won't be easy. At least I suspect it won't be."

"It will be easier than facing death." Girion shrugged.

The lads now rejoined Paskasha, Fergus and the princess, and Girion announced, "We have made our decision. We shall take the soldiers with us and simply trust that we can arrive at Paanu Assagwa before sunset. But we have one condition to add to the matter."

"What might that be?" Langwana inquired.

"Princess, as you are planning to risk your life in breaking the ashaska, Aradis and I will be doing the same," Girion declared.

"Not ye too!" Fergus moaned. "Why don' we all just go in at this rate? Crannadacks!"

No one else standing there had any idea what this word meant, but they were quite certain it wasn't an agreeable expression.

Paskasha looked hard at the Menfolk and asked, "You do know what breaking the ashaska means, do you not? You know that you probably won't make it five steps into the sanctum before you are killed by King Thornoak's guards?"

"Yes, of course," Aradis answered, drawing from the power of the fire that was still burning within him. "But we cannot let the princess face death alone."

"Oh, if we weren' so pressed for time, I'd wring ye two silly," Fergus swore, "but, seein' as so much grief has already run amok, I'll agree to yer madness jus' so we can get on wit this festival o' folly."

"Have we your permission to join you, Princess?" Girion inquired.

"Of course," Langwana solemnly declared. "Aradis and Girion, you shall come with me into Paanu Assagwa. Now, Paskasha and Fergus, ready your troops. Let the bell be rung to summon them. Whoever's out there waiting for us can readily surmise that we'll be coming, and when we leave this place, we cannot do so in secret, so we may as well let them hear the bright pealing of our hope. For such shall sound from the bell of the guardians of Iswa Hanahoma in this, their finest hour."

As soon as Langwana had finished speaking, Paskasha and Fergus began rushing about the ward, calling out orders to their subordinates.

The course to the Konaskwa had been charted, and now it only remained to be seen how perilous it would prove to be.

CHAPTER EIGHT

The Course to the Konaskwa

uring the next few minutes, there was a great deal of hustle and hubbub as everyone prepared themselves for the journey to Paanu Assagwa. All the while, a great bell tolled out resoundingly in a cupola above one of the wooden buildings to the north. When all was said and done, there were forty of Paskasha's Ingan warriors assembled by the gates of the Guardians' Quarter, all holding glinting spears and formidable vine whips. Many of them also had leather slings tucked into their belts, along with small burlap bags filled with stones. The Questmongers Fergus had brought were all standing at the rear of the guards, inspecting their various weapons.

Meanwhile, a soldier had brought the Siloans back their packs and weapons. Also, several soldiers had saddled the four tonquit from Shalkanu Ataqua. These animals were massive and majestic; slightly larger than elk, they had glossy, sable fur and enormous antlers, appearing almost to be made of bark, that were partially swathed in dark-green moss. Also, they had long, jet-black beards that hung down almost to their knees. As their backs were so high up, Aradis and Girion had to be helped up onto their saddles by Paskasha, who assured them that the beasts were very well-trained and that the lads could use the reins on them just as they would on a horse. When Paskasha had gotten the lads settled, he began lashing their packs to the sides of their tonquit.

As he was doing this, Fergus went up to the princess, who was mounting her own tonquit. "Where are you a-keepin' the pieces o' the medallion?" he asked.

"In here," the princess replied, tapping a little leather pouch attached to a girdle that was fastened around her dress.

After Paskasha had finished trussing the Siloans' packs to their mounts, he came over and handed Langwana a vine whip, saying, "Take this spinescourge, Princess – just as an extra precaution – though I dearly hope you won't have to use it. The safety of you and the Menfolk is our utmost priority, so let our troops guard you in case of attack and only fly or fight at greatest need. If there is anything we can do to protect you, rest assured that we will do it. Indeed, you are most precious to us, Princess."

"Thank you, Paskasha," Langwana said, nodding courteously to him, as he patted her tonquit's nose. He nodded courteously in return, then climbed onto his own beast.

As soon as Paskasha had mounted his tonquit, several Ingans who were staying behind opened up the gates, the bell ceased its tolling and the company passed out onto the verge that lay in-between Iswa Hanahoma and the eaves of the forest to the east. Ingan soldiers, all in light armor, were jogging in columns in front of, behind and to either side of the four riders. All of the Questmongers were dispersed randomly throughout the group – all of them, that is, except for Collic McGarrus the Leprechaun and Sarranil the Timber-Elf, who were running some distance ahead, just as they had that morning, in order to keep an eye out for ambushes.

The company traveled at a swift pace down the path that led back east to Konassu Road. Much to the troop's relief, the first three miles of the nine-mile journey to Paanu Assagwa passed without incident, and they arrived at Konassu Road as the sunlight was beginning to take on a soft, red tone.

"We're going to be too late," Langwana whispered to Paskasha.

"Nay, milady," Paskasha returned, then shouted to the company, "All right, we've got to pick up the pace. Come on, soldiers!"

Those on foot immediately went from jogging to running, as they veered northward onto Konassu Road to finish the last six miles to Paanu Assagwa. Collic and Sarranil picked up speed as well, as they ran along the margins of the forest, peering into the shadows of bushes and trees.

The company proceeded for another ten minutes, and then Sarranil suddenly shouted, "Ambush!" An instant later, he leapt back, narrowly dodging a deadly arrow. Then three more arrows came flying out of the forest, seeking to pierce the nimble Timber-Elf. Spectacularly, he dodged all of them and began racing at full speed back toward the main company, as did Collic. A few more arrows sailed past the fleeing Questmongers, as Sarranil shouted, "It's an ambush! Prepare for an attack!"

The company, of course, had expected that something like this might happen and was almost instantly ready to engage in combat.

"How many are there?" Fergus yelled, as he rushed to the front of the company.

"Thirty, at least," Sarranil called.

Just then, a motley squadron of around sixty Barada plunged through the underbrush on the eastern edge of the road, yelling a wild battle cry. This force consisted of Timber-Elves, Menfolk, Ingans, Leprechauns and Wood-Gnomes carrying bows, arrows and swords. All were attired in green and brown, such as would blend in well with woodland terrain. As they were running toward the troops from Iswa Hanahoma, they loosed a shower of arrows at them, which felled three of Paskasha's soldiers.

"Charge them!" Paskasha ordered, and the company began pounding forward.

Quite shortly, the two forces crashed into each other, and a raucous melee ensued. Paskasha trampled to death four of the bandits with his tonquit, while his front guards burst through the jumbled ranks of their foes, skewering several of them with their spears, though, in the process, many received nasty slashes from the bandits' swords. The Menfolk and the princess, meanwhile, were harbored at the back of the company, protected by a handful of soldiers who were not directly engaged in battling the bandits.

As for Fergus and the Questmongers, they bounded forward, all at the exact same speed, and with incredible, almost magical, synchronization, they broke into the midst of the bandits like a whirlwind. Aradis and Girion had never seen anything like it. The efficiency and skill with which the Questmongers had dealt with Quagga and his goons at the Banaka Gate was child's play compared to this. Chula was spinning his exotic blade with unbelievable speed and cutting down many a bewildered foe. As for Fergus, he was slicing the legs of anyone within the reach of his curved sword, while all the rest of the Questmongers were executing equally spectacular, lethal maneuvers.

This combat had been going on for less than half a minute when there came from the woods, just to the west of the road, a great deal of commotion. Howling triumphantly, another fifty bandits appeared out of the forest with swords raised, and they raced into the company's exposed left flank, killing three more of Paskasha's soldiers. Several of this new group of bandits were launching arrows toward the company, and a few of these hit Langwana's tonquit in its head and neck. The beast roared in agony, then began to fall sideways. The princess tried to steady her mount, but this effort proved fruitless, so she rolled out of her saddle. She only barely avoided having her leg pinned under the tonquit's body, as it landed on the ground with a heavy thud.

As soon as Paskasha saw this, he spurred his steed toward Langwana, yelling, "You must take mine, Princess! Then you and the Menfolk must ride for your lives to Paanu Assagwa!"

Rapidly, he dismounted, and Langwana leapt up into the saddle. Then Fergus raced back out of the fray and panted, "Beware, all o' ye! There may be more ahead! Don' let 'em catch ye off guard! An' remember, ye've got to make it to Paanu Assagwa alive or Argonis is doomed!"

Just as he finished saying this, several bandits broke through the line of defense and tried to attack Langwana's new mount. It reared up, striking them with its mighty hooves and knocking them to the ground.

"Come, Aradis! Come, Girion! For the kingdom!" Langwana shouted, as she launched her steed northward, skirting around the fracas.

The lads followed swiftly after her, and, as they left the company behind, they heard Fergus call after them, "Fret not for us! Tink o' the king! Ride for him! Ride for Argonis!"

The three Barada and their mounts thundered down the road, soon leaving the furious battle far behind them. As they rode, their eyes intently searched the trees on either side for any enemies who might be concealed there. But then, at a section where the road curved slightly, they realized that it was not their enemies' objective to hide themselves; rather, they were waiting for them in plain sight. For there, several hundred feet ahead, were three formidable creatures: a large brown bear, a huge, muscular, black wildcat and a wolf with a big gash in its side.

"That's Gornok!" Aradis exclaimed in dismay. "He must have known they'd send us on alone!"

"The bear and the tashkala are undoubtedly Druids as well," Langwana said. "Quickly, into the forest!"

Already, the three animals had begun to run toward them, their paws beating the road with a horrible, savage rhythm that was rapidly increasing in tempo. As the princess and the Menfolk charged eastward into the dense forest, which was diffused with the light of reddish sunbeams, they reached up to protect themselves from low-hanging branches. Desperately, they began weaving back and forth through a maze of fallen limbs and thick underbrush.

As straight as she could manage, Princess Langwana was now leading the lads to the northeast, hoping to reach the road that ran a little more than four miles from Konassu Road directly to Paanu Assagwa. But the beasts were quickly gaining on them, plowing madly through the forest, snorting, snarling and panting with bloodlust. Up ahead, the trees were much taller, and the spaces between the trunks were greater, but this was of little consolation, for there the chase would come down to raw speed. This was especially disconcerting with regard to the tashkala, which was racing through the woods at an incredible pace and vaulting over logs, even very large ones, seemingly with tremendous ease.

"We've got to split up!" Langwana shouted to the Siloans, as they entered a spacious area of the forest populated by tall elms. "If we all go in different directions, they'll have to pick who they're going to follow."

"Yes, but there's one of them for each of us," Girion pointed out, "so it won't do us any good."

"It may," the princess rejoined. "Tonquit have great endurance and can match the speed of a bear or a wolf. Whoever the tashkala chooses to take after most likely won't make it, but the other two have a chance."

"Are we all still going to head for Paanu Assagwa?" Aradis asked, ducking under a large bough.

"Yes," Langwana replied. "The road that will take us there is not very far to the north of here. If you just follow it to the east, you will come to the gates of the sanctum."

"Let's do this, then," Aradis sighed. "And may the Danna be with us all."

Urging his mount forward with all haste, Aradis veered off to the east. Girion went in a more northeasterly direction, and Langwana directed her tonquit to go straight north. Growling with rage, the three animals chasing them broke off from each other; the bear swerved toward Langwana, the tashkala sprang after Girion and the wolf darted after Aradis.

Soon, the Siloans and the princess lost sight of each other, as they rode wildly on through the forest. Each of their Druidic pursuers was drawing closer, bit by bit, bounding on through bushes and brush, ferns and foliage, with ravenous ferocity. Paanu Assagwa was but a few miles away, and the beasts knew they would have to reach their quarry before their quarry reached the sanctum, for there were many soldiers there, and the beasts would thus be badly outmatched.

Langwana was the first to reach the road to Paanu Assagwa. Her tonquit sprang out onto the dirt track, and she immediately directed it eastward. Then, to her horror, she heard the murderous cry of a kapaqua, a large, predatory bird with glossy brown plumage, somewhat bigger than a vulture and certainly uglier than one. Glancing over her shoulder, she saw one diving down toward her, its grisly beak wide open in a scream. Just as it was about to reach her, she struck at it with her vine whip. The bird narrowly dodged the vicious lash, then swooped on toward Girion, who had just appeared ahead of Langwana on the road.

"Girion, watch out for the kapaqua!" she screamed. Looking behind him, Girion very quickly learned what a kapaqua was. In the nick of time, he swung his staff and knocked the bird away from him. It wasn't a clean hit, however, and it flapped back up above him and dove again.

By this time, the bear had come onto the road and was racing along just behind Langwana. The princess, realizing that the bear was really quite close, close enough that she could almost feel its hot breath, jerked her tonquit into the woods to the north of the road, where it sprang over a sizeable mess of brambles. The bear was not quite able to make the jump, so it was delayed in getting back on the princess' tail.

Meanwhile, Aradis was speeding through a grove of maple trees, with the wolf not far behind. Snarling ferociously, it burst forward with a sudden surge and began running right alongside Aradis' tonquit. Then, keeping pace with the tonquit, it moved closer and closer. Aradis sharply yanked the reins to direct the tonquit to the right, so that it would trample the wolf. But the beast leapt up at the tonquit, and as it did so, there was a flash of blue light. Now, where the wolf had been, there was the Druid Gornok, who looked just as he had the day before when the lads had known him as Kelwyn Faircrest; he was even wearing the same clothes. Gornok grabbed Aradis' saddle with both hands the very instant he took on his Druid form and attempted to hoist himself up onto it.

Though completely caught off guard by this maneuver, Aradis still managed to use his free hand to push on the Druid's face, simultaneously kicking him in the stomach with the hard sole of his boot.

Gornok grunted, "Die, Manfilth!" as he seized Aradis' leg with his right hand.

The lad rapidly turned the tonquit so that it would run directly by a large maple tree. As they barreled on by its stout trunk, Aradis struck Gornok's face with his fist, and the Druid, to avoid smashing against the bole, let go of the saddle. There was another burst of blue light, and, an instant later, the wolf reappeared, dashing after the fleeing Aradis.

Back on the road, Girion was wondering what had become of the large wildcat that had been chasing him. He could see Langwana off to the north of the road and now a little ahead of him but still being pursued by the bear. There was no sign of Aradis. As for the kapaqua, it had flown some hundred feet above the trees and seemed to be keeping an eye on the whereabouts of the tonquit and their riders. As his mount raced out of a little hollow, Girion spotted a large stone complex up ahead, cloaked in ivy and vines, with trees growing out of its domes. At the back end of the complex, gray, timeworn towers rose up into the reddening sky. That place, he concluded, must be Paanu Assagwa; he was almost to safety.

Suddenly, Girion heard the terrible scream of what could only have been the tashkala and realized that it was now ahead of him. He actually spotted it leaping along just inside the trees at the forest's edge and knew that, as soon as it decided to come over to the road, he would be done for. "Go, go!" he yelled at his tonquit. "We're almost there!"

Paanu Assagwa drew ever closer, but so did the terrible tashkala, hissing and spitting frightfully. Girion could actually see the figures of guards by the gates now, dressed in barkcloth kilts. He bent down all the way to the tonquit's mane and urged, "Come on! Please! Heaven and earth, tonquit, you've just got to make it!"

But the tonquit could go no faster. And the tashkala was now just ahead, racing up a large rock on the south side of the road. Roaring at the top of its lungs, the beast launched itself off the boulder from a full sprint and sailed through the air toward Girion. But, just before it reached him, a shining spear flew through the air and pierced its right flank. The tashkala gasped, fell just short of its mark and lay stricken upon the ground. An instant later, there was a blaze of blue light, and, instead of a tashkala, there was now the corpse of a brown-robed Druid with a javelin sticking out of it.

Girion was so shocked that he could hardly grasp what had just happened, but he spied a guard ahead with an outstretched arm and knew that he must have been the fellow who had just saved his life.

As soon as the tashkala was felled by the javelin, the kapaqua screeched and wheeled back to the west, while the bear cut off its pursuit of Langwana. And, a moment later, Aradis, mounted on his tonquit, bolted onto the road just ahead of Girion. Behind him, there echoed a lonely howl through the forest.

"To the gates!" Langwana cried, riding on at full speed.

Galloping up to the soldiers standing there, the three Barada swiftly dismounted and raced up to the soldier who had thrown the javelin, who seemed to be their leader. Meanwhile, several other sentries rushed to take the bridles of the tonquit and tie them to nearby trees. Langwana handed her spinescourge to a soldier standing nearby, as she said something to him in Asla'gu. She then directed the Menfolk to give their weapons to another soldier. The lads were not certain of the cause for this instruction but guessed it might be because Paanu Assagwa, like Iswa Hanahoma, was a sacred site and probably had some sort of ban on arms. Whatever the case, judging from the earnestness and urgency of the princess' voice, they deemed it would be best to comply without delay, and so they handed the sentry all their weapons.

Together, the rest of the soldiers bowed slightly, reciting, "Masku, Tagwan, Hanidosha, Yaggawat."

"Pessanagwa," Langwana blessed them, her right hand uplifted. She brought her hand down, and the soldiers put their hands together in the customary manner for this blessing, stretched them skyward and then lowered them.

"Taga me hanadwa quastahogwelasha makelu ekque?" the lead guard asked. "Higo'i nasiqua?"

"There's no time to explain everything, Chelashu," Langwana hastily replied in Daiga, of course for the Menfolk's sake. "My father is going to take his own life in just a few minutes, I fear, and we must go in and stop him."

"I'm sorry, Princess," Chelashu firmly declared, "but your father has extended the ashaska to you as well. It is forbidden for you to enter Paanu Assagwa, upon pain of death. I sent a message to you about the matter this morning, and the runner told me he delivered it to you personally. Was he lying?"

"Not at all," Langwana returned. "I am fully aware of the ashaska, but I cannot abide by it, for if I do so, my father will die."

"If you break the ashaska, so will you," Chelashu asserted. "I cannot ignore my duty, even if that means I must kill you." With this, he grabbed a javelin from one of his fellow sentries and used it to block Langwana's path into the sanctum.

Undaunted, the princess took the two pieces of the medallion out of her pouch and handed them to Aradis, saying, "Take these. You are the one who brought the missing fragment of the amulet to Argonis, and you shall be the one who shows my father that we now have both halves in our possession."

"Is that … is that the Amulet of the Akwarna?" Chelashu gasped. "It cannot be! How … or where did you find the other piece of it?"

"The Menfolk brought it from across the sea," Langwana explained, as she pushed his javelin aside and began marching toward the huge, ancient stone archway that led into Paanu Assagwa.

"You would not dare violate the traditions of our people!" Chelashu yelled, hoisting his javelin into ready position. All of the other soldiers also aimed their spears directly at the princess.

"We cannot allow you to enter Paanu Assagwa and live," Chelashu insisted. "And I should very much like an accounting of how the Menfolk came by the other piece of the medallion. Am I really to believe that these two Eskagwan are responsible for fulfilling the Sign of the Sengara – the sign we've been awaiting for five thousand years?"

Langwana turned and looked Chelashu squarely in the eyes. "Yes, they have fulfilled it. But there's no time to give an accounting of it now. And, as for your threat to slay me for my breach of the ashaska, I know you to be an Ingan of your word, Chelashu. I know you will not hesitate to kill me or to kill the Menfolk if we try to enter. And that is your prerogative. Now, you know that I hold our people and our traditions just as dearly as you do. But I also recognize that there are things greater and higher than these, things which we must hold more dearly still. Two of those things are life and freedom. A life will soon be lost if we fail to act, and the freedom of our land will vanish not long afterward. Therefore, for me, the greater concern must swallow up the lesser. Life is a precious gift, and if I must spend it now, at least I shall not have spent it in cowardice or in flinging aside a duty more sacred even than keeping the traditions of our ancestors."

Chelashu had nothing to say in reply to this. He merely kept his javelin poised and tried to maintain an intimidating countenance.

"Come, Aradis. Come, Girion." The princess waved for them to follow her.

With trepidation, they began to do so, uncertain if they were about to be slain. However, they were roughly pushed back by several guards, who then seized them. Aradis struggled against them, but Girion simply let himself be held by firm Ingan hands.

"Hinder them not!" Langwana cried, holding up her hand.

"They are Eskagwan!" Chelashu spat. "No Eskagwan has ever entered this sacred place. If they do, they must die."

"Of course." Langwana nodded. "As must every Barada someday. They have already risked their lives many times attempting to save our kingdom. If this is where all their labors end, at the hands of supposed guardians of the very land they are trying to rescue, then it will be a bitter end, but not a craven one. You yourself saved one of them from death ten breaths ago, but if you would now reverse that decision, I cannot keep you from doing so. But I swear to you that these Eskagwan may be the very last hope Argonis has. Extinguish that, if you will, Chelashu, but I cry unto the Sacred Quinary that they will see your folly for what it is and have pity upon you for it."

Chelashu's expression hardened even more, and he looked as if he might hurl his javelin at the princess' heart at any second. Then, unexpectedly, his grimace softened just slightly, as he lowered his weapon and said, "Quastasemna'ieku hanadwako."

The guards, with some hesitancy, released the Menfolk and parted so that they might pass.

Chelashu now looked at the princess, glowering darkly, as he warned, "The teskagwe will strangle the Menfolk for certain, and all three of you will incur the wrath of the machaswa, for it is their duty to protect what is sacred. In fact, I fear that even I and the soldiers, who also bear responsibility for this grievous act, shall be punished by them."

As the Menfolk joined her, Langwana sharply returned, "If what we are about to do riles the machaswa, then, naturally, we will suffer the consequences they apportion to us, which may well involve being slain by them. Yet I will trust to the essential awareness of and adherence to that which is good that our traditions claim reside in them. Surely they will understand what is at stake and know that it is necessary for us to violate the ashaska in order to rescue my father and the kingdom. Then again, perhaps they will not. I cannot claim to know for certain. The sun is dying, as will be my father soon, and I cannot tarry to ponder such things. If ill befalls us, then so be it. Death will not keep me from my duty."

With that, she turned and walked briskly across the crumbling, moss-clad stones of the entry courtyard, which was devoid of any ornamentation except for a few carvings of geometric shapes that had been made on the worn stone walls. The lads, despite being nearly paralyzed by fear, managed to trot along after her, though they half-expected spears to sink into their backs at any moment.

Once they had passed the arch, they stood in a much larger courtyard, which was scattered with big, rough slabs of stone, all swathed in lichen. The walls of the place featured friezes of strange swirls and misshapen faces. Up ahead, there was a great, gray-barked tree growing out of the stone ramparts. Its wild, grasping roots surrounded a large set of wooden doors with a huge keyhole in the left portal.

The princess hastened up to the doors and unlocked the gates with a key she pulled from one of her dress pockets. Then she beckoned for the Menfolk to follow her into a dark passageway. They did so, trembling slightly, and took the passageway straight to the east more than a hundred feet, going toward the red, fading glow of sunlight at the end of it.

The passageway exited into a courtyard that was bigger still than the one before it. This one had large steps going down to a grass-covered area in the center. The edges of the courtyard were shaded by an arcade with massive stone columns, each of which was carved with reliefs of fantastic, exotic beasts. In niches in the walls of this courtyard, there were statues of grotesque beings looking somewhat like sickly, emaciated, demented Ingans with sloped foreheads and wide-open mouths with horrific, long sharp teeth. The figures were all clad in tattered robes and had thin, skeletal hands and fingers.

A number of doorways led out of this courtyard, but the princess took the Siloans to an especially large entrance that was directly across from where they stood. The passage it led into ran some two hundred feet before branching off in two directions. Meagerly illuminated by a few reddish beams of Marda, the walls of the entire passageway were covered with dark brown vines that had inserted themselves in every crack and crevice and hung menacingly down from the ceiling.

Taking a deep breath, Langwana cautioned, "Be wary in these hallways. These are the teskagwe that Chelashu spoke of."

"Yes, I was going to ask you what he meant by 'the teskagwe will strangle the Menfolk for certain,'" Girion said. "What are teskagwe and what do they do?"

"They are motillids, plants with the ability to move. They have an acute sense of smell and will attack anyone whose scent they don't recognize. Ingans have long used them in places where they wanted people kept out who didn't belong because the motillids could be counted on to seize and strangle intruders."

"Well, that's exactly what we are," Aradis pointed out, "so how are we going to keep from being taken by them?"

"We're going to run as fast as we can," Langwana said. "There's a maze ahead and very little light, but I know the way, as I've been through here many times to see my father."

Aradis and Girion looked at each other uneasily. Then the latter declared, though not without reluctance, "Lead the way then, Princess."

Breathing heavily once more, the princess took off down the passageway, and the lads raced after her. Almost immediately, vines began stirring, then rapidly shooting out from the walls and uncoiling from the ceiling, making grabs for the speeding Siloans.

"Keep running!" the princess shouted. The lads needed no encouragement in this regard.

Down they ran through passageway after passageway, with only stray ambient light from purple pachacuri lamps to guide them, for they were deep within the complex. All the while, the lads felt the sticky, slimy vines grabbing at them from all directions, and they knew that if they hesitated for even an instant, the vines would have them. As it was, they were nearly held fast on several occasions but managed to rip themselves away.

After several minutes, they saw red, fading rays of Marda through a doorway up ahead and sprinted into a fourth courtyard, just barely escaping the grasp of an especially dense colony of teskagwe. This courtyard was more spacious than all the others and planted with a number of extremely old, weathered trees, under the shade of which there were various stone monuments.

"Just ahead is the Shrine of the Machaswa," Langwana explained, gasping for breath. "It's through that small door on the opposite side of the courtyard. There are three long halls, which are all mausoleums, for there the Konaskwas of old are interred. Beyond the final hall, there is a passageway that spirals down into a great, hollow place. That, I believe, is where we will find Thornoak. And we've got to hurry. Sunset is nearly ended."

Jogging past the trees and monuments, Aradis, Girion and Langwana came to the small doorway she had spoken of. It led into a dark passageway some thirty feet long. Beyond it, there was a great hall with a high ceiling, which was just barely visible in the light of the purple pachacuri lamps, which were encased in mounted iron sconces. The walls of the place were covered with tombs, all inscribed with bizarre symbols.

No sooner had the party entered the hall than they felt an absolute dread fall upon them. There was terrible darkness here, that of some heinous and awful presence. They froze in their tracks, not daring to go on. After several moments, Langwana whispered, her voice quavering, "They've come for us. They have come to avenge our trespass. Behold, the machaswa."

The lads' breath caught in their throats, and a ghastly chill seized them, as they caught sight of the beings of which she had spoken. At the far end of the hall, hovering just above the floor, there were hazy specters having the appearance of decrepit, sallow Ingans, shrouded in dark robes. They were very much like the statues they had seen in the third courtyard; they had the same twisted faces, the same malevolent teeth, the same hollow eyes. Their malformed hands were eagerly outstretched toward the Baradic intruders, and their faces glowed with a nauseating light.

"It cannot be!" Girion gasped, nearly choking on the words. "This cannot be. We must be imagining them." But this prospect became increasingly difficult to maintain, for as the specters floated closer and closer, they began to moan with unearthly anguish.

"We must face them!" Langwana asserted, though her voice still shook. "We cannot be deterred now. We're so close."

As the princess stared at the spirits, she seemed to be struck by a sudden, bracing realization. "We have always been taught that the machaswa are worthy creatures, though frightening to mortal eyes, for they are beings of the Haedra," she whispered, her rhythm swift and anxious, as if her thoughts were tumbling out in a turbulent cascade. "And frightening they are. But I cannot believe that these particular machaswa before us are either worthy or decent in any regard, for if they were, they would not attempt to thwart our passage, for our cause is higher and nobler than the taboo these things are here to uphold. Hence, we have both the right and the duty to banish them, so that we may proceed," she finished decisively.

Now, with incredible resolve, she began walking across the hall, shouting at the spirits, "You cannot hinder us, foul machaswa! These Menfolk have been sent in fulfillment of the Sign of the Sengara. They have come hither through great trials and terrors. Death has hunted them but found them not, for Palquanoga's vow to the Wennatoga cannot be thwarted. You dare not harm those upon whom the favor and protection of the Sky Lord is bestowed. Now, in the name of Palquanoga, he who alone dwells beyond the grasp of time, I command you to return to the darkness. Be gone, wretched wraiths!"

The apparitions screamed at her, and as they did so, their mouths seemed to grow larger and larger. The hall echoed with their ghastly shrieks, and the dull, violet light of the pachacuri lamps was swallowed up by a voracious darkness, so that only the lurid, luminous bodies of the machaswa could be seen. Then, all of a sudden, a cold wind swept through the room. The phantoms' wailing went on in a massive crescendo, but as the wind struck them, they were carried off into the walls and vanished. Their screams faded into nothingness, the darkness lifted and the threesome now stood alone in the subtle, lilac glow of the pachacuri lamps.

"What just happened?" Aradis asked breathlessly.

"I know not, save that the machaswa have fled," Langwana replied, turning to look at the Siloans, "but we haven't a moment to lose. It may be too late already."

Dashing onward, she led the Menfolk through the other two hallways, which, just like the first, were lined with tombs. After the third hallway, the spiral passage began. It was quite broad and had small windows on the left-hand side that looked out over the hollow into which it was descending. Each time the passage ran all the way around the rim of the hollow, it got a little narrower and its loop tighter, as if it were drawing in toward the center of the hollow like a whirlpool, fortunately making it faster to go all the way around on each successive run.

As they were running down the passage, they heard a strange, low, mumbling voice echoing up from below. It was speaking in Asla'gu, it seemed, and chanting in a steady, slow rhythm.

"That's my father!" Langwana abruptly whispered. "He's chanting a poem, a very old poem about a warrior named Pennosqua who slew himself after a battle, having failed to protect those he was charged with. The warrior kills himself at the end of the poem, and my father will undoubtedly do the same. Come on! We must hurry!"

Now they ran faster and faster down the passageway, and the footfalls of the three Barada resounded on the ancient stone. By now, the sunlight was very dim indeed, and what little light there was almost didn't reach the sides or bottom of the hollow. The chanting voice went on, growing louder as they descended. The lads' hearts raced madly in their chests, as they listened to the dark incantation.

Suddenly, they came to the bottom of the passage, and Langwana ran into the hollow, which was open to the darkling sky and covered with many compact layers of decaying, wet leaves. The air was exceedingly heavy here, and there was a sense of tremendous antiquity. Around the open area, there was a tall arcade, supported by alternating arches and stout pillars.

To the east, across the hollow, there was a carven throne of gray stone with a crude stone altar in front of it. On the throne, there sat an Ingan who looked as if he were almost a corpse, so pale was his withered visage, which was shrouded in the shadows that lay just beyond the reach of the final beams of Marda's Farewell. His weariness was practically tangible. His bark-skin was wrinkled and leathery, and his eyes were nearly shut. With his back bent and arms sagging, he looked almost as if he had fused to the throne from sitting there too long. The Ingan's moss-hair and eyebrows were silver, with hints of green in places, and his long, stringy hair fell below his shoulders, looking as if it hadn't been combed or washed in ages. He was wearing a long, black robe featuring various abstract geometric patterns sewn in blue thread. Upon his brow sat a crown of hard, black wood; it had four protuberances, one on each side of his head, and a jewel was set in each of these: one emerald, one yellow topaz, one ruby and one sapphire. The topaz was over his brow. All around the band of the crown, there were little, sparkling diamonds. This crown, it seemed, was all that remained of the splendor and glory that had once been the mighty Thornoak, Konaskwa of Argonis.

Thornoak had a dagger in his feeble hand, the hilt of which was made of the same black wood as his crown. The blade itself had been carved from a sharp piece of pale, white bone. Still muttering the poem, Thornoak began to raise the dagger and hold it in front of his chest, ready to pierce his bosom the moment he completed his chanting.

Langwana suddenly rushed forward and shouted, "Kaskeku sahekwanaita!"

Thornoak immediately ceased his incantation and looked up at Langwana, who was standing at the western edge of the hollow. His face was colored by a sudden, menacing rage, as he yelled, "Tashaknawe'et ashaskako. Megwenasu taquanu genacha."

The Siloans, of course, had no idea what was being said, but they could tell that this exchange was exceedingly hostile and that Langwana was about to break down into tears.

"Ar-ghan-is keta'olgahacha. Paga 'olgahacha," the princess pleaded.

"Paga Ar-ghan-is osnawe'et," Thornoak bellowed, rising from his throne. Then, seized with what seemed almost to be a desperate madness, he shouted, "Maslanasu bana toga ketasindase malesaku kosa pagasaku, chanu hakwa!"

"No!" Langwana cried, bursting into tears.

Just then, Thornoak noticed the two Menfolk standing in the shadows. Glaring at his daughter, he roared, "Langwana, not only have you broken the ashaska like a senseless heathen, you have brought these two Eskagwan Menfolk into our holy place!"

"Father, you must listen to me!" Langwana cried. "I did not violate the ashaska on a whim nor did these Menfolk. You were going to take your life, and there was no other way to stop you. And, just as I told you that Argonis needs you, Argonis needs these Menfolk. They have come from across the sea, halfway across Orona, to deliver this kingdom, risking their lives many times over to do so. At least hear us out!"

"There is nothing to be heard," Thornoak growled. "You have trampled upon the honor of your ancestors. I wonder greatly that the teskagwe did not choke them to death and that the machaswa did not strike both you and them dead."

"And rightly should you wonder," Langwana returned hotly. "We survived because of the grace of the Sacred Quinary, and that alone should be an indication to you that our cause is not ignoble."

"Bah," Thornoak spat. "Disdaining our ancestors and our traditions could never be viewed as anything but ignoble." Then, drawing up to his full height and strength, in such a manner as it became hard to fathom that he had looked so impotent and frail only moments ago, he addressed the Menfolk. "Who are you? Why have you trespassed here?" he yelled.

Aradis and Girion swallowed hard, but remained where they were, terrified of the mad Ingan monarch.

"Speak!" Thornoak shouted angrily, and his voice echoed throughout the hollow and up into the approaching twilight.

There was silence for a few more moments. Then Aradis felt a strange spark within him, and he stepped forward into the hollow. Looking directly into the eyes of the Ingan lord, he declared, in as bold a fashion as he could muster, "I am Aradis Kingblade, and my companion is Girion Ringmark. We are peasants from the Kingdom of Velaris in eastern Quarana, and we have come here to help save your kingdom."

"They brought the other half of the Amulet of the Akwarna," Langwana explained. "The prophecy of Janura has come to pass – they have fulfilled the Sign of the Sengara." The princess looked at Aradis, then prompted him, "Come on, Aradis. Show him the pieces of the medallion."

Aradis nodded, reached into his pocket and pulled out the two precious fragments. The piece he had borne was still fastened to its thin chain, but the other was attached to nothing; it was simply a fragment, the edges of which fit perfectly with Aradis' half. The lad stepped forward and held them in the miniscule amount of light that reached the bottom of the hollow.

Thornoak regarded these artifacts with an expression that was hard to decipher but most akin to a mixture of bewilderment and skepticism.

"Come closer," the king beckoned.

Aradis reluctantly obeyed, taking slow, careful steps across the damp leaves. He stopped when he could feel the Ingan lord's heavy, pungent breath on his face. Now he could see quite clearly every wrinkle of the king's furrowed brow and the silent energy of his intent, gray eyes.

"Who are you?" Thornoak quietly asked.

"Aradis Kingblade," the lad repeated.

"Why have you come all the way here to Argonis? Who sent you?" Thornoak pressed.

"We were sent by the Danna, he who was called Telyon by the Menfolk of old," Aradis replied, with great conviction.

Thornoak suddenly got a queer look on his face, and murmured, "Telyon. Yes, Telyon. The Danna. Palquanoga." Then, turning his back to the lad, he declared, "I know of this Telyon you speak of. He is not pleased with my people, nor with me. This I know. And it is right for him to be angry. Especially after what I've done."

Whirling about to face Aradis again, he revealed, "In my efforts to combat evil, I myself became evil. To battle Daegar, I delved in Daegar, and I have paid the price for it. And a terrible price it was. My people, too, have paid a terrible price, in part because of my foolishness in the last few years but also for their own accumulated folly over the ages, for they have forgotten what they once knew. They once knew the truth, but they became enslaved to empty traditions and myths. Though remnants of the light remain, they are clouded. We have forsaken the Danna, and thus he is right to turn against us. Your efforts to help Argonis, whatever they may have been, are laudable, but pointless. The Danna cannot help us now, for he is obliged to let our doom overtake us."

"Who are you to say what the Danna will or will not do?" Aradis retorted. "We received a message directly from him, a commission to deliver this land from ruin and destruction. And if you summon the Verdinnion, that will be the first step in bringing about that deliverance. Let the kingdom reunite and then exert its full strength against the Witch. Girion and I are ready and willing to journey all the way to Blackbough Woods to vanquish her, for that, too, is part of our quest. And there is, as you see before you, a sign that we are speaking the truth – this medallion, which has so long been broken. Now the two halves are brought back together, and the amulet can be remade."

After this address, Thornoak's face almost seemed to shed its melancholy and desperation. Then, like a flash, his visage darkened and he shouted, "Folly! This is all folly! Do you not see it? It is too late. The darkness is not coming to swallow us up; it already has. The kingdom is fractured beyond repair. All that remains are petty factions and rancor, contempt and bad blood. Bandits and beasts have claimed all the woodlands, and Anganor is filled with spies, cutthroats and rabble. Blackwings keep watch on us from the west and north, while Dwarves are massed on the south and east. Ravinia will soon find a way around the Greenwall, and then, exulting in her hideous triumph, she will bring the hordes of the Fell Alliance swarming down upon us – Blackwings, Yetis, Dwarves and Druids. Then we will all drown in her terrible, black Deathwash. Yes, the Sannadosh, the Great Adversity, is at hand. All the signs are present and clear. There is no doubt about that, but there is also no deliverance from it. It is over! Argonis is finished, slain, destroyed! Ruin and woe are all that remain! Ruin! Ruin! Ruin! Ruin and *death*."

Now Girion stepped forward into the midst of the hollow and asserted, "You're right, Your Majesty – partly, that is. Many of the things you said were true, but your conclusions are by no means certain. We did not come to offer you a bright future. Time alone can bring forth such a thing, and for us, a bright future can only exist once it has arrived. What we came to offer both you and Argonis is hope. And hope has little value until things are quite dark. In fact, the more the shadows lengthen, the more hope shines through them, and the more precious it becomes. We cannot give you the dawn, only a solitary ray of light. Will you not accept the light that has come to you, meager though it may be in your eyes, as a promise of greater light to come? See, before your very eyes is a sign – a sign, I believe, from the Danna himself."

"What sign? The amulet?" Thornoak scoffed. "Yes, it has returned to us. I'll even admit that you have fulfilled the Sign of the Sengara. But what does that matter to us now? That thing is useless to us while sundered. We need to summon Janura in order to defeat Ravinia, and we cannot do such a thing until the two halves of the medallion are joined together again. In fact, the restoration of the amulet is probably the only thing that would dissuade me from my course of ending my own miserable life." With this, he picked up the dagger, which he had set upon the altar in front of the throne.

"You could fuse the medallion back together with your magic!" Langwana insisted.

"*My* magic!" Thornoak disdainfully rejoined. "The magic that killed your mother? The magic that brought the curse of the Sacred Quinary upon us? I think not. Besides, magic doesn't work the way you think it does. I couldn't make the medallion whole again even if I tried."

"But no one else can do it!" Langwana contended.

"Perhaps not, but neither can I," Thornoak callously replied.

"But you can!" Langwana cried. "It's our only hope."

Thornoak shook his head despairingly at his daughter, as he returned, "Then it is a false hope. We are doomed. That's all there is to be said about the matter."

"These Menfolk have come from the east, from across the sea," Langwana offered desperately. "They are seeking to bring you back to Anganor. Do you not understand what that means? Do you not remember the prophecies of Janura?"

She began frantically, earnestly reciting the last stanza of the rhyme encapsulating Janura's ancient words:

"Fear not, O Children of Argonis! For Palquanoga will verily lift you up.
As the Sannadosh comes crashing down, you will rise bright and free.
The foe will meet a sudden end; look for a hand from across the sea.
As the shadows lengthen in the west and doom comes tumbling down,
Look to the east for this hand to come and bring back the absent crown.
Aye, look to the east for this hand to come and bring back the absent crown."

As Langwana's voice, strained yet bold, was ringing throughout the hollow, Thornoak was growing increasingly stoic. His eyes glazed over, his breath slowed and his skin seemed to take on a pallid hue. The lads wondered if some spell had come over him, either at his own command or that of another, for he looked very strange indeed – almost unnatural, in fact. And the more they reflected on this, the more they became aware that the entirety of the Shrine of the Machaswa was being enshrouded in some dark presence. There didn't seem to be any visible signs of it, but the air felt increasingly heavy all about them, to the point that it was almost smothering.

Having finished the verses, Langwana stared at her father in dismay, realizing that he was completely unmoved by the poem.

"These Menfolk – they're the ones in the prophecy," she insisted, as tears again formed in her eyes. "Do you not see it?"

"We have been abandoned," Thornoak replied in a low, cold, lifeless voice, his lips barely moving. "Argonis is as good as dead, Langwana. Even Palquanoga himself cannot lift us up from this wretched condition. The ancient prophecies have failed. The medallion is broken and cannot be remade, not by my power or that of any other. And without it made whole, there is no future for us."

As he raised the dagger high into the air to plunge into his breast, he said, his voice now colored by a dark fatalism, "Make the proper sacrifices when you return to Iswa Hanahoma."

"No!" Langwana screamed.

"Aradis, do something!" Girion shouted.

Aradis, who was the only one close enough to actually be able to do something before it was too late, had a sudden and desperate urge to press the pieces of the medallion together. He could not ascertain whence this instinct arose, but it was mighty indeed. Crying out, he touched the two halves to each other. Instantly, brilliant rays of green light shot out from the amulet in all directions, and a strong wind rushed through the hollow. Thornoak was swept back into the throne by the wind, and, as he stumbled backward, the dagger fell from his hand and landed on the soft leaves below.

After a few moments, the wind died down and the green light ceased, save for a few traces of peculiar, labyrinthine markings and inscriptions on the amulet itself, which was still lit with a very faint, almost indiscernible, green glow. To everyone's astonishment, Aradis was now holding a perfect, unbroken amulet, a full, emerald, egg-shaped leaf with silver edging. Aradis was perhaps the most astonished of all.

"What did you just do?" Girion asked, incredulous.

"I have no idea," Aradis declared, looking around in bewilderment.

"You've saved my life," Thornoak gasped.

Langwana and the Siloans looked at the heavily breathing monarch and saw that the shadows seemed to have fallen from his countenance. He still looked very old and worn, but there was a keen gladness and nobility in his face now. Indeed, his eyes had brightened, as if he had tasted some delectable honey after many days of famine, and he looked to have shed the accumulated decay of his long exile, even as a snake sloughs off an old skin. Strength and health, which had been long absent, now coursed through his veins once more. Shillelagh McDasher had spoken to the lads of what Thornoak had been like in his glory days, and now they could see that Thornoak returning in a way, before their very eyes. The Konaskwa, who had for years been naught but a mournful ruin, a mere shadow and mockery of what he had once been, had been roused and quickened by a glorious infusion of new life.

Also, though there had been an aura of evil permeating the Shrine of the Machaswa a few moments ago, that was now quite vanished, replaced with a sense of pure serenity. The bizarre, malevolent weight in the air had lifted, and the oppressive darkness that had enveloped the hollow had been rent from top to bottom. The place seemed to no longer be so close or damp, as if it could finally breathe again after being stifled for ages.

Rising slowly from his throne, Thornoak announced, "The kendarill has flown back to us. Light has returned." Smiling at his daughter and the two Menfolk, he said, in a rich, noble voice, "And I must return to Anganor, that the absent crown might be absent no longer."

Langwana looked at the Menfolk, her eyes sparkling, and then smiled back at her father and knew that, indeed, hope had returned to Argonis.

CHAPTER NINE

A Summons from the South

A solemn dusk had now fallen over Paanu Assagwa, and Thornoak and Langwana were speaking to each other softly in Asla'gu. Aradis and Girion, though unable to understand the content of this conversation, felt its almost mystical cadences of reconciliation, delight and renewal wash over them. The Konaskwa embraced his daughter, then strode majestically across the courtyard, his strength growing with each step as he motioned for the Menfolk to follow him.

"Will you return to Anganor with me?" he asked over his shoulder. "Would you be willing to speak to the Verdinnion?"

"You're going to summon the Verdinnion?" Aradis asked, practically dizzy with elation upon hearing the Konaskwa utter these words.

"Indeed," Thornoak returned.

"Of course we'll come back with you," Girion said, likewise delirious with jubilation from what he had just heard.

"Good. Then we must return to the entrance," Thornoak said, as he entered the spiral passage leading up out of the hollow, "for there are many matters about which I must confer with Chelashu, the captain of my personal guard. And Langwana and I must speak of much as well. Indeed, I expect the two of us will have precious little in the way of sleep tonight. However, the two of you may rest until dawn. You will be spending the night in the guards' lodgings just outside Paanu Assagwa. In the morning, I intend to depart for Anganor."

Thornoak continued, "It is my hope that, ere the afternoon has waxed long tomorrow, you will be standing in the Hall of Cascades, the great hall of Strongbranch Citadel. I was informed this morning of some disconcerting affairs in Anganor involving the rebel Quagga, but that insolent upstart shall not hinder my return. Of that you can be certain. And, as soon as we reach the Citadel, I will send messengers to summon the Verdinnion, for it is imperative that its members cooperate in order to formulate and carry out a plan to end the threat of Ravinia once and for all and to keep our kingdom safe in the meanwhile. Four days from now, I hope to host the Verdinnion at the Citadel, for we daren't delay that meeting any longer than is necessary. In the meantime, you will stay there as my guests, and we shall converse at length, Menfolk from across the sea."

"Th-thank you, sire," Aradis stuttered, still held captive by wild amazement at all that had transpired in the last few minutes.

No more was said for a time, as the company wound its way back up to the top of the Shrine of the Machaswa. When the four of them entered the halls with the tombs, the lads were aware of not only the acute absence of evil there, but of a strong presence of solace and benevolence. They found this to be both extraordinary and inexplicable but welcomed this comfort heartily after all they had been through.

Soon, they came to the maze with the teskagwe, and Thornoak assured the lads that the malicious vines would not harm them now, for he would keep them from doing so. He explained that they had, in fact, been trained to remain dormant at the release of a certain scent, and he produced a potent vial with the odor necessary to placate these particular vines.

After making their way through the maze and the series of courtyards, they came at last to the front gates of the sanctum, where Chelashu and the other sentries gawked at them in utter astonishment. There was a great deal of excited discourse in Asla'gu for the next few minutes and a fair amount of enthusiastic gesturing toward the Siloans. Eventually, Thornoak spoke to the Menfolk in Daiga and requested that Aradis impart the medallion to him, as he wished to examine it closely that evening. The lad did so quite readily, though, as he handed it over, he noticed that the mysterious markings on it were still visible, outlined in pale, green light.

"Sire, do you know what all those strange lines are?" Aradis asked, as the Konaskwa placed the amulet's silver chain around his neck and tucked the medallion itself into his robe.

"We shall see," Thornoak replied. "That was one of the things I was planning on investigating this evening. If I do discover what they are, I shall tell you when we have a proper opportunity to discuss them."

The Konaskwa then commanded one of the soldiers, whose name was Sannasok, to take the Siloans to their lodging for the night. Thornoak and Langwana expressed their sincere gratitude to the Menfolk for everything they had done, bid them a good night and then began speaking with Chelashu again. Meanwhile, an Ingan soldier had gathered the lads' packs from their tonquit, and another had gone and gotten the lads' weapons from the spot where they had been stored while they were in Paanu Assagwa.

Sannasok now came up to the Siloans, thanked them for their bold deeds on behalf of Argonis, then began escorting them northward along the walls of the complex. When they came to Paanu Assagwa's northwest corner, he led them toward a large, wooden structure, two stories high, that lay just to the northeast. The Ingan opened a heavy wooden door of the structure, which was guarded by several sentries, and ushered them into a spacious hall with a low fire in a ring of stones. There was a table there laden with grilled fish and game, fresh fruits and berries and bowls of golden tapusa. Sannasok invited them to partake, then left them alone to do so. As he departed, he informed them that their packs and weapons would be placed next to their beds for the night and that he would show them to these right after supper.

After the lads had relieved themselves, they supped, and their hearts were warmed by food and fire. Yet they spoke little, for they felt as if they had been tossed about by many savage waves for ever so long, and now they had washed upon the shore of some kind, tranquil isle. They were safe at last but terribly exhausted.

Just as the lads finished their meal, Sannasok returned and said, "Menfolk, there is someone outside to see you." He waved for them to join him at the door.

Wondering who it could be, they stepped out into the night-blanketed forest and saw, to their great surprise and delight, a familiar figure. It was Fergus the Fearless, looking worn and weary but equally overjoyed to see them.

"Bonnie bless'd be ye lads!" he exclaimed, as Sannasok withdrew.

"Oh, Fergus!" they cried, falling to their knees and grasping his hands.

"I had a-taken it for certain that I'd ne'er see ye again," he laughed, "but here ye are, an' Tornoak an' Langwana livin' too. An' I hear Tornoak's a-goin' back to Anganor tomorrow. An' the medallion ha' been made whole again. I shouldn' wonder now if I shall be gettin' a whole palace full o' jewelcakes for me birt'day! O, happy day this is! But for the lives lost in the battle on

Konassu Road, that is." The giddy Leprechaun's expression fell at this last thought.

"Tell us about the battle," Aradis insisted. "How did you fare?"

"Seventeen o' Paskasha's troops were lost," Fergus sighed. "An' one of our own Questmongers – Redgarth the Ingan. It's been a difficult few days for ol' Fergus O'Brannadon, for I've lost Redgarth an' Mordie, learned o' Landrig's demise an' seen the unmaskin' o' that monster, Gornok. But many o' the bandits fell, an' the rest were driven back an' scattered. An', tanks to Chelashu, a Druid was slain as well, as ye know. The guards ha' taken a gander at his body but found nuttin' o' use in identifyin''im. But it doesn' take a genius to surmise tha' he was one o' Ravinia's lot, an' that's the importan' ting, as she's got one less spy in the kingdom now. Regardless, I've got to look into the matter o' the other Druids, the bear an' the kapaqua, when a wee bit o' time comes me way."

"Oh, an' what else is there to tell ye? Ah, o' course. Paskasha an' his troops, bein' the best-trained garrison o' southern Mentasqua, are a-stayin' here to help guard ye, the princess an' the Konaskwa but also to escort ye to Strongbranch on the morrow. Yet now, me an' the Questies are headed back to Anganor." He motioned to a number of dark figures standing under the trees about twenty yards off. The silhouette of Chula, which was instantly recognizable, was doing odd toe-touching exercises.

"I spoke of matters wit Tornoak an' Langwana just a few minutes ago, an' the Konaskwa wants us to find out what's afoot wit tha' pesky Quagga," Fergus went on. "No word o' happenin's in Anganor ha' come to us today, on accoun' o' the city bein' shut up as 'tis. At the very least, we'll be a-needin' to make sure Tornoak an' the rest o' ye can get into the city when ye arrive. But we'll also need to use a secret route to get up pas' the Sentinels' Strand an' go alert Hoarstaff to all that's transpired out here down sout. Now, if tings are really bad – an' I mean if an' only if they're *really* bad – me an' the Questies may need to go after Quagga an' the rest o' the ringleaders o' this mischief ourselves, an' Hoarstaff will mos' likely have to send out some troops from Strongbranch as well, e'en though Tornoak's a-comin' back to the city tomorrow. Whate'er the case may be, though, there'll be quite a lot for this ol' Leprechaun to see to an' that on naught but a mite o' sleep."

The Questkeeper shook his head wearily, then laughed, "Ah, but tomorrow shall be a jolly day – a day I've awaited many a year. For Tornoak shall be a-comin' back to Anganor. Oh, an' I canna wait to see Tornoak put Quagga in his place! Ten tousan' rumbadinnies to one I'll give ye tha' Quagga blusters an' blatherskites right up to the end, e'en to the Konaskwa his-self, but, when it comes to it, he won' have the gumption to back it all up. Then he'll be shown to be the little heap o' pigeon-hearted triptrap he really is."

"I won't take you up on that," Girion chuckled, "first, because I haven't got any rumbadinnies to spare, and secondly, because I think you're exactly right."

"O' course I am," Fergus proudly proclaimed. "I'm the Questkeeper. It's me job to be right more often than not. Well, I better be a-goin', an' ye best be a-slumberin'. Savin' a kingdom in't exacl'y a stroll tru the afternoon market."

"You're right about that too." Aradis smiled.

"Off to bed wit ye!" Fergus called, as he went over to join the waiting Questmongers.

"Good night and a safe journey to you," the Siloans called in return.

Sannasok now returned to the lads out of the darkness and took them back into the lodge, then up broad, wooden steps to the second story. He showed them to a room on the north side of the building and there bid them lie upon two long, low beds next to a window, through which a cool evening breeze was blowing and soft summer starlight was shining.

"You needn't worry about anything tonight," he assured them. "There are several hundred of Thornoak's finest soldiers nearby, and they won't let any harm come to you here. Someone will personally come wake you ere dawn, so you can prepare for your ride to Strongbranch. Sleep well, Menfolk from across the sea."

As soon as Sannasok left the room, the lads threw themselves onto the beds and pulled the barkcloth covers tight around themselves.

They had been lying there for only a few moments when Girion quietly asked, "So what actually happened back there with the medallion? Do you really have no idea?"

"I haven't a clue," Aradis declared, as he stared up at the dark, timbered ceiling.

"I didn't know you had it in you," Girion laughed softly.

"Neither did I," Aradis said. "But don't go thinking I had anything to do with it. I think if anyone had stuck the pieces of the medallion together right then, the same thing would have happened."

A few moments passed, and Girion replied, "Perhaps. But you were the one holding them, and I rather think it was meant to be that way. But don't worry; it's not as if I think you've turned into a magician or something."

"Good, because I haven't."

"That's a relief," Girion returned, burrowing farther under the covers. "I wouldn't be sure what to make of a magic-wielding Aradis."

"I wouldn't want to be anywhere near him," Aradis said. "To be perfectly honest, magic rather frightens me – even if it's good magic."

"I know precisely what you mean. It's as if, by its very nature, it's bound to make the Barada uncomfortable. Thankfully, our encounters with it have been rather limited in number."

"Indeed."

The lads lay there in silence for a bit, and then Girion asked, "Aradis, did you notice?"

"Notice what?"

"We're in beds, Aradis. *Real* beds. Beds that were actually made for Barada that are reasonably our size. Where was the last place we slept in proper beds?"

"Siloa, I reckon," Aradis replied. "I'm not counting the berths on the *Meridot* and the *Blue Moon* because a proper bed shouldn't roll back and forth while you sleep."

"Agreed," Girion concurred.

After that, the companions lay there, pondering all that had befallen them that day. However, their thoughts soon faded into a haze, and they slipped into an unbroken slumber.

When the night was just beginning to be colored by the approach of Marda the next morning, an Ingan soldier, who introduced himself as Senniquet, entered the room where Aradis and Girion were sleeping and called to them that a breakfast had been prepared for them and that they would be riding for Anganor in around half an hour. The lads rolled out of their beds, grabbed their packs and weapons and went back down to the room where they had taken supper the previous evening. The table was spread with piles of bread fried in oil and topped with herbs, bowls of some kind of steaming, mashed, orangish vegetable and sizzling strips of dark meat.

Aradis and Girion thoroughly enjoyed this repast, though their conversation was again minimal, as they were both still quite overwhelmed by all the momentous events of the past few days. After breakfast, they washed up outside and stretched their limbs, then followed Senniquet back to the entrance of Paanu Assagwa.

There a large company of some one hundred and twenty soldiers was waiting for them. These troops had evidently been summoned from garrisons in the area during the night. At the front of these six score was Paskasha, outfitted in resplendent armor, sitting astride a tonquit. Next to him, though on foot, stood Chelashu, spear in hand. Just behind them were three more tonquit; apparently, an additional mount had been brought some time during the night. Thornoak sat upon one of them, which had creamy, whitish fur and a silver chanfron, a magnificent piece of head armor. The lads did not recognize the beast from the day before and thus deduced it was the new arrival.

The Konaskwa was attired in a gray kilt and a silver-colored tunic, upon the chest of which had been emblazoned the symbol of a verdant shield with a deep-green emblem of Strongbranch in its center. The monarch's crown was upon his head, but it seemed not to weigh him down, as it had the night before. Rather, its bright stones shone like a beacon from his brow in the light of the rising sun. Langwana was on the tonquit next to him, dressed in the flowing yellow dress she had been wearing when the lads first met her. The last tonquit, which had been Girion's steed the previous night, bore no one presently; the Menfolk guessed it would likely serve as their own mount.

Senniquet now beckoned for the lads to come with him toward the riderless tonquit. Just then, he and the Siloans looked down the road to the west and saw a strange Barada approaching the company, striding along with a crude black staff with a green jewel at the top. Senniquet motioned for the Menfolk to stop, as he watched the stranger approach.

The stranger was a moderately aged Ingan, tall and thin, almost unhealthily so, and he was wearing a black loincloth held up by a belt of red, blue and yellow beads with several green stones set in it. Over his shoulders was draped a dark-green cape with a black lining and a silver hem. Strips of dark cloth were wrapped around his legs. His chest was bare, but from his neck there hung a string of long, curved teeth and a medallion of polished green stone that had a square in the middle and four semicircles surrounding it, one curving out in each direction. Set around the sticklike projections upon his head, there was a beaded band with large, green feathers sticking up out of it. The Ingan's face was narrow and had rather sharp features, and it currently wore an expression of tremendous surprise, bordering on bewilderment.

Thornoak was gazing at this Barada with a look that was rather difficult for the lads to interpret; somehow, they gathered that the Konaskwa knew this individual, but they could detect neither animosity nor endearment in his appraisal of him. And yet, there was great intensity, even communication, in the two Ingans' viewing of each other, though neither of them had spoken a word or made a gesture.

The stranger walked forward until he stood about twenty feet from Thornoak's tonquit. The Konaskwa lifted his right hand, and then the stranger went down on one knee, bowed his head, and said, "Masku, Tagwan, Hanidosha, Yaggawat."

"Pessanagwa," Thornoak replied, after an awkward delay of several seconds. A moment later, he lowered his hand.

The Ingan put his hands together and lifted them up, then brought them back down. Then he raised his head and stood, and the Konaskwa said, "You look rather astonished, Noggaset. Perhaps you did not expect to find me departing from Paanu Assagwa?"

"Yes, although I ought to have expected precisely that," the Ingan replied.

"Is that so?" Thornoak queried. "Have you come from Hadoga Taquenassa?"

"Indeed, I have," Noggaset answered.

"And what would lead you to believe I would be departing from the sanctum? I sent you no word to that effect."

Noggaset regarded the Konaskwa somewhat nervously for a few moments, uncertain of his current disposition, then returned, "Tannemoc and Mannetoc sent me here to give you a message and bid you come to them at Hadoga Taquenassa. They insisted that you would not only have emerged from the sanctum but that you would be returning to Anganor as well. I did not believe them, as usual, but they were so adamant about the matter that I consented to come. And I only agreed to deliver their message to you if I found you engaging in the course they had predicted. It seems that condition has been met."

Thornoak now sat, swaying ever so slightly in his saddle, seemingly muted by this news.

"They came to me shortly after sunset," Noggaset continued, "and said that the Sign of the Sengara had been fulfilled and that the shadow over you had lifted. They also said that you had seen a vision the night before last, which they referred to as the Fivefold Vision, as it had five segments."

Rather abruptly, Thornoak asked, "And what were they?"

"They said you would ask that," Noggaset said. "They were scenes of these things: the Gates of Iron, the Altar of Dust, the Brooding Marshlands, the Fiery Fortress and the Flowering Mound."

As soon as Noggaset uttered the first of these descriptions, Thornoak's face was visibly seized by shock and amazement, which became more pronounced with each additional scene that Noggaset named. The Konaskwa breathed heavily but said nothing. He only stared at the Ingan before him, wrestling with what he had just heard.

"Father, is this true?" Langwana asked, as she looked concernedly at Thornoak. "Did you have such a vision?

"Yes," Thornoak answered reluctantly, the word finally escaping his throat, which had become rather dry. "It is the reason why I decided to … why I decided on the course that I did, which you and the Menfolk only narrowly averted."

"The Menfolk?" Noggaset said, amazed. "So, is that, too, as Tannemoc and Mannetoc said? Were two Menfolk truly the ones who brought the Sign of the Sengara to pass? Where are they?"

"We're right here," Aradis called, stepping out from behind Senniquet.

Noggaset peered at him, blinking, and shook his head in disbelief. Then, turning back to address the Konaskwa, he declared, "You know how I feel about Tannemoc and her sister, but I cannot deny that their words have been fulfilled to the letter. Thus, most esteemed Konaskwa, I request on their behalf that you and the Menfolk return with me to Hadoga Taquenassa to speak with them. There, they will unfold to you the meaning of your vision and deliver their oracle to the Menfolk, for they have a message for them as well."

Aradis and Girion both felt a strange shudder run through them upon hearing this announcement. They wondered what these sisters would have to say to them and whether they could even trust such a message. Also, the conversation from the previous night came rushing back to them, and they feared they would soon be embroiled in an encounter with magic again.

"Did they say what their message to us was about?" Aradis called out impulsively.

"No," Noggaset answered, still regarding the Menfolk with a certain sense of incredulity. "They only stated that it was extremely important."

"Who did the sisters say all these messages came from?" Thornoak asked. "Palquanoga?"

"You surmise correctly, sire," Noggaset returned. "And you know how I feel about that as well."

"Of course," Thornoak sighed. Then, after deliberating for a few moments, he said, "Your naming of each segment of my vision has utterly persuaded me that I must go see them, but I am deeply anxious for Anganor's sake, for a wretched fellow named Quagga has taken control of the city, and his foolish deeds may cost the lives of some of its citizens. How can I in good conscience ride far to the south to ease my troubled mind regarding the Fivefold Vision, while my people may be perishing at the hands of a fool who I could easily and swiftly subdue upon my return to Anganor? Let me go first to set matters aright in Anganor, and then I will return."

"The sisters also foretold that you would speak as you have," Noggaset said, "and they declared that their words to you, in part, are regarding what you must do when you return to Anganor. Thus, you must see them first. Also, they told me to assure you that no lives would be lost in the city before your return on the morrow. Make of that what you will."

Noggaset now stood, patiently regarding the Konaskwa, awaiting his decision.

Thornoak looked at Noggaset, then back at Paanu Assagwa, then north to Anganor and finally up at the bright firmament above.

"I will come with you to Hadoga Taquenassa," Thornoak said at last.

Immediately, there was a great weight lifted from the company, for they had all been drawn into the tension that had been developing since the moment Thornoak and Noggaset had laid eyes on each other. However, Aradis and Girion felt knots tighten in their stomach as they thought again of what the sisters might possibly tell them.

"You must have walked the nearly six leagues from there to here through the night," the Konaskwa said to Noggaset. "Do not be ashamed if your legs will not carry you back. Come, ride upon Hayarwassa."

"How can I accept such an offer?" Noggaset asked quite earnestly. "I am not of such a station that I am worthy to share a tonquit with my Konaskwa."

"Better it would be for you to wonder how you could reject it," Thornoak returned. "Your Konaskwa *demands* that you accept it," he added graciously.

"Then accept it I must." Noggaset bowed his head, approached Thornoak's tonquit and took the Konaskwa's hand that was extended down to him. Then he leapt up on the animal's back and sat behind Thornoak.

Meanwhile, Senniquet had been lashing Aradis and Girion's packs to the sides of their own tonquit. He helped them up onto its back, with Aradis sitting in front and Girion holding onto his comrade's sides. As Senniquet handed the younger Siloan the reins, he said, "Quennashoc is a good mount. Just give him a little tug, and he'll do whatever you need him to."

Aradis urged the creature forward, until it halted next to the tonquit bearing the princess.

Thornoak called to a young, lithe Ingan, whom the Siloans recognized as a Questmonger, and said, "Ashworthy, I want you to run as swiftly as you can back to Anganor and inform Fergus of this change of plans. Since I don't know what the state of Quagga's revolt and of the city has been for an entire day, it's difficult for me to judge how he ought to advise Hoarstaff or what he ought to do himself. Though Tannemoc and Mannetoc have sent word that no lives shall be lost prior to my return, I would still seek to exercise as much wisdom as I may in this matter. Tell Fergus that I would prefer to end the rebellion personally when I return, as I believe I can manage it with no bloodshed or, at least, very little. Thus, if there is any way at all to keep folk from getting more agitated until I reach the city, let him pursue that. If Hoarstaff sends out soldiers, it could only push the pot to boiling, so have him hold out on that course unless it is utterly necessary."

"Also, we will not be returning to Paanu Assagwa this afternoon, as the journey would be too far. I plan to have the company sleep at the Royal Manniog tonight, so if Fergus needs to send me a messenger, have his courier go there. It is my hope that we will arrive at the Quannamet Gate just a little before the Crown of Marda tomorrow. Oh, and of course, you'll need to tell Fergus to contact Hoarstaff and have him move the arrangements for our arrival at the Citadel accordingly."

"I will be off at once," Ashworthy declared, "and if Fergus has any word to send you, I will ensure that I or one of the other Questmongers come to you as soon as we may." As soon as he had finished speaking, he bowed to the Konaskwa and dashed off down the road.

The Konaskwa then called several Ingans in the company to him and spoke with them briefly in Asla'gu. These nodded in assent to what Thornoak was saying and then returned to their former positions.

Now, at last, Thornoak turned to the company behind him and announced, "Let us be off to Hadoga Taquenassa. On the morrow, we shall reclaim Anganor. That much I promise you."

With that, he set his tonquit to trotting westward. The company let out a shout of joy and promptly set out after him, much delighted that the Konaskwa's long exile from Anganor would finally be coming to an end. Paskasha spurred his tonquit on, and it galloped a number of yards in front of Thornoak's, then slowed down to a trot. Chelashu ran up to where Paskasha was and continued walking by his side. The other tonquit followed close behind that of the Konaskwa, and the soldiers on foot embarked at a brisk pace behind them. Several Ingan scouts ran ahead to watch for any ambushes, seeking to avert a repeat of the incident that occurred the previous evening on Konassu Road. However, the prevalent view among the company was that another attack would be unlikely, since there were three times as many soldiers present today, and it was probable that the bandits would have difficulty organizing another ambush so soon, especially one of greater scale and secrecy.

Before they had gone very far, Thornoak greeted the Menfolk and asked them how they had slept, how their meals were and so forth, and they exchanged several pleasantries. He promised that he would try to converse with them more that evening but said that he currently had many things to talk over with Noggaset. The Siloans replied that this was perfectly all right and that they were looking forward to speaking with him more later on.

As the company traveled down the road through the tall timbers of Mentasqua, Aradis and Girion thought of how they had come this way just the night before and with such incredible haste. Of course, they had hardly been able to appreciate the beauty of the forest then, so they were making up for it now, trying to put the potentially unsettling meeting with the oracular sisters out of their minds, at least temporarily, by breathing in the magnificent woodland air and gazing about at the ancient trunks cloaked in thick, green moss.

As for Thornoak and Noggaset, they were riding some distance in front of the lads, conversing in Asla'gu, while Langwana was riding next to them, deep in thought.

After they had traveled about halfway to Konassu Road, Girion whispered to Aradis, "Move over a little closer to the princess. I want to ask her about some things."

Aradis obliged, and, as they drew nearer to her tonquit, Girion said, "Princess Langwana, I was wondering if you could tell us more about this place we're going. What exactly is Hadoga Taquenassa?"

Langwana raised her head, emerging from the realm of intense contemplation in which she had been roaming. "Hadoga Taquenassa is one of the sacred sites of the Honnamec Valley," she said. "The Honnamec has its sources in the Taggawasha Uplands and is the river that runs at the feet of Malinoc Hill, upon which stands Strongbranch Citadel. Of old, my people, the Wennatoga, settled in the Honnamec Valley only a few years after coming to Argonis. More specifically, they dwelt in Kassimaw Forest, which extends south from Anganor to the Taggawasha Uplands in an area bordered by the Honnamec on the west and the Pastures of Seruga and Mannewug's Weald on the east. Thus, all of Argonis' ancient and most revered sites are to be found here in Kassimaw Forest in the Honnamec Valley."

"Anyway, Hadoga Taquenassa is a place some distance to the south of here. The name means 'The Colony of the Oracles.' Technically, it means 'The Colony of the Oracle,' for long, long ago there used to only be one there. Times have changed, but the name has not. Early in the Years of Yore, there was a single oracle who lived alone in the Nachagwa, which is our name for the area of unique rock formations in which Hadoga Taquenassa lies. The chieftains of Argonis would go to that oracle for counsel and advice, and he or she would then speak with Palquanoga to see what he would say about those matters. When the oracle died, another would take his place."

"Then, at some point in the midst of the Years of Yore, the oracle in residence at the Nachagwa took a number of apprentices. These were instructed in the ways of the Haedra, and the oracle issuing their training began to communicate with the other members of the Sacred Quinary: Masku, Tagwan, Hanidosha and Yaggawat. Since that time, there has always been a head oracle, a Chief Taquenassa, and many apprentices. Noggaset is the current Chief Taquenassa, and thus he is over all the rest of the oracles at Hadoga Taquenassa, all of whom must undergo rigorous trials to be allowed to reside in the colony."

"Ah, I see," Girion said. After pondering all this for a few moments, he asked, "So nowadays, do all of the oracles, even the apprentices, usually receive messages from the Sacred Quinary? Or is it only the Chief Taquenassa who receives them?"

"All of them do, but there are certain privileges and responsibilities that belong to the Chief Taquenassa alone," Langwana replied. "Also, most of the time, the oracles don't hear directly from the Sacred Quinary – or see them, for that matter – at least not these days. More often than not, it is the machaswa they consult. Also, they no longer speak to Palquanoga – more correctly, I should say that he does not speak to them. In fact, toward the close of the Years of Yore, the denizens of Hadoga Taquenassa claimed that Palquanoga had become silent and withdrawn, and so they turned increasingly to the other four of the Sacred Quinary and to the machaswa for guidance."

"But didn't Noggaset confirm that it was Palquanoga that these two oracle sisters got their message from?" Aradis asked.

Langwana looked ahead at her father and the Ingan sitting just behind him, then turned to the Menfolk and said in a low voice, "Yes. That is what they claimed, anyway. But there is quite a bit of controversy about these sisters and their communication with the Sky Lord. As a matter of fact, Noggaset bears a great deal of ill will toward them on account of it."

"If you are not at liberty to speak of this matter, then you need tell us no more," Girion assured.

Langwana glanced at the riders in front of her, who were still engaged in vigorous conversation, and then quietly replied, "I will speak more of it, but I would rather that Noggaset not hear us discussing the matter. He will not take kindly to it, I think."

The princess now prefaced her response, "Most of what I am about to tell you I learned from my father, so just know that you will largely be hearing his perspective on things, not my own, unless I state otherwise."

Sighing, she explained, "The two oracles that requested to speak with you and Thornoak are twin sisters named Tannemoc and Mannetoc. Some thirty years ago, they came to Hadoga Taquenassa from the Sassanog Enclave, which is a region to the west of the Honnamec, but east of the Quarinoc, the river that divides Mentasqua from Songalwa, which is western Argonis. They passed all of the initiation rites necessary to enter the company of the oracles, and Noggaset took great personal care in their instruction, for they showed tremendous promise from the very beginning of their training."

"The sisters, it seems, found special favor with the Haedra, for they were in frequent conversation with the machaswa, and they even claimed to have seen and spoken to Masku and Hanidosha themselves. That is a rare thing even among the oracles nowadays, as I said earlier."

Girion, who was rather puzzled at this remark, asked, "Did not you yourself go to seek the counsel of the Sacred Quinary yesterday at Iswa Hanahoma?"

"I did," Langwana replied, "but I am no oracle, and I have never heard their voices or seen them in any form. Rather, when I meditate, I remove all thought from my mind, using a practice called kanapacha, which is dictated by the Taquenar, the sacred body of traditions and practices of my people. Then I wait for sensations to form, and what comes to mind is taken as an answer unto my reaching out to the Sacred Quinary. The oracles, however, actually hear voices and see things, often the machaswa, although, as I said, it is rare for the Sacred Quinary to make themselves visible or audible to them."

"Was last night the first time you had ever seen the machaswa?" Aradis inquired, shuddering as he thought of the foul creatures that had confronted them in the dark halls of Paanu Assagwa. In fact, he was so disturbed by his grim memory of the machaswa that he regretted even asking about them.

"It was, and I hope it shall be the last, though that does not mean that I do not revere them," the princess replied rather curtly. "I just would prefer not to see them again, for reasons I think you can fully relate to." She evidently didn't want to dwell on the matter either.

"Oh, where was I?" she wondered aloud, then resumed her tale. "Ah, yes. But, as I was saying, on account of their remarkable resonance with the Haedra, the sisters rose to prominence in the colony rather quickly, even though they were relatively young. However – and this is something I'm not entirely clear on – for some reason, the sisters began to doubt the soundness of their oracles, as well as the source of them, and they started trying to communicate with Palquanoga. Noggaset frowned upon this, for he considered it unwise to seek after the Sky Lord. After all, it was Palquanoga himself who had ceased communication with the oracles ages ago. Of what account, then, were the Barada, that they should trouble him if he did not wish to be troubled? In any event, twenty years ago – and this I remember quite well or at least remember my father telling me about it at the time – my father was going to appoint a new Ayonashka, a new chief minister, for the old one had died. So, he came to consult the oracles at Hadoga Taquenassa about whom he should select to replace the deceased Ayonashka. His two choices were Hoarstaff and a very bright and well-spoken Ingan named Yennapuc."

"The twin sisters claimed that Palquanoga had told them that my father should choose Hoarstaff and beware of Yennapuc, while every other oracle said that Yennapuc was the better choice and avowed that the machaswa had confirmed this decision. My father took the advice of the vast majority of the oracles and appointed Yennapuc the next day. Three weeks later, Yennapuc tried to poison him, but the plot was discovered and thwarted by one of the servants of the Citadel. Yennapuc was executed shortly thereafter, and Hoarstaff was made Ayonashka. Thus, the recommendation of Tannemoc and Mannetoc was vindicated."

Checking once more on Thornoak and Noggaset to make sure they weren't aware of her discourse, Langwana went on, "After that incident, the sisters became much more vocal about their adherence being solely to Palquanoga, and they openly denounced the rest of the Sacred Quinary, as well as much of the Taquenar. They said the machaswa were fraudulent, evil spirits and that all the rest of the oracles were liars and traitors to the Sky Lord."

"Eventually, Noggaset felt that action had to be taken, for they were creating a great deal of friction among the oracles. He could not expel them from the community, for they had done nothing to explicitly violate the age-old codes that govern the oracles, which were mostly concerning things they would or would not do with regard to diet, behavior toward certain animals and so forth. It may have merely been an oversight on the part of those who crafted these codes to not include verbal denunciations of the machaswa and the Sacred Quinary as forbidden, since they would never have dreamed that an oracle of Hadoga Taquenassa would engage in such blasphemy. At least that is my guess concerning the matter."

"But, in any event, the case was that the sisters had done nothing against the oracular codes. Hence, Noggaset himself would be breaking the codes if he expelled them without just cause. So, he decided to punish them severely and in a way that he thought would put an end to their visions of Palquanoga." The princess paused, and a heaviness fell across her face. Quietly and rather hesitantly, she concluded, "Though it pained him, for he had seen so much potential in them in their earlier years, he had their eyes gouged out."

"That's horrible!" Aradis gasped, his mouth dropping open.

"Shh," the princess whispered, nervously glancing ahead. The Konaskwa and the Chief Taquenassa had not heard Aradis' outburst, thankfully. "Perhaps now you understand why all of this is such a sensitive matter to discuss around Noggaset."

The lads nodded grimly.

Langwana then said, "Noggaset did not, I think, wish to take such an extreme measure as that which he did, but they refused to leave the community, though he strongly urged them to do so. Thus, he had to do something that he thought would deter them from their public decrying of the Taquenar, the machaswa and the four seasonal monarchs of the Sacred Quinary, as well as their insistence on proclaiming messages purported to be from Palquanoga. In addition to putting out their eyes, which was meant to keep them from seeing further visions, he also moved them to the dwelling at the farthest rim of Hadoga Taquenassa. In this manner, he made their ostracization even more apparent."

"Yet their visions continued and even occurred with greater frequency. And their voices were neither softened nor silenced, for they still called out their messages from their place at the edge of the settlement. Consequently, it is not surprising that, since that incident, there has been continuous and concentrated animosity between them and Noggaset, as well as the other oracles."

"Hence, it is all the more startling that Noggaset came all the way to Paanu Assagwa to deliver a message on their behalf. I would imagine that they pressed him so unrelentingly and emphatically about it that he couldn't stand it any longer. Surely they would have come themselves if they were able, but, of course, their blindness would prevent them from doing so. Perhaps Noggaset felt some guilt about that as well. Whatever the case, Tannemoc and Mannetoc have once again been vindicated, it seems. Indeed, Noggaset's naming of the five portions of my father's vision certainly persuaded my father of that. And my father's verification that the portions were accurately named seems to have persuaded Noggaset of the same thing."

"Do you think those two sisters are genuine oracles?" Aradis asked. "That is, do you think they can really see secrets of the present or the future?" He was still feeling rather anxious about himself and Girion having to go and speak with them and was hoping that the princess would answer in the negative, for that would make it much easier to simply disregard the oracles' proclamations, whatever they might be.

Langwana stroked her tonquit's head softly, as she replied, "The Taquenar's teaching about oracles in general is that they can all see such things, at least in part, but some see them better than others, and some understand what they are looking at better than others. Personally, I think it would be hard to deny that Tannemoc and Mannetoc both see and understand such things better than most, if not all of the oracles of Argonis. Yet that troubles me, for they also speak ill of much that I and my people hold dear. But, for that matter, so does my father."

"How is that?" Girion inquired. "What specifically is he opposed to that you uphold?"

"Do you not remember what he said last night in the Shrine of the Machaswa? He said that the Wennatoga had become enslaved to empty traditions and myths. By that, he meant the Taquenar; I am almost certain of it because I cannot think of anything else that he could have been referring to. He has told me before that he has some doubts about it, though I'm not certain whence such skepticism came or how deep it ran. Still, he had never spoken so openly against it as he did last night. In fact, his statements sounded rather like something the twin oracles might say. The most puzzling thing, though, is that my father also said things last night that could be taken as an endorsement of the Taquenar, such as when he accused me of being a heathen and dishonoring our ancestors."

"That is very strange indeed, now that you mention it," Aradis said. "How could he both denounce and defend the same body of beliefs?"

Langwana's face became somewhat drawn. "I don't think any sane person could do such a thing. But I am persuaded that my father wasn't entirely sane last night. I can only hope that his railing against the Taquenar was a product of his madness and that he has now come to his senses. Regardless, I intend to broach the subject with him sooner rather than later in order to find out where his mind truly lies on the matter."

The princess and the Siloans now fell silent for a while. The Menfolk were then left alone with their own doubts about the twin oracles, which had only become more complex and heightened after hearing more of their story. Indeed, there seemed to be such a strange and dubious history surrounding them that both the lads felt a keen apprehension about the whole matter. For, if the oracles were giving deceptive messages, their conversation with them might still serve to conjure a cloud of misgivings over their quest. But, if their messages were truthful, and if they really came from Palquanoga, and if Palquanoga really was the same as Telyon, then that might prove even worse, for their message might be one of doom. And a doom from a true oracle would be an inescapable one. Yet all was so uncertain and unknown, they again pushed the matter from their minds.

A little while later, the company came to Konassu Road and turned left, heading southward toward the Taggawasha Uplands. Two miles farther on, they came to the turnoff to Iswa Hanahoma, but they kept bearing south and slightly west on Konassu Road. When they were not far past the turnoff, the lads noticed that the forest bordering the road hosted many representatives of a particular variety of tree, tall and slender, with long, thin leaves having a slightly golden tint to them.

"What is that type of tree called?" Girion asked the princess, as he pointed to one of them.

"Those are garlens," Langwana answered. "The garlen is ultimately where Argonis gets its name, you know, since they are so prevalent in this land. Ar-ghan-is, which has been put into Daiga as Argonis, means 'Land of the Garlen Grove.'"

"Someone told us that before," Aradis recalled. "Shillelagh perhaps?"

"It was Goldquiver," Girion corrected. "Argonis is sometimes even called Garlenwood, isn't it?" he asked Langwana.

"Yes," she replied, "but folk over in Asquamot – that is, eastern Argonis – are the ones who most frequently use that term. Asla'gu usage is very scarce over that way, giving Barada from that region the impression that Asla'gu is in greater decline than it actually is. But, as a result, they call many places by their Daigan equivalents. For example, the Barada of Asquamot are wont to refer to Anganor as Trunktown."

"Aye, several of the Leprechauns, including Shillelagh, called it that," Girion said.

"In some cases, though, nearly everyone uses the Daigan equivalents nowadays, not just those from Asquamot," Langwana explained. "For example, my father's Asla'gu name is Assartanu, but practically everybody calls him Thornoak, which is what Assartanu means in Daiga. Actually, calling an Ingan by his Daigan name can in many instances be a way to express endearment, especially among those who are not of Ingan stock. Other times the Daigan version simply rolls off the tongue well. Some Ingans don't care a bit which name you call them by, while others are very insistent on being called by their Asla'gu names. The situation simply varies from case to case."

"Very interesting," Girion remarked. "I wish I knew more Asla'gu, so that I could translate the names of various Ingans we've met or heard about. And I'm just curious now – what does your name mean in Daiga, Princess?"

"Radiant Meadow," she answered softly. Then, with a tinge of sorrow, she added, "My mother chose that name."

"It's very fitting," Girion said, both courteously and quite truthfully. He felt bad asking about Langwana's name now, though, as it had stirred up a pang of sadness over her mother's death. Thus, he resolved to change the subject.

The lad admired the garlens about them for a few moments, then remarked, "These trees are really quite magnificent. I wish we had some of them in the forest close to our village in Quarana. Princess, do you know if garlens grow anywhere else besides the Elder Forest?"

"As far as I am aware, they can only be found in this particular region – that is, Argonis and the area immediately surrounding it," she returned.

"And for that reason, we feel a special connection to them. The Taquenar teaches that the souls of trees can sing, though they generally do not do so in words that can be perceived by mortals. Anyway, it is said that the song of the garlens is also the secret song of the Wennatoga, but we can neither hear nor understand it in waking life. Ever it penetrates us, but it is only in death and dreams that we are aware of it. For there we wander in the Shadowed Garlens, where such things as the music of souls can be clearly heard and even seen."

"The Shadowed Garlens?" Girion asked. "And what are those?"

"The other side," Langwana replied succinctly. "The place where spirits stalk."

"Ah," Girion said. The brevity with which Langwana had addressed his inquiry seemed to indicate that she was ill at ease discussing the matter further, at least presently. Girion thought that it might perhaps be because there was a connection between the Shadowed Garlens and the machaswa.

Now looking over his shoulder at the road behind them, which led back toward Iswa Hanahoma, Girion asked, "How much farther do we have until we come to Hadoga Taquenassa?"

"We have about seven miles more on Konassu Road, and then we'll take a road that runs south by southeast roughly four miles into the heart of the Nachagwa, that area of rock formations I told you about. All told, we have a journey of perhaps four and a half hours remaining, as the terrain is more taxing in the Nachagwa. Thus, we will come to our destination during the Dance of Marda."

"What does the word 'Konassu' mean?" Girion asked. "Is that just the name of the road or is there an additional sense to it? And what does the name 'The Nachagwa' signify?"

The princess laughed, then replied, "You are a Barada of many questions, Girion Ringmark. You have an eager mind, I perceive, one that treasures knowledge quite highly. That is commendable."

Girion blushed slightly, and Aradis remarked good-naturedly, "You don't know the half of it, Princess. Girion is like a child at a pastry wagon when he has a source of knowledge before him. And you are certainly that. But, unlike a child at a pastry wagon, Girion shares his pastries with everyone else. On account of the fact that the two of us spend so much time together, I'm a frequent recipient, and often I get more than I bargain for."

"You should cherish Girion's pastries as much as he does," the princess advised. "They will serve you well. My mother taught me something that I remember and hold fast to even to this day. Knowledge is a fountain whose waters are sometimes sweet and often bitter but are always filled with untold riches. For he is rich indeed who draws closer to awareness of that which is. And true knowledge is precisely that – understanding of things as they really are."

"But, to answer your questions, Girion, 'Konassu' is actually rather difficult to translate into Daiga. It refers to something that once was glorious and majestic, but has faded, and yet retains its potency deep down. The nearest thing I can think of is 'memory'. But that doesn't really do it justice at all. Konassu Road is named as it is because long ago, many sites along it, which now are heavy with years, were young, bright and vibrant. Now, like Paanu Assagwa, they are subject to decay and are overgrown and sometimes even forgotten. But that does not mean that their worth or significance has vanished. It is only cloaked and dimmed."

"The Nachagwa are much easier to explain. A rock of peculiar shape is called a 'nachaga,' and 'nachagwa' is the plural of that."

"Thank you, Princess," Girion said. "Your explanations are much appreciated." Of course, he had many more questions going through his head, but he felt it would be imposing upon Langwana to inquire more, even though she had praised his pursuit of knowledge. So, he contented himself with relishing the idyllic woodland scenery of Kassimaw Forest that lay on either side of them.

A mile past the turnoff for Iswa Hanahoma, they passed a road that ran to the southeast. Here a few Ingans separated from the company and went off down this road. The lads realized they were the ones with whom Thornoak had spoken just before they departed from Paanu Assagwa. When Aradis asked where they were going, Langwana informed the Siloans that this smaller road led to the Royal Manniog, where they would be spending the night. She said that the Ingans who had just left were going there to oversee preparations for food and such that evening.

Girion had stilled his inquisitive tendencies for a short while, but he couldn't resist seeking a proper explanation of what a manniog was.

"It is essentially a stockade," the princess responded to his query about the matter, "although oftentimes manniogs are divided into various sections – enclosures within enclosures, if you will, although the Royal Manniog isn't partitioned in that way."

"I suppose Anganor is rather like one huge manniog, then, isn't it?" Girion said.

"It is," Langwana confirmed. "That is certainly where the design for the city came from, anyway. In olden days, many of the Ingans of Argonis dwelt in manniogs for protection, and the population of each manniog often numbered five hundred or more. Inside the manniogs, the Ingans lived in dwellings called gannogets; you will see some of them tonight. They are great, long houses built of saplings, vines and tall grass that traditionally housed around fifteen families, though in some cases they would house as many as twenty-five. The Royal Manniog has been around for ages in one capacity or another, functioning as a home away from home for Konaskwas who were attending to business in Kassimaw Forest. Like Paanu Assagwa, Iswa Hanahoma and Shalkanu Ataqua, the Royal Manniog has a retinue of Ingans that live there permanently to see to upkeep and such and to be ready for the reception of any royalty or dignitaries in the event of either a brief visit or a more extended stay. Those fellows who just left us were simply going to alert the servants at the Royal Manniog of our coming tonight and to supervise such tasks as need to be tended to."

"Ah, I understand now. Thank you." Girion nodded, then fell silent again.

As the morning wore on, the company passed through woods that grew somewhat thicker and wilder, with trees that were taller and stouter, but flanked by all kinds of bushes and vines. Five miles beyond the road that ran to the Royal Manniog, there was another road, this one going to the northwest, and Langwana said that it went to Shalkanu Ataqua, the large enclosure where all of the Konaskwa's tonquit were stabled.

When they had gone just slightly over a mile past this point, they turned onto a dirt path that struck off quite boldly into the forest to the south. A short way into the woods, the path grew narrower and more rutted, but it still bore signs of frequent use. Accordingly, due to the decreased width of the trail, the soldiers had to spread out, but now there were scouts running along both in front and to the sides of the company to compensate for this more exposed arrangement.

After the troop had followed this trail for about a third of an hour, the terrain became somewhat uneven, and large boulders draped in dark-blue lichen could be seen on either side of the path, while the forest became increasingly populated with peculiar varieties of evergreen trees and shrubs, although the majority of the plant life was still deciduous. A little farther on, the path climbed up a hill and then fell into a deep hollow. This pattern continued for some time, but the farther south they went, there were more and more strangely shaped rocks, for they had now ventured into the Nachagwa.

Here, the hollows had old stone pillars, hewn out of local rock and covered with bizarre inscriptions and imagery. Back under the shadows of the trees, there were occasionally little, dome-shaped huts of stone, long abandoned, with dark, yawning entrances half-blocked by dense spider webs. Up on the ridges, there were weathered stone pavements with jagged marks chiseled into individual stones. At the center of some of these pavements, there had been placed large rocks with curious indentations or hollows carved into them. The overwhelming sense of the Nachagwa was of a place both primitive and pristine, wild and seductive, filled with arcane secrets that now perhaps only silent stone could tell. It was a forlorn place but one where ancient memories still whispered in the winds on the hilltops.

Some three miles from Konassu Road, the company descended into a great hollow that broadened to a valley. The path ran onward as the hills on either side of the valley closed in and became considerably steeper. There was a shallow brook not far away to the right of them, winding through the forest, and the sound of trickling water could be heard up ahead of it. Thornoak halted his tonquit, dismounted and then requested that the others do the same. Noggaset, Langwana, Aradis and Girion all leapt down from their tonquit, and nearby soldiers took them by their bridles and led them toward the brook.

The Konaskwa then spoke with Chelashu and Paskasha for several minutes. When they were finished, the two captains went off to give directions to their soldiers, and Thornoak called to another Ingan, a porter it seemed, who handed the Konaskwa two bundles of garments upon his request. Thornoak then beckoned to his daughter, and the two of them went away into the forest for a few minutes. They came back wearing much less splendid attire than that which they had worn on the southward journey that day. Thornoak was dressed in dark-brown breeches of animal hide and a loose, gray linen shirt, while Langwana had donned her barkcloth dress from the previous evening. The duo handed their other clothes, along with Thornoak's crown, to the porter and then walked over to Noggaset and the Siloans.

"You'll need to leave your weapons here," Thornoak instructed the Menfolk. "It is a law among our people that such things are not to be brought into Hadoga Taquenassa by those seeking to receive an oracle. The oracles themselves are all unarmed, and therefore, those who come to them must also be thus."

The lads nodded. They were rather used to this by now, after having had to leave their weapons behind at both Iswa Hanahoma and Paanu Assagwa. Aradis removed his sword and dagger, Girion took his staff and they handed all these to an Ingan attendant who approached them.

"Here we leave the company behind and proceed on foot, for the way is too difficult for tonquit," Thornoak now told the lads. "Keep your footing up ahead, for there is water running over the path we shall take."

Noggaset strode on just in front of Thornoak, Langwana followed her father and Aradis and Girion walked along at the rear. The path meandered up to the end of the valley, where the brook issued from a series of rock shelves over which clear water was flowing. Each was only a bit higher than the one below it. Noggaset stepped into the shallow brook and then onto the first shelf and proceeded to use the shelves as stairs to ascend toward a narrow opening at the southern terminus of the valley. The rest followed.

When the lads stepped into the water, the cool spring splashed and flowed around their boots, and they took care not to slip on the smooth rock. There was watercress growing here at the head of the stream, as well as a long, stringy aquatic plant, waving lazily in the water, and there was luxurious, soft moss draped upon wide, rounded stones sticking up out of the water. Up the shelves the lads went, and, when they had gone up a number of feet, they looked back down into the valley and saw the company from Paanu Assagwa sitting down among the large mushroom-shaped rocks strewn throughout the forest and opening up their provisions to have a bit of lunch.

Noggaset led the group to the very top of the rock shelves, where two high rock faces flanked a narrow opening. When the three Ingans and the two Menfolk passed through this, they stood in what would have been a grotto were it not open to the sky. A waterfall trickled over the south rim of this area, feeding the spring that tumbled over the stone shelves to the north, and a narrow stone staircase led off to the east, then turned sharply south. Noggaset took this staircase up and the others came after him, pressing their hands against the cold stone walls on either side to steady themselves, for the stairs were steep and not entirely level.

The stairs soon emerged at ground level and the company went through a small stretch of forest, with the little stream that fed the waterfall springing down through the woods just to their right. There was another rock face in front of them, and a narrow ravine, only a few feet across, ran straight through it, with nearly vertical walls of stone on either side. Just to the west of the ravine, there was yet another cascade, where water came over the stone lip above and spilled down to the cool stream beneath it.

They entered the ravine and trod on straight for a bit until a staircase appeared on the left, though the ravine itself kept going. After taking this staircase up through the rock, they came out at a path leading steeply up a wooded slope to the south, bordered on either side by large, roughly triangular stones. The party climbed this until it leveled off at a plateau of sorts and then came out from under the shady boughs of the forest to stand gazing upon a most remarkable sight, for they had reached Hadoga Taquenassa.

CHAPTER TEN

The Twin Oracles
of Hadoga Taquenassa

here before the party were a number of large rock formations, variously shaped like beehives, mushrooms or other odd, lumpish masses. Smoke came out of openings in the tops of many of these, and there were doorways cut into quite a few of them. Also, Ingans in garb rather akin to that of Noggaset, though having less flair and distinction, were wandering around the area, tending to fires set in circles of stones or passing in and out of their rock dwellings. In open areas among these peculiar lodgings, there were what looked to be stone altars and tall, carved wooden posts with prominent notches in them. There were also trees growing here and there among the rock houses of Hadoga Taquenassa, and crude statues rested underneath the foliage of several of them. Above all this sprawled a clear summer sky.

"Welcome to Hadoga Taquenassa, the Colony of the Oracles," Noggaset ceremoniously addressed the Menfolk. Then, turning to Thornoak, he inquired, "Now, sire, will you and your companions take some refreshment before you go to speak with the sisters?"

"We will," the monarch returned, looking about at the oracles attending to their business.

"Splendid. Follow me, please. You can eat outside my quonniot."

Noggaset took them to the rock dwelling, evidently referred to as a quonniot, that was nearest to where they were standing and bade them sit on smooth stones that served as seats by the fire that was burning away just outside of it. He entered the dwelling and emerged shortly thereafter with a number of clay bowls and spoons fashioned from bone that he passed out to each of them. Then he went over to a neighboring quonniot and spoke with several Ingans standing there. As they talked, the Ingans turned and looked at Thornoak, Langwana and the Menfolk with great amazement. Thornoak's presence seemed to especially astonish them. After a minute or so of further conversation with Noggaset, they hurried off and came back not long afterward with a kettle of stew, which they then portioned out in the clay bowls to the Konaskwa, his daughter and the two Menfolk.

"This is tokenowga stew, along with boiled chulekot and kandahoga," Noggaset told them.

Aradis and Girion gave him puzzled looks, so he explained, "The tokenowga is a wild game bird of the Taggawasha Uplands, and chulekot and kandahoga are a native root and vegetable, respectively."

Addressing Thornoak, Noggaset then inquired, "Sire, who will be going to see Tannemoc and Mannetoc first? You or the Menfolk?"

"I will see them first," Thornoak quietly replied. His mood had grown definitively pensive and melancholy.

"Very well," Noggaset returned, bowing his head.

For the next few minutes, the foursome simply ate their stew in silence, while Noggaset occupied himself within his dwelling. When Thornoak finished, Noggaset returned, and then he and the Konaskwa spoke for a minute in Asla'gu. Thornoak said something to Langwana, also in Asla'gu, and then he and Noggaset walked off to the south through the village.

"What was that all about?" Aradis asked. "That is, if you don't mind my asking, Princess," he added, after noticing a rather disapproving look from Girion.

"Oh, my father was just telling Noggaset that he wanted to go in to speak with the sisters alone. Noggaset, of course, said he would comply, even though he doesn't trust them. Then my father said he thought their messages were genuine, for how else could they have known about his vision or revealed what they did about him and you Menfolk? Noggaset responded that they must have learned such things from some great power, though he suspected it was an evil one, since they speak out against much of the Taquenar. My father agreed that the source of their knowledge must be a great power indeed, but not necessarily an evil one, then said that he wished to speak with the sisters immediately."

Girion tapped his spoon absentmindedly on his bowl, as he remarked, "With regard to these twin oracles, I see quite clearly what you were talking about earlier today, Princess. Indeed, there's really a lot of strife stemming from varying opinions about them. I just don't know what to make of it, and, honestly, I'm a little leery about going to talk with them." This was, in fact, a considerable understatement, for Girion was really quite concerned at this point, since it would be his and Aradis' turn to go speak with the oracles as soon as Thornoak got back.

"Yes, there is a great deal of contention about them," Langwana concurred. "At least if you go see them yourselves, you can come to your own conclusions. I only hope that their messages to my father and you are ones of encouragement. Even with all that happened last night, we still need a good deal more of that."

The princess set her bowl and spoon down, then got up and abruptly walked off into the forest.

"She probably just wants to be alone," Girion said, as Aradis stared worriedly at the departing Langwana. "There's a lot for her to think about, you know. There's a lot for all of us to think about, really."

"Oh, there's a tremendous amount," Aradis agreed, "though I'll tell you what, Girion. I'd really like to head back down those stairs and get out of here right now, sure as rain, as Fergus would say. I have an absolutely awful feeling about going to see those oracles. I'm actually quite spooked, to tell you the truth."

"So am I," Girion admitted, somewhat abashedly. "When I said I was leery about going to see them, I wasn't quite putting the full extent of my anxiety out there. Frankly, I just didn't want the princess to know how jittery I really am about this whole thing."

"That's quite understandable," Aradis replied. "But you needn't feel too ashamed about it, at least not when compared to me, for I would imagine that I'm far more uneasy about it than you are."

"Perhaps," Girion said.

"I just can't stop thinking about it," Aradis sighed. "There are so many things that are just downright worrisome about it. I mean, how do we know whether to trust these sisters or not? And, supposing we can trust them, what if they tell us something terrible? I know that lots of people say they'd like to know the future – I'm sure I've said things to that effect before – but here we are, perhaps about to find out something about the future, and I'd just rather not know. If it's good, that'll be wonderful. But if it's not, I'd just as soon let it hit us when it comes. The way I see it, knowing something bad is going to happen and not being able to do anything about it is far worse than the bad thing just happening."

"I agree with you on all points," Girion said. "And I've already admitted that I'm terribly nervous about the matter, but we wouldn't be doing ourselves or Argonis much of a service by scuttling off like a couple of scared rabbits just because we didn't want to have a conversation with two blind Ingan maidens."

"You say that now ..." Aradis retorted.

"Let's just try not to think about it until we have to go see them," Girion counseled. "Obviously, while we're there, we'll have to think about it. If it's a pleasant message, so much the better. But even if it's a bad one, it will be over soon enough. It's like a splinter. If you dig and pull it out, it hurts like mad, but then it's gone, and you're the better for it. That's the way it is with oracles, I think."

For what seemed like an excruciatingly nerve-wracking forever and a half, but was really only an hour, Aradis and Girion sat there on the rocks outside of Noggaset's quonniot. They alternated between their own internal reflections and sparse conversations about their adventures up to this point, which were a definitive attempt to keep them from thinking about the matter at hand. At last, Noggaset came walking back through the village and approached them.

"Where's Thornoak?" Aradis asked. "Is he still with the sisters?"

"No," Noggaset replied. "He finished his business with them and is walking about in the forest now, not far off. He is close enough that he can see the village, anyway. He said he wanted to be alone for a while but that you could go ahead and speak with the sisters. He will likely return when you have completed your conversation with them."

"Lead the way, then," Girion said, standing, though he wanted very badly to have stayed sitting and just politely informed Noggaset that he and Aradis had jointly decided they weren't going to go see the sisters after all.

"Very well. Come with me," Noggaset said.

Aradis looked anxiously at Girion, then he also rose, and they walked off to the south after Noggaset.

Noggaset took the lads through the heart of the village, winding through various quonniots and fire rings, and every single oracle they passed stared at them, astonished.

"There evidently haven't been any Mannish visitors to this village for quite some time," Aradis mumbled to his fellow Siloan. "They're looking at us as if we had six eyes or something."

"To my knowledge, no Manfellow has ever set foot in Hadoga Taquenassa until today," Noggaset declared. "There's no taboo against it; there's just never been any reason for Menfolk to come here."

Aradis' face reddened, as he was somewhat embarrassed that Noggaset had overhead his comment. Then, wanting to divert the Chief Taquenassa's thoughts elsewhere, he inquired, "Did Thornoak tell you of our tale?"

"We spoke of it," Noggaset replied, "although he said that there is much of it that he does not yet know himself. However, I gathered that you are rather remarkable lads, Menfolk from across the sea."

None of the three said anything after this until they reached the quonniot of the twin oracles, which was a beehive-shaped rock at the very southern edge of the village, next to a rim where the plateau fell off into thick forests below. There was a marvelous view of the Nachagwa here. Looking out, the lads could see other, similar plateaus of gray stone, decorated with picturesque, but bizarre collections of rocks, rising out of the green woodlands. Only a few miles beyond the Nachagwa, the more regular rise and fall of the Taggawasha Uplands began, marching off toward the southern border of Argonis.

Aradis thought to himself that it was a wonderful panorama from up here and pitied the sisters that they could not see it whenever they stepped outside their quonniot.

The sisters' dwelling itself had a stark, rectangular opening cut into it, and there was a low fire that had nearly burned out altogether smoldering inside. To the Siloans, that opening was a doorway into doom.

"This is the quonniot of Tannemoc and Mannetoc," Noggaset announced. "When you enter, let them address you first. Then you may speak to them at will. Also, it is customary to kneel while you receive the words of an oracle and to not depart until he or she dismisses you. You may ask questions, but if they refuse to answer, do not press the matter. I will be waiting over yonder." He motioned toward the center of the village.

As Noggaset walked away, Aradis and Girion looked at each other, took deep breaths, then stepped into the darkened dwelling of the twin oracles.

As their eyes adjusted to the gloom, they saw two long-haired Ingan figures in rags kneeling on the far side of the quonniot. They couldn't make much of any of their features, though, for the dwelling was quite dark. However, the lads did note that there were two beds in the quonniot, one off to each side, and a number of earthenware vessels next to them, as well as a few piles of garments and blankets. Other than these things, the dwelling was, it seemed, completely barren. There was a hole cut into the ceiling as an outlet for smoke, but, due to the sun's position in the sky, little light fell to the floor of the quonniot from there, and not much came in through the open doorway either. The depth of the darkness wouldn't make any difference to the sisters anyhow, the lads thought to themselves, for it was always night for them.

"Fearful are your footfalls, Aradis, son of Darion, and Girion, son of Dugamar," came a soft, female voice from one of the figures, the one on their left. "I am Tannemoc, and this is my sister Mannetoc."

"How … how did you know our fathers' names?" Aradis stammered, as a shiver ran down his back.

"We are oracles of Palquanoga, are we not?" a voice came from the figure on their right.

"Yes, about that … " Girion said, but he was promptly cut off by the oracle on their left.

"Come, sit," she urged. "Don't be afraid. Not of us, anyway. We are but two blind Ingan maidens. What harm can we do to you?"

Girion's similar words by Noggaset's quonniot around an hour ago suddenly came back to the lads, as did Aradis' response. Still, Girion struggled to reconcile his current fears with the soundness of his prior remark, and Aradis felt more ill at ease than he had been even a few moments ago. Nevertheless, the lads forced themselves to kneel on the rock floor in like manner to the oracles they were facing.

Gulping, Aradis said, "It's not the two of you that we're afraid of, so to speak. And by that, I mean no offense. In truth, we are concerned about whatever it is that you have to say to us. Before you give your oracle, will you at least tell us whether it's good or bad?"

"Good or bad?" Tannemoc, the maiden to their left, repeated the words curiously. "Oughtn't you first inquire whether it is true or false?"

"Well, yes," Girion returned. "We do inquire that, then. How can we know that the words you will be speaking are true?"

"What would convince you that they are?" Mannetoc asked, probingly. There could only be heard the soft hissing of the coals in the fire, as the Siloans sat, pondering this question.

"Would an incursion of the Haedra win you over? A show of magical power?" Tannemoc pressed. "Would that do the trick? If so, then you might be easily led astray, for the Haedra has beings both good and evil. Within it dwell both liars and speakers of truth."

"Why are you here?" Mannetoc suddenly inquired.

"At Hadoga Taquenassa?" Aradis asked, feeling terribly bewildered by all these questions.

"No, in Argonis," Mannetoc said. "You are from the village of Siloa in the Kingdom of Velaris, Menfolk from across the sea. Why did you leave that village to come to this place so far from home?"

Aradis and Girion turned toward each other in the darkness, struggling to find words, and then Girion said, "We both spoke to a Hadathi, who commanded us in the name of Telyon to come here and save this land. Aradis was the one who was actually given the quest, though, and I was offered the opportunity to come along if I wished, that I might provide aid to him in his journey."

"How do you know you really saw a Hadathi?" Tannemoc asked.

"Because we ... " Aradis began, then halted, thinking. "Because we weren't the only ones that saw him. Girion's parents saw him, and my father had met him before. Besides, he was in the tavern in Siloa where everyone could see him. So, we didn't just imagine him. Also, he showed me his true form. That's when I really knew he was a Hadathi."

"Cannot the minds of the Barada play them for fools?" Mannetoc inquired. "Don't people see strange things that aren't really there?"

"Yes, but that doesn't mean that people don't also see strange things that are really there," Girion returned.

"Still, that doesn't mean that they do," Tannemoc declared.

Aradis, who was getting rather frustrated, heatedly replied, "Well, people who see strange things that aren't really there don't get objects from those so-called strange things like I did, they don't get very specific information that turns out exactly as the so-called strange things said it would and they don't fulfill five-thousand-year-old prophecies by turning up in a kingdom halfway across the world at exactly the right time just because the so-called strange things sent them on a quest there."

"That was put quite well, Manfellow," Mannetoc stated, with great satisfaction.

"Is that all of your questions? Are you going to give us your oracle now?" Aradis asked impatiently.

"No, not yet," Mannetoc succinctly returned.

"Was this Hadathi good or evil?" Tannemoc asked, as soon as her sister finished speaking.

"Good," Girion asserted.

"How do you know?" Mannetoc countered.

Again, the lads labored to think of a reply to this. At last, Aradis answered, "I asked the Hadathi the same question, and he said that the good Hadathi – I don't remember what they're called – anyway, they all follow Telyon."

"Yes, Telyon," Tannemoc repeated the name eagerly. "He is the hinge upon which all of this turns. Who is Telyon? And how does one know? And how does one know if a Hadathi is an emissary of Telyon or not? For evil Hadathi could certainly claim they were his servants even if it were not so. And how do you know if Telyon is really good, after all? Have you pondered these things?"

"Of course we have," Girion affirmed. "But I do not know if we could answer those questions to your satisfaction. We simply don't know enough about Telyon or the Haedra or Hadathi in general to be able to give a full account of how we know what we know."

"*Yet*," Mannetoc added. "You cannot perhaps give such an account *yet*. But that will come in time."

"What do you mean by that?" Aradis demanded. "And why are you so interested in Telyon anyway? We were told that you were oracles of

Palquanoga. Are Telyon and Palquanoga one and the same? If not, then who is Palquanoga?"

"As for what I meant when I said you would be able to give an account of how you know what you know in time, that is quite self-explanatory," Mannetoc said. "You currently cannot answer the questions my sister gave you, but there will come a day when you will be able to answer them. That may not seem to be much consolation to you now, but all things must come at their appointed time. Sometimes patience is not merely a virtue – it is a necessity."

"And we are interested in Telyon because he is the only dawn for the Barada," Tannemoc explained. "All else is night. We have both embraced the night before and know the utter futility of that. Never shall we return to it."

"And, as for your questions about Palquanoga, it is very important that you understand something about Telyon before we answer them," Mannetoc declared. "Telyon is the name of the Danna as he truly he is, not as he is sometimes falsely perceived. But Telyon is an ancient name and one of the old Mannish tongue. Yet Telyon is known by Barada all over the world, and yet they do not all call him Telyon, for not all know the old Mannish name."

"Do not misunderstand us," Tannemoc cautioned. "One cannot affirm that a person knows Telyon merely because he seeks after one by that name. If he knows Telyon as he truly is – well, then he knows him; that much is plain. But if he has fashioned some other version of Telyon in his mind, a false one, then he does not really know him, even if he should call him by that name."

"Also," Mannetoc continued, "if one knows Telyon as he truly he is, but calls him by another name, it may not be said that he does not know him. The tongues of the Barada are many and varied, but where you find one who knows Telyon as he truly he is, then such a person knows him, even if he knows not the name of Telyon. All over Orona, there are peoples who once had clear knowledge and memory of Telyon's works of old, but these have become wrapped ever more in mist and forgetfulness as the ages have passed. In some instances, the loss has been more grievous than others."

"But, to answer your original question," Tannemoc said, "Telyon and Palquanoga are, in a sense, one and the same; that is, Telyon is identical with Palquanoga as he was originally known to our people, the Wennatoga, long, long ago. Since then, their perception of him has been altered somewhat, but a sizeable kernel of truth still remains. Nevertheless, you must always employ discernment toward anyone or anything that is claimed to have a connection to Palquanoga, for that name can be put to ill or errant use just as the name of Telyon can."

The lads sat silently, trying to grasp all that the oracles had said, until Girion finally asked, "If the Wennatoga once knew Telyon as he truly is, but some of that knowledge has been lost or tainted, then how did you come to know him?"

"Ah," Tannemoc exclaimed. "We were hoping one of your minds would come to that inquiry. For, if our account of our acquaintance with Palquanoga is sound to you, then you will better be able to trust that our message from Palquanoga is genuine. That is to say, if you know that we really do know Telyon, then you will also know that our words to you should be heeded."

"Draw the curtain," Mannetoc suddenly instructed.

"Which … what curtain?" Aradis asked, trying to make one out in the dimness of the hut.

"The one by the door," Tannemoc said. "What we are about to tell and show you must be made as clear as possible for your eyes and ears. Of course, we cannot see the room anyhow, but the darkness will help you to see as we do. Also, when sight is dim, Barada often pay better heed to that which enters their ears. We know this quite well from personal experience, for more acutely have we heard since our eyes left us."

Hesitantly, Aradis got up and fumbled around by the door, finding a heavy canvas that was bunched back behind a series of hooks. He pulled up the drape, then let it fall over the doorway. Now they were in near blackness, and their eyes fell upon the mysterious, red glow of the embers in the fire. Aradis returned to Girion's side and knelt down.

"Watch carefully, Menfolk from across the sea," Tannemoc directed.

From the dying fire before them, there arose a few, pale wisps of smoke, a ghostly gray against the hazy black behind them. All of a sudden, these coalesced to form a shimmering image of sorts, which was instantly recognizable as Hadoga Taquenassa. The lads gasped and felt their palms begin to sweat.

"What you see will not hurt you," Mannetoc assured. "It is for your instruction. Yes, it is magic. Magic, if enacted through wicked Hadathi or by what wicked Barada would consider to be their own power, is always of an evil nature. It is Daegar. But magic that is an act originating in Telyon or those who serve him is pure and undefiled. So, fear not. The image is not of our making, but of his."

Tannemoc now related, "When we were only fifty-eight years of age, which is rather young by Ingan standards, we came to this place to embark upon the path of becoming oracles. Noggaset, the one who brought you here, saw skill and eagerness in us that he said was unparalleled, so he taught us many things that other apprentices would have to wait much longer to learn."

The shimmering image now shifted to show the two sisters sitting in their quonniot, as they were now, but their hair was elaborately braided and their eyes were bright. They were leaning over a fire with their hands upraised.

Mannetoc now spoke. "We learned the songs of the machaswa, and we would call to them, and they to us. They took us deeper and deeper into the Haedra and showed us many dark treasures of knowledge and power."

The phantom image now morphed into a mass of swirling red and black forms like serpents intertwining and slithering over each other.

"Doors were opened that should have been left closed," Tannemoc lamented. "We saw and heard things which no living Barada should meddle with. And, in our foolishness, we sought to know the Naqua Senkawa, the Masters of the Seasons: Masku, Tagwan, Hanidosha and Yaggawat."

Now the smoke fractured into thin figures of these four, which the lads recognized from their statues in the pavilions at Iswa Hanahoma.

"Yes, they are real," Mannetoc asserted. "Of that be assured. In the semblances you see before you, they showed themselves to the Wennatoga of old, and this persuaded them to revere them. But these forms you see are only guises. Their real forms are utterly hideous. We have seen them, at least those of Masku and Hanidosha. In truth, the Naqua Senkawa are dark, deceptive creatures. They are Kalathar; that is, wayward Hadathi."

The shapes of the Naqua Senkawa dissolved and were replaced by dark creatures ringed in fire, each with many arms and eyes.

"In much of the Taquenar, the Wennatoga are mistaken," Tannemoc said mournfully. "They imagine that images wrought by their own hands of various materials of Orona may, in fact, aid them in their time of need. That is folly. But there is an error of thought which claims that because this is so, there is nothing of consequence happening when the Wennatoga fall in awe before these likenesses or present offerings to them. Nothing could be further from the truth."

Mannetoc explained, "When the Wennatoga venerate these things of stone and wood, the Kalathar are in attendance, eagerly receiving this veneration, and if a Barada feels the Haedra acutely, he will be aware of their presence."

Aradis suddenly had a realization. Abruptly, he blurted out, "When we were in the pavilions in Iswa Hanahoma, looking at the statues there, I was certain I felt a malevolent presence nearby. Was that the Kalathar, then?"

"I do not doubt it," Tannemoc returned. "For they often linger near the engines of their deceit."

"We were once deceived, just as many of the Wennatoga still are," Mannetoc said, "for we thought that the mere presence and power of beings of the Haedra was sufficient to warrant our allegiance to them. We talked to scores of machaswa, all of whom originally claimed to be ancestors of our people, but we soon learned that the forms in which they showed themselves were merely a ruse, as was their claim to be deceased Ingans. They demanded that we portray them as the spirits of the dead to those who came to consult us but informed us that they were nothing of the sort. Rather, they were mighty beings native to the Haedra who, if we wished to retain our own powers, we were obliged to serve and venerate. In revealing this, they did not think that we would betray that knowledge, for they thought we were wholly and utterly given over to them and that this fuller revelation would only serve to seal our bondage even further. You see, the machaswa, too, are nothing but Kalathar, wayward Hadathi." The ghostly image now showed the horrific, disconcerting forms of machaswa transforming into images still more horrific and more disconcerting: bloated, bestial things with glowing tongues and eyes.

"It is when we realized this that we sought desperately for some source of true light in the Haedra," Tannemoc narrated, and the smoke presented a picture of the white Pavilion of the Ages in Iswa Hanahoma. "In the

Taquenar, there was always something distinct about Palquanoga. There was a particular otherness to him that could not be found in anything else. So, we sought as much knowledge about him as we could get."

"Otherness, yes," Aradis whispered, almost inaudibly, as he recalled that it was the exact word he had used to describe the feeling he had experienced in the Pavilion of the Ages the previous day.

Now the smoke molded into the pillar inside the pavilion with its mysterious flame at its apex.

"We had been told that he had withdrawn from the affairs of Orona," Mannetoc related, "but we sought further and discovered much about the legends of the Sannadosh, the prophesied time of terrible trial, as well as the omen of deliverance from it, the Sign of the Sengara, which seemed to be an indication that Palquanoga had not fully separated himself from the doings of Orona after all. We inquired first of Noggaset and of the other oracles and then spoke to every authority in the Taquenar that we could about the matter, including the chalgunas – that is, the shamans – at Strongbranch Citadel and several scholars in the Taquenarium, the great repository of lore in the very roots of Strongbranch. One of these scholars in particular was conversant with Wennatogan legends of incredible antiquity, some of which had been inscribed on timeworn monuments during the Years of Yore at a site some thirteen miles to the southwest of here, at the very sources of the Honnamec. The place is called the Standing Stones of Kennemec Ridge, where it is said that our first fathers, those who first set foot in this great land we call Argonis, carved true tales with their own hands. For thousands of years, this startling testament to our own history has remained graven on stark, jagged fingers of rock on a windswept ridge at the edge of the Taggawasha Uplands, and yet we have drifted ever farther from the truths to which they bear witness."

Blurring for an instant, the image refocused as the scene the oracle had just described. Set against a pale sky, tall rounded stones stood upon a grassy hillside.

Mannetoc paused to reflect on this sorrowful state of affairs she had outlined, then went on, "In any event, at the roots of the Citadel, we learned one of the oldest teachings of the Taquenar about Palquanoga, one which was written on those stone monuments of which I spoke. It is this: Palquanoga is never very far from any of the Barada, and if one reaches out for him, he will assuredly find him. When we learned this, hope was again kindled in us. Perhaps there was a way out of enslavement to the machaswa after all, we thought. So, we sought night after night to call to Palquanoga and to defy the machaswa, although we were but their pawns and prisoners."

Tannemoc continued excitedly, "At last, our cries were answered, for he spoke to us late one night in the stillness of our quonniot. We asked how we might know it was truly him, for we had learned quite well that there are many deceptive beings in the Haedra. He told us that Thornoak would soon come to seek counsel at Hadoga Taquenassa, and the advice he would give us to impart to Thornoak would contradict that of all the other oracles, who were receiving their counsel from the machaswa. Yet Palquanoga's word would prove true and that of all the others false, and by this, we might know that he was the source of true light."

Girion, recognizing that the sisters must be referring to the event Langwana had related to them earlier that day, remarked, "The princess told us of an incident in which you advised Thornoak to appoint Hoarstaff as Ayonashka, and all the rest of the oracles told him to appoint someone else. Was that the affair in which Palquanoga's message to you was vindicated?"

"It is," Mannetoc responded. "After that, we trusted wholeheartedly in Palquanoga and turned completely away from our dealings with the Kalathar, much to their burning rage and fury. We spoke against the twisted portions of the Taquenar, of which there are many, and advised those who came to us seeking guidance to abandon practices encouraging enslavement to the Kalathar. These were things such as yasachama, which is the lighting of many candles as a plea to garner some particular favor from the machaswa. Another such harmful practice is chasakara, the pouring out of bowls of tapusa as a demonstration of one's devotion to the machaswa. But worse than either of these is kanapacha, a so-called emptying of the mind that is intended to make room for messages from the Haedra. It is regularly practiced by many of the Wennatoga, unfortunately. In their assumption of how kanapacha works, they are actually quite correct. When they remove all thought, they create a void which is filled quite eagerly by the subtle whispers of beings of the Haedra. Much to their woe, it does not occur to them that only evil beings work with that emptiness; Palquanoga and his emissaries do not ultimately seek to bypass rational thought but, rather, to strengthen and purify it. That does not mean that they never employ the Touch of the Haedra, which is in many ways incomprehensible to the Barada, but that their final objective and their customary operations involve interaction with the rational nature of the Barada."

"But our opposition to the corrupted components of the Taquenar did not stop with the counsel we gave to our patrons," Mannetoc continued. "We actually condemned quite publicly Noggaset and the other oracles' insistence on consulting beings that many of them knew to be deceivers even from their own interactions with them. That ended up costing us our eyes," she sighed.

"The princess told us of that affair as well," Aradis said morosely. "We're so sorry you had to bear that fate."

"It was a cost well worth paying," Tannemoc boldly asserted, "for though Orona is now hidden from our sight, the truth of the Haedra is not. And still we receive visions, though we could not tell you how, except to say that it is by the power of Palquanoga. And that is the same power that has enabled you to do what you have done."

The vapors over the fire now showed the sundered Amulet of the Akwarna joining together and brilliant green light springing forth from the medallion, as it was made whole.

"You, Aradis Kingblade," Tannemoc said quite pointedly, turning her face to the lad, though of course she could not see him, "have fulfilled the Sign of the Sengara, but it was not in any measure by your own strength or power. Telyon is the one who brought you here and the one who enabled you to accomplish what you did."

"And you, Girion Ringmark," Mannetoc said, "have played a great part in enabling Aradis to do what he did. Were it not for your wisdom, your encouragement and your quiet strength, Aradis would have faltered long ago. Yet even this is from Telyon. When you departed from Siloa, the matter was presented to you as one of your own choosing, and it was. You *did* choose to accompany Aradis, but, had you not, the quest would have failed."

Girion shook his head in bewilderment. "But ... but ..."

"The Well of Palquanoga is deep, Manfellow," Mannetoc declared. "Be not troubled if you cannot see the bottom of it. There are none but he who can."

The image above the fire now changed to one of deep, rippling water, then faded. Remarkably, the quonniot then became filled with shimmering, blue light, which danced cryptically on the walls. It looked now as if the whole place were underwater but only illuminated by a few beams of sunlight from far above. The lads stared at the Ingan sisters and saw that their cloth was poor indeed. Their bare hands, arms, legs and feet were all scratched and covered in dirt, bearing visible marks of a life filled with toils and difficulties. Where their eyes once were, there were heavy scars, and the Siloans felt a poignant sting of grief when they saw them. The torment of past tribulations were written upon their faces, which were seemingly indistinguishable from each other, and yet they somehow still looked young and serene, washed clean in the almost indigo glow of the magical light that filled the dwelling.

"However, though we cannot see the bottom of the Well, we shall now gaze into it," Mannetoc proclaimed at length.

"Aye. We shall now give you the oracle for which we summoned you," Tannemoc said, shuffling forward on her knees toward the fire.

Her sister followed suit, and then they both reached out and each took a coal from the fire. They did not cry out nor did their hands seem to be burned whatsoever, though the coals were still glowing.

"Take these," Tannemoc commanded, as the sisters extended their hands toward the Menfolk.

"We cannot," Aradis asserted, drawing back slightly. "We'll be burned."

"Have we been burned by them?" Mannetoc asked.

"No," Girion replied, somewhat reluctantly. "But you're oracles."

"Indeed," Tannemoc agreed. "And if we really are oracles of Palquanoga, then no harm will come to you when you handle them. This is a matter of trust. If you do not trust us in this, then we will not ask you to trust our message to you."

The lads swallowed hard.

"Do you trust us?" Mannetoc pressed. If she had possessed eyes, the Menfolk thought, they would have been piercing them straight through, laying even their souls bare.

The Siloans looked at each other, and their eyes met in the rippling blue half-light of the quonniot. Trembling, they slowly but simultaneously stretched their hands forward, directly under the hands of the oracles.

Smiling at this gesture of faith from the Menfolk, the sisters turned their hands over and dumped the coals into Aradis and Girion's palms. Tannemoc's fell into Aradis', and Mannetoc's fell into Girion's at the exact same instant. The lads cried out in anticipation of pain, but, to their great astonishment, they felt that the glowing coals were cool to the touch.

"He who handles fire will be burned," Tannemoc intoned, "save the Wielder of the First Flame and those under his protection. For he who is master of all things cannot be ruled by any of them. And if you are under his shield, no harm can penetrate it."

"We do not mean to assure you of invincibility, for death and harm are very real dangers," Mannetoc cautioned. "Rather, we mean to prompt you to boldness and to kindle your courage. You will soon come against foes and adversities that will seem to you to be insurmountable and unconquerable. But, just as you hold these tokens of fire in your hands and are yet unscathed, so shall you vanquish these future trials and yet come through alive and well in the end. But you must have the boldness and the courage to confront them. If you cower before the darkness, it will swallow you up. If you march forward into it bearing the light, the darkness itself will be driven back."

Her words were now graphically enacted in the swirling smoke above the fire, in which appeared a terrible gloom rent by a beam of piercing, white light.

"From the beginning, your quest has been aimed at a bitter darkness," Tannemoc asserted, "for you are destined to face Ravinia herself." The smoke flowed into the shape of a monstrous raven that was flapping its fell wings and opening and closing its grisly beak. "And she is far more perilous than hot coals from any fire of Orona, for she herself is a Kalathar."

Both of the Siloans' jaws dropped at once, and they felt their hearts skip a beat.

"Ravinia's a Hadathi?" Aradis exclaimed, his voice quavering. His skin had gone ice cold, and his heart was racing.

"Indeed," Tannemoc returned. "Did not your heart tell you this long ago?"

"Y-yes," Aradis stammered. "But I was afraid to consider that it might really be so."

"How can we assail a Hadathi?" Girion asked, terribly unsettled.

"How can you hold hot coals and not be burned?" Mannetoc asked, directing her eyeless gaze at Girion.

The lads looked down at their hands and marveled yet again that they were not the least bit singed, though the coals glowed as though they had just been plucked from the heart of a great flame.

"Nonetheless, be wary, Menfolk from across the sea," Tannemoc advised. "Ravinia knows of you and has guessed your quest, for she too knows of the ancient prophecies about the Sannadosh. And, even as we speak, she is desperately seeking a means of ensuring that you are slain."

"What we feared has come to pass then," Aradis said solemnly. He shivered as he uttered these words.

Mannetoc responded, "If what you feared is that she might have learned much about you, then yes, that has come to pass. She was alerted to the incident in Gorondil, and she has also received news of you from the Ravenstaff. That was enough for her to deduce a great deal. And now she is determined that the prophecies from the dawn of Argonis should not prevail. These words:

Fear not, O Children of Argonis! For Palquanoga will verily lift you up.
As the Sannadosh comes crashing down, you will rise bright and free.
The foe will meet a sudden end; look for a hand from across the sea."

Now, to the lad's great relief, the image of the raven melted away and they saw the *Meridot*, the ship they had taken to the Fontskals from Velaris, skimming across the surface of an ocean glinting in the light of midday.

"You are the hand from across the sea," Tannemoc declared, pointing at Aradis.

The lad now felt his skin run even colder. He didn't like the idea one bit of being a pawn in a prophecy, as if he had to fulfill it, no matter what. "But what does that mean?" he asked. "There's another line in the poem about the hand from across the sea, one about bringing back the absent crown. I think I understand that part now. It seems to be referring to us getting Thornoak to go back to Anganor. At least that is my guess, anyway. But what does the portion you just recited have to with Ravinia? And why – "

"As the hand from across the sea, your coming is the signal that the foe will meet a sudden end," Mannetoc explained. "That is why Ravinia so adamantly wants you destroyed."

Then, angling her face toward Girion, she said, "But do not think any the less of yourself for not being the primary agent in this matter, Girion Ringmark. Your fate is bound up with Aradis' in this, both for good and for ill. As I already declared, without you, Aradis could not have gotten this far, and without you, the prophecy would not have been fulfilled. But also, Ravinia wants to destroy you for your involvement in this, just as she wants to destroy Aradis."

In response to this, Girion swallowed hard and then sat in silence.

After a few moments, Aradis, feeling nearly all hope and strength drain from his soul, said, "This is much for us to bear. You tell us not to be afraid and then speak of terrible and fearful things. What would you have us do? How can we proceed with such great shadows before us?"

"Have you not just come through deep shadows?" Tannemoc asked. "How did you pass through them?"

"Are you referring to what happened in Paanu Assagwa?" Aradis inquired.

The oracles did not answer. The vision of the *Meridot* above the fire now blurred into a gray haze.

"Well, yes, I suppose that was a pretty perilous business," Aradis mused, deciding on an answer to his own question. "In that instance, we knew what needed to be done. Thornoak had to be rescued, so we just passed each obstacle as it arose. When the guards threatened to kill us at the gates, we simply went forward, although I don't know if we would have done so were it not for the boldness of Princess Langwana. And when we got to that maze of nasty vines, we ran through it as fast as we could. But we wouldn't have made it to the other side had it not been for the princess.

And then there were the machaswa. They tried to stop us, but Langwana cried out against them, and they were swept away. And right when Thornoak was ready to kill himself, I fused the medallion, though I have no idea how." Aradis stopped and scratched his head. "I don't understand how going through all that was supposed to help me figure out how we're going to proceed. It rather seems like we wouldn't have made it very far at all if we didn't have aid. In fact, we'd probably be dead."

"Yes, you came close to death a number of times," Mannetoc confirmed. "And of that you should take heed. You should note that death has earnestly pursued you but has been turned aside again and again. Does that not embolden you to continue?"

"No, it frightens me out of my wits," Aradis returned, somewhat irritably, although with complete candor.

Tannemoc spoke again. "Menfolk from across the sea, there are more powers at work than Ravinia that are trying to thwart your quest. Indeed, it was no happenstance that the machaswa stationed themselves to waylay you just before you reached Thornoak nor was it a confirmation of Ingan superstition or taboos. The machaswa were there to keep you from saving the Konaskwa. And though Princess Langwana seemed to drive them off by her invocation of Palquanoga's name, the matter was not quite so simple, for she knows not Palquanoga as he truly is and thus could not rightly claim him as your defender. Nonetheless, her invocation was heard and aid was given, not due to any power or knowledge in her, but so that the name of Palquanoga might be upheld and his superiority over the machaswa demonstrated. Yes, creatures of the Haedra, both good and evil, have a vested interest in your deeds. Hence, you must recognize that what you see occurring here in Orona is not the full sum of your tale. Surely, Aradis Kingblade, you did not think that you fused the medallion back together by your own power?"

"Of course not," Aradis replied, almost indignantly. "But how was it made whole again?"

"Are there not both good and evil Hadathi?" Mannetoc inquired. "Was it not evident to you that both were at work in the Shrine of the Machaswa?"

The lads, who were already overwhelmed by so much the oracles had told them, found their heads spinning at this revelation.

"Do you mean to say there was some kind of invisible war going on all around us last night?" Girion asked.

"There is such a conflict going on around you now; indeed, the machaswa are not far off from this very hut. The Haedra and our own realm are woven together quite closely, perhaps more so than you would care to think," Tannemoc said. "But fear not, for the good is stronger. So must it always be in the end."

"But what exactly are *we* to do?" Aradis asked, greatly unnerved at the thought that there were machaswa nearby. "If so we're so critical in the unfolding of all this that even the Haedra is practically swirling around us, it would seem that we should have some clearer direction from the Danna about our course. What are we going to do to defeat Ravinia? When you had me explain how we succeeded in our mission in Paanu Assagwa, it became apparent to me that the only reason we did so is that we had help. And we didn't know how we were going to accomplish our task either. That just seemed to fall into place as we went along."

"Have you not spoken to your own inquiry, lad?" Mannetoc said, raising her eyebrows.

"How so?" Aradis returned, perplexed.

"I think I know what you're after," Girion stated slowly, as he studied the oracles' faces. "The reason that we entered Paanu Assagwa in the first place is that we knew *what* it was that we needed to do, and we were determined to do it. But we didn't know *how* to do it. In every single instance, though, that part of it was taken care of, in most cases by Langwana. But almost our entire journey has been like that. We've been trying to do *what* it was that we needed to do, but we haven't known *how* to do it, and yet help has always been provided in one way or another. We've had many come to our aid along the way – Harlin Halehand, Felding Starwash, the Fall-Elves, Shillelagh McDasher and quite a few others."

The oracles smiled.

"So *what* we need to do next, then," Girion continued, unraveling his thoughts, "is see to the summoning of the Verdinnion. Thornoak already intends to do that when we get back to Anganor. And then I suppose we'll need to seek that body's advice on how we may proceed to our greater task of destroying Ravinia. We'll learn *how* that can be done as we go along, and if we need help – and we almost certainly will – we can trust that it will be provided."

"You yourself could be said to be a sage of sorts, Girion Ringmark," Tannemoc remarked, with a wry grin, "for your perception is keen and your insight powerful. What you have given is wise counsel. Now, we are only mouthpieces and cannot speak beyond what we are told, so we cannot give you all of the answers that you seek. Aye, note this well – Telyon can never be forced to give answers, so we must take the messages from him that we have already been given and let them be our guide. Also, we can readily rule out any conflicting messages that come along later, for Telyon does not contradict himself. Happily, in your case, you received a clear course for your quest in a general sense on the very night you set out on your adventure, and that ought never to be in question. You must cling to it unwaveringly."

The oracle continued, "Unfortunately, we cannot tell you *how* to complete your quest, but we can affirm what you already know – that you must, as Girion said, speak to the Verdinnion and then go on to defeat Ravinia. If you had begun this matter of your own accord, it would certainly fall upon you to find the specific means of carrying it out. But you did not begin it, and thus, it is not your duty to contrive on your own the means of completing each stage of your quest. Rather, the manner in which you will contend with each and every difficulty will be revealed to you at the proper time, just as it has been in your journey up to this point."

"But we do have a word of caution for you," Mannetoc abruptly declared.

"And what is that?" Aradis asked.

"Whatever happens, you must not abandon your quest," Tannemoc insisted. "Very soon, it will be proposed that you do exactly that. Do not – and I repeat – do not back down. And be warned – it may well be that the fiercest pleas to forsake your venture and the greatest urges to do so will come not from the outside, but from within."

The oracles were eerily silent for a few moments after these weighty admonitions. Both the lads felt rather disquieted as they considered what Tannemoc had just said, but Aradis felt especially unsettled, for he was certain that, had Tannemoc yet had her eyes, they would have been fixed directly on him, peering into doubts and apprehensions that were hidden even from him.

"Indeed, your quest must be seen through to the end," Mannetoc said at length, "but you must also seek fulfillment of an even greater quest."

"Yea, though Telyon has sent a message directly to each of you," Tannemoc continued, "neither of you yet know him as you ought. He is still largely hidden from you. If you find Telyon, you will find the dawn, as we have. As it is, you are still in the night."

"How can we find him? Where is he?" Aradis asked in great earnest.

The smoky haze over the fire, which had been dormant for a while, now transformed into the image of an ancient forest with old, gnarled, moss-clad trunks and fallen logs. In the middle of this scene stood a great, elongated boulder, also cloaked in moss.

"Is that where Telyon is?" Aradis inquired. "That doesn't look anything like Erdion, at least not what I envisioned it to look like."

"What do you see?" Tannemoc asked. "What is the image before you?"

The lads were quite startled by this inquiry. "Don't you know?" Girion returned.

"No, we're blind," Mannetoc reminded him. "And we're not making the images appear either. That's the doing of Telyon. Many of them we have seen in our minds, but this one is hidden from us."

"There's a forest with a mass of stone in the midst of it," Aradis said, staring at it intently. "The trees are rather close and dark all around it – they're of a kind I don't fully recognize – and there's a bush with berries of a deep, purple hue growing next to the stone. The stone itself is a long, rounded boulder, perhaps twelve or fifteen feet tall. It has a very complex surface, it seems to me, with lots of cracks and folds and so forth, and much of it is covered in dark-green moss."

"That is where you will find the Voice of Telyon," Tannemoc declared. "Speak to the one with the book."

"Is he the voice of Telyon?" Girion inquired.

"In a way, but the Voice you should truly seek is the book itself," Mannetoc asserted.

"This is terribly important. Do not let what you have seen just now slip from your minds," Tannemoc warned, "for you must come to that place not only to find the Voice of Telyon, but also to bring your aim of vanquishing Ravinia to fruition. Remember that. Remember what you have seen."

"What will happen when we arrive there that will help us defeat Ravinia?" Aradis asked, his mind practically exploding with questions now.

"Remember. Remember what you have seen," Mannetoc said, echoing her sister, her voice fading into a whisper. From the tone of her voice, Aradis gathered that no further answer would be given to his query or to any others for that matter.

Both of the sisters now shuffled back toward the far wall of the quonniot, still on their knees, and Tannemoc said, "Now, place your coals back upon the fire."

The lads turned their hands over, and the coals dropped into the dying fire. Immediately, it sprang to life. The image of the great stone in the forest vanished instantly, as did the blue light filling the dwelling. Darkness returned.

"Our oracle is ended," Tannemoc announced. "Go with our good will and with bright courage as your blade."

"Do not turn from your path, and be not afraid to grasp coals that are thrust into your hand. But do not forget to seek the book, for it is only there that you will find the dawn." These words, Mannetoc's parting admonition to them, filled the quonniot with a sense of tremendous solemnity and finality. And, with a potent, yet indescribable sensation, the lads felt that they were engraved deeply in their minds.

The Menfolk gazed for a few moments at the crackling, red fire, took one last look at the twin oracles and then slowly rose and made their way out of the quonniot. They felt as if, during their conversation with the sisters, they had left Orona and entered a world of dreams and strange, writhing mists and fantasies. Now they found themselves awake, yet quite exhausted, at the very edge of Hadoga Taquenassa, with warm, bright sunlight beating down on them just beyond the dwelling's doorway.

CHAPTER ELEVEN

Beyond the Shadowed Garlens

s Aradis and Girion stood there outside the sisters' quonniot, their eyes again growing accustomed to Marda's light, a strange feeling of disquiet came over them. They suddenly noticed that, some forty yards to the north, back toward the center of the village, nearly half a hundred oracles were gathered in a tight cluster. They were standing eerily still and staring sharply, almost ominously, at the lads. Among them, Noggaset was nowhere to be seen, and there was no sign of Thornoak or Langwana either. The Siloans looked uneasily at each other, as they began walking toward the group of oracles, hoping to gain news of their host's whereabouts.

"What's all this about?" Aradis muttered.

"I don't know, but they don't look like they'd do very well in a 'Friendliest Oracles of the Year' contest," Girion returned.

Aradis raised his hand in greeting and called out to them, "Excuse me, but you could tell us where Noggaset's gone off to?"

One of them, who was standing at the front of the group, a tall, brawny Ingan with a metal pin through his nose and four red streaks on his forehead, stepped forward and said, "You have spoken with the sisters. They have given you their oracle. Now we must give you ours." His voice had an uncanny, hollow quality to it.

The lads halted, uncertain of how to react to this statement.

Just then, Noggaset appeared from behind a quonniot, seeking to quickly make his way to the front of the cluster of oracles. "Hold, Kantasosh!" he cried.

The Ingan who had been speaking turned around and retorted, "It is our undeniable duty to deliver this sacred message. You of all people should know and uphold this, Noggaset."

"I do, I do," Noggaset panted. "But give me a chance to speak with the Menfolk before you do."

Kantasosh grunted irritably as Noggaset reached him, and the latter huffed, "Aradis and Girion, I must apologize. I ought to have been here to greet you when you emerged, but I went looking for Thornoak and Langwana. Alas, I haven't found either of them yet."

"No harm done," Girion assured. "We only finished a minute or so ago."

"What Noggaset means to say," Kantasosh cut in, "is that he went looking for Thornoak because he wanted him to command us not to give our oracle. But, of course, he knows that when the machaswa have spoken, we are obligated to impart their message, and that's something even the Konaskwa can't override."

The lads now had a rather strong suspicion about what the sisters were referring to when they said the machaswa were not far off. Apparently, Kantasosh and the other oracles had received a message from them while the Siloans were in the sisters' quonniot.

"Yes, of course I know that," Noggaset snapped, "which is why it's utterly foolish for you to suggest that I went looking for the Konaskwa in order to prevent such an outcome."

"Good. Then we shall give our message without delay," Kantasosh said. "Now, if you would, Menfolk, be so kind as to come with me and enter my quonniot." He motioned to a hut back toward the northern end of the village. "There you must kneel so that you can receive our oracle."

Aradis and Girion looked at each other, filled with misgivings, and stood there for a few moments uncomfortably. Then Aradis declared, "I'm sorry, Mister Kantasosh, but, if it's all the same to you, we'd rather not hear your oracle."

"It is *not* all the same to me," Kantasosh returned rather waspishly. "We are bound by sacred tradition to give you our message. Now, come with me to my quonniot."

Girion looked hard at him and said, "Again, we're very sorry. But I'm afraid we're not going to either enter your quonniot or receive any oracle from you. It may be your sacred tradition, but it isn't ours. And, more importantly, we have some very serious qualms about listening to anything the machaswa have to say."

Kantasosh's eyes flashed. "Your minds have been poisoned by those wretched sisters, haven't they? They and the spirits they consult are nothing but irreverent, self-serving liars. Undoubtedly, they coaxed you into their web of deceit with their sorry tale of how they learned the truth about the machaswa and the Masters of the Seasons, the Naqua Senkawa, claiming that Palquanoga himself demonstrated this powerfully to them. Well, Noggaset put their eyes out for a reason, didn't he? Their minds are blind to the truth of the Taquenar, and thus it is only fitting that their eyes have been blinded as well."

Noggaset, who was growing extremely agitated, objected, "That's not all there is to it, Kantasosh. First of all, I didn't actually put their eyes out. You did."

"But you were the one who gave me that order," Kantasosh shot back. "And anything else you have to say right now is irrelevant. You're just trying to stall until Thornoak returns."

"I really think you ought to reconsider this matter," Noggaset insisted. "I do not doubt that the sisters have told the Menfolk lies, as they peddle their falsehoods to everyone who comes to see them. Nevertheless, what these Menfolk have accomplished in fulfilling the Sign of the Sengara should make us pause before … well, before telling them what the machaswa said. We may need them here yet."

"Says who?" Kantasosh scoffed. "Why would you trust your own feeble hesitations over the clear word of our ancestors?"

Noggaset forcefully replied, "It is not I alone who feel this way. Thornoak told me on the way here that he thinks these Menfolk – well, regardless of what he thinks, it is a fact that they have fulfilled several of Janura's prophecies about the Sannadosh. First of all, they have brought the other half of the Amulet of the Akwarna. And the fair-haired one made the amulet whole again."

Aradis was by no means appreciative of the fierce and instant attention that this statement garnered for him from the gathered oracles. All of them seemed to be scrutinizing him, assessing whether he was the sort of fellow who could even perform such a great deed. Based on their expressions, their analysis seemed to have arrived at rather negative results.

"How do you know that for certain?" Kantasosh brashly demanded of the Chief Taquenassa. "Did you see him do it? Have you seen the Amulet of the Akwarna since it was supposedly made whole again?"

"Yes, I have, actually," Noggaset replied crossly. "Thornoak showed me the amulet this morning on our ride here. But no, I wasn't there when the Manfellow restored it, since he joined the pieces together last night."

"Hm," Kantasosh sniffed. "Well, even with that being the case, there's still no reason to withhold the words of the machaswa from them."

"These Menfolk have done more than merely fulfill the Sign of the Sengara," Noggaset returned, disregarding Kantasosh's last remark. "They also fit the description of the hand from across the sea, the one coming from the east – the hand that will bring back the absent crown. Thornoak in no uncertain terms told me that they are the reason he is ending his exile and returning to Anganor. That's why I think it would be prudent to at least let the Konaskwa hear your oracle before you give it to the Menfolk. He might have some reservations about the matter. And, to be perfectly honest, I myself have several, some of which I have already voiced to you."

Kantasosh laughed dismissively, spat and exclaimed, "That may well be, Noggaset, but this still comes down to you putting the opinions of two Barada – yourself and Thornoak – against the word of the machaswa. That is a contest I think you know better than to engage in. Also, the truth has come out, though you still haven't stated it openly. You really *do* think it would be better if we refrained from giving our oracle altogether, and you really *were* looking for Thornoak in order to let him have his say and convince the Menfolk that they ought not to depart."

"Depart?" Girion pressed. "From where? What is all this about?"

Ignoring the Siloan's inquiries, Noggaset got right up in Kantasosh's face and ranted, "So maybe I was looking for Thornoak to let him counsel us in this. And maybe I don't think we should deliver this particular message of the machaswa. But I am the Chief Taquenassa, after all, and that ought to at least count for something. I do believe the machaswa give us accurate revelations – generally. But you and everyone else standing here know that their messages aren't always interpreted correctly. This may be one of those times. And just because I'm not so close-minded as to exclude that possibility from the outset doesn't mean that – "

"Even if we have misinterpreted their message, we're still obligated to present it," Kantasosh interrupted, gritting his teeth and glaring at Noggaset. "As Chief Taquenassa, you must uphold our traditions. We will not be dissuaded from giving the Menfolk our oracle," he snarled, with dark resolve. "The machaswa have commanded it, and we will obey."

Noggaset stared back at the seething Kantasosh for a good long while. Though the other oracles certainly could have said or done something at this point, they felt as if the affair was firmly in the hands of Noggaset and Kantasosh to decide, and it was not their place to insert themselves into it.

Meanwhile, the Menfolk had an urge to retreat into the sisters' quonniot, though they weren't sure what the sisters could do to help them, and another urge to just leave the village altogether. However, judging from the intense looks on the oracles' faces, it seemed that if the lads pursued either of these courses, every last oracle in the glowering throng would readily chase them down and drag them before Kantasosh to hear his message, even if it had to be practically shoved down their throats.

At last, Aradis' patience expired, and he blurted out, "If you're bound and determined to give us this stupid oracle from the machaswa, then what can we do to stop you, in truth? If you've got something to say to us, the lot of you, then why don't you just go ahead and say it?" He wasn't sure how Girion would feel about this concession, but the way he saw it, there was no way these oracles were going to let the matter rest unless they had their say.

Kantasosh turned his burning stare to the Siloans. The other oracles turned as well, fixing their eyes piercingly on the lads.

Last of all, Noggaset turned to them, his shoulders sinking in defeat. "So be it," he said gravely. "But I will have no part in this affair." With these words, he stepped resignedly to the side of the oracles.

Kantasosh snorted contemptuously at this remark, then loudly addressed the Menfolk. "If you would receive our oracle, then come with me to my quonniot. There we can observe the customary procedure. You and I will kneel and – "

"We *wouldn't* receive it if we had any choice in the matter. But we don't," Girion interrupted sharply. Evidently, he agreed with Aradis' assessment. "It's bad enough that we have to listen to this business at all, but we already told you weren't coming to your quonniot, and we meant it. And, for your information, we're not going to kneel either. So, give your oracle and be done with it. We'll take it standing up – right here and right now."

"Bah," Kantasosh scoffed. Then he proclaimed, "If you insist on being foolish heathens and refusing to receive the oracle in the proper manner, then let your guilt be on your own heads. But here is our message."

"While you were in the sisters' quonniot, the machaswa whispered this great oracle to all of us – all of us except for Noggaset, that is. But I was appointed as the one who would deliver it. Now I will give you the machaswa's esteemed and judicious counsel, so that you and those you care for may be kept from needless harm."

The lads braced themselves for whatever it was the Ingan had to say. They were certain the message was going to be rather dismaying, based on how adamantly Noggaset had fought to keep Kantasosh from presenting it.

Now, speaking in a weird, strained voice that seemed to be coming almost from the air itself, rather than from his throat, Kantasosh began his oracle, intoning, "You have completed your quest, Menfolk from across the sea. You have done what was necessary for you to do. But now, others must see to the end of the matter. Surely, if you go on to face Ravinia, you will die. The choice is yours, but if you seek her out, death will claim you. Do not deceive yourselves by thinking that course can be averted if you journey on to Blackbough Woods."

As Kantasosh was speaking, the Siloans felt a sinister tingling commence in the very atmosphere around them. This highly disturbing sensation crawled all over their skin and made their blood run cold. In addition to this, the lads felt a horrid sensation arising from within; indeed, a great darkness was welling up inside them, for Kantasosh's words had filled them with raw, aggressive fear and anxiety. Although they had strong reasons to believe that the machaswa were impostors and liars, both Kantasosh's message and its delivery were so forceful that they felt their knowledge and resolve inadequate to protect them from its power.

The voice continued in even greater earnest. "Aye, beware! Beware! Your families are in terrible danger, Menfolk from across the sea. But if you return to them now, you can save them. Provision will be made for you to reach them in time. However, if you linger here or foolishly journey westward, they will all die. Every last one of them. You are the only ones who can rescue them. Turn back now, before it's too late. Don't let them suffer – "

"Cease this rubbish!" a mighty voice called out. It was Thornoak. At the sound of his voice, the Siloans' fears hissed a final venomous curse and then dissipated, like steam from water poured on hot stones. Whatever captivating spell or bewitchment the oracle had put upon them, its hold was broken. The ominous tingling in the air vanished, and they felt a sudden warmth and health flow through them. The lads could not help wondering if the battle of unseen powers that the sisters had spoken of had not just nearly broken through into Orona.

The Konaskwa strode toward the cluster of oracles, his face lit with rage. "What is this nonsense?" he demanded. "And exactly when did you decide you can give your oracles in whatever manner you please, Kantasosh?"

All the oracles, including Noggaset and Kantasosh, turned around to face the Konaskwa.

"Answer me, Kantasosh," Thornoak commanded. "Since when do you give your oracles standing up, out in the open? And to those who are not kneeling to receive them? Have you no concern for custom or tradition? Would you spit upon the souls of your fathers?"

"Th-they would not comply with our traditions," stammered Kantasosh, who was furious that his oracle had been interrupted. "They blatantly refused either to come to my quonniot or to kneel. Yet, it was necessary for me to give our oracle, so I did what I had to do."

The Konaskwa stood and stared at Kantasosh, his keen gray eyes boring into him. "So the machaswa gave these words to all of you just a short while ago?" he asked.

"Yes," Kantasosh curtly returned. "We all heard them – all of us except Noggaset – and I was elected to present them to the Menfolk. And, as for your chastising my violations of custom, what right have you to barge in during the delivery of an oracle? Just because you're the Konaskwa doesn't mean – "

"I would have interrupted you even if I weren't the Konaskwa," Thornoak said hotly. "These lads have already done many hard things in seeking to complete their quest. You certainly don't need to make things any more difficult for them than they already are by planting seeds of doubt in their minds."

Turning to Aradis and Girion, he said, "Now, if I were you, I wouldn't accord that preposterous message even the slightest mite of credence. That whole thing was just a pile of drivel and dung, which isn't at all surprising, considering the fact that it had its origin in the machaswa."

Before the lads had a chance to respond, Kantasosh narrowed his eyes and roared, "Drivel and dung? You dare speak ill of the machaswa? And immediately after denouncing me for dishonoring our ancestors, no less?"

"Do you not know what the machaswa are?" Thornoak asked rather savagely, suddenly whirling to face Kantasosh again. "They are unwholesome, murderous, conniving creatures who seek only to unjustly garner our adoration and ensure our ultimate destruction. Anyone who consorts with them is a traitor to the only truth that remains in the Taquenar."

The oracles were all stricken with shock and utter incredulity, but Aradis and Girion couldn't keep from noticing how closely Thornoak's appraisal of the machaswa resonated with that of Tannemoc and Mannetoc.

"Wh-wh-what are you saying?" Kantasosh spluttered. "Have you gone completely mad? Have you no fear to insult our blessed forefathers? You're the Konaskwa. You can't denounce the Taquenar. Why, that's absolutely absurd. Such a thing has never been done."

"Your Majesty, I don't understand how you could say such things," Noggaset protested. "I myself have doubts about the messages of the machaswa, or at least our interpretation of them. And this is only reasonable, since the Taquenar allows for a margin of error in that regard. But that fact does not by any means warrant the diatribe you just spewed. Frankly, I think your railing against the machaswa in this manner is taking things much too far. What has become of your former reverence for the Taquenar? In the past, have you not valiantly defended it before all the heathens who live among us that give it little or no regard?"

"I have, and unwisely so," Thornoak replied.

"This is the doing of those accursed sisters, isn't it?" Kantasosh exclaimed. "They've infected your mind, haven't they?"

Thornoak shook his head. "No, I discovered all this for myself, though others had a hand in preparing me to do so. During those bleak seven years in which I sat all alone in Paanu Assagwa, the Haedra lay heavy upon me, and I suffered the oppression of the machaswa there. I know far more about the machaswa than I would ever care to admit, and I would be ashamed to admit how I learned it. Thus, you shall get no confession of the matter from me here. But I also learned that there is light in the Haedra, and I now know whence it comes."

The Siloans were watching this dispute proceed with almost as much astonishment as the oracles, for they were taken aback by the great fervor, and, in some cases, vehemence, with which Thornoak was addressing the group.

Just then, they noticed that Langwana was walking up behind her father. Her mouth was open in disbelief.

"Father," she called timidly.

The Konaskwa turned around to face her and, with his tone softening considerably, said, "Langwana, I – I would rather you had heard this from me in private."

"But instead, you're declaring your rejection of core elements of the Taquenar in front of one of the most ancient and solemn bodies of its guardians," she returned.

The Konaskwa sighed loudly, then replied, "It was going to come out very soon, anyhow."

"What does all this mean?" Langwana asked, as tears began running down her face. "Have you really abandoned the ancient way of the Wennatoga, your own dear kin?"

Thornoak turned back to face the oracles, who were staring at him with expressions ranging from fury to bewilderment to sorrow.

The Konaskwa straightened up, cleared his throat, and then announced, "I do not deny that I have, in former days, been passionately dedicated to the defense and upholding of the Taquenar. And I still am dedicated in that manner to a portion of it. But I simply cannot adhere to things I know to not be true. I have learned what the machaswa are. They are not our ancestors, as the Taquenar claims. And, as a source of knowledge, they are not to be trusted. The same goes for the Naqua Senkawa – yes, for Masku, Tagwan, Hanidosha and Yaggawat. They are not what the Taquenar would lead us to believe they are."

"Wait just a minute," Kantasosh burst out, sensing that Thornoak was about to continue. "If the machaswa aren't our ancestors, then what do you think becomes of Barada when they depart from Orona?"

"That is another matter for another time," Thornoak said darkly.

Kantasosh was obviously unsatisfied with this response, but a certain edge to the monarch's tone persuaded him that he oughtn't pursue the matter further right now.

"But it is imperative that you not misunderstand me in this. I do not think the Taquenar is errant in all matters," Thornoak assured, returning to the main trajectory of his discourse. "For at its heart and guiding all of its most ancient tenets, there is truth. Though many have forgotten the most sacred and primal beliefs held by the Wennatoga of old, the land of Argonis has not wholly abandoned those memories. They are still written in stone not far from here, on Kennemec Ridge."

The Siloans now perceived that, regardless of whether or not Thornoak had been swayed to his current views by Tannemoc and Mannetoc, his thought certainly aligned with theirs.

"But there are none who can read the Standing Stones there," Noggaset objected. "Their meaning survives in tradition alone, and the interpretations are varied. No one knows for certain what they actually say."

"Not so," Thornoak returned adamantly. "The true, original knowledge of them has been preserved in the Taquenarium at Strongbranch Citadel. There the tale they tell remains undiluted. They speak of the very oldest legends and teachings of our people, such as those involving our journey to the Elder Forest from the northern lands. The Wennatoga did indeed come from the far north, from the Shrine of Sorrows, as the common legends tell, in the years after the Veil of Calamity covered all that once was. And our flight from that place was because of a quarrel with Palquanoga. The Standing Stones and the Taquenar are in agreement on these matters. But, contrary to what the Taquenar teaches in its current manifestation, we have not always venerated the Naqua Senkawa. At first, we only sought after Palquanoga, that we might mend the relations with him that we had marred. In the Standing Stones of Kennemec Ridge, there is no mention of the Naqua Senkawa, no mention of the machaswa nor any admonition to engage in a whole array of practices that are now associated with these beings I have just mentioned. In fact, it is written that true reverence should be presented to Palquanoga alone. Thus, if you would truly honor our ancestors, pay them heed and seek out Palquanoga and no other. Call me a madman and a traitor to the Taquenar if you will, but Kennemec Ridge bears witness that I speak the truth and that you and all the others are in error."

Thornoak now stood, his chest heaving, as he looked penetratingly at each oracle in turn. The air hung heavy over the village, and the lads hardly dared to breathe for fear of defiling the immense weight and solemnity of the near silence. All that could be heard was the distant buzzing of insects in the surrounding forests, a few stray birds calling in the woods beneath the plateau and the crackling of fires strewn throughout Hadoga Taquenassa.

At last, Thornoak spoke once more. "I do not expect you to take my word for these things. I was once as you are and know that I would not have done so. But I urge you to seek the ancient truth. It may be difficult to find, but it is not lost. And there has of late come forth proof that the old tales ring true. The Sannadosh is upon us, just as it was foretold long ago, but the Sign of the Sengara has been fulfilled. The Amulet of the Akwarna has been made whole again, and it is here for all to see."

The Konaskwa produced the amulet from his robe and held it up on its chain, dangling in the sun. It gleamed in Marda's afternoon rays, but there was no outline of symbols in green light, faint or otherwise, to be seen on it now. All stared at the amulet in amazement, even Aradis, Girion and Langwana. Though they had been present when its halves had been joined, there was something undeniably majestic about seeing it held aloft as proof before the oracles that ancient prophecies of the Taquenar had been fulfilled.

Thornoak turned to face the Siloans and said, "And you have these lads to thank for it." All the oracles' eyes now came to rest on them. Even Kantasosh seemed to regard them with some degree of wonder.

"Did I not tell you it was so?" Noggaset said quietly to Kantasosh, who frowned slightly, as he again stared at the amulet.

"You oracles all claim to be believe the old prophecies of the Taquenar," Thornoak resumed his address, "but when you see that they have actually come to pass, you are speechless. But for that I do not fault you much, for I myself long claimed to believe them and was yet astonished when they were fulfilled. Still, we all can rejoice that what was foretold has come to fruition, for that heralds that our deliverance is nigh. Nonetheless, we still must part ways in the matter of the Taquenar's current teachings."

"And lest you think that this amulet lends credence to the whole of the Taquenar," he went on, "I advise you to look into the matter more closely. The prophecy of Janura about this artifact was given early in the Years of Yore, at the time I mentioned when Palquanoga alone was held in reverence and esteem. She was a sengara, one of *his* emissaries, and the prophecy was linked to *his* deliverance of the Wennatoga. This amulet thus vindicates *his* word alone, not that of the machaswa or the Naqua Senkawa. Therefore, I will continue to believe the words of Palquanoga as given to Janura but reject the proclamations of the other beings I mentioned. Aye, for your part, you may listen to the whispers of the machaswa, those who are said to roam the Shadowed Garlens, the vast and gloomy woodlands of the Haedra. And you may hearken to the counsel of the Naqua Senkawa if you wish. Such is your prerogative. But for my own part, I will heed only him who dwells beyond the Shadowed Garlens, holding court atop the Hill of Ten Thousand Streams. Palquanoga alone will I hearken to, and that is my prerogative."

For some time, the oracles did not respond to any of this discourse, for they were still reeling in shock from all that the Konaskwa had said and from seeing the Amulet of the Akwarna in its entirety with their very own eyes.

Finally, Kantasosh seemed to have collected his thoughts or at least reached some conclusions about what Thornoak had said, and, motioning to the Siloans, he asked, "What is to become of these Menfolk, then? If you have determined to scorn the warning of the machaswa to them, what is it that you intend to do with them?"

"They are not mine to do with as I please," Thornoak tersely returned. "They are by no means indebted to me, but I certainly am to them. However, they have agreed to come with me to Anganor and to speak with the Verdinnion there. That, at least, is a start. But they have also expressed a desire to journey to Blackbough Woods to destroy Ravinia. Of course, that is precisely why your counselors among the machaswa specifically tried to frighten them out of doing exactly that – because they knew of their intentions."

"Of course they knew of their intentions," Kantasosh snapped. "And they wouldn't have warned them unless they had a compelling reason to do so."

"I fully agree with you in that regard," Thornoak declared, much to Kantasosh's surprise. "I do believe the machaswa had a compelling reason to give the message they did. It is evident that the machaswa don't want the Menfolk to address the Verdinnion or attempt to assault Ravinia because –" He halted, cleared his throat, then said rather abruptly, "Aradis and Girion, it's time for us to be going."

"The machaswa don't want the Menfolk to do those things because of what?" Kantasosh demanded, glaring at the Konaskwa.

"You should be able to deduce that based on what I've already said," Thornoak replied. "One kapaqua recognizes another, after all."

Kantasosh did not by any means appreciate Thornoak's usage of this very unflattering proverb. His eyes got very narrow indeed, and he hissed, "Just exactly who are you calling kapaquas? Us and the machaswa or what? Us and Ravinia? The machaswa and Ravinia? Are you really suggesting that our benevolent ancestors are allied with that beastly Druidess in some capacity? Are you out of your mind?"

Thornoak did not answer. Instead, he turned, muttered something in Asla'gu to his daughter, then began walking toward the northern end of the village. Langwana followed after him, and Aradis and Girion did so as well, veering around the oracles gathered before them.

"We weren't finished giving our oracle!" Kantasosh shouted after the departing Thornoak, as he malevolently eyed the Siloans.

The Konaskwa did not turn around, but he called back, "As a matter of fact, I believe you were. And if the machaswa have more to tell the Menfolk, they can tell it to them themselves – without your help."

Kantasosh fumed, but neither he nor any of the other oracles made a move to waylay the Menfolk as they passed. Noggaset, however, ran after Thornoak. He eventually caught up to him, slowed down by his side and began speaking to him in Asla'gu.

When Thornoak, Langwana, Noggaset and the Siloans came back to Noggaset's quonniot, they halted, and Thornoak spoke to the Chief Taquenassa for a few minutes, still in Asla'gu. It was, of course, impossible for the lads to decipher specifics of what they were talking about, but their conversation was of an intense and earnest nature. The Menfolk guessed they might be discussing Thornoak's public defamation of the Taquenar. As the two Ingans were speaking, Langwana seemed to be getting more and more irate. Her tear-stained face took on a pronounced scowl, but she did not enter their exchange.

Eventually, the two Ingans ceased their dialogue and stared at each other disappointedly, though with mutual esteem. They seemed to have reached an impasse of sorts. At last, Noggaset bowed his head, then said in Daiga, "Would you like for me to accompany you and your party back down to the valley below, sire?"

"No, that's all right," Thornoak replied. "You've been more than courteous today in so many regards. And despite the things I just said, that does not change the fact that I have great respect for you. We must speak more extensively of these matters soon. I will send word to you to come to Strongbranch after things are resolved there."

"Kanassoka," the Chief Taquenassa declared, bowing his head once more.

"Kanassoka iwe," Thornoak returned, smiling.

"Come," the Konaskwa said, beckoning to the Menfolk, as he started toward the forest to the north.

"Thank you for everything today, sir," Girion said to Noggaset.

"Yes, thank you," Aradis echoed.

The Chief Taquenassa nodded humbly to them, replying, "May every stream be your comrade, every ray of Marda your ally, every tree your companion and every stone your friend, Menfolk from across the sea. Argonis shall ever be in your debt."

"May we soon meet again," Aradis returned, certain he couldn't come up with a farewell of even remotely comparable eloquence. Truthfully, he was somewhat puzzled by the fact that Noggaset had given them such kind parting words, as he and Girion had spoken little with him. The lad surmised that Noggaset's warmth toward them might well be based on things Thornoak had told him about them.

The Siloans and Langwana now trotted quickly after Thornoak into the woods. When they had gone a fair number of paces, Aradis mumbled to Girion, "The sisters said that people would soon try to deter us from our mission. I didn't know it would be this soon."

"Oh, I imagine the opposition has only just begun," Girion replied grimly.

Langwana, who had overheard these remarks, said, loud enough that Thornoak could clearly hear her, "Well, at least the two of you aren't afraid to share things you heard from the sisters." She shot a scathing glance toward her father. The Konaskwa kept marching ahead with no visible reaction. Of course, he couldn't see Langwana, but her voice was more than sufficient to convey her extreme displeasure.

Girion, recognizing that Langwana was hankering to engage in an argument with her father about some matter (or several of them), tried to tactfully change the subject. "Ahem, yes. Now, I was just wondering if anyone here could help me with some Asla'gu. What does 'kanassoka' mean?"

He was expecting Langwana to answer, but it was Thornoak who addressed his query. "It means 'debt,'" he replied quietly.

"And 'kanassoka iwe'?" the lad inquired tentatively.

"No debt,'" Thornoak returned, as he walked onward. "Noggaset was thanking me for arriving when I did. He knew that the oracle from the machaswa was for you to terminate your quest and return home; he didn't want you to hear that and was glad that I cut that message off and publicly spoke against it."

"On our ride down here this morning," he continued, "I told Noggaset such of your adventures, deeds and intentions as I was aware of, many of which I learned from Langwana last night, for she had heard them from Fergus the day before. Noggaset was convinced, as I am, on the basis of some statements in Janura's ancient prophecies, that you might yet have important business here in the Elder Forest. Of course, he has his doubts about aspects surrounding the matter and does not appreciate Tannemoc and Mannetoc's involvement in this affair. Nevertheless, he thought it unwise for Kantasosh to – how can I put it? He thought it unwise for him to dampen your spirits and give you cause to abandon your errand."

"Well, we very much appreciate your stepping in when you did," Girion said. "The things Kantasosh was saying weren't terribly reassuring or inspiring, I must say. I have a feeling they were only going to get worse. We're fortunate you didn't come any later."

"Where were you, anyhow?" Aradis asked, immediately afterward realizing it may have been a slight breach of etiquette to put this question so bluntly to the monarch.

"He was off in the woods on the plateau," Langwana brusquely declared. "I wandered about in the forest until I found him, and then, when I inquired about the message Tannemoc and Mannetoc had given him, he refused to tell me anything about it. Indeed, he wouldn't share a single word of what they'd told him. He insisted that he needed some more time alone, so I left. And then, not long after that, I heard loud voices in the village, so I went to investigate. And what did I come upon? I was privileged to arrive just in time to hear my own father renouncing the very foundations of his thought and life," she finished bitterly.

They had now reached the section of the slope where the path was edged by sizable triangular stones. Thornoak stopped and turned to face his daughter. "Langwana, did I not already tell you that the sisters' message was too heavy of a matter to share with you now?" he asked, with a hint of irritation in his voice. "I can hardly bear it myself. I am not keeping it from you to be unkind, but to protect you until you are in a better frame of mind to receive it. And, as for what happened back there with the oracles, I really didn't have a choice. I had to intervene on the Menfolk's behalf then and there. Also, I already told you that I would rather have revealed to you my current views on the Taquenar in private."

"That may have been your preference, but that wasn't how it turned out, was it?" Langwana crisply returned, as she stopped a few feet from him. The Menfolk halted several yards behind her.

"No, it wasn't," Thornoak replied. "But, as I said, it was going to come out very soon anyhow."

"And what exactly did you mean by that?" Langwana demanded.

"Merely that these things I now know cannot indefinitely remain hidden from the kingdom."

"What?" the princess exclaimed. "You're going to tell the whole of Argonis that you've become some kind of mad heathen?"

"I must," Thornoak answered resolutely, then turned and began walking down the path again. Langwana promptly started out after him. The Menfolk stood there for a few moments, feeling very awkward indeed that they had been present for this dispute, but they figured that Langwana wouldn't have pursued the conversation in the first place, much less in Daiga, if she minded whether they heard it or not.

"Come on," Girion urged, as he sighed and continued down the slope. "Let's get back down to the valley."

Aradis jogged after him, and both quickened their pace until they were not far behind the princess.

Soon the foursome came to the stone steps that led down into the upper ravine. Thornoak descended the stairs and had nearly reached the ravine's floor when Langwana called to him, "So that's simply that? I'm just supposed to accept that you're going to proclaim your wanton heresy and lunacy in front of the entire kingdom?"

Thornoak did not reply until he had gone down several more steps. Then he staunchly answered, "You can choose not to accept it if you wish, but it must come to pass, nonetheless."

"Father, I don't understand what's going on with you," Langwana huffed, as she proceeded down the stairs. "Last night, when we were in the Shrine of the Machaswa, you said several things that lay squarely within support of the Taquenar. But you also said things that were clearly opposed to it, for what else but the Taquenar could you have been referring to when you claimed that our people are enslaved to empty traditions and myths? And only a few minutes ago, you spoke as one who curses nearly all that which the Taquenar enjoins us to hold dear, even going so far as to suggest that the machaswa are in league with Ravinia. That is what you meant by quoting that proverb to Kantasosh, wasn't it? I would just like to know – have you abandoned belief in the Taquenar or not? Does this have something to do with what the sisters told you?"

"I was not in my right mind last night, if you must know," Thornoak sighed, as he reached the bottom of the stairs and turned into the ravine. "Dark visions had haunted me all day yesterday, and I was a desperate, delusional Ingan if ever there was one. The truth is that I have increasingly come to believe over the last few years that much of the Taquenar is erroneous. However, I shared my doubts with hardly anyone, though I, of course, have told you a little about them before, as you may recall. Thus, my rejection of the Taquenar is not ultimately the sisters' doing, and it certainly didn't come about simply because of my conversation with them this afternoon. In fact, I had already concluded it was false before going to see them. I just hadn't made that publicly known."

The Konaskwa now halted in the ravine.

"Last night, I stood at once in two worlds," he murmured, reflecting. "In one sense, I was fettered to the old lies and despaired of ever escaping from the power of the machaswa, even if I knew them for what they truly were. In the other, I had unimpeded sight of what was really true but hadn't the strength nor the hope to hold fast to it. I hope that you will see that I was clearer in thought a few minutes ago, standing in front of all the oracles of Hadoga Taquenassa, than I was yesterday at the dying of Marda, down in the Shrine of the Machaswa, with a dagger ready at hand to plunge into my breast."

Thornoak turned to face Langwana, who was now standing at the bottom of the stairs, staring at him.

"I'm sorry, Langwana," he said, looking dolefully at her. "I truly am. I'm sorry that you discovered in the way and at the time that you did that I have turned my back on the current beliefs of the Wennatoga. I am willing and desirous, of course, to discuss all of this with you in detail when we return to Strongbranch. I understand completely how you feel and how heartbroken you must be."

"Do you?" Langwana asked, her voice beginning to melt from anger into grief. "Do you really know what it's like to have your father consign himself to a death beyond death? To reject the very ancestors who are his only hope for joining them in peace in the realms beyond?"

The Konaskwa bowed his head, breathing deeply. "No, I don't know what it feels like," he replied, with as much solace as he could muster. "But I know what it means to you, and I know what it means to our people. Be assured that I have not severed my own bonds with such things lightly."

The Siloans once again found themselves in a very awkward position. There they were, standing on the stairs, witnessing this very serious and incredibly personal disagreement unfold between the Konaskwa and his daughter. They had certainly neither asked nor desired to be included in this discord and now wanted nothing more than to excuse themselves from it to spare themselves from what they perceived was an embarrassing situation for all involved.

"We can go back up to the woods for a few minutes if you need to talk alone," Girion politely offered.

"No, that's all right. You can stay," Thornoak called to the Siloans, who were just within his sight, several stairs from the ravine's floor. "In fact, I would actually prefer that you be present for this discussion. This matter concerns you in a way as well, though you may not now see how that is so. I will explain it to you later tonight. I promise."

"All right, then," Girion replied, giving Aradis a quick glance, as if to say, "I tried."

"Indeed, this matter concerns many, Father," Langwana asserted, her voice shaking slightly. She was so dismayed by the matter at hand that she hardly took any notice of this brief interruption by the Menfolk. "The Wennatoga look to you for guidance. What will it profit either you or them for you to lead them astray? Why not just leave well enough alone?"

"Tell me, daughter of mine," Thornoak softly urged, "if you knew something to be false, would you continue to believe it anyhow?"

"No," Langwana retorted. "But I do not believe you know the Taquenar to be false."

"Lay that thought aside for a moment. If you yourself knew, beyond the shadow of a doubt, that the Taquenar was false, would you still believe it?"

"Of course not," the princess replied, clearly exasperated.

"Such is my predicament," the Konaskwa said.

"But what *do* you believe, then?" Langwana asked. "When you fall into the slumber from which Barada awake not, what will you become of you, according to this new, twisted Taquenar of your own invention? Do you expect me to care nothing for your final destiny?"

"What does the Taquenar teach about those who depart from Orona?" Thornoak queried gently.

"You know quite well," Langwana returned, still wavering between anger and sadness.

"Yes, but I want to hear it from you," Thornoak said. "In detail, preferably. The way I taught it to you when you were a little girl."

"Why are you asking me to do this right now?" she asked, somewhat annoyed.

"Please, just oblige me."

Langwana looked at him for a few moments, puzzled, and then began, "Well, the Haedran essence of each Barada falls into the Waters of Shammaquen upon death. If he has engaged in much evil or if he has transgressed some serious boundary, he will sink to the bottom and there ever dwell in blackness. But if he has sought to do good in Orona and has venerated those who came before him, then he shall have strength to swim until he comes ashore at the Shadowed Garlens as a machaswa. Then he may occasionally pass through doorways between that place and Orona. If he seeks to accomplish ill in Orona or among the machaswa in the Garlens, he may be drawn back to the Waters of Shammaquen and at last be drowned, so even that which remains of him will vanish. But if he continues to pursue virtue even in the Shadowed Garlens, he may, through that virtue and through the aid of his descendants, make his way across those great woods until, at last, he comes to one of the Sengwa Senkawa, the Palaces of the Seasons, residing at the home of whichever of the Masters of the Seasons he has honored most ardently. There he shall stay until all the world has grown weary and then make his last stand with the Sacred Quinary against the demons of the far north, who will issue from the heart of Akannuwet, the flaming mountain. But if a Barada behaves with exceptional nobility and piety both here in Orona and in the Shadowed Garlens, he may come to the Hill of Ten Thousand Streams, where Palquanoga dwells, and there he will ever be safe and content, well-fed and watered and always at peace. When the bitter struggle comes, he will be exempt from it, and he will be master over many in the ages that follow."

"You have learned the teachings of the Taquenar well," Thornoak declared. "I wish I could be proud that I had taught all of that to you. But alas, I think much of that reckoning is mistaken. Let me ask you this – based on all this, how do you hope to someday reach the lands beyond the Shadowed Garlens?"

The princess pondered this a bit, then said, "As long as I am bound to Orona, I will venerate the Sacred Quinary and honor the machaswa properly to aid them in their own journeys, and then they shall aid me in mine. I will follow the Taquenar until I at last fall into that dark slumber of which we spoke, and then I will have vitality enough to reach the dark shores of the Shadowed Garlens. There I will seek to be as worthy and benevolent of a machaswa as I can, and, though it may take me a great count of years, I hope that I will ultimately come to some bright resting place."

Thornoak looked hard at Langwana, his countenance deeply troubled. "According to the Taquenar, do you know that you risked losing all that on my account?" he asked probingly. "Last night, you broke the ashaska and entered Paanu Assagwa to save my life. And you told me you banished the machaswa that sought to hinder you, the very same machaswa that you are so insistent we pay proper honor to. Had you any guarantee that you would not founder and be lost in the Waters of Shammaquen?"

"No," Langwana returned, biting her lip and becoming very solemn indeed. "I thought that – well, that they were evil machaswa and needed to be banished and that there was some good greater than the ashaska that needed to be seen to – that of saving your life and the kingdom."

"Ah." Thornoak nodded. "So you didn't think you would drown in the Waters of Shammaquen?"

"I wasn't sure one way or the other," Langwana replied hesitantly. "But I hoped that my noble aims would buoy me up if I did perish in Paanu Assagwa."

"I appreciate tremendously you taking that risk on my behalf, make no mistake," Thornoak said. "But there are several things I want you to note about what you did. First, it demonstrates that you believe, deep down, that there is a guiding light that is higher or greater than the Taquenar. That is to say, when it came down to it, even though the Taquenar demanded that you not violate the ashaska, you thought it was misguided on that point, since you held that keeping me from killing myself and seeking to aid the kingdom constituted a greater good. In this estimation, I think you were correct. Regardless of that, though, *you* thought you were correct. And so, though you may not like to admit it, you also do not fully trust the Taquenar. I just trust less of it than you do."

"But secondly," he went on, "I want you to be aware of the fundamental uncertainty that the Taquenar offers regarding what happens in the Waters of Shammaquen and the Shadowed Garlens. Even with as much of the Taquenar as you are aware of – and you are an extremely well-educated young lady in that regard – you weren't certain if the violation of a single taboo would negate all of the labor you've put forth your entire life in seeking to do what is right. Do you not find that problematic?"

"Well, yes, but I don't understand what you're aiming at," Langwana returned abashedly. She was obviously quite disconcerted by the line of thought her father was pursuing.

"This," Thornoak said, looking affectionately at his daughter, his silver hair, shot with green, catching stray light that entered the ravine. "The Taquenar, as it now stands, isn't worthless. It isn't to be cast aside altogether. There are fragments of truth and goodness in it. But it isn't sufficient to kindle any such thing as hope – not real hope. It can provide no sure passage to the lands beyond the Shadowed Garlens or even out of the Waters of Shammaquen, if such places exist. Even you recognize that. The Taquenar claims that those who are virtuous shall reach the dark shores, and if they are able to maintain their noble deeds, they may come to distant places of light. But how much virtue is enough? And how much evil is enough to condemn one to drowning in the Waters of Shammaquen? If one replies that the matter is based merely on the degree of effort, on how hard one tries to do what is right, then how much effort is enough? The Taquenar does not say. I have studied it my entire life, and yet, I could not give a proper answer to any of these questions."

"And furthermore, none can claim to have observed the Taquenar entirely without fault, not even Kantasosh, for he attempted to give his oracle out in the open, and neither he nor the Menfolk were kneeling. If the Taquenar was given to us by beings of the Haedra, it is to our shame that none in all the ages of this world have ever kept their virtuous code without fault. And if it was made by the Barada for their own guidance, then it is an even greater shame that we cannot keep our own rules of conduct, try though we might."

Thornoak sighed heavily, then said, "As for the matter of the machaswa, both you and the Taquenar are open to the possibility that at least some of them might be ill-intentioned toward the Barada, abusing the forms they take when they come to the Shadowed Garlens, though tradition demands that we still venerate even such as these. But the incident at Paanu Assagwa last night should have at least planted some doubts in your mind about whether the machaswa should be worthy of such adoration. Did not the machaswa seek to bar you and the Menfolk from coming to my aid? And though you banished those in the halls above, were you not aware that, right before Aradis united the pieces of the medallion, machaswa surrounded me and sought to darken both my sight and my mind?"

With a sudden chill, the lads recalled the bizarre changes that had come over the Konaskwa the previous evening when Langwana had been reciting the lines from "The Signs of the Sannadosh."

"No, I did not see them," Langwana replied, with a look of deep perplexity crossing her face. "Could *you* see them? If so, how could it be that they were visible to you but not to us?"

"That is the way of such creatures. They can take various forms at will and reveal such forms only to those whom they desire to see them. That is precisely why so many have been persuaded that they are our ancestors, for they can take the guise of the deceased and speak thus clad. I am well aware that the Taquenar teaches that, although a few machaswa may work mischief on occasion, the majority of them are benevolent. Yet, in my opinion, the proofs offered for this conclusion are weak. Often, any good occurrence is attributed to the machaswa without any sound evidence that they are the cause of it. Of course, there are those who would dispute that, but you and I needn't get into all of that now. We certainly shall later, I'm sure. But for now, if nothing else, I want to make my beliefs on this matter unmistakably clear and hopefully convince you of them in the days to come."

"There are many reasons to suspect that machaswa are, in fact, creatures of a horribly deceptive and perverse nature. Thus, prostrating oneself before them and observing rituals for their sake will grant no aid to the Barada when death takes them. Indeed, one cannot escape the Waters of Shammaquen by draining bowls of tapusa upon sacred stones in the woods nor can the Hill of Ten Thousand Streams be reached by reveling in the murmurs of the machaswa."

"You are truly lost, then," Langwana said, her voice quavering, as tears began to gather in the corners of her bright-green eyes. "If a Barada will not properly honor his ancestors, he cannot hope to escape being swallowed by that sea of blackness. He will never reach the shore of the Shadowed Garlens."

"My daughter," the Konaskwa tenderly replied, "you are so concerned with me reaching the Shadowed Garlens, but I myself am concerned about what lies *beyond* the Shadowed Garlens. For there dwells Palquanoga, and I believe that he alone is able to draw me out of the sea. And I do believe there is a way to reach him or at least a way for him to reach us. But it is not through observance of the Taquenar."

The princess was visibly and grievously distraught by this statement, but she allowed her father to continue.

"I love you, Langwana," Thornoak went on, "and I want more than anything for you to understand why I believe what I do, and I want you to believe it as well. But I want you to believe it for the same reason that I do – because it's true. You may be angry at me if you wish. You may weep if you wish. Such things are quite natural and understandable. But you must know that I care very deeply for you. You're all I have left, Langwana. I killed your mother with my wanton folly and, through my accursed passivity, drove your brother to march gallantly, but foolishly, into the merciless net of Ravinia and her dark legions. And for the past seven years, I have let the kingdom slowly crumble while hiding away in Paanu Assagwa, nursing my grief. Yes, I am a wretched father and a wretched king. And by all rights, if the Taquenar as it is currently taught is true, then I should be swallowed up by the Waters of Shammaquen. I know that, but please forgive me for these failings if you can. Yet I do not ask you to forgive me for seeking truth. I only ask that you accept that I really do love you. I always have, my dear Langwana, and I always will."

Langwana stood, holding back the dam of her sorrow as best as she could, but it broke. She began sobbing, and Thornoak walked to her and wrapped his arms around her. They stood there, embracing in the narrow ravine for a good minute or so, until Langwana finally whispered, "I know you love me, Father. I know you do. I love you too, and I forgive you for all the times you have failed both our family and the kingdom. And though I'm deeply grieved that you have rejected the Taquenar, I'm so glad you've finally come back out of the darkness after all these years."

She looked up at him, mustering up as much of a smile as she could manage in her current, heavy state. It wasn't much, but it was utterly heartfelt, and Thornoak recognized it as such. He smiled warmly in return.

All this while, the Siloans stared at the ground, overwhelmed by the raw poignancy of this interaction of the Konaskwa and his daughter.

"Let us rejoin the company,"Thornoak said at last, releasing Langwana from his embrace.

Then, looking solemnly at the Menfolk, he said, "Hopefully you can forgive me as well, Aradis and Girion. You've certainly gone to a lot of trouble to rouse me out of my seven-year stupor."

"All is forgiven, sire," Girion assured.

"We're just happy you're alive and ready to return to Anganor," Aradis said.

"I am ready," the Konaskwa breathed, gazing up at the thin strip of bright, blue sky that was visible from the bottom of the ravine.

Turning northward, Thornoak now led the way out of the ravine, down the slope to the next set of stairs, then back into the near-grotto with its waterfall. The foursome passed through the gap that opened onto the shelves of spring water, and they carefully made their way back down to where the company was assembled. The daylight was now taking on the rich, golden tone of late afternoon, and most of the Ingan soldiers were sitting down and conversing in small groups. A few of them happened to look up and see that the Konaskwa had returned, so they alerted their fellows to this fact. Almost immediately, the whole company began making preparations for departure.

Meanwhile, Thornoak, Langwana and the Siloans relieved themselves and took a few refreshments that were brought to them by some of the soldiers. The attendant who had taken the Menfolk's weapons returned them and told the Siloans their mount had had a good bit of food and a rest while they were gone and had been made ready for the ride to the Royal Manniog. The lads thanked him for attending to these things, then washed their hands and faces in the cool waters of the stream.

As the Siloans were walking back to their steed, Aradis remarked, "I wish we'd stayed down here with our tonquit and just had a good bit of food and a rest like he did. Consider this, Girion – if we were tonquit, we could have just lain down on the grass and had a nap that even Neldon Broadbuckle would be envious of. That certainly wouldn't have been so

tiring or nerve-wracking as what went on up there on the plateau."
He glanced up with a definitive degree of dislike in the direction of
Hadoga Taquenassa.

"There are definitely some benefits to being a tonquit," Girion
remarked. "They don't really have to worry about oracles and prophecies,
Witches and machaswa, the Taquenar or any of those kinds of things. All
the same, I think I'd rather be a Barada."

"To each his own," Aradis said. "Being a Barada can be a rather difficult
business. Personally, I'd prefer to be a tonquit." He was only half-joking.

CHAPTER TWELVE

Rhennian's Rhyme

t was not long before Thornoak, Langwana and the Siloans had mounted their tonquit and the entire company was making its way back northward through the Nachagwa, with Chelashu and Paskasha again leading the troop. As they went along, the four Barada who had gone up to Hadoga Taquenassa earlier that afternoon spoke little, for the events of that day and the previous one pressed rather heavily upon them.

As the Menfolk again rode past the stone huts and strange, worn stone monuments, they tried to sort through the mind-boggling tangle that had been their afternoon thus far. They sifted through as much of their conversation with Tannemoc and Mannetoc as they could recall and tried to form a proper understanding of a number of things Thornoak and Langwana had spoken of in the ravine. Yet, even with all this to occupy their thoughts, they found that Kantasosh's oracle kept surfacing in their musings, gnawing at them sporadically and stirring dark waters of fear and doubt in the depths of their minds.

Nonetheless, despite this sinister undercurrent, their overall outlook on things was rather optimistic. The admonitions of Tannemoc and Mannetoc had given them a certain sense direction for their future endeavors, and their revelations about Palquanoga, the Naqua Senkawa and the machaswa had swept away a great many cobwebs of confusion and dismay. For that, at least, they could be grateful, though there was much that was still incomprehensible and unsettling to them.

As the afternoon wore on, the company came back to Konassu Road and embarked to the northeast, following the road back toward Anganor. They passed the turnoff for Shalkanu Ataqua and then went another five miles north by northeastward until they came to the path that led to the Royal Manniog. Here they veered sharply to the southeast, passing under the eaves of Kassimaw Forest as a fiery, red-gold sunset lit up the woods of Mentasqua. By the time they reached the Royal Manniog, which was a mile off the main road, Marda's parting, crimson rays had faded to the subtle, deep blue of twilight.

Before the company, to the east, stood a tall stockade built of great, pointed logs, which was accessed only by a set of broad wooden gates. These portals opened on their arrival, and they were greeted by several Ingan soldiers, all of them bearing torches to guide them in the growing darkness. The Konaskwa, his daughter and the Siloans all dismounted, and, after the Siloans had gotten their packs from their tonquit, they were escorted by the Ingans toward a series of large structures, the frames of which appeared to be built of saplings; their exteriors were mostly covered in long grass and bark. Each structure was about one hundred and fifty feet long, twenty feet high and twenty feet wide. The dimensions of some of these varied, but mostly in length, as a number of them were quite a bit shorter than one hundred and fifty feet, and a few were considerably longer than that. They were all shaped rather like upside-down cradles, with slightly slanted walls and gently curving, rounded roofs. The lads realized these must be the gannogets Langwana had spoken of earlier that day.

"Ah, there's Shallamec," Thornoak exclaimed, noting an Ingan in rather rustic attire who had just come out of one of the gannogets.

"Shallamec is the chief steward of the Royal Manniog," Langwana explained to the Menfolk. "He, his family and a number of others live here and care for the grounds, looking after the gardens, rethatching the gannogets and such."

Thornoak halted and raised his hand as Shallamec approached, and the latter bowed his head, reciting the names of the Naqua Senkawa as he did so. The Konaskwa issued the customary "Pessanagwa," though there seemed to be an odd reluctance in his pronouncement of it. Thornoak put his hand down, and Shallamec went through the usual procedure with the lifting and lowering of his hands.

Then Shallamec said, "It's such a pleasure to see you, sire, for long it has been since last you came to see us here at the Royal Manniog. Rest assured, your welcome here is as warm as ever. Indeed, your quarters have been made ready, and food awaits you there. Please, come with me." Nodding to Langwana, he added, "You as well, Princess."

"Thank you, Shallamec," the Konaskwa responded. "You can go ahead, Langwana." He motioned to her. "I'll be along in just a moment."

Langwana bid the Siloans a pleasant evening and then followed Shallamec toward the gannogets.

When his daughter was out of earshot, Thornoak turned to the Menfolk and quietly said, "I want to apologize for that business in the ravine earlier. You likely felt as if you were intruding, by no fault of your own, on a discussion that was of a deeply sensitive and personal nature. I really did want you to stay and hear it though, so you needn't feel bad on my behalf – or Langwana's either. Honestly, I don't think she was upset by you being present for our dispute, or if she was, it was a minor matter compared to the fact that the dispute was happening in the first place. Actually, what she seemed the most distraught about was the confrontation up in the village. But that's neither here nor there, as far as you're concerned. I'm the one who needs to try and help her see why that was necessary."

He went on, "Now, I promised you that'd I'd explain what that conversation in the ravine had to do with you, and I intend to do that later on tonight. But we can all take our supper first and have some time to just enjoy the evening. That, I think, will be beneficial for all of us, for the day has been rather long and taxing."

"You'll be staying in a gannoget with a number of the guards from our company. I want to make sure that you have proper protection, as we can't be certain that any of the bandits from the attacks yesterday won't come after you, although you can alleviate your fears for the most part regarding that matter. You see, should they wish to attempt something, they'll have to get into the manniog first, and that will be no simple matter."

"Aren't you worried they might come after you or Langwana?" Aradis asked.

"Oh, don't worry about us," Thornoak replied. "Chelashu and some of his finest warriors will be on guard at our gannoget."

The Konaskwa beckoned to a nearby torch-bearing Ingan from the group that had escorted them from the gates of the Royal Manniog. The fellow walked over, and Thornoak instructed, "Passagwon, take these Menfolk to their gannoget and see that they receive their supper."

The Konaskwa told the Siloans, "Passagwon will be staying in your gannoget tonight. So, if you should have any inquiries or requests during your stay here, you can direct them to him. And, if need be, he can fetch Shallamec, Langwana or myself, as he'll know where to find us."

Before the Ingan led the Menfolk away, Thornoak encouraged them, "Eat heartily tonight, Menfolk from across the sea, for tomorrow we ride for Anganor. And, as I said, I will come by this evening to speak with you about the matter from the ravine. Oh, and I have some other matters to converse with you about as well – deeper matters," he added enigmatically. And with these words, he walked off into the twilight.

Passagwon now walked a few paces ahead of the Menfolk, guiding them between the gannogets until they came to an average-sized one in the midst of a number of others.

As they passed through the dwelling's rounded doorway, the lads saw a number of fires blazing away in stone rings placed down the length of the gannoget. On the walls to their right and their left, there were long benches fixed at several heights, with ladders enabling access to the higher ones. Many of these benches had barkcloth blankets cast upon them and seemed to serve as beds. Others had stores of food, drink and other commodities, and many had large, woven baskets or piles of spears on them. Tall, stout log pillars rose from the floor up to the ceiling, and hooks had been attached to these, from which hung garments of various kinds. At their bases were large clay pitchers, drinking bowls and cups.

A great many Ingans were present in the gannoget, engaging in various tasks. Some were tending the fires and others the victuals cooking over the fires. Still others were polishing their weapons or carrying items about in preparation for supper. The place was filled with quiet murmurs of the jagged rhythms of Asla'gu, the smell of wild game simmering in savory broth, the sweet, dancing lights of low fires and the pleasant aroma of kuringa, which was wafting from lamps hanging from the log pillars.

"Come, eat," Passagwon urged the Menfolk, as he set his accoutrements down by one of the benches.

The lads followed him to the fire at the rear of the gannoget and sat on the dirt floor next to several Ingans. There they were presented with a stew called saquot, which had a deer-like animal named tugassa as its main element, along with chunks of a fish called gassawot, a gray, hearty vegetable called bannacheg and various native herbs of Kassimaw Forest.

There was also a fried bread called quennic, sprinkled with some sweet powder, and for a beverage, they had classic Ingan tapusa.

When the Siloans had finished their dinner, they were taken to one of the benches nearby, which was at the back left of the gannoget, and told they could sleep upon it. The lads placed their packs and other effects next to the bench and then went and sat by the closest fire to wait for Thornoak to come speak with them as he had promised. Passagwon walked by and assured the Menfolk that he was at their disposal if they should need anything; he then headed to the front portion of the gannoget to attend to some duties with his comrades. A number of Ingans had already begun to lie down for the night, and the Siloans were, in fact, the only ones at their particular fire now, though other fires still had small clusters of Ingans around them.

"What have we gotten ourselves into, Girion Ringmark?" Aradis sighed, as he stared at the red blaze before him. "Do we really have any business being here? Maybe that Kantasosh fellow and his dratted machaswa advisers were right. Maybe we have done everything we can do, and it's time for us to go home. Thornoak's going to go put things right in Anganor tomorrow and then summon the Verdinnion right after that. Surely Argonis can deal with Ravinia after all that's been seen to. We can't destroy a Hadathi. You know that. And maybe our families really do need us."

Girion poked the fire with a stick that was lying nearby. "On the ride here, I entertained all those thoughts as well," he admitted. "But I know I shouldn't have. And you shouldn't either." Then he shook his head and chastised, "Have you already forgotten what the oracles told us? We are destined to face Ravinia. Do you not remember holding the coal in your hand? What more of a sign do you need, Aradis? We've been given so many already. We ought to take Thornoak's advice and not give credence to a single word of that message from the machaswa."

"Yes, I suppose you're right," Aradis conceded, somewhat sheepishly. "But confound all this adventuring just the same! I miss my family, Girion. And I know you miss yours. Really, I miss home and everything about it. We've been gone for so long."

"We did the right thing in coming here," Girion assured. "Thornoak would have died had we not come. And then how would Argonis have fared?"

"I know, I know," Aradis said. "But what if our families really do need us? If they're alive, that is. I just hate not knowing where they are, how they are, what they're doing and so forth. We should have asked Tannemoc and Mannetoc about them. They could have told us everything we wanted to know, I'll wager. Oh, bratbangles! Why didn't I think of that?" he cursed.

"I don't think their powers work like that, Aradis," Girion said. "They even said as much, basically – that Telyon can't be forced to give answers and that they can only speak what's been revealed to them. And for some reason, I don't think the information you're after is something they'd be privy to."

"I wish we'd asked them just the same," Aradis replied sullenly. "I just can't help wondering about everything. I wonder whether my father is any better or if he's only gotten worse. I wonder if my mother is able to bear all the burdens that my father can't. I wonder if Mellora is holding up all right; I absolutely hate to think of her suffering. And I wonder if blasted Teric has gotten his act together."

"And I miss our friends too," Aradis went on. "Corim and his antics. Tallis and his good sense. Darmon and his jokes. And Neldon and his ..."

"Downright absurdity," Girion finished, chuckling. "Give that lad five minutes and he'll make a wreck of any situation. And when he does, it always provides entertainment for years to come."

Throwing his stick into the fire, Girion said, "I miss them all as well. But I believe that someday we'll come back to Siloa and rejoice with all of them and make the merriest merriment that ever was made. Still, we've got to finish our business here in the Elder Forest first. It was appointed to us, and we've got to see it through. We've had help of an extraordinary nature up to this point, and I believe that will continue to be the case. That means we really can do this thing, Aradis. We just have to take it one step at a time."

"Well, the last few steps have been pretty rough," Aradis declared wearily. "We've had hope kindled recently in several ways, but if we hadn't,

I don't think I personally could have made it through the trials we've just come through."

"To be perfectly honest, I don't think I could have either, but here we are," Girion said. "What we had was sufficient, as has been the case all along. Just one step at a time, Aradis. One step at a time. Today's today, and tomorrow is tomorrow."

"I know. I know. My father used to say that all the time. He loved quoting the Sayings of the Sages," Aradis sighed.

"Aradis. Girion," a voice quietly called.

The lads turned and saw Thornoak standing only a few feet away from them, illuminated by the low firelight in the gannoget.

"Oh," Aradis exclaimed, mildly startled. "Hello, sire."

"Would you join me for a walk outside?" the Konaskwa inquired.

"Certainly," Girion replied, and the lads rose and followed Thornoak to the entrance of the gannoget, passing by many a slumbering Ingan, a handful of guards standing on duty next to log pillars and a few who were yet consuming their saquot or sitting and chatting.

When they stepped outside, the air was pleasant, but just a bit warm, since it was the height of summer. There were Ingan sentries posted at the gates of the compound and others patrolling outside the gannogets. The stars were out, birds cooed softly to each other from the boughs of trees surrounding the stockade, and the air was filled with the hum of insects performing their nightly symphony.

"Before we discuss what I came to talk to you about, I want to thank you again," Thornoak said, as he began strolling with the lads toward the eastern edge of the cluster of gannogets and the greensward beyond it. "I am most sincerely in your debt, Aradis and Girion, for you saved my life."

"Your daughter must share part of the gratitude as well," Girion insisted.

"Yes, but she wouldn't have been able to do it without you," Thornoak replied.

"And we wouldn't have been able to do it without her," Aradis said.

"Fair enough," Thornoak granted. "Nonetheless, you have my thanks and the thanks of the entire Kingdom of Argonis. Even if many of its citizens know nothing yet of what transpired at Paanu Assagwa last night, when they learn of it, they will certainly thank you."

"We are honored," Girion said. "If we have been of any aid to this kingdom, it is not our own doing, but that of him who sent us."

"Telyon," the Konaskwa murmured. "Palquanoga."

"Yes," Aradis confirmed. Then, stricken by a sudden burst of insight, he inquired, "Where did you learn that name? Telyon, that is. Very few people on our travels have been familiar with it, as it seems to be of somewhat obscure Mannish origin."

"It is," Thornoak said quietly. "But as for how I came to learn it, for now, let us simply note that I did and leave it at that. That, anyway, is not a matter for tonight."

The lads found the Konaskwa's reluctance to discuss this subject quite peculiar but sensed that it would do no good to press him about it presently.

"Very well," Aradis replied.

"If you don't mind us asking, how is Langwana doing this evening?" Girion asked, endeavoring to rekindle the conversation. "Has she brightened up a bit since this afternoon?"

"She is reserved and rather somber," Thornoak answered, "but I think she's all right. She's doing better than she was during our argument in the Nachagwa, anyway."

"Speaking of that," the Konaskwa said, "now that you have had some time to consider the matter, do you know why I wanted you to stay and hear our dispute?"

"I honestly haven't figured it out yet," Girion replied. "Have you, Aradis?"

"No," the younger Siloan answered. "I actually had a difficult time even following several parts of the conversation, much less discerning what they had to do with us. The segment about the dark waters and the Shadowed Garlens and all that rather lost me, I'm afraid."

"Hmm," Thornoak hummed. "No matter, for I will divulge the connection to you now."

Taking a deep breath, he continued, "I would have explained it to you then and there in the ravine, but that was already a touchy situation, and it would have undoubtedly made things worse if I had. Even if your knowledge of the Taquenar is rather limited, I'm sure you gathered that the things I said to the oracles were considered absolutely heretical by them and by my daughter. According to their teaching, my refusal to pay proper homage to the machaswa and the Naqua Senkawa practically ensures that my soul will be lost when I die. It was already hard enough to say the things that I did in front of the oracles, but, in truth, it was even more difficult to be confronted about them by Langwana."

"I tried to make the best case I could to her that the machaswa are wicked deceivers, but it was not for her benefit alone that I presented those arguments. It was for yours as well, for if you could be persuaded that the machaswa are not to be trusted, then you could more easily disregard Kantasosh's malicious oracle. I haven't any idea how much you know about the machaswa or what you believe about them, yet I would suspect that you don't adhere to the Taquenar, coming from outside of Argonis and not being Ingans and all. But when I consider that you have become embroiled in many strange events here and that you have already encountered the machaswa, I just want to make certain that you are not disposed to heed their message to you for any reason whatsoever."

"Ah, so that's it!" Girion exclaimed, as they began walking through a series of vegetable gardens that began just beyond the easternmost gannogets. "You wanted us to hear exactly why you believe the machaswa are untrustworthy, so we could be immunized against their warnings. Well, you needn't fear that we are beguiled by the machaswa, sire, for we were amply warned about them by Tannemoc and Mannetoc. Besides, the run-in that Aradis and I had with them in Paanu Assagwa had left a far less than favorable impression of them already. But we do very much appreciate your concern for us and your wanting us to know additional reasons why hearkening to the machaswa ought to be avoided. Also, for the record, yesterday is the first time we even heard of the Taquenar; we know only a little bit about it and therefore could hardly be considered adherents of it."

Thornoak heaved a sigh of relief, as he said, "I'm very glad to hear that such is your view of the matter. I simply didn't know one way or the other, as we've had so few opportunities to converse. Honestly, I don't know where the two of you stand on a lot of things. But I hope we may amend that condition when we return to Strongbranch. We certainly must converse again before the Verdinnion, for I shall want to know your minds well ere that meeting occurs, and you shall likely want to know mine. That would,

I think, be advantageous for both of us, for a number of reasons. Yes, we shall speak of many things at the Citadel. But I have yet one important inquiry regarding your reception of Kantasosh's oracle."

Thornoak stopped and looked intently at the lads. They stood still and waited for him to speak. "Now, I want you two to be honest with me about this," the Konaskwa said. "Though you have indicated your awareness of the fact that the machaswa are not to be trusted, is there any part of you that fears that their warnings might be valid? If there is even the smallest inkling of that sort, I want to know about it, so we can address it."

The threesome stood there in silence for a few moments before Aradis hesitantly began, "Girion and I have actually only discussed the machaswa's oracle briefly, and we are in agreement that there are very good reasons not to believe it. But if I were to be completely forthright, I would say that, though I don't wish to believe it, there is a part of me that still very much fears that it should be heeded. Actually, when Kantasosh was in the midst of delivering it, I felt as if I was being gripped by some ... well, by some strange darkness, and though that sensation departed when you called out to interrupt him, suspicions that Girion and I ought to abandon our quest and return home keep rising within me. They have all afternoon, as a matter of fact."

"You felt that too?" Girion asked. "That weird stirring in the air?"

Aradis nodded.

"That was from samayanta," Thornoak said abruptly. He then turned and started strolling across the greensward again.

"Sama ... sama-what?" Aradis asked, as he and Girion followed after the Konaskwa.

"Samayanta. It is when a being of the Haedra comes upon an oracle and speaks through him, seizing his voice as it were. The voice you heard was not that of Kantasosh, but of the machaswa that had taken hold of him. I have seen for myself on several occasions that the voices of the machaswa can accomplish queer things in Orona, and the machaswa were almost certainly behind whatever it was that you felt in the air. In fact, I do not doubt that some ill effects of hearing that voice may yet be lingering in you."

The lads shuddered at this last remark.

"Is there anything that can be done to remove those effects?" Aradis asked concernedly.

"Untruth must be fought with truth. No other weapon will do," Thornoak replied.

They had already passed the last of the vegetable gardens and were at a spot on the greensward partway between them and the eastern edge of the manniog. Here Thornoak stopped again, turned to the Menfolk and, with tremendous earnest, said, "Aradis and Girion, I know that you already know the truth about the machaswa if the sisters have revealed it to you, as you said they did. The machaswa are nothing but Kalathar, malevolent Hadathi. But, though you may know that, you must remind yourselves of it again and again, for lies, even absurd ones, have a way of creeping back out of exile and working their mischief in subtle ways. Bit by bit, if not properly combated, they can begin to take hold and infect your thoughts."

The Konaskwa spoke with even greater earnest now. "Please, do not think yourself safe from those lies by any means. That sensation of false security is precisely what they will seize upon in order to worm their way into your minds. You must avoid at all costs the great dangers of complacency and thoughtlessness, which are all the more dangerous, since they are natural urges within you and, indeed, within all Barada. Although you seem to have been mildly affected up to this point, comparatively speaking, I rather suspect that much worse is yet to come. If you harbor even the least inkling that the lies are true, fear will be birthed in you. And once that fear begins to grow, your minds will become clouded, and the lies will only be strengthened more and more. It is a truly vicious cycle. So, you must resist both fear and lies with all the strength you possess."

"We'll try, sire," Aradis promised, although he was rather doubtful of his or Girion's ability to carry that promise out. For there was, in his reckoning, much to be afraid of, even without the machaswa's oracle to worry about.

"We'll do our very best," Girion added.

"Good. Now, I want you to completely and permanently disregard that ludicrous oracle that Kantasosh gave," Thornoak urged. "Simply do not believe it. It is most definitely *not* certain that you will die if you go on to fight Ravinia. And I do not believe your quest is done by any means. As for the assertion that your families are in danger, that may be true, for all

I know; I won't pretend to know their situation. But there are a number of factors that should give you pause for thought before accepting that as truth. First, the machaswa don't know everything; they can only be in one place at one time, though their kind can travel far and fast, and they may converse with others of their sort. The fact is, nonetheless, that they may not even know where your families are. Also, even if they did, they are not benevolent beings by any stretch of the imagination, as you have seen for yourselves, and could hardly be expected to be concerned about your welfare or that of your families. And finally, eastern Quarana is thousands of miles from here. It would be very difficult to pass through Sarganath to the coast of Byram, as you already know all too well, and it is very unlikely that you could help your families in time even if they were in danger. That is not to say that I do not care about the welfare of your kin; I am merely stating a fact of the matter."

The Konaskwa then added, "Oh, and to further demonstrate my point that the machaswa are ill-intentioned and manipulative to the core and therefore simply cannot be trusted, I might ask – do you know why I didn't show up to speak in Anganor the morning of the day before yesterday?"

"Hoarstaff basically said it was because you weren't feeling well or something like that," Aradis replied.

"I *wasn't* feeling well," Thornoak confirmed. "Not well at all. But that is not why I didn't come. That's just the part I chose to send to Hoarstaff. The real reason is that the machaswa came to me and told me not to go because it would only make matters worse for the kingdom, and I was fool enough to listen to them."

"Really?" Girion was astonished. "The machaswa were behind that too?"

"Indeed," Thornoak said. "I had spent weeks convincing myself that I needed to go back to Strongbranch, and when I had fully resolved to go, I dispatched messengers throughout the kingdom to apprise my people of this. Yet, when those odious creatures came to me and showed me their ghoulish faces, whispering softly in the darkness, I was lulled into trusting them again, as I had been many times before. Take note, lads. It is very unwise to underestimate the power and the draw of their words, whether they are articulated by the machaswa themselves or by one of their representatives among the Barada."

"But, as I said, I wouldn't give that torrent of lies that Kantasosh rained upon you even a passing thought, for they were truly naught but the venomous work of the machaswa. So, if misgivings rise because of what you heard, slay them. Rehearse the truth again and again, as often as the lies return. You must not doubt your quest. Your task is not yet accomplished. Argonis needs you – desperately. Do not forget that. This land cannot survive now without a tarnadin."

"And that brings us to the deeper matters I spoke of," Thornoak said, as he turned and headed toward a collection of flower beds at the far eastern end of the manniog. The Menfolk followed, walking several paces behind him.

"Do you know what a tarnadin is?" Thornoak asked, as he strode forward.

Girion promptly answered, "No. I've never encountered that word."

Aradis, however, replied, "Tarnadin? Yes, I've heard the term before. I only learned of it rather recently, though. When we were in Harnabrig, Masterfarmer Mackle mentioned that you had said something at the last meeting of the Verdinnion about Argonis needing a tarnadin."

"I don't remember that," Girion declared. "When did he say that?"

"When I talked to him a little before dawn on the morning we left," Aradis answered.

"What did he say the term meant?" Thornoak inquired, as he glanced up at a passing firefly.

"He said – " Aradis paused, thinking. "He said it was a person who gave up everything for others in order to help them – to deliver them in some way."

"Yes, that is the general drift of it," Thornoak confirmed. "The term itself is very old. It's a Vasornic word, actually. Vasorna was the language of the Manusians, who were an Elven people that lived along the shores of southwestern Tassaru in the Apex of Archaea. In any event, there was a renowned Manusian poet and scholar named Rhennian who used it in a rather famous poem called 'The Way of the Tarnadin.' It's about a particular tarnadin – *the* Tarnadin, you might say – but many of its principles ring true wherever and whenever there is someone who gives his all to provide aid to others who are in desperate need."

The Konaskwa went on, "When I was wandering in the woods on the plateau while you were in the sisters' quonniot, the words of that poem were running through my mind, for the sisters had said that you were to be tarnadins of the Elder Forest. And I am fully convinced they were speaking the truth."

"They really told you that we were going to deliver this land? And you believed them?" Aradis asked, marveling. "I mean, they told us the same thing, essentially, and, of course, the reason we've come here all the way from the other side of the world was to save Argonis. But the fact that you, the ruler of Argonis, are persuaded that we can actually accomplish our quest is just … it's just … "

"What Aradis means to say, Your Majesty, is that your vote of confidence means ever so much to us," Girion gushed. "With you on our side, perhaps it will be easier to gain the Verdinnion's support in sending us against Ravinia."

"I fear that little about the prospective, forthcoming meeting with the Verdinnion will prove to be easy," Thornoak said quite dejectedly. "When I spoke with Fergus briefly last evening, he told me that you had won Shillelagh, Mackle and Gronk to your cause, but there remain feuds that must be settled between those three before they will cooperate, I would strongly suspect. And though Galadin Greycloak of the Timber-Elves is a generally levelheaded fellow, both Arctelius, the leader of the Sky-Gnomes, and Goldquiver, whom I was told you have already met, are certain to oppose almost any plan we put forth. This is especially so in Arctelius' case. And it's not that we can't proceed without their approval, but I think that it will take all of the strength that Argonis can muster to weather the coming storm. Whether we like it or not, I think we're going to need the aid of both Goldquiver and Arctelius, for the Sannadosh is not yet ended. It is only coming to a head. Fortunately, in fulfilling the Sign of the Sengara, you have already given us assurance from Palquanoga that when the clouds burst, though the flood will come, the waters will spend their fury and then be gone. Aye, at last, there will come a day when the full light of Marda will shine once more on this kingdom."

The lads were greatly uplifted by this last statement. Indeed, they found great consolation in Thornoak's words, even though they also contained grim forebodings of great trials ahead.

Aradis sighed, as he looked up at the wide, starry sky over the manniog. "Oh, that the day you just described were already here! I'm afraid there is going to be so much darkness, so much heaviness, between that day and this. Did the sisters tell you anything that might be of comfort to us? What else did you learn when they gave you their oracle?"

"Oracles are burdens laid upon both the ones who give them and the ones to whom they are given," Thornoak returned somberly. "Each must bear the burden as it is bestowed, and if he shares the oracle with someone else, he places that burden on him as well. The majority of my oracle is too great of a burden even for me at this time, and so I cannot bring myself to lay it upon you also. But I will tell you that you have already brought about the first portion of my vision – the Fivefold Vision that Noggaset mentioned this morning at the entrance to Paanu Assagwa."

"Oh, yes," Girion recalled. "I can't remember what the first part was, though."

"The Gates of Iron," Thornoak said.

"What were those?" Aradis inquired. "That is to say, what was the first part of your vision?"

Now they had come to the flower patches at the manniog's eastern edge, and Thornoak veered northward, roughly following the fence of the manniog, as he replied, "The night before last, a mist came upon me in my sleep, and I found myself standing in a great, windowless stone dungeon lit only by dying flames set high in a few of the walls. There was no way out of that cold, miserable prison, save through massive, iron gates. These were standing open but only ever so slightly. When I realized that only through these gates could I escape that horrid hall, I began to run toward them. But my legs buckled beneath me, and I fell to the floor. Then I found that I could barely crawl forward and that only with great pain could I move at all. And what's more, to my grievous dismay, I heard a hideous grinding and saw that the gates were closing.

It would have been impossible for me to reach them in time; my doom was sealed. I despaired of both hope and life."

"But then, all of a sudden," Thornoak continued, his voice rising, "there was a shout of exultation beyond the doors, and blinding light shone through the tiny gap between them. A moment later, there was a great crack, as if the earth had been rent asunder, and the gates burst into ten thousand fragments. Light engulfed me, and then mist came upon me once more."

The Siloans found themselves nearly breathless when Thornoak finished this account, for he had given it with such passion and remarkable diction that they almost felt as if they had been there with him in his dream.

"If I had had such a vision, I would be shaken for days," Girion declared, with complete sincerity. "Even just hearing you speak of it, I am rather shaken. But how did *we* fulfill that vision?"

"The sisters explained its meaning to me," Thornoak replied. "The dungeon was that of my despair. I had given up hope for both myself and Argonis. The little light that remained was dying, and my confidence that help would come from the outside had all but withered. Such was represented by the closing of the gates. The shout was that of Palquanoga coming to my aid, and the light was your fulfillment of the Sign of the Sengara and fusing of the medallion. So, take heart, Menfolk from across the sea. You have, in part, already brought light back to Argonis. You may not have become tarnadins for the entire kingdom yet, but you have already become tarnadins to me. And that thought certainly occurred to me while I was pondering the words of 'The Way of the Tarnadin' in the woods surrounding Hadoga Taquenassa."

"Your revelation of these things certainly does provide encouragement," Aradis said. "And we very much appreciate your sharing them with us."

"Of course," Thornoak returned graciously.

The Konaskwa and the Siloans walked a few more paces across the greensward, angling slightly away from the edge of the manniog, and then Aradis asked, "You recited that poem, 'The Way of the Tarnadin,' to the Verdinnion the last time it assembled, didn't you? At least that's what Mackle told me when he recited a part of it, the part that got lodged in his mind."

"I did,"Thornoak returned. Then, smiling, he remarked, "And I am glad Mackle remembered a segment of it. That is another sliver of light to me. I have been terribly worried about that fellow."

"What made you suspect that Argonis needed a tarnadin, so much so that you felt compelled to recite that poem?" Aradis pursued. "Wasn't the last time the Verdinnion met years ago? Were things just as bad back   then?"

"They are worse now," Thornoak replied, as he began walking back toward the middle of the compound, where all the gannogets stood. These were rather distant now, standing on the far side of a broad tract of ground covered by low grasses.

"But, even back then, I knew we needed a tarnadin because no one in Argonis was both willing and able to do what needed to be done to save our land. It is true that many were willing, but none were able. Besides, Janura's prophecy specified that the other half of the amulet had to return from across the sea and that the evil in the west would only perish after the coming of a hand from across the sea. It was obvious that we needed help from the outside. Deliverance would not come from our midst. Someone would have to take up our cause, join us as if he were one of our own and set out to vanquish a foe that none of us could. That is the way it was with the True Tarnadin," he finished cryptically.

"Who is the True Tarnadin? What do you mean by that?" Girion pressed.

The Konaskwa stopped and turned to the lads, his gray eyes resting upon their puzzled faces.

"Alas, that is not a tale for tonight," he replied, sighing. "I'm not sure I understand the tale fully myself or if I believe it fully either. I'd like to. But it's … well, it's a very deep matter, far deeper even than the fate of Argonis. I'm afraid we shall have to let it rest at that for now."

"Will you at least tell us the poem?" Girion asked earnestly. "Maybe that will help us to understand."

"Yes, I will recite Rhennian's Rhyme," Thornoak said, "for it is what prompted me to interrupt Kantasosh's oracle the way I did. Its words have much relevance to your quest, I believe, and thus, it is quite appropriate that you should hear it in its entirety."

Thornoak's voice now entered a mode that only a Konaskwa's could, and, with a swelling richness and depth, he spoke into the summer night of the Royal Manniog,

> *"The Way of the Tarnadin is a road of woes,*
> *A path that is harrowed by grievous foes;*
> *E'er it is troubled by darkest night,*
> *Yet he who would tread it must put fear to flight.*
>
> *For the Tarnadin's task is clear and plain:*
> *He must battle darkness for others' gain.*
> *Indeed, for himself he must have no regard,*
> *But passing through fire, he will emerge uncharred.*
> *He takes up the cause of those who are weak,*
> *Though he himself be the meekest of the meek.*
>
> *When the powers of shadow upon flesh bear down,*
> *And the cries of all mortals in anguish are drowned,*
> *The Tarnadin stands in their stead to fight*
> *As a bearer of hope, a bearer of light.*
>
> *When the strength of the strong has at last come to naught,*
> *It is clear that a Tarnadin must then be sought.*
> *Indeed, all are in need of the Tarnadin.*
>
> *The Way of the Tarnadin from mercy proceeds,*
> *Then on through shadow and flame it leads,*
> *Yet Death's Blade will be shattered and night be no more;*
> *And the Tarnadin will stand in glory e'ermore."*

"Rhennian wrote that in Manusian, of course, but it's since been translated into Daiga," Thornoak said. "I've tried rendering it in Asla'gu, but that has proven difficult," he lamented.

"I'm afraid that didn't clarify things about the True Tarnadin for us, or at least for me," Aradis said glumly, "but it was a very nice poem. It's got a fair amount of darkness in it, though."

"Yes, it's very nice indeed, and it is quite dark in places," Thornoak agreed. "But the darkness is broken at the end, as Ravinia shall be. Be assured of that. The prophecies of Janura cannot be denied. Indeed, their fulfillment has already begun, and you have played no small part in them."

"Sire!" a voice called from over by the gannogets. Thornoak turned to see an Ingan soldier running toward him.

"Sire," the Ingan repeated. "We've been looking all over for you. A Questmonger has arrived from Anganor. Fergus sent him to let you know that Quagga somehow got wind that you are returning to the city tomorrow. He's stationed himself and a great many of his followers inside the Quannamet and plans to keep you from getting into the city."

"Oh, he does, does he?" Thornoak said, with tremendous annoyance. "Whom did Fergus send, and where is he?"

"Limberleaf, sire," the Ingan replied. "He's up by the gate, and he has a good deal more to his message than what I just told you."

"You must excuse me, lads," Thornoak said to the Menfolk. "I'm going to have to discuss some things with Limberleaf, formulate a plan and then send a message back to Fergus tonight."

After Thornoak had dismissed the Ingan soldier, he turned to the Menfolk one final time and declared, "I know you have come through a great many difficulties and accomplished so much already, but there are undoubtedly even greater difficulties and tasks before you, not the least of which is facing Ravinia. However, even if the whole kingdom were to doubt you, I will not. I believe you are the ones who will save this land, and I will not be shaken from that. I swear it by Palquanoga himself. Rest well this night and let your strength be renewed, Menfolk from across the sea."

After he had said this, he walked off toward the gannogets and was joined by several other Ingans, who escorted him toward the front gates of the manniog.

The Menfolk stood out under the stars for a minute, reflecting on what Thornoak had said to them. His tremendous vote of confidence somehow made the possibility of them actually defeating Ravinia so much more real. But they could not help thinking that, even if it really were true that they were destined to defeat Ravinia, they must pass through many dark toils and hardships to get to her. Indeed, even the poem Thornoak had recited had stated that the path of the tarnadin must lead through shadow and flame.

"Well, even tarnadins need sleep, don't they?" Aradis sighed, at last.

"I suppose they do," Girion said. "Come on. Let's find our gannoget."

The lads set out across the field and came to the cluster of buildings. There they wandered around for a few minutes, searching for their gannoget unsuccessfully in the dark, for they had not paid terribly close attention to where it was when they were first taken there. Fortunately, an Ingan soldier recognized them and offered to show the way. He took them on a little path that meandered through the large dwellings until they came to the one where they had supped. Then he ushered them to the door and bade them a good evening.

Soon, the lads were lying at the rear of their gannoget on their designated berth. They pulled a thin barkcloth blanket over themselves, then fell asleep to the quiet music of the dying fires lining the middle of the gannoget. Though there was certainly enough to keep both their minds occupied for hours, their bodies had the last say in the matter, and they were more than ready for a decent slumber.

When dawn came, many of the soldiers had already vacated the gannoget. Aradis and Girion awakened feeling truly refreshed, a condition they hadn't experienced in quite some time. Hastily, they got ready for the day's journey and hurriedly ate some quennic that had been left for them on trenchers by their berth. After this brief breakfast, they grabbed their equipment, rushed outside and saw that the company was nearly ready to depart.

The troop looked much the same as it had the day before, but there was a different feeling in the air. This time, they really would be going to Anganor. There would be no more diversions.

The lads ran up to their tonquit, and a soldier helped them tie their packs to its flank.

"Good morning, Quennashoc," Aradis cheerfully greeted their steed. The beast brayed good-naturedly in reply.

After the Siloans had mounted Quennashoc, again with Aradis in front and Girion just behind him, they rode up directly behind Thornoak and Langwana, who were in the same attire they had been wearing the previous morning when they left Paanu Assagwa. Thornoak, in his silver tunic and kilt and with his crown gracing his brow, looked even more regal than he had the day before, as did Langwana in her magnificent yellow dress.

"Are Menfolk always such late risers?" Langwana chided playfully. She seemed to be in much better spirits today. Perhaps her sleep had done wonders for her, just as the Siloans' had for them.

"I'm afraid I kept them up for a while last night talking," Thornoak said, as he smoothed his tunic. "But I hope our conversation proved worthwhile."

"It most certainly did," Girion assured.

"Good," Thornoak returned, smiling.

"Were you able to come up with a plan for dealing with Quagga?" Aradis asked.

"Indeed," the Konaskwa replied. "Limberleaf brought an excellent suggestion from Fergus regarding our possible course of action, and I contributed a few touches of my own. What we came up with is, I believe, quite satisfactory. When we finished conversing, Limberleaf departed for Anganor and should have arrived there several hours ago. Fergus will be in the midst of making preparations now, even as we speak, but I fully trust that when we arrive, everything will be suitably arranged."

"What's the plan, then, sire?" Girion inquired.

"You'll see for yourself when we get to Anganor," Thornoak answered, with a twinkle in his eye. "I don't want to spoil the surprise. I can tell you for certain that Quagga isn't going to like how things turn out, though. However, the two of you won't need to worry about a thing. You see, everything will already be taken care of."

Then, moving his tonquit around to face the company, Thornoak raised his voice and cried out, "Good Barada of Argonis! Today this land shall have a Konaskwa again, reigning from Strongbranch Citadel. I am dreadfully sorry that I abandoned you for so long, but I am back now, and I intend to put things right. Today we shall reclaim Anganor, and whatever stands in our way, be it Quagga or ten thousand Quaggas, shall not hinder us, for today the crown of Thornoak Assartanu shall shine in the light of Marda again."

The Konaskwa now took the Amulet of the Akwarna from around his neck and held it up for all to see.

"Behold!" he cried. "In my own hand, I hold the sign of assurance that the Sannadosh, this time of terrible adversity, will soon come to an end. As you have heard, the Sign of the Sengara has been fulfilled by these courageous Menfolk. But gaze upon the Amulet of the Akwarna with your own eyes and rejoice that the ancient words have run true. And let honor be given to Aradis Kingblade and Girion Ringmark, the brave Menfolk from across the sea!"

A great cry of jubilation rose up from the company, as they raised their hands and hailed the Siloans, who were utterly overwhelmed by this exuberant show of appreciation.

"Do not forget this day in the days to come," Thornoak said to the Menfolk quietly. "Your labors have not been in vain," he assured.

They nodded at him in return.

Then, addressing the company once more, Thornoak shouted, "Let us go forth, valiant folk of Argonis. Forth to Anganor!"

Now the Konaskwa turned his mount to face forward. Another mighty cheer went up from the company. The gates of the Royal Manniog were opened, and the troop passed through them onto the way that led back through the forest to Konassu Road, with Paskasha and Chelashu at the front, Thornoak and his daughter just behind and the Menfolk right behind them.

"In all seriousness, Girion Ringmark," Aradis said, glancing at the rows of armed Ingan warriors behind him, "what have we gotten ourselves into?"

"If you would have just stayed home instead of going down to the Ploughman's Shanty on that night back in Elaya, none of this would have happened," Girion laughed.

"Oh, I'll wager Nagello would have found me no matter where I went that evening." Aradis grinned. "Anyway, it's too late for regrets now. I suppose we'll have to make the best of it. So far we've been doing all right, all things considered."

"We have indeed," Girion returned thoughtfully, looking up at the bright sky overhead.

As Marda rose above Mentasqua, the company came out from the shade of Kassimaw Forest onto the open swath of Konassu Road. Then it turned north, toward Anganor. A kindly summer breeze danced through the woods, and morning rays glanced off the spears of the soldiers and the jewels in the Konaskwa's crown. But no light in that splendid array was as bright as the hope that had been kindled in the hearts of the company, for they had seen with their very own eyes that there were now powers at work to bring about the deliverance of Argonis. That deliverance, which had once been naught but a desperate dream, now seemed really and truly possible.

Nonetheless, there was still much darkness ahead for the kingdom, for it was yet troubled both within and without. However, on this particular morning, at least for Aradis and Girion, that coming darkness seemed far-off. Though there were formidable tasks yet before them, they had found new strength and vigor in the victories that had just been accomplished. The Sign of the Sengara had been fulfilled, and Thornoak was going back to Anganor. Though the Barada of Argonis had not fully reunited and Ravinia had not been defeated, the lads had begun to turn the tide against her. Both they and Argonis had needed hope to carry on. And, for now, what they had was enough.

THE END

Author's Note on the Appendices

As was stated regarding the appendices of this saga's previous volumes, the following appendices are included for the sake of the reader who is interested in the sorts of information they contain, information which some readers may, I fear, find dull and boring. However, the careful reader of Appendices 3 and 4 in particular will be pleased, I think, to discover connections therein to the adventures of Aradis and Girion.

As before, I have been obliged to write these appendices, but no one is obliged to read them. They contain linguistic, cultural, geographical, historical and chronological information and the like – things which are of great interest to Oronic loremasters and persons of that ilk. However, it must be made very clear that one may ignore the appendices altogether and still find the main story rich and satisfying.

Sincerely Yours,
Jarrett J. Skaddisson

Glossary of Useful Terms

The following glossary, which is by no means comprehensive, has been included for three purposes:

- To act as a quick reference guide for terms which are either used frequently in the story or are of great importance to it.

- To provide the reader with descriptions of entities that have been explained in the previous volumes of this saga, but which are not explicitly exposited in the main text of this current volume.

- To provide additional information about certain entities which the reader may find to be of interest.

The reader may note that several items which are presented in the main text are left unexplained here in the glossary; this is intentional on the author's part, especially as regards things pertaining to the Deep Lore of Orona, as it would be imprudent to reveal elements critical to the unfolding of the Kingblade Chronicles prematurely. Hence, for the time being, the reader must be left as perplexed about some things as are Aradis and Girion. Please note that items pertaining to timekeeping in Orona (such as the names of ages, months, days of the week and times of day) are not included in this glossary, as they are dealt with in Appendix 2.

Agleri – A region in central Velaris which encompasses nine barolli, one of which is Feldryn, wherein lies Siloa. The primary geographical feature of the area is the Plains of Agleri.

Anganor – The capital of the Kingdom of Argonis. Anganor is also known as Trunktown, which is a rough translation of its name from Asla'gu, a now little-used tongue of the Ingans of the eastern Elder Forest.

Aradath (adj. Aradathian) – The Southern Moiety of Orona. All those regions of Orona, which lie south of the Bushbelt. It contains the Neathmarda of Byram, Quarana, Fenrost and the Eldritch Isles.

Aradathian – A Barada from Aradath. The term is also the adjectival form of 'Aradath.'

Aragest – The capital city of the Kingdom of Velaris and a port of international significance. It lies on the northeastern shore of Cape Loresso.

Argonis, Kingdom of – A relatively small Ingan kingdom in the eastern region of the Elder Forest. Argonis is also known as Garlenwood, which is a rough translation of its name from Asla'gu, a now little-used tongue of the Ingans of the eastern Elder Forest.

Ashaska – A taboo among the Wennatoga. An ashaska can be due to the perception of either an entity's sacredness or profanity, but in all cases, it involves the idea that certain things cannot be said, done or touched without consequences, which will either be inflicted by Barada or beings of the Haedra. There are different levels of severity or intensity for different ashaskas, depending on each case and what it involves. Some are serious enough to warrant death as a punishment for their violation, while others merit only public shaming.

Asla'gu – An Ingan language of the eastern Elder Forest. It is the native tongue of the Wennatoga of Argonis, but its usage has declined considerably in the last few centuries of the Latter Epoch due to Huldionization.

Asquamot – The eastern region of Argonis. It lies east of the Teraska.

Assartanu – A personal name in Asla'gu. In Daiga, it is rendered as 'Thornoak.'

Bannymagracket – A monster featured in the Leprechaun folktale, *The Nine Lasses of Mellany Mountain*. This monster remains sedate and harmless unless it consumes a spoonful of plum marmalade, at which point it becomes ferocious and bloodthirsty.

Barada (sing. Barada; adj. Baradic) – The intelligent inhabitants of Orona, as opposed to the Telnari, the animals. When preceded by the definite article, the word can refer to all Barada as a whole, a group of Barada or an individual; the meaning must be determined by context.

Barolla (pl. Barolli) – One of 27 counties, or districts, of the Kingdom of Velaris.

Bippledrops – Small, smooth, pastel-colored candies coming in various shades and made by the Sky-Gnomes of Argonis.

Blackbough Woods – A region several hundred miles to the west of Argonis, where the Witch Ravinia dwells.

Blackwings – See 'Farga.'

Blunderbob – A Leprechaun term referring to a person who unwittingly causes a great deal of trouble for others, generally due to a lack of attention and sometimes a lack of intelligence.

Bratbangles – A rough translation of the Daigan exclamation 'thalma-thernanna', which expresses either frustration, annoyance or disgust, depending on the context.

Brightbeam – Aradis' sword, given to him by his father on the night he left Siloa.

Bushbelt, The – One of the Neathmarda. It separates Huldion and Aradath, circumscribing the entire world of Orona, lying roughly along its equator, which is called Sabakwani's Girdle. It is covered by dense jungle, steep mountains and regions of active volcanism and is several hundred miles wide at all points. The Bushbelt is occupied by savage, aggressive Barada and strange, terrifying beasts; thus, it presents a formidable barrier to movement between the Moieties of Orona. Consequently, almost all travel through the Bushbelt occurs along established routes, which are protected by cooperative garrisons of Barada from various kingdoms in both Huldion and Aradath. This cooperation occurs primarily for the advancement of trade interests.

Byram – One of the Neathmarda. It lies in Aradath, to the west of Quarana. The Kingdom of Argonis lies near the eastern coast of Byram.

Cape Loresso – See 'Loresso, Cape.'

Crannadacks – A Leprechaun expression signifying extreme frustration or indicating that the matter to which the word is applied is exceedingly ruinous or detrimental. The term originated from a type of biting insect native to Murnia called a crannadack that occasionally plagued the homes of Leprechauns there.

Daegar – Dark magic and/or dealings with evil beings of the Haedra.

Daiga (adj. Daigan) – Historically, the language of the Pine-Elves of Murnia. However, due to the wide geographical and cultural interaction of the Pine-Elves with other Barada, Daiga was used increasingly as a lingua franca throughout Orona in the 2nd-7th centuries of the Latter Epoch. By the opening of the 8th century of the Latter Epoch, it was widely spoken in every Neathmarda, though not by culturally-resistant or isolated populations. Daiga is the daily language used in both Velaris and Argonis.

Deathwash, The – Ravinia's enchanted black tears, which instantly kill anything they touch. The term also refers to the black rain summoned by Ravinia, which, likewise, immediately kills anything it touches.

Deep Lore – Lore of Orona which pertains to either matters of the Haedra or to those matters of the Haedra which affect Kazamar. The term is also used to refer to events of great significance in the former ages of Orona, some of which have been largely forgotten by the Barada.

Dorganinka – An extremely sluggish, light gray rodent of the eastern Elder Forest. They are, on average, around nine inches in length and burrow in open meadows or glades, although they are frequently found hunting for insects in heavily wooded areas far from their dens.

Druids (adj. Druidic) – One of the Narthanna. Druids are extremely human-like Barada, possessing height within the normal human range of variance and having an average lifespan of around 400 years. Notably, Druids mature physically more quickly than humans and retain a high level of fitness into their fourth century of life.

Dwarves – One of the Narthanna. Dwarves are short, human-like Barada, between 4 and 4 ½ feet tall, with an average lifespan of 130 years. They have thick skin and round noses, and their bodies are stout and muscular.

Elder Forest, The – One of the Five Fabled Lands. The Elder Forest lies in eastern Byram and is characterized by various types of woodlands. In the north, semitropical forests prevail; the central regions are dominated by deciduous forests; the southern regions contain primarily coniferous forests. The Kingdom of Argonis lies in the eastern region of the Elder Forest.

Eldritch Isles, The – One of the Neathmarda, an archipelago of large islands that lies in Aradath, far to the west of Byram and far to the east of Quarana.

Elves – One of the Narthanna. Elves are extremely human-like Barada, although they are slightly taller than humans as a general rule, possess an average lifespan of 300 years and have pointed ears.

Emerald Run, The – The primary home of the Leprechauns of eastern Argonis. It is an extensive system of tunnels under the Balgorra Hills, which are in Argonis' northeastern corner.

Eoreth – The moon of Orona.

Erdion – One of the realms of the Haedra and the dwelling place of Telyon.

Farga (sing. Farga; adj. Fargese) – One of the Narthanna. Farga are human-like Barada with many bat-like characteristics, possessing height within the normal human range of variance and having a lifespan of around 60 years. They are distinguished from all other Barada by large, leathery wings that protrude from their shoulders. Their ears are like those of a bat, and their noses are a hybrid between bat and human noses. Many parts of their body are covered with hair. They are also known as Blackwings.

Farren, The – A plains region stretching from the port of Gorondil on the Indurian Deeps nearly all the way to the eastern border of Argonis. It is dotted with large, bizarre rock formations.

Feldryn – A barolla in the Agleri region of Velaris. The village of Siloa is on the western edge of Feldryn.

Fell Alliance, The – The legions of Druids, Blackwings, Yetis and Dwarves of the eastern Elder Forest that have allied themselves with Ravinia.

Fenrost – One of the Neathmarda. It lies in Aradath, to the south of Quarana.

Five Fabled Lands, The – The five regions of the Neathmarda of Byram. These are the Elder Forest in the east, Pollona in the northeast, Rannadalf in the southwest, Soyawat Piyani in the northwest and the Wide Lands in the southeast.

Fontskals, The – A group of rocky islands in the southern Indurian Deeps, which is inhabited primarily by Menfolk. The term is also commonly used to refer to the nine largest islands in the group.

Forebounder, The – The official title of the leader of the Leprechauns of the Emerald Run.

Garlen – A kind of tree native to the eastern Elder Forest. Garlens grow throughout the Kingdom of Argonis and, due to their predominance there, have actually given that land its name. Their trunks are tall and thin, and they have elongated green leaves with a golden tinge to them.

Garlenwood, The Kingdom of – See 'Argonis, the Kingdom of.'

Gnomes (adj. Gnomish) – One of the Narthanna; short, human-like Barada, between 3 and 3 ½ feet tall, with an average lifespan of 150 years. Gnomish morphology varies considerably; Gnomes can have faces ranging from squarish to triangular, and their body frames can either be skinny and nimble or broad and muscular. Their ears can be, variously, indistinguishable from Mannish ears, slightly pointed or shaped almost like a conch shell.

Goblins (adj. Goblin) – One of the Narthanna. Goblins are shortish, human-like Barada, between 4 ½ and 5 feet tall, with an average lifespan of 90 years. They generally have rather gangly, slender frames and possess large, triangular ears. Their noses can be a range of shapes or sizes, and their skin color can vary considerably.

Goldquiver – The current leader of the Fall-Elves of Mendalas.

Greenwall, The – A high barrier of magical green energy that rises from the floor of the Chasm of the Erynos and serves to keep the Fell Alliance from entering the Stony Wilds via Blackbough Woods. The Greenwall was created by a mysterious utterance of King Thornoak at the battle known as the Sundering of the Erynos.

Hadathi (sing. Hadathi) – Powerful beings of the Haedra.

Haedra, The (adj. Haedran) – The immaterial realm in the universe of Orona.

Huldion (adj. Huldionite) – The Northern Moiety of Orona, all those regions of Orona, which lie north of the Bushbelt. It contains the Neathmarda of Tassaru, Estereth, Murnia and Jassuna.

Huldionite – A Barada from Huldion. The term is also the adjectival form of 'Huldion.'

Huldionization – The promotion and/or implementation of various aspects of Huldionite culture.

Indurian Deeps – The ocean which lies between the Neathmarda of Byram and Quarana.

Ingans (sing. Ingan; adj. Ingan) – One of the Narthanna. Ingans are tree-like Barada, generally between 7 and 7½ feet tall, with an average lifespan of 250 years. Their morphology is essentially that of a tree with human-like features: eyes, ears, nose and a mouth, along with jointed, bark-covered legs and arms. They are also known as Treefolk.

Jassa – A goat-like creature, though rather larger and more agile than goats; jassa are used as mounts by the Ogres of Longarnu and the surrounding settlements.

Jewelcakes – Cakes made by the Leprechauns of the Emerald Run by mixing jewels from the mines below their main passages with the waters of Shamrock Lake. The preparation of jewelcakes is a somewhat involved process wherein numerous ingredients are added to the initial combination of jewels and lake water.

Kassimaw Forest – The forest to the south of Anganor.

Kazamar – The material realm in the universe of Orona.

Kendarill – A bird native to the eastern Elder Forest and an ancient symbol of Eastern Argonis. Its morphology is rather like a hummingbird, but its tail is more elongated, and it possesses a distinctive, rounded crest. The bird is, on average, about the size of a large robin. Primarily active at night, the kendarill glows with a subdued silver light, which helps it lure insects and small fish to the surface of lakes and streams. The Ingans of Argonis maintain that they were first led by a single kendarill into the area that currently constitutes Eastern Argonis.

Konaskwa, The – The official title of the ruler of the Kingdom of Argonis, who must be an Ingan.

Konassu Road – The main road leading south from Anganor through Kassimaw Forest. A number of miles south of Anganor, it curves to the west and runs over to the Quarinoc River.

Kuringa – A red plant material, rather like peat, that is burned by the Ingans of the eastern Elder Forest to provide both light and heat. Many Ingans also burn it for its aroma, for which they have a great liking.

Leprechauns (adj. Leprechaun, Leprechaunish) – One of the Narthanna. Leprechauns are short, human-like Barada, between 2 ½ and 3 feet tall, with an average lifespan of 200 years. They have a generally slender build, and their faces are characterized by wide noses, slightly pointed ears and sharp chins.

Longarnu – The primary Ogric settlement in the Kingdom of Argonis. It is located in eastern Mentasqua.

Loresso, Cape – A prominent cape on the northeastern coast of Velaris. The term also refers to a region of Velaris which encompasses six barolli on the cape.

Luminous Meridian, The – The most northerly point in all Orona.

Maena (pl. Maenas) – A term designating a female individual who is one of the Menfolk.

Machaswa – Beings of the Haedra believed by the Wennatoga to be the spirits of their ancestors.

Mamgaburra – A tree native to the swamps of the Goblin lands of northwestern Quarana. It grows to be approximately forty feet tall and has an extremely fat, gray-barked trunk and numerous twisting branches.

Manfellow (pl. Manfellows) – A term designating a male individual who is one of the Menfolk.

Marda – The sun of Orona.

Mardelac Forest – A great forest just to the north of the Kingdom of Argonis that extends nearly all the way eastward to the Indurian Deeps.

Marlassi Coast, The – A region in southeast Velaris which encompasses four barolli. The Marlassi Coast, which stretches from the southern end of Cape Loresso to the southern border of the Kingdom of Velaris, is the primary geographical feature of the area.

Masters of the Seasons, The – See 'Naqua Senkawa.'

McDasher's Mirth – A celebration hosted by Shillelagh McDasher in the Emerald Run. These can be held for practically any reason whatsoever and always involve feasting, dancing and music.

Mendalas – A small region on the eastern edge of the Kingdom of Argonis. Though it is technically outside Argonis, it is still under the sovereignty of that land.

Menfolk (masc. sing. Manfellow; masc. pl. Manfellows; fem. sing. Maena; fem. pl. Maenas; adj. Mannish) – One of the Narthanna. Menfolk are human Barada, possessing height within the normal range of human variance and having an average lifespan of 70 years.

Mentasqua – The central region of Argonis lying between two rivers, the Teraska on the east and the Quarinoc on the west.

Moieties of Orona, The – The northern and southern hemispheres of Orona: Huldion and Aradath.

Naqua Senkawa – The Asla'gu name for the Masters of the Seasons: Masku, Tagwan, Hanidosha and Yaggawat. These are the four ontara of the Sacred Quinary who preside over spring, summer, autumn and winter, respectively.

Narthanna (sing. Narthaya) – In the singular, the term for one of the distinct varieties of Barada, such as Menfolk, Druids, Elves, Dwarves, Gnomes, Ingans, etc. The plural refers to several or all of the varieties of Barada.

Neathmarda (pl. Neathmarda) – A translation of the Daigan term 'dhar-marda', which literally means 'situated under Marda'. The Neathmarda are the nine most populated landmasses of Orona. Technically, one of them is actually a collection of landmasses rather than a single landmass, as it is a group of islands. The nine Neathmarda are Tassaru, Murnia, Estereth, Byram, Quarana, Jassuna, the Eldritch Isles, Fenrost and the Bushbelt.

Nippi-nappa – Shaggy, white-haired, three-horned, antelope-like creatures herded and kept for their meat by the Ogres of Argonis.

Northern Moiety of Orona, The – The northern hemisphere of Orona, another name for Huldion.

Ogres (adj. Ogric) – One of the Narthanna. Ogres are large, human-like Barada, between 8 and 9 feet tall, with an average lifespan of 60 years. They have thick skin, big ears, broad noses and are extremely muscular.

Ontara – In the Taquenar, particularly mighty beings of the Haedra.

Orona (adj. Oronic) – The world of the Kingblade Chronicles.

Otterloo – Otter-like creatures with glowing wings that dwell in the subterranean waters of the Emerald Run. They are kept as pets by the Leprechauns there, who also raise them for their milk, from which they make butter and cream.

Outhedge, The – An approximately fifty-foot-tall thorn hedge that surrounds the Kingdom of Argonis on its eastern, northern and western boundaries.

Pachacuri – A bioluminescent moss used to illuminate both the interior and exterior of various dwellings and other structures in Argonis, particularly in Anganor.

Palquanoga – An ontara of the Sacred Quinary. Unlike the others, who each preside over one of the four seasons, Palquanoga presides over timelessness.

Pastures of Seruga, The – A tract of rolling meadows in Argonis granted to some Ogric mercenaries by Thornoak's father. They lie in-between the Teraska River and Anganor.

Perinac River – A river that begins in the Arkanian Mountains, several hundred miles to the west of Argonis, and flows into the Indurian Deeps. It forms the northern boundary of the Kingdom of Argonis.

Ploughman's Shanty, The – The tavern in the village of Siloa.

Pollona (adj. Pollonan) – One of the Five Fabled Lands, Pollona lies in northeastern Byram. Its terrain consists of deserts, savannah, mountains and tropical forests.

Quarana – One of the Neathmarda. It lies in Aradath, to the east of Byram and to the north of Fenrost. The Kingdom of Velaris lies on the eastern shores of Quarana.

Quarinoc River – The river that divides Mentasqua, which is the central region of Argonis, from Songalwa, the western region of Argonis.

Quennic – A mild bread fried in oil and topped with kantarec, a sweet powder made from a woodland plant of the eastern Elder Forest called yammequon.

Questmongers, The – An organization of secret, highly skilled agents in the direct service of the Konaskwa of Argonis. They are called upon to carry out missions of particular importance or difficulty and also to investigate, expose and eradicate any and all covert operations against the Konaskwa or the kingdom.

Quonniot – A rock dwelling of one of the oracles at Hadoga Taquenassa, the Colony of the Oracles in south central Argonis.

Rashty Pie – A savory pot pie featuring elk and a number of other ingredients. It is a highly favored dish of the Leprechauns of the Emerald Run.

Rayalta – The Star-Realm – i.e. the region of Kazamar, which lies beyond the sky of Orona.

Rendanna (sing. Rendaya) – In the singular, a subdivision of one of the Narthanna; that is, a particular variety of a particular Narthaya. E.g., Shore-Elves are a Rendaya of Elves.

Rimwold – A region in western Velaris, which encompasses six barolli. The primary geographical feature of the area is Rimwold Forest.

Sabakwani's Girdle – The equator of Orona.

Sacred Quinary, The – The five ontara most revered by the Ingans of Argonis: Masku, Tagwan, Hanidosha, Yaggawat and Palquanoga.

Salnagok – A traditional celebration of Aradathian Ogres involving bonfires and feasting, customarily observed on the twenty-third day of every other month.

Sannadosh, The – A prophesied time of great distress that will befall the Wennatoga and the Kingdom of Argonis. It was foretold that it would be accompanied by particular signs.

Sardolia, The – A government organization of the Kingdom of Velaris. The agents of the Sardolia act as tax collectors, constables and a standing army. The Sardolia has barracks in the capital of every barolla in Velaris.

Sarganath – The name for all the lands under the sway of Ravinia. Sarganath completely surrounds the Kingdom of Argonis.

Sayings of the Sages, The – An ancient collection of Mannish proverbs.

Semmoquaw – A Konaskwa of Argonis, reigning from LE 271 to LE 363. He is particularly notable for his Huldionizing influence (i.e., his promotion and implementation of various aspects of Huldionite culture).

Sennec – A variety of deciduous tree, often growing near water. Its sap is used in the making of a mead called tapusa.

Shamrock Lake – A subterranean lake in the Emerald Run.

Shore-Elves – A Rendaya of Elves hailing from the Eldritch Isles, though their original homeland is in Huldion. They often have olive-colored skin and are generally perceived by other Barada as being somewhat odd.

Sky-Gnomes – A Rendaya of Gnomes living in Argonis, having small and spindly frames and ears shaped like conch shells.

Southern Moiety of Orona, The – The southern hemisphere of Orona; another name for Aradath.

Sparlag – A lively Leprechaun dance with fast footwork and occasional leaps.

Stony Wilds, The – A wild, forested, hilly region lying between the Kingdom of Argonis and the southernmost stretch of the Arkanian Mountains, which are several hundred miles west of Argonis.

Sundering of the Erynos, The – A great battle between the forces of Argonis and the Fell Alliance that took place on a high ridge known as the Erynos Divide, which lies at the western edge of the Stony Wilds. At the climax of the battle, Ravinia summoned the Deathwash to slaughter her enemies. King Thornoak responded by speaking a mysterious word of power, which caused the Erynos Divide to collapse into a great chasm, sending many of both Argonis' and the Fell Alliance's forces to their deaths. Also, as a result of Thornoak's utterance, a high barrier of magical green energy known as the Greenwall rose up from the floor of the newly-created gorge, the Chasm of Erynos, which now serves to keep the armies of Ravinia from entering the Stony Wilds.

Tapusa – A golden mead made with sap of the sennec tree.

Taquenar, The – The body of traditional beliefs, practices and lore of the Wennatoga.

Telnari (sing. Telnara; adj. Telnaric) – Refers to the animals of Orona, as opposed to the Barada, the intelligent beings of Orona. The word applies specifically to animals with blood and bones and thus includes mammals, birds, reptiles, amphibians and fish.

Telyon – An ancient Mannish name for the Danna.

Teraska River – The river that divides Mentasqua, which is the central region of Argonis, from Asquamot, the eastern region of Argonis.

Treefolk (masc. sing. Treefellow; masc. pl. Treefellows; fem. sing. Treemaena; fem. pl. Treemaenas; adj. Treeish) – See 'Ingans.'

Triptrap – A Leprechaun term that refers to someone or something that is worthless or of no account.

Trolls (adj. Trollish) – One of the Narthanna. Trolls are large, human-like Barada, between 8 ½ and 9 ½ feet tall, with an average lifespan of 50 years. Some aspects of Trollish morphology vary considerably; they can have faces ranging from oblong to triangular, their ears and noses can either be round or pointed and the skin colors of different Trollish Rendanna can be quite diverse. However, Trolls' body frames are generally more slender than stocky, and they are consistently muscular.

Trunktown – See 'Anganor.'

Tyracus – The great, blue South Star, often used to aid in navigation in Orona.

Vastia the Pathfinder – The renowned Elven explorer who pioneered a route through the Bushbelt from Huldion to Aradath. The Latter Epoch is considered to have begun the year after he returned from his expedition. In fact, his opening of the way through the Bushbelt is the event which launched the present age of Orona.

Velaris, The Kingdom of (adj. Velarisian) – An Elven kingdom in eastern Quarana, having substantial populations of Elves and Menfolk, as well as pockets of Gnomes, Dwarves and Druids.

Verdinnion, The – The council of Argonis' leaders that represents the primary varieties of Narthanna and Rendanna that reside therein: the Ingans, the Wood-Gnomes, the Fall-Elves, the Leprechauns, the Timber-Elves, the Ogres and the Sky-Gnomes. The Verdinnion is led by the Konaskwa.

Walls of Ancient Wrath, The – An enormous cliff, three thousand feet high, that runs roughly four hundred miles from east to west, forming the southern boundary of the Kingdom of Argonis and the Stony Wilds.

Weggimnawa – The proper name of the stump building where the Gnarly Stump Tavern and the Questmongers' Den are housed.

Wennatoga – The principal Ingan tribe that inhabits the Kingdom of Argonis.

Yetis – One of the Narthanna. Yetis are large, ape-like Barada, between 6 ½ and 7 feet tall, with an average lifespan of 60 years. They are covered in thick hair, usually white in color, and are extremely muscular.

Timekeeping in Orona–
The Manus-Romelliad Calendar

A Brief Note on the Manus-Romelliad Empire

Early in the Third Age of Orona, which is known as the Apex of Archaea, two great Elven empires arose in the Neathmarda of Tassaru. These were known as the Manusian and Romelliad Empires. Through a series of national upheavals, political intrigues and great battles, they were unified into what was undoubtedly the most powerful political construct of the Apex of Archaea: the Empire of Manus-Romella. Manus-Romella held sway over much of Tassaru and many lands beyond for a great many centuries, disseminating its cultural, philosophical, political, artistic, architectural and societal institutions, models and values throughout Huldion. For this reason, it is regarded by many Oronic historians as the single most important political entity in the history of Orona. In fact, so significant was the Manus-Romelliad Empire that its sundering and subsequent transformation marked the close of the Third Age of Orona.

One of the entities which was inherited by the Barada from the Empire of Manus-Romella is the Manus-Romelliad (M-R) Calendar. This is used to mark the five ages of Orona, the twelve months of the year, the seven days of the week and the various times of day. This appendix details the divisions of the M-R timekeeping system, which is used to describe the transpiring of events throughout the Kingblade Chronicles.

The Five Ages of Orona

In the standard M-R reckoning, there are five ages of Orona, which are as follows:

The First Age of Orona: The Mists of Old (MO or simply 'The Mists') has no specified commencement point, and its length is much disputed by the learned Barada of Orona. Dates are only occasionally attached to events which are believed to have transpired in the Mists of Old. When they are, they are cited as having occurred a certain number of years before the termination of the age. Thus, the notation MO 130 would signify the year 130 years prior to the commencement of the Second Age of Orona. [NB: those Barada who accord credence to the Mannish volume known as the Elyrion refer to the First Age of Orona as The Forgotten Days (FD) and assign it a specific duration. Dates for the Forgotten Days are listed forward in time from FD 1, the first year of that age, to FD 2312, its final year.]

The Second Age of Orona: The Years of Yore (YY or simply 'Yore') are reckoned as having begun in the year after the founding of the great Druidic fortress city of Grath. The end of the Years of Yore is marked by the destruction of the ancient Mannish capital city,

Yaruzadar, by the Druids of Grath, which occurred in YY 1895. This particular date was chosen by Oronic loremasters because of the extent and significance of the Druid kingdom and its successors, which rose to prominence as a result of the defeat of the Menfolk. [NB: adherents of the Elyrion mark the start of the Years of Yore as having occurred 209 years before the date used in the M-R calendar. Consequently, in that system, the date assigned to the Fall of Yaruzadar is YY 2104. In cases where clarification between the two systems is needed, the Mannish system is prefaced by the indication EYY, with the E standing for Elyriac, the adjectival form of Elyrion.]

The Third Age of Orona: The Apex of Archaea (AA or simply 'Archaea') began the year after the Fall of Yaruzadar and ended with the sundering of the Empire of Manus-Romella, which occurred in AA 1087. The term 'Archaea' refers to the southern and central regions of Tassaru, which is where the great empires of this age flourished.

The Fourth Age of Orona: The Bridging of the Tides (BT or simply 'The Bridging') is determined to have commenced in the year after the sundering of the Manus-Romelliad Empire; it was concluded in BT 1290 by the return of the great Elven explorer Vastia the Pathfinder from his expedition to find a viable route through the Bushbelt. The name of the age comes from the expression coined by the renowned Manus-Romelliad statesman Salarna, who famously said, "Time is a tide; someday our children will reach the latter days, and what stands between us and them will be a bridge across the tides."

The Fifth Age of Orona: The Latter Epoch (LE or simply 'The Latter') began the year after the Elven explorer Vastia the Pathfinder returned to Huldion from his fabled expedition into Aradath. Aradis and Girion's departure from Siloa for the Kingdom of Argonis occurred on the 10th of Elaya in the year LE 717.

A Note on the Commencement of Ages in the Manus-Romelliad Calendar

Even though the events which triggered the onset of a new age occurred during the middle of each of the respective final years of the age in which they occurred, the following age, primarily for the ease of scribes' and loremasters' calculations, is determined as beginning on the first of Bellin which most closely follows the event which heralded the new age. Thus, even though Vastia the Pathfinder returned from his expedition some time during the year BT 1290, it was not until the first of Bellin, the beginning of the next year, that the Latter Epoch began.

The Ages of the Manus-Romelliad Calendar in Brief

1—The Mists of Old

2—The Years of Yore 1-1895

3—The Apex of Archaea 1-1087

4—The Bridging of the Tides 1-1290

5—The Latter Epoch 1-the present (717)

The Months of the Manus-Romelliad Calendar

The Manus-Romelliad calendar is both lunar and solar, using twelve months consisting of 30 days each and a special set of five days called the Middings (also called Pelarond), which are placed in-between the first two months of Huldion's summer (Aradath's winter) in order to complete a 365-day solar year. The Middings is celebrated all over Orona as a five-day holiday with festivities, parades and joyous feasting. The Manus-Romelliad year begins in the springtime, and the first month is roughly equivalent to our month of March. Though to be entirely precise, it begins in the last few days of our February—February 21st to be exact. Very minor adjustments have been made to the calendar periodically throughout the centuries in order to maintain astronomical integrity, much like the case of our own calendar, but in Oronic reckoning, the extra days have always been added to the Middings. Customarily, every eight years, two days are added to the Middings for a total of seven days for Pelarond on the eighth year. Such years are called Years of the Middings. The names of the generally correspondent months are as follows:

Bellin (March)—30 days

Serona (April)—30 days

Alareth (May)—30 days

Landrenna (June)—30 days

Pelarond [also known as 'The Middings'] (end of June)—5 days

Ularos (July)—30 days

Galrim (August)—30 days

Ferenos (September)—30 days

Derrig (October)—30 days

Elaya (November)—30 days

Tannaril (December)—30 days

Harasa (January)—30 days

Ildurion (February)—30 days

The Days of the Week in the Manus-Romelliad Calendar

The Manus-Romelliad calendar uses a seven-day week. These seven days are as follows:

Vardis—Sunday

Jurdis—Monday

Cordis—Tuesday

Nardis—Wednesday

Ragdis—Thursday

Maldis—Friday

Yawandis—Saturday

NB: the particle 'dis' does not actually mean 'day' but comes from the Vasornic (adjectival form of Vasorna, the language of the Manusians) word 'dissa,' meaning 'charge, entity placed under the protection of someone or something.'

The Times of Day in the Manus-Romelliad Calendar

The names for different times of day come from corresponding Vasornic expressions, which have been loosely translated into Daiga. According to the common parlance throughout Orona, the times of day may be arranged sequentially as follows:

Call of Marda—the first hint of Marda's impending arrival

Song of Marda—the first appearance of Marda's rays over the horizon

Marda's Glory—early morning

Marda's Feast—late morning

Crown of Marda—noon

Dance of Marda—early afternoon

Journey of Marda—late afternoon

Marda's Farewell—sunset

Marda's Passing—twilight

Dawn of Eoreth—early evening

Eoreth's Tale—late evening

Scepter of Eoreth—midnight

Hour of Rayalta—another name for midnight

Palace of Eoreth—the hours right after midnight

Eoreth's Lament—the hours just before dawn

NB: Marda is the sun of Orona, Eoreth is the moon and Rayalta is the Star-Realm.

NB: the M-R Calendar reckons days as beginning at the Call of Marda and thus does not correspond to our own commencement of days at midnight.

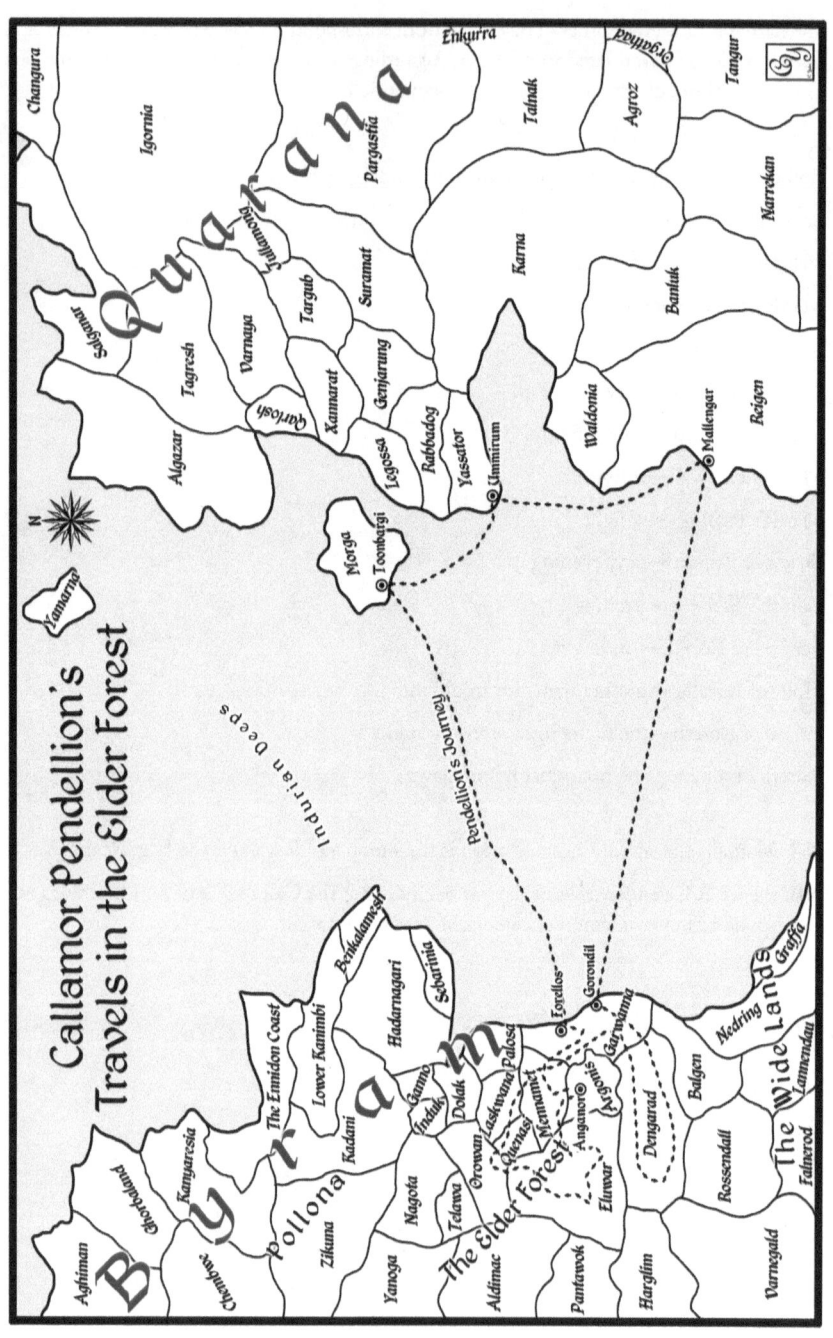

Callamor Pendellion's
Travels in the Elder Forest

A Travelogue of Anganor in the Days of Semmoquaw – The Document and its Author

Anganor is a city with a rich and complex history, and within its stone walls and high hedges, much can be found to startle and amaze any visitor. However, the magnificence of this place is scarcely known abroad in Orona, even in Aradath, save in vague murmurs around the fires of distant taverns. And even in these, it is spoken of only as a half-fantasy, a place of which some people have heard, but hardly anyone has seen.

Almost paradoxically, although Argonis has a substantial variety of Narthanna within its borders, including Ingans, Gnomes, Leprechauns, Elves, Dwarves, Ogres and even Menfolk, it has often been rather inaccessible to foreigners. The foremost reason for this is the fact that it is surrounded on all sides by formidable natural barriers – staggering cliffs and monstrous hedges of thorns. Argonis has, due to these obstacles, taken on a rather insular and reclusive nature over the centuries. Within its bounds, it has developed without much regard for the outside world, except for certain periods where its leaders have allowed or even encouraged an influx of foreign ideas or commodities. These have been mostly confined to three areas – the usage of Daiga, the institution of the Manus-Romelliad calendar and the imitation of certain Huldionite architectural styles. As for large-scale immigration of foreign persons, the various Narthanna who now reside in Argonis (save for the Ingans, who are truly indigenous) came by explicit invitation from its rulers. Argonis has never been inclined to let just anyone enter who wishes to do so and has only admitted foreign populations under rather extenuating circumstances. In practice, this has meant that foreigners generally didn't even bother journeying to Argonis unless they received some sort of prior indication that they would be welcomed there. As a result, precious little has been written about the kingdom by outsiders.

Nonetheless, there remains a rather vivid and detailed account by an outsider of the kingdom of Argonis and the city of Anganor in particular. The account dates from the early fourth century of the Latter Epoch and can be found in a work entitled *Wanderings in the Woodlands: An Aradathian Elf's Travels in the Eastern Elder Forest*. This volume was penned by the famous Elven ambassador, historian, ethnologist and linguist, Callamor Pendellion, or Gunnapeg as he was affectionately known to the Goblin peoples of eastern Xannarat, a land in northwestern Quarana, with whom he worked most intimately. Pendellion's book describes his eight-month sojourn in the Eastern Elder Forest, in which he sought to establish lasting trading links between the Ingans in that region and the Goblins dwelling on the island of Morga, which is offshore from Xannarat. Several chapters in the middle of the work present his travels and observations in Argonis and Anganor.

301

A Brief Biography of Callamor Pendellion, the Author of the Aforementioned Travelogue, with Specific Regard to the Circumstances Surrounding Its Composition

Callamor Pendellion was born in LE 131 in the Goblin village of Gamdakgan in the extreme south of Varnaya, which later merged with the land of Tagresh to form the present-day kingdom of Tagresh Varnaya. His parents, Medrinos and Hamarnia, published scholars in their own right, were Vine-Elves from the island of Tambari, which lies between the Neathmarda of Murnia and Tassaru. They had cultivated a prodigious enthusiasm for research in Goblin antiquities at an academy in their homeland and had decided to go to Varnaya to study such things firsthand, while collecting and preserving them for their academy back in Tambari.

Medrinos and Hamarnia arrived in Quarana in LE 116. In the first several years in which they traveled in Varnaya and the surrounding Goblin countries, they were met with fierce animosity and were frequently driven from village to village. The Goblins of northwest Quarana were relatively hostile to Huldionites at that time, and especially so to Elves, as they almost exclusively viewed them as profit-hungry scoundrels or pillaging barbarians; often they were accused of being both. However, as the Vine-Elven couple learned more about the Goblins' languages and cultures, they employed this knowledge to win friends among them, and they gradually came to be seen as earnest and sincere inquirers into the Goblins' views about themselves and their history. Consequently, they were eventually adopted into a Goblin tribe, the Yongaban, among whom Callamor was born.

From an extremely young age, Callamor showed both remarkable ability and interest in his parents' field of study – namely, all things Goblin. During his lifetime, he learned no less than 63 languages, 54 of which were Goblin tongues (and it must be noted that this was an exceedingly impressive feat, since Goblin languages are notoriously difficult to learn, although, of course, Pendellion had learned several of these natively). Also, he wrote an astonishing 278 books, many of which were penned in Daiga for the benefit of scholars in Huldion. Most of these were works on Goblin-related matters, including collections of folk-tales, grammars of different languages, catalogues of artifacts, geographies and much more. Among his works were his published journals and several notebooks of poems written in his native Tambari, as well as four fictional stories about a character named Jumankurra, a Goblin hero he set in the early Bridging of the Tides.

Pendellion was described by both Goblins and by other Narthanna he encountered in his travels as well-spoken, brilliant, tireless, extraordinarily perceptive and possessing an unquenchable thirst for knowledge. Most of his life was spent in Aradath, primarily in northwest Quarana, although he did journey to Huldion on three occasions. On the latter two of these trips, he gave lectures on his extensive findings at academies in the Neathmarda of Murnia and Tassaru. These had mixed approval, as many scholars were (and still are) rather disdainful of the native Narthanna of Aradath and disregarded their cultures and histories out of hand. Although some hailed Pendellion's research as singularly valuable and groundbreaking, most viewed it as badly tainted, since Pendellion seemed to regard many of the Goblins' stories and traditions as having a basis in fact.

Due to the controversial nature of Pendellion's views, some scholars even went so far as to claim that he had fabricated much of his data, and one infamously described him as 'hopelessly addled by Aradath.'

These experiences left rather a sour impression of Huldionites on Pendellion, and this is evidenced by his negative commentary on Huldionite scholars in many of his later works. Nonetheless, he recognized that there were some individuals among their ranks who were deeply appreciative of his labors, so he continued to write in Daiga that they might have access to his material.

In contrast to his rancorous reception by Huldionite scholars, Pendellion was widely respected among the Goblin peoples, so much so that he was considered to be one of their own. This earned him the name 'Gunnapeg,' which means 'true native' in Bajjarun, a lingua franca used among various Goblin tribes, primarily in in the land of Xannarat. Due to Pendellion's tremendous degree of familiarity with all aspects of Goblin society, as well as his close personal association with many Goblin leaders, he was appointed as an ambassador for the Goblin kingdom of Morga by Wullunga Bandugong, its High Gurrajan (a widely-employed Goblin term for a ruler). Bandugong was keenly interested in setting up trade associations with the Ingans of the Elder Forest, as there were a number of resources there that he wanted to be able to sell to Huldionite merchants in order to enrich his own domain. As the Ingans and the Goblins had not been on good terms for many centuries, Bandugong asked Pendellion to represent Morga to the Ingans of Byram. Although Pendellion was considered by the Goblins to be one of their own, he was, technically speaking, an Elf, and Bandugong hoped this fact would help downplay his Goblin associations.

Pendellion embarked from the port of Toonbargi in Morga, and in Ularos of LE 305 he arrived in the land of Garwanna, which lay along the Byram coast, just east of Argonis. He spent several months building favorable relations with Ingan tribes to the east and north of Argonis before he was granted an unexpected means of gaining access to that fabled land. A chieftain among the Tasquenash, a tribe of Ingans living just north of the Perinac River, was deeply impressed by Pendellion, so he gave him a tawmpah – a token of friendship and good will that acted something like a letter of recommendation among Ingan peoples. This particular chieftain was allied at the time with Semmoquaw, the Konaskwa of Argonis in those days, and Pendellion was told that the tawmpah he had been given would enable him to secure an audience with Semmoquaw through his associations with the Tasquenash.

When Pendellion showed the tawmpah to the sentinels of Argonis at its central northern gate on the banks of the Perinac, they agreed to provide him with an escort to Anganor and bring him before Semmoquaw. Several days later, Pendellion and his escort arrived in Anganor, where he was taken to Strongbranch Citadel. There he spoke at length with Semmoquaw, who, like his friends among the Tasquenash, was greatly impressed by the Vine-Elf.

Semmoquaw agreed to let Pendellion speak with the ministers of Argonis about specifics of trading arrangements with the Goblins of Morga, and these negotiations were conducted at Strongbranch Citadel over the next few weeks. During that time,

Semmoquaw also designated some of his servants to act as guides for Pendellion and show him the marvels of both Strongbranch Citadel and the city of Anganor.

After nineteen days in Anganor, on the 22nd of Ferenos, LE 305, Pendellion had concluded all of his trade discussions and forged a historic commercial alliance between Argonis and Morga, which has since been dubbed the Pendellion Pact, after its chief negotiator. Pendellion was then given additional guides by Semmoquaw, who took him through several regions of Argonis before he departed from that land via the same gate that he had entered.

Pendellion then went farther inland to speak with more Ingan peoples, although, due to the breakout of a tribal war, he was forced to flee north. There he sought to converse with still more Ingan clans. He was able to persuade a few of these to trade with the Goblins, although most of them were unremittingly hostile to the idea, so much so that Pendellion found himself in considerable danger on quite a few occasions. Ultimately, this leg of his trip proved the most difficult and the least successful.

Pendellion concluded his time in the Elder Forest by making his way down to the Tannaquaw Plains south of the Walls of Ancient Wrath, where he met with the local Ingan tribes and secured several agreements to initiate trade with Morga. Among all the Ingan peoples that Pendellion visited, he was most fascinated by the Kinnegwah tribe, who dwelt in this region, and he dedicated a full, separate volume to their culture and legends.

Pendellion's finances actually ran out completely while he was among the Kinnegwah, but they supplied him with ample provisions and a substantial enough gift that he was able to purchase passage on a Dwarven ship departing from the Garwanna coast. Although this ship was bound for the port of Mallengar in the Dwarven kingdom of Reigen over in Quarana, Pendellion found some Goblin merchants there who agreed to take him back to Morga free of charge, since he was an ambassador and because they were utterly astonished by his own command of their native Goblin tongue, Wargapurg (he actually spoke it better than they did, and he had no distinguishable foreign accent), the usage of which was restricted primarily to a few thousand Goblins in a small, remote area of the Goblin land of Yassator.

When Pendellion returned to the port of Toonbargi in Morga, his sponsor, Bandugong, was so delighted by his success that he awarded him the Amethyst Angujap, a medal featuring a vaguely dolphin-like creature native to the waters around Morga. This medal had never before been given to anyone but a Goblin, nor has it been presented to anyone but a Goblin since.

Years later, when Pendellion died in LE 398 of jibkanagga fever in the Goblin village of Bungarung in eastern Xannarat, his remains were dealt with according to his wishes, which were to have them interred using a traditional Goblin burial method called gamundi. His body was left on a murrugan, a Goblin death altar, until only his bones remained. These were then painted with gray earth and placed inside a wooden box, along with the Amethyst Angujap and a number of other gifts from Goblin leaders. A mamgaburra tree in Bungarung was cut open, and the box was placed inside so that the trunk might grow back over it. That tree is still there in Bungarung to this day, surrounded by countless tokens of memorial placed there over the years by Goblins from all over northwest Quarana.

Additional Notes on Pendellion's Travelogue of Anganor

What follows is a direct excerpt from Callamor Pendellion's book, *Wanderings in the Woodlands: An Aradathian Elf's Travels in the Eastern Elder Forest.* This volume is available in most academies and libraries in Orona that house works on Ingan studies, although it is sometimes published under Pendellion's native Tambari name, Bennio Lorenzari. [His parents' Tambari names were Sandorio and Laguenna Lorenzari; their other names, like Callamor's, were rough translations of their Tambari names into Daiga, taken for the purposes of journeys to other lands, as was (and still is) common practice. Such a Daigan traveling name is known as a dendaya (pl. dendanna).]

Pendellion's book is structured as a sequential narrative, although it occasionally deviates from this for the sake of including largely topical content; e.g. when presenting background information of a cultural or historical nature. It also features Pendellion's trademark practice of including frequent running commentary, clarifications and additional lore stuffed into parenthetical remarks. The section below begins right after Pendellion's chapters on his initial meeting with Semmoquaw and his description of Strongbranch Citadel. In his book, it is followed by his detailed reports on his trade negotiations with Semmoquaw's ministers, although that material is not presented here, as it is not directly relevant to his description of the city of Anganor.

Also, it should be noted that the Daigan renderings of the names of the districts in Anganor that are almost universally employed today actually originated with Pendellion. Pendellion gave these translations in his book, a copy of which eventually found its way into the hands of Semmoquaw's son, Menniget, who reigned as Konaskwa after him. Menniget thought very highly of Pendellion, and, consequently, whenever he conducted dealings in Daiga, he referred to the districts of Anganor using Pendellion's translations. These usages spread throughout the populace during his reign and came to be regarded as standard.

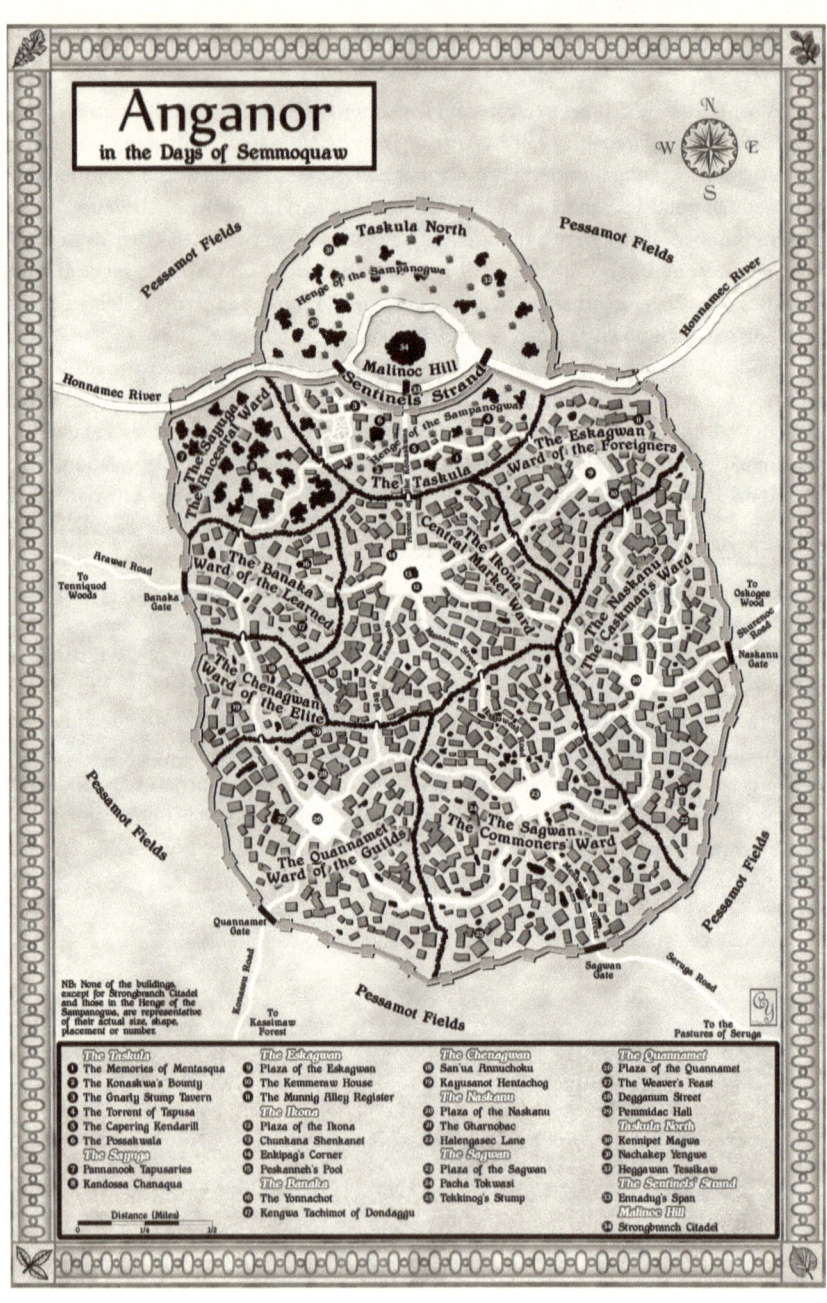

The Marvels of Semmoquaw's City –
The Divisions of Anganor

An Overview of the City

The city of Anganor, as I have mentioned before, is surrounded by high walls of stone, and its interior is divided into different sections by tall, green hedges (although it should be noted that there is a stone wall, not a hedge, in-between the Taskula and the Sentinels' Strand, as well as between the Taskula and the banks of the Honnamec to the east and west of the Sentinels' Strand – I will describe these places in more detail below, and the interested reader is also advised to consult the sketch of the city I have included in this book). This design, I later found out, is an imitation of a type of Ingan settlement called a manniog, although personally, I rather wonder which came first: Anganor or the manniogs. The city is absurdly old, I believe, although I could never get a straight answer on exactly how old. My nearest guess would be around four and a half (or perhaps five) thousand years, based on information I have collected from the Ingans, although I rather suspect that Anganor was a much smaller settlement in those days, if indeed the Ingans had arrived in these parts as early as they say they did. (Of course, if we are to believe the Huldionites, the Ingans actually came here a lot earlier than that. But I have already made my views on Huldionite scholarship perfectly clear in this volume, so here I will refrain from further comment.)

If I had to describe Anganor in only a few words, I simply would not; there is too much to say, and I really don't feel as if I could do the place justice in any of the tongues I know. Nonetheless, solely for the sake of the reader, here I will make an attempt, clumsy though it may be, to paint in broad, crude strokes the sentiments that the city stirred within me. As I walked through its streets, I perceived all these things: Anganor is ancient and yet not decrepit, drenched in memory and yet neither dazed nor distant, echoing with hearty laughter and yet cloaked in sobriety, brimming with both the unexpected and unfamiliar and yet not unsettling. It is an eruption of antiquity and creativity, a poem of heroism and wild enlightenment, a place sprung forth from boundless imagination and exotic finesse. Anganor is, in short, both unforgettable and indescribable.

What follows are my notes on my excursions into each of Anganor's separate districts, or okwalu, as the Wennatoga, the Ingans of Argonis, call them. (Technically, 'okwalu' is the singular and 'okwalwu' is the plural, but the Wennatoga often use the singular form to denote both the singular and the plural in the case of this particular word.) In the customary reckoning, there are nine of them. Although there are really three additional segments of the city beyond these nine, these last three are quite different from the others, and that is the reason for their exclusion from the tally. The nine okwalu are the Taskula, the Sayuga, the Eskagwan, the Ikona, the Banaka, the Chenagwan, the Naskanu, the Sagwan and the Quannamet. The additional three areas I mentioned are Taskula North, the Sentinels' Strand and Malinoc Hill.

Semmoquaw had promised me that, during my stay at Strongbranch Citadel, he would arrange for me to see every district of Anganor in detail. These visits, he decided, would be on days that I couldn't speak with his ministers about our trade proposals, as they would be occupied with other matters. The reader will, I trust, remember Tahonagga, one of my guides from the previous chapter. With his extensive knowledge of the history of Argonis and Anganor, he was, Semmoquaw deemed, the natural choice to accompany me on these excursions. The four days set aside for these were the 8th, 11th, 16th and 19th of Ferenos.

The Taskula

At midmorning, on the 8th of Ferenos, with Marda in a merry mood, I was taken by my guide, Tahonagga, from Strongbranch Citadel down to the bridge across the Honnamec and then to the gates leading from the Sentinels' Strand to the Taskula, which lies directly south of Malinoc Hill. The Taskula, I was told, was the very oldest district of the city, being the closest to Malinoc Hill and Strongbranch Citadel.

Of course, where possible in this work, I have tried to give the Daigan equivalent of Asla'gu words, phrases or expressions. Here I will endeavor to do that for the name 'the Taskula,' though I don't think I shall quite succeed. Tahonagga struggled greatly to supply me with a clear rendering of its meaning, but the best he could do was explain the two components from which it was formed. 'Tas,' he said, is a word that refers to a place that is of considerable importance and may be thought of as being interwoven with the Ingans themselves in some way. 'Kula,' the second portion, is a term describing a thing that has been deliberately preserved. Thus, the most adequate translation I could come up with, based on his explanations, is that Taskula means 'The Significant Place of the Remnant.'

As for what this 'remnant' component is referencing, one could readily deduce this, in my opinion, from just looking around the district; there are no less than twelve stumps of enormous girth and height situated throughout it. These are all that remain of a grove of sampanog trees, which can grow to be staggeringly tall, I was told by Tahonagga, though they could not attain to the height of Strongbranch. The Goblins of Qarlosh (who were the Goblins most inclined to exploration in the days of old) have stories about trees of absolutely fantastic height being found in the heart of Ingan lands, in forgotten forests in the Byram interior. Undoubtedly, these tales originated from the aforementioned sampanog trees, which perhaps grew over a rather large area in ancient times. I do not know if they still flourish anywhere, but I am quite sure that many of our northern friends up in Huldion would not believe in them even if one were cut down and brought before their very noses.

These sampanog trees in the Taskula were once all like smaller versions of Strongbranch Citadel; that is, they were whole trees filled with passageways and rooms and constituted the dwellings of persons of importance within the city. But near the commencement of the Bridging of the Tides, there was an incident called the Felling of the Sacred Sampanogwa, which is the Ingans' own account of how these trees were reduced to stumps. However, I will reserve that for a later section on the legends of Argonis. Suffice it to say here that the stumps I saw were perhaps half a hundred to three quarters of a hundred feet high. That should give the reader a possible idea of the original height of the trees, as well as the magnitude of the aforementioned calamity which reduced them to mere stumpery.

If one is looking for sights to investigate in the Taskula, there are many to choose from. Just wandering through the district, one can see that there is a considerable spectrum of both activities and attractions. There is a museum of sorts called the Memories of Mentasqua that contains artifacts from commoners of Argonis dating from the reigns of various Konaskwas and sorted accordingly. I call it a 'museum' for the sake of my Daigan readers, simply to describe what it is most similar to in Huldionite thought. For the Ingans, a museum would be a very strange concept indeed; for them, to remember is to revere, and that means that any museum, as such, must serve some kind of meditative or devotional function. I am not certain about the matter, but I think that they believe the artifacts at this 'museum' in some way help them to connect with their ancestors in a rather direct sense. For my part, though, it was a fascinating window into the history of the kingdom.

In the Taskula, there are also a fair number of curiosity shops (again, the term doesn't quite fit with the Ingans' mentality, nor does its implied function). The Wennatoga call them tapagwenna. These tapagwenna contain particular objects (dubbed wentapa) that would certainly be considered curiosities anywhere else, but the Ingans regard them in a very utilitarian manner. They are not seen as fetishes or charms, I perceive, but they are viewed in a way somewhat similar to those things. Lamentably, I have not, as of yet, been able to untangle all the subtleties of Wennatogan belief.

As for food and drink, the Taskula hasn't a great number of establishments that supply such things, but the ones that do are quite excellent. An eatery called the Konaskwa's Bounty is first-rate (I know this from experience), and the favorite taverns seem to be the Gnarly Stump and the Torrent of Tapusa (affectionately referred to as 'the Stump' and 'the Torrent' – apparently, there is considerable feuding about which of the two is better). There is also a particular inn in this district called the Capering Kendarill that is claimed to have been around for more than 900 years. It is the natural place to stay for persons who are not considered worthy enough to be housed in Strongbranch and yet have business there.

As the Taskula was the very first district of Anganor, much of its architecture is distinct from that of the other districts, displaying features peculiar to the Wennatoga of old. Besides the fact that it has sampanog stump buildings, it also has a number of stone buildings carved with glyphs of some kind. (These glyphs are known as gandahnwa.) Supposedly, these structures and their markings date from the Apex of Archaea, although the purposes of the buildings themselves have changed numerous times. Nowadays, some are used as residences, others as businesses and still others for ceremonial or government functions. In many cases, a single stump building hosts an assortment of these things I just mentioned. Oftentimes, one cannot go from one to another inside the stump building, though (say, from apartments to a government office), and must go outside and then come through another entrance to access different portions. (I neglected to mention this previously, but the Wennatoga have a special word for these stump buildings – nawakonwa. The singular is nawakona.)

After Tahonagga and I had walked through much of the Taskula, stopping at a number of these sites I have mentioned, we passed on into the Sayuga, the district to the west of the Taskula.

The Sayuga – The Ancestral Ward

Translation of 'the Sayuga' is rather more manageable than that of 'the Taskula,' but it is still a bit tricky. It is probably best to just call the place the Ancestral Ward, although it must be noted that the term 'ancestral' is not intended to be perceived as the adjectival form pertaining to the Ingans' forebears themselves; rather, it refers to their way of life.

According to Tahonagga, walking into the Sayuga is like walking into a Wennatogan settlement of bygone days, and yet, in my perception, it feels neither staged nor stale. The residents of the Sayuga have managed, quite remarkably I think, to preserve both the precise mode and the vitality of their ancestors' civilization. One gets a sense that rhythms of life there are either suspended or else drastically slowed. There is often music in the air, that of low, reedy flutes and solemn chanting, occasionally accompanied by the hollow thud of drums, and this mirrors the Sayuga perfectly. The Ingans there are certainly engaged in chores and tasks of the day, but they are all incredibly focused, doing their work slowly and deliberately, speaking little. They eschew anything, be it novel inventions, Daiga or aught else, that might alter this simple, reflective and somber way of life. The rest of Orona, I would guess, is of little or no concern to them; at the very least, that is the impression they exude.

Nearly all the dwellings there are of a kind known by the term 'kahonasi,' which are essentially great huts that employ the trunks of osguna trees as an integral part of their structure. Osguna trees, which are native to the eastern Elder Forest, have multiple trunks that rise up a score or more of feet and then converge into one great trunk. To fill the gaps between these lower trunks, the Ingans make curving walls of sticks and mud, and they always leave a hole or two in the top of the kahonasi to let light enter and smoke escape. I had seen these dwellings in other districts in Anganor but nowhere in such predominance as in the Sayuga. Tahonagga related that practically the entire city was once populated with kahonasi, but previous Konaskwas, due to Huldionite influence, had gradually supplanted these with the conventional timber and stone structures of Huldion.

As for establishments and attractions, this district has few, as it is primarily residential. The main attraction, as it were, is to witness the Ingans carrying on daily life according to their ancient traditions, which is, in and of itself, both ravishingly enchanting and immensely fascinating. However, the Sayuga is not wholly devoid of specific items or locations of interest to visitors, as it bears the distinction of hosting Anganor's most renowned tapusa breweries, also known as tapusaries. The singular of this term is tapusary. (The reader will recall that tapusa is a mead flavored with sap from the sennec tree; it is the Wennatogan beverage of choice, consumed with practically every meal.) These breweries, known collectively as the Pannanook Tapusaries, can be found at the west end of the district inside kahonasi of especially grand size (that particular area of the Sayuga is referred to as Pannanook).

On our way out of the Sayuga, Tahonagga stopped to show me Kandossa Chanaqua, a series of altar stones near the center of the district that were dedicated to local payagwannah, which are guardian spirits of communities and settlements (as opposed to nennasakwa, which seem to be viewed as guardian spirits of individual families). These were surrounded by notched wooden poles, called tengawwa, which Tahonagga said were used to make specific requests of the payagwannah. I gathered that the system of notches is some kind of code, likely of great antiquity, though I don't suspect it was ever used for anything other than interaction with denizens of the Haedra.

When Tahonagga and I had finished in the Sayuga, it was late in the afternoon. We passed into the Taskula, then went eastward across its breadth to the adjacent district, the Eskagwan.

The Eskagwan – Ward of the Foreigners

Idiomatically, 'Eskagwan' means 'foreigner,' but it would be put literally as 'person from beyond the hedge.' 'Es' is 'hedge', 'ka' is a postposition meaning 'beyond' and 'gwan' is a term for 'Barada.' The hedge that is being referred to is the Outhedge, of course, which surrounds much of Argonis. When applied to a person (as opposed to the district of Anganor), the term 'Eskagwan' can be employed either pejoratively or neutrally; the sense is given by tone of voice and context. Also, in certain cases, the word is used to refer to anyone who is not an Ingan born in Argonis. Thus, a Wood-Gnome who was born in Argonis and has lived there all his life or an Ingan who was born just outside the bounds of the kingdom may be called Eskagwan, but this usage is somewhat infrequent.

The Eskagwan, which had formerly been an area for mixed Ingan and Wood-Gnomish residents, gradually came to be a more exclusively Gnomish area in the middle of the Bridging of the Tides. This transformation did not take place under any formal auspices but was simply due to the Gnomes having a culture in common and tending to settle in that district with their own kin. The Ingans in the Eskagwan, for the most part, moved to other districts around the same period and for similar reasons. Since that time, the Eskagwan has hosted primarily non-Ingan Barada. Nowadays, its population is mostly made up of Wood-Gnomes, but there are some Fall-Elves and a handful of Leprechauns also living there. There are a few Ingans too, most of whom are of non-Wennatogan descent.

As might be expected, due to the presence of a mixture of non-Ingan Barada, both the architecture and the ambience in the Eskagwan reflect rather eclectic influences. There are some dwellings such as the Ingans have, but many are of a Wood-Gnomish sort – neatly trimmed cottages with thatched roofs. Just southeast of the Plaza of the Eskagwan (which is in the district's center), there is, in fact, a tenement that has different architectural styles for each floor. The ground floor shows obvious signs of Fall-Elf workmanship, with many intricate carvings in the wood, while the second has a more rustic, practical Wood-Gnomish look to it. The third floor is an ode to the Leprechauns, as it is cleanly whitewashed and has brightly painted, round windows. This particular set of apartments is known as the Kemmeraw House. 'Kemmeraw' means 'cake' in Asla'gu, and the place is aptly named, for there is an excellent bakery on the ground floor.

In the northeast area of the Eskagwan, there is a lane known as Munnig Alley. A stone wall in the alleyway has been appropriated by certain former and current residents of the district to record their names for posterity. Initially, this practice of writing one's name there had neither official sanction nor prohibition (it began spontaneously about a hundred years ago, Tahonagga said), but now it has reached the status of tradition, and the people of Anganor are rather proud of it. One can see, scratched in the gray stone, the names of Wood-Gnomes from as far back as the opening of the prior century all the way to those of Leprechauns who probably only inscribed them there a few weeks ago. If you are in the Eskagwan, it is definitely worth paying the Munnig Alley Register a visit. I'll have to admit that I couldn't resist adding my name to the mix there, so esteemed reader, if you ever look through the register, do try to find it and then add your own.

Upon finishing our stroll through the Eskagwan, we returned to the Citadel, for it was then some way into the evening.

The Ikona – The Central Market Ward

On the 11th of Ferenos, we were again graced by benevolent weather. Tahonagga and I set out quite early from the Citadel, passed through the Taskula and came to the Ikona, which is the district at the very center of Anganor. I will render the Ikona simply as 'the Central Market Ward,' which is an apt description indeed, for that is precisely what it is (although it has much housing for commoners as well).

The heart of activity in the Ikona is the Plaza of the Ikona, which lies at its center. In the middle of the plaza is a great tree, of a species known as shenkanet. And on this tree, known as Chunkana Shenkanet ('chunkana' means 'grandmother' in Asla'gu), there grows a special type of moss, related to the pachacuri I have previously described. However, this moss is golden in color and is known as sannekway; it is considered sacred by the Wennatoga. At the base of Grandmother Shenkanet, there are four large stones shaped rather like thumbs – these are known as yanqua – and each one is dedicated to a member of the Naqua Senkawa, the Masters of the Seasons, of which I have informed the reader previously. According to Tahonagga, the yanqua serve as contracts with the beings to whom they are devoted. The one east of the tree is consecrated to Masku, the one northward to Tagwan, the one westward to Hanidosha and the one southward to Yaggawat.

All around the tree and the yanqua, there are ponds with fish, likewise dedicated to the Naqua Senkawa. There are also many magnificently sculpted vertical hedges, if one may call them that. These vertical hedges are known as mankawotchee (that is, the type of hedge itself is known by that term, regardless of whether it is sculpted or not). They consist of multiple segments stacked on top of each other, with each segment trimmed into the shape of a particular entity, usually botanical in nature. These representations are called innaket and are believed to curry favor with beings of the Haedra associated with the objects that are represented. (Both the representations individually and a collection of them stacked on top of each other are called innaket, although it is also possible to refer to a stack of them as a yasna-innaket.) Innaket can be formed from various materials:

stone, wood, metal, clay or, in the case of those in the Plaza of the Ikona, hedges. The innaket are kept neatly trimmed by specially trained gardeners called innaket-awaktu (innkaet-shapers), who use ladders of various lengths to reach different levels of the hedges. Watching them work is really quite a treat, I assure you.

On the perimeter of the plaza and also distributed throughout it, there are merchants selling items of all kinds, although victuals are the predominant wares. In the northwest extremity of the plaza, there is a spot known as Enkipag's Corner (named after a particularly notable and ostentatious merchant of the first century LE who hawked his wares there). There, in the mid-morning on certain days of the week (and I was privileged to be there on one such day), a competition is held in which vendors prepare their finest morsels for randomly selected onlookers to try and rate; each must select only his very favorite. Whichever merchant wins the competition that day is then given what is considered the prime spot in the Plaza of the Ikona from which to sell his wares. He retains this position until the next contest.

Also of interest in the Ikona is a place known as Peskanneh's Pool, an extremely deep well housed in an old stone structure with a small dome on top of it. It can be found in the district's southwest sector. This well was believed to have been filled by the tears of an oracle named Peskanneh back in the late Apex of Archaea. The cause for the sorrow that produced all his tears is unknown, but Ingans experiencing grief will often collect their tears in a vial or bowl and then pour them into the well, hoping that the spirits there will aid them in their anguish, as it was said that the same spirits brought solace to Peskanneh long ago.

Tahonagga and I had procured ample nourishment from sampling various comestibles at the Plaza of the Ikona, so we did not stop for a luncheon, but rather proceeded westward into the district known as the Banaka.

The Banaka – Ward of the Learned

The word 'Banaka' refers to a learned person, so I have chosen to put the district's name as the Ward of the Learned. Apparently, there is another word that refers to a scholar of greater caliber, but that is reserved for outstanding scholars at the Taquenarium, the great store of lore in the roots of Strongbranch. It is actually every scholar's aspiration to work there, but only a few are selected by the Konaskwa and the resident librarians of the Taquenarium for such a position.

The Banaka is the intellectual epicenter of Anganor (in saying this, I am excluding the Taquenarium from my reckoning, since it isn't in Anganor proper, per se). Any Barada of Argonis who show exceptional capabilities in the study of lore are admitted to one of the various academies housed in this district. These academies – or konnewec, as the Wennatoga call them – all have a similar look to them; they often have great stone pillars in the front, supporting high arcades. Some of these institutions specialize in the study of plants and animals, while others focus on Wennatogan traditions. Still others offer training in politics and oration; it is often from these konnewec that ministers of the kingdom are drawn. (Before proceeding any further, lest the matter slips my mind, I should note that the Banaka contains several government offices and some residences for commoners; it is not solely occupied by academic edifices.) Each konnewec has several tutors, called bengwa (the singular is benga, a very respectful title), and each only admits a handful of students, dubbed chanutwa (the singular is chanuta, also a very courteous term). Thus, it considered exceedingly prestigious to be admitted into a konnewec.

Several of the konnewec concentrate on the study and production of art (all devotional in nature, for Wennatogan art inevitably carries such a function, I think), and one of these has a set of rooms, collectively called the Yonnachot, set aside for the display of such art, which includes paintings (mostly portraits), carved wood, sculpted stone and carefully and intricately woven grass mats, in which various grasses are dyed different colors. There are some stunning tapestries as well.

Some of the konnewec have what are known as 'kengwa tachimot,' which I will, for the sake of simplicity, translate as 'libraries.' At Tahonagga's request, I was granted admittance to one of these, of course by virtue of my status as an ambassador and a guest of Semmoquaw. That one was specifically dubbed the Kengwa Tachimot of Dondaggu, who was the founder of the particular konnewec where it was housed. Dondaggu had died in the early years of the Latter Epoch after amassing a collection of records from the previous two hundred years or so and founding the konnewec to instruct others in the study of that period. The place had a number of large slabs of bark with writing inscribed on them. Most of them are of relatively recent provenance (when compared with the whole of Argonis' history), dating from the close of the Bridging of the Tides and from the first century of the Latter Epoch. However, since Dondaggu's death, the collection has been augmented by some records from the 9th and 10th centuries BT. I was not allowed to touch any of the bark slabs, but I did get a good look at them. Had I more years than are granted to an Elf (and I know Elves already have a fair number more of these than do certain types of Narthanna – I hope they do not begrudge us that), I would apply at this konnewec, seek to learn the old Asla'gu writing and then pore over these texts to my heart's content. As the reader has already been made well aware, I am an ardent devotee of all kinds of lore, but I find Ingan lore almost as fascinating as that of the Goblins.

When Tahonagga had finished ushering me through the halls of the Kengwa Tachimot of Dondaggu, we departed for the Chenagwan, the district just south of the Banaka.

The Chenagwan – Ward of the Elite

I will readily translate the Chenagwan as the Ward of the Elite, for that is the plain sense of it, and it is obvious that the district is named well as soon as one enters it. Everything is clean and elegant, and much in the Chenagwan is merely meant as an embodiment of prestige, rather than functioning in some pragmatic capacity (although it does host some specialty shops that certainly serve what could be seen as practical use, some might regard them as frivolous). The folk who reside there are Ingans of considerable means and high standing in the city. Even being escorted by Tahonagga, I almost felt I shouldn't be there, as if my station were too meager to merit my treading the immaculate streets of the Chenagwan. Though Barada could potentially pass through the

Chenagwan on their way from the Banaka to the Quannamet, the district to the south of the Chenagwan, they usually don't, as such an act would be generally frowned upon and seen as quite cheeky. (Of course, there are always individuals who relish opportunities to be impertinent, so there is occasionally non-Chenagwan traffic in the area.) Also, the Chenagwan is one of only two districts that has no gate to directly access the Ikona (the other is the Sayuga). Presumably this is to reinforce the impression of the Chenagwan's exclusive and rather segregated status.

Tahonagga was given permission by the owner of an annuchoku, which is essentially a bathhouse, for us to enter and have a look about. The place isn't open during the daytime and is only frequented in the evenings by wealthy inhabitants of the Chenagwan. (Incidentally, I suppose those are the only sort of inhabitants the Chenagwan has.) The annuchoku was built of stone and had several round basins raised high above the floor. These were accessed by sets of wooden stairs and had pipes running out of them. The pipes all had sluice gates that could be operated to either keep the water in the baths or let it run out. Each bath is filled one bucket at a time by Ingans carting them up the stairs. Consequently, by the time the baths are ready, the water is rather cold, although the Ingans don't seem to mind (I gathered this from comments made by Tahonagga and the owner of the annuchoku). In my opinion, the whole system isn't terribly efficient, but it gets the job done.

After investigating the annuchoku (that particular one was known as San'ua Annuchoku, after the type of flowers, called san'ua, that were planted all around it), Tahonagga and I sojourned to a hentachog. (The particular hentachog we visited was called Kayusanot Hentachog, also after the variety of flower growing outside, dubbed a kayusanot; this naming of places based on their botanical accompaniments seems to be a standard Wennatogan practice, at least in Anganor, as it is applied to establishments in other districts of the city as well, such as shops in the Ikona and apartments in the Eskagwan.)

I must apologize here for the inclusion of so many Asla'gu terms, as the reader may be finding them burdensome to follow, but I must admit that, as a linguist, I was relishing the veritable cascade of Asla'gu nomenclature that Tahonagga was pouring upon me. In some cases, the Asla'gu terminology could probably be bypassed with a rough Daigan substitute, but, with that being said, I could never bring myself to do much of that sort of thing, as I would feel as if I were cheating the reader out of some precious gems of knowledge. But in the case of the word 'hentachog,' translation is a vain endeavor. I do not believe there is any acceptable Daigan translation of that word. Indeed, it would be far more preferable to describe what occurs at one of these places rather than to give it a simple label in a language or culture that has, frankly, almost nothing to do with Asla'gu or the Wennatoga.

At the hentachog, persons of illustrious pedigree and expansive income sit drinking various mixtures, some intoxicating and some not (many of them are rather like herbal teas), as they discuss financial matters. Whilst doing these things, they also play a game called gennucha, which involves the trading of small stones with markings on them. I shall not pretend to understand this game, as when Tahonagga began to explain it, my comprehension was beset by a formidable haze. In any event, perhaps now the reader will see why I could not give a decent rendering of hentachog in Daiga. For my part, I simply drank what was offered to me and left it at that. I neither spoke of financial matters nor tried my hand at gennucha, for sampling the variety of beverages offered to me was more than enough to occupy both my capacities and my senses.

At last, as night was falling, Tahonagga and I bid the proprietor of the hentachog a good evening and returned to the Citadel.

The Naskanu – The Caskman's Ward

An hour or so after daybreak (and a sumptuous breakfast) on the 16th of Ferenos, Tahonagga and I set out for the Naskanu, which is the district south of the Eskagwan and to the east of the Ikona. We reached the Naskanu by passing through the Taskula and then the Eskagwan, entering the district at its northern gate.

The word Naskanu is composed of two elements: 'nas,' which refers to a container for liquid, and 'kanu,' which is a designation for a person who has extensive familiarity with the thing preceding it. Hence, I would (admittedly, rather idiomatically) translate the Naskanu as the Caskman's Ward. When the Naskanu was first added on to Anganor (that addition occurred in the 7th century of the Bridging of the Tides), it was populated with a number of inns and guesthouses, along with their associated workers, and it was also home to a fair number of liquor merchants, which is how it acquired its present name. In those early days, it was actually quite a nice place, but, sadly, it has deteriorated considerably since then in many regards.

The Naskanu is, in essence, the antithesis of the Chenagwan. It is home to all the most destitute and downtrodden of Anganor, and the buildings, streets and so forth readily reflect this fact. There is much want of care and repair in the Naskanu, but no one who is concerned enough to do anything about it has either the time or wherewithal to address the problem. It certainly doesn't help matters that the place has a rather notorious reputation, this being on account of the many knavish and crooked persons who carry out their illicit businesses there.

As the reader has surely gathered by now, there isn't much of note to see in the Naskanu, not even in the Plaza of the Naskanu, at the district's center, but one can find pleasure in simply witnessing the interactions of the Barada there; these are invariably mundane and often coarse, but they are also thoroughly genuine, a feature which I found to be quite attractive.

However, there were some places Tahonagga knew of where we could see some of the more recreational elements of life in the Naskanu. Down in its south section, I observed two strapping Ingan lads wrestling in a shallow pit known as the Gharnobac. Apparently that is a descriptive term used for any such pit for wrestling, but that one was known as '*the* Gharnobac' since it was the only one in the Naskanu, or in Anganor for that matter (there are others in the forest villages of the Wennatoga). The manner of wrestling employed has special characteristics and rules, as well as a unique name, which is yenkawash. Although most denizens of the Naskanu have hardly any coinage to spare, they will gladly spend some of it to bet on their favorite contender in the Gharnobac on any given day.

Near the Gharnobac is what is known as Halengasec Lane, where Ingan children can frequently be found playing a game called rachu and mokwet, which involves one individual throwing special stones called rachu through a netted wooden hoop known as a mokwet, which is tossed up into the air to make the rachu-throwing more difficult. The netting is woven in such a way that there is only a smallish hole in the middle of the hoop that the rachu can actually pass through. There is a variant of this game called rachu and kachu, which involves throwing a spear (a kachu) at a rachu that is thrown in the air.

After observing some games of rachu and mokwet for a while, Tahonagga and I headed west into the Sagwan.

The Sagwan – The Commoners' Ward

Translating the 'Sagwan' is a simple matter. It could be put quite straightforwardly as 'the Commoners' Ward.' It is, in fact, where a great many of Anganor's commoners live and lacks any special virtues or characteristics that the other districts possess. But, in that regard, it could be said to capture the most authentic and quintessential feeling of the city and its people. It represents, I think, what today's city-dwelling Wennatoga are like when they are being quite themselves, not necessarily trying to follow any particular, predetermined way of life. They needn't cope with the hardship of poverty in the Naskanu nor with the equally grueling misfortune of stifling affluence in the Chenagwan. They are not upholding the ancient ways, as are the Ingans of the Sayuga, nor are they seeking to cultivate the diverse ambience of the Eskagwan, the sober intellectual environment of the Banaka or the sense of prestige and historical propriety found in the Taskula. They needn't even worry about all the bluster and activity of the Ikona, although that place functioned rather like a commoners' ward before the Sagwan was built. The Barada of the Sagwan can really and truly be themselves, I believe, in a way that other residents of the city cannot.

Much as the case had been in the Naskanu, I found myself relishing mere observance of the Barada of Anganor engaged in their daily business. However, Tahonagga wanted to make sure I visited particular points in the district, so we made our way to the Plaza of the Sagwan, which lies at the district's center. Just west of there, we came to a place known as Pacha Tokwasi, which translates as 'the Meditation Shelter.' It consisted of two stone breezeways, the roofs of which were held up by unadorned stone pillars. These breezeways intersected at a perpendicular angle, and where they met, there was a modest rotunda. Somewhat surprisingly, there was nothing underneath this save for a mosaic of a white flower known as a sigwalu. At the ends of the breezeways, which corresponded to the cardinal directions, there were largish statues, one for each terminus. These images were of the Naqua Senkawa, the Masters of the Seasons, and each member of that group was positioned in the spot associated with his or her cardinal direction. Thus, the statue for Masku, the River Princess, was at the eastern end of the lateral breezeway, Hanidosha, the Forest Queen, was at the western end, Tagwan was to the north and Yaggawat was to the south. The two breezeways were actually situated in the midst of a green lawn surrounded by buildings on all sides, so the place had a rather secluded feeling to it. Ingans go there to meditate and pay homage to the Naqua Senkawa in thought or in word, but no offerings are made at Pacha Tokwasi.

Leaving the solemnity and tranquility of Pacha Tokwasi behind, Tahonagga and I proceeded to what is known as Tekkinog's Stump. This is a large stump in the southwest corner of the Sagwan that has been appropriated as a stage for various musicians. Both instrumentalists and vocalists frequent the spot, but there are rather more of the former; vocalists are often accompanied by either percussion or some kind of flute. Any Barada that wish to perform there may, provided they wait their turn. Passersby will stop for a short while, and others will stay for much longer. Though many Barada will enjoy the music without giving anything in return, enough Barada in the audience show their appreciation in a monetary manner that it is worth the musicians' while to play or sing at Tekkinog's Stump. Local merchants take advantage of this attraction by setting up their stalls nearby, so I treated myself to some kwantu on a stick (a kwantu is a type of bird, often served with various herbs and butter spread over it).

After listening to the marvelous artistry of an elderly Ingan flautist, I deposited a few bannagums in her money bowl (the bannagum is the foundational unit of Argonis' currency). Then Tahonagga and I had to be on our way to the last district we were to tour, the Quannamet, which is just to the west of the Sagwan.

The Quannamet – Ward of the Guilds

The Quannamet could be dubbed in Daiga as the Ward of the Guilds. It is the center, not of commerce (for that is the province of the Ikona) but of skill. The majority of the city's craftsmen live and work in the Quannamet, and even those who don't probably got their training there originally. However, the Quannamet also houses a large sector of commoners who are not necessarily involved in any of the guilds.

As Tahonagga and I were both rather hungry when we entered the Quannamet (my kwantu on a stick was only an appetizer, the reader must understand), he took me to an eatery called the Weaver's Feast, which is right next to a cluster of several different weaving guilds. I was thoroughly impressed with both the food and the experience and heartily recommend the Weaver's Feast to anyone exploring what the district has to offer.

After our rather late lunch, we went to one of the nearby weaving guilds, where we watched a public demonstration of yaquashenda, which is the Wennatogan art of grass-weaving. There was one master weaver and several apprentices, but I was astonished even by what the apprentices could do. The deftness and speed with which they worked was certainly to be marveled at, and on display before them and available for purchase was a seemingly endless array of items they had made. There were bowls, trays, baskets, satchels and many other entities for practical use, all with intricate patterns and colors. There were also quite a few ornamental pieces, some of which were quite abstract, while others were in the shapes of different kinds of trees, flowers and animals.

When the yaquashenda demonstration had ended, Tahonagga and I took a stroll down Degganum Street, which runs north from the Plaza of the Quannamet. This plaza, like all the others in Anganor, lies roughly in the middle of its corresponding district.

Degganum Street is where all the most practiced craftsmen of the Quannamet have their wares on display, either in shops or in stalls lining the lane. At the north end of the street is what is known as Pemmidac Hall, where assorted guild leaders meet to discuss guild politics, including guild regulations, standards for apprentices, various means of advancing guild interests and so forth. Pemmidac Hall has quite engaging architecture, both on the inside and outside, and it has a distinctly Wennatogan flavor to it. I would elaborate on that statement if I could, but the reader may have to spend some time among the Wennatoga himself to really understand what I mean.

At last, Tahonagga and I finished our grand tour of the Quannamet and returned to the Citadel that evening by way of the Ikona and the Taskula.

Taskula North

The 19th of Ferenos dawned clear and very pleasant indeed, and Tahonagga and I exited the front gates of Strongbranch and went down to the Sentinels' Strand, the narrow strip between the Honnamec River and the walls that mark the northern boundary of the Taskula. (The attentive reader will recall that the Honnamec runs around the base of Malinoc Hill, upon which the Citadel stands.) We then went to the western end of the Sentinels' Strand and crossed another bridge over the Honnamec into Taskula North at a point just west of where the river splits at Malinoc Hill's western base. (There is actually a bridge over the Honnamec just beyond Malinoc Hill's eastern base as well; that bridge is also accessed from the Sentinels' Strand and leads to Taskula North.)

The reason that Taskula North is dubbed thus is that it is the other half of the great grove of sampanog stumps from which the Taskula derives its name; just as in the Taskula, there are a number of sampanog stump buildings there. However, Taskula North lacks the density of other kinds of buildings that the Taskula has. Also, it has thirteen stump buildings, which is one more than the Taskula. The stumps' positions in the two halves of the Greater Taskula (a term for the combined area of the Taskula and Taskula North) mirror each other, as it were (a fact, which I find to be exceedingly odd), save for the additional stump in Taskula North, which lies directly north of Strongbranch.

As I remarked in the opening of this chapter, I have not included Taskula North in my tally of the districts of Anganor, since it doesn't really function as a part of the city – at least not the 'civilian' portion of it. In fact, it is only accessible from the Sentinels' Strand, which is not open to the general public, as it serves as a defensive bank for Strongbranch Citadel.

It would perhaps be easiest to describe Taskula North as a park, for it has many wildflowers and lovely trees. Certain portions of it are more cultivated than others, and there are sections of it that are used regularly for various activities, but it is rather like a preserve, a sacred precinct of sorts. Gazebos, benches and small orchards can be found throughout it, and there are some little ponds as well. Semmoquaw occasionally strolls through it, I am told, whenever he is in need of respite or quietude, and previous Konaskwas have used it in much the same way, as a sort of retreat from the constant demands of the Citadel.

In an area just north of where we entered, there was a collection of old, dome-shaped stone huts, known as Kennipet Magwa. These huts were built in the early Apex of Archaea as residences for a special group of sages known as the Kennipet. That body has long since dissolved, but early rulers apparently depended heavily on them. The huts are considered hallowed, so I was not allowed to set foot beyond their thresholds or touch them, but I did get a look inside from a distance. There was nothing there but old fire rings and a few clay pitchers and bowls, unless the darkness concealed aught else from me.

Up in the northwest region of Taskula North, I was shown a very ancient tree, hollowed out early in the Bridging of the Tides. Sacred artifacts of revered ancestors were stored there, but, due to a Wennatogan ashaska, or taboo, I was not permitted to enter this tree, which is known as Nachakep Yengwe, the Storehouse of Revered Objects (I know the name reads a bit clumsily in Daiga, but it was the best I could do. If the reader were acquainted with Kumkummur, my favorite Goblin language, I would render it as Ag-Wiwsut Jubbu to put the name more precisely, less awkwardly and, in my opinion, more euphoniously. Alas, I fear that few, if any, of my readers shall know Kumkummur, on account of its small population of speakers and the general inaccessibility of materials on it.)

Our final stop in Taskula North was in its eastern sector. There we visited Heggawan Tessikaw, the training grounds and barracks of the core army of Argonis, which is known as the Tessikaw (hence, the place's name, which means 'grounds of the Tessikaw'). Soldiers were conducting drills on fields there with various types of weaponry, including spears, bows and arrows, halberds, spinescourges (whips of thorny vines) and several other weapons unique to the Ingans. They were also practicing maneuvers on large, antlered animals called tonquit (there were stables for these nearby). The soldiers' barracks were well-kept and amply outfitted, and I was quite impressed by the poise and dignity of the commanding officers who ushered us through them.

Upon concluding our sojourn through the barracks of Heggawan Tessikaw, Tahonagga and I crossed the bridge over the Honnamec to the eastern end of the Sentinels' Strand.

The Sentinels' Strand

The Sentinels' Strand is a narrow segment of land, covered by neatly trimmed grass, that is bordered on the south by the walls of the Taskula and by the Honnamec River on the north. It is accessed from the city proper by a single set of gates from the Taskula, and it has, as I have related, a bridge at its eastern end leading to Taskula North and a bridge at its western terminus doing the same. In the middle of the Sentinels' Strand, there is a bridge across the Honnamec leading directly to Malinoc Hill and to the road which climbs the hill up to Strongbranch Citadel. The remarkable thing about this bridge is that it is actually formed by one of Strongbranch's roots. Whether it was trained to arc over the river as it does or whether it grew that way naturally I do not know, but it is a stunning sight nonetheless. It is nicknamed Ennadug's Span. Apparently, Ennadug is the name of the root itself, which the Wennatoga think of as being a spirit person of sorts who acts to protect the Citadel.

The Sentinels' Strand is called as it is because guards from the Citadel are posted there to man the gates to the Taskula. If there were ever an attack from within the city (and there have been several of these in Argonis' history, but I will not enumerate them here), the Sentinels' Strand could accommodate a fair number of soldiers, who could climb the stairs to the ramparts of the Taskula wall and assail their enemies from the battlements. Also, if a force ever approached Anganor from the north, soldiers from Strongbranch could quickly make their way down to the Sentinels' Strand and then cross over into Taskula North to aid the army there if need be.

I had, of course, seen the Sentinels' Strand many times before, but I have included its description here since I decided to group all of the portions of Anganor that do not really qualify as districts on this final day of my touring.

Malinoc Hill

In the midst of the Honnamec River and just north of the Sentinels' Strand, Malinoc Hill rises up around four hundred feet, looming over the city. The hill is roundish, I would say, but also quite steep. It is covered with a carpet of soft, green grass and white, eight-petaled blossoms called sigwalus. (The sigwalu is a flower considered sacred in some capacity by the Wennatoga; it is also the symbol of Anganor.) There is a road ascending from the bridge from the Sentinels' Strand all the way up to the gates of Strongbranch, which are south-facing. Also, roots of the Citadel erupt from beneath the earth in certain places on the hill and then dive back into it lower down.

As I climbed the road to the Citadel at the conclusion of my last guided excursion into Anganor, I thanked Tahonagga profusely for his excellent services in showing me all of the marvels of Semmoquaw's city. Certainly, I shall never forget the fantastic sights, sounds and experiences that Anganor had to offer, and hopefully, now that I have set them on parchment, they will not be forgotten to the world either.

Questmongers Lore

The following appendix contains seven sections, each explaining a different facet of Questmongers lore. These sections are as follows:

1) The Founding and Development of the Questmongers
2) Notable Quests of the Questmongers
3) Positions and Placement in the Questmongers
4) Famous Questmongers
5) Rooms in the Questmongers' Den
6) Artifacts Housed in the Questmongers' Den
7) Chronological List of Konaskwas During the Operation of the Questmongers

It must be understood that the information presented in this appendix is by no means comprehensive. It is only intended as an introduction to the lore of the Questmongers, merely the front vestibule in a grand castle, as it were. If the reader wishes to access further information on these matters, he is advised to consult the extensive records kept in the Questmongers' Den in Anganor, for he may learn many times more than he will here. Of course, permission to study these volumes will have to be granted by the current Questkeeper, but he is said to be a decent fellow, so the acquisition of such an allowance should be quite manageable.

1 – The Founding and Development of the Questmongers

Though the Questmongers ultimately came to be known as an illustrious institution functioning in a number of diverse capacities, it first had a rather narrow and odd purpose. Indeed, the organization was first established merely to indulge the fancies of a Konaskwa of Argonis in the late Bridging of the Tides. This particular Konaskwa was Nachoonateg the Dreamer, so named because he often had dreams that he took very seriously, even to the point of allowing them to dictate his kingdom's policies. He was obsessed with ancient Ingan artifacts and spent much time in the Taquenarium, the great library beneath Strongbranch Citadel, researching the possible whereabouts of legendary items, especially ones featured in stories from the early Apex of Archaea and the Years of Yore.

One particular item caught his attention more than any other, and that was the Spear of the Silver Pashakway. Several ancient texts, as well as legends circulated among the Ingans of Argonis, stated that this spear belonged to an outstanding warrior named Quessitoc, who lived in the opening centuries of the Apex of Archaea. The weapon's title came from an extremely swift bird, the silver pashakway, and it was said that Quessitoc could throw this spear as fast as a diving pashakway and from a hillock on one bank of the Perinac River to one on the opposite bank.

When Quessitoc grew old, he gave a farewell speech to the people of Anganor, claiming that the Shadowed Garlens were calling him, and his time in Orona was at an end. He took his spear in hand, crossed the Teraska and was never seen again. None knew where he had gone, how he had died or where the Spear of the Silver Pashakway lay. So the stories went.

However, Nachoonateg discovered what he believed to be a record of Quessitoc's farewell speech in the Taquenarium, and it mentioned a strange riddle he had given the people:

"A leader once was I, but now I must be led.
Long ago I touched the soul of a lonely tree;
It sang to me and I to it. Now it sings again;
I hear its songs in shadow, where twilight reigns.

Root to root and branch to branch its body stands;
Longing, it stares into the darkened mirror.
Now, I must pass that way at last,
And my mighty spear shall pass with me."

Nachoonateg was certain that this riddle was what had led the Wennatoga to conclude that Quessitoc thought himself bound for the Shadowed Garlens, for its imagery might well convey an embrace of death. However, he suspected that the riddle might have been misunderstood. Legends concerning the early portion of Quessitoc's life related that he had seen, heard and touched a sennuraga somewhere in Asquamot, which is the eastern region of Argonis. A sennuraga was believed to be a tree's soul manifesting in a visible form akin to an orb of slightly luminous moss. Anyone who touched one was said to be destined for mighty deeds, and this incident was reputedly what had launched Quessitoc's career as a valiant warrior. Since Quessitoc seemed to be alluding to the sennuraga in his riddle, Nachoonateg thought the warrior was referring not to a journey to the Shadowed Garlens, but to the place in Orona where he had seen the sennuraga, namely Asquamot.

No amount of research divulged the specific location within Asquamot of this sennuraga encounter to the obsessive Nachoonateg, but he did discern what he thought were descriptive elements in Quessitoc's riddle. The line about 'shadow' and 'twilight' indicated to him that Quessitoc had entered a cave, and the 'darkened mirror' might then be a reference to a subterranean pool. Since the tree from which the sennuraga came was described as being 'root to root and branch to branch,' Nachoonateg deduced that a tree growing next to such a pool and having drooping branches might look as if it were connecting to its own reflection, root to root and branch to branch.

Once he had struck upon this idea, he was determined that he should send forth a party to find such a place, and he would direct this group to begin its search in the Balgorra Hills, since they were in Asquamot and riddled with many grottoes. So, in the year 828 of the Bridging of the Tides, he selected particular servants from his retinue at Strongbranch Citadel and told them of his discoveries and musings, bidding them maintain complete secrecy in all these matters, lest anyone learn of his deductions and steal away the spear before they could reach it. Then he dispatched them with all haste to the Balgorra Hills to begin their search for the Spear of the Silver Pashakway. And thus was born the organization known as the Questmongers.

As it turned out, Nachoonateg's conjectures were correct. After several months of searching, the party he had sent came upon a cave with a small pool with an ancient tree of an exceedingly strange variety next to it. On the bank of the pool lay the fabled spear, matching precisely with its description in old legends. There was an Ingan skeleton there as well, which they presumed to be that of Quessitoc.

When the party brought the spear triumphantly back to Nachoonateg, he dubbed them 'the Questmongers' and immediately began planning other expeditions for them to find lost artifacts. Proud of their new standing with the Konaskwa, they took the tree and its reflection from the cave where Quessitoc lay as their secret symbol and mark of their fraternity, since none but they and Nachoonateg knew the meaning behind it. (The symbol is referred to as the Nannaqued Tree, meaning 'the tree of the riddle' – this riddle of course being a reference to that of Quessitoc – and the Questmongers have used it throughout the centuries to conduct covert communications. Its given meaning is the loyal service of the Questmongers to the Konaskwa, along with the Questmongers' willingness to go to any length to accomplish their objectives; of course, it also signifies their founding and the completion of their first quest. When the symbol is drawn in haste, it is often stylized as merely a tree with its roots curving up toward its branches and its branches curving down toward its roots. However, in more official capacities, the Nannaqued Tree is depicted as a rather close replica of the original.)

For the remainder of Nachoonateg's reign, the Questmongers existed solely to fuel his artifact acquisition addiction, but his son and successor, Bangurasa, employed the hardy band in a different capacity. He had not the penchant for legends and relics that his father had. Rather, he was beset by harrowing concerns of the present. A number of guilds in the Quannamet, a district of Anganor, had taken an extreme disliking to him as soon as he had ascended to the throne. He suspected that some of the heads of the guilds might have close ties with his ministers at Strongbranch, and he was worried that a cabal might be forming against him. Thus, instead of disbanding the Questmongers, he repurposed them, dispatching them as informants who would gather whatever intelligence they could from the councils of the guilds. They performed magnificently in this capacity, and Bangurasa subsequently used them for further tasks of this nature. In order to better facilitate their anonymity, he had them move from their quarters in Strongbranch Citadel to the second floor of the Gnarly Stump Tavern in the Taskula, the oldest district of Anganor, where they still meet to this day.

Bangurasa's son, Yenkasona, continued to expand the Questmongers' roles and reputation and had them take charge of not only collecting information about threats to him, but also constructing plans to overcome such threats. In the Malgennaquin Thickets, which are in the southwest corner of Argonis, there was a faction of rebels rising against Yenkasona. The Questmongers were assigned to infiltrate these rebels' camps, assess their defenses and then formulate a means for Yenkasona to capture all the insurgents. Once again, the Questmongers accomplished their mission with flying colors, and Yenkasona afterwards engaged them quite regularly in ventures requiring high levels of skill and intelligence.

Yenkasona was succeeded by his son, Kechkuna, who frequently used the Questmongers for missions involving espionage, special operations and the like, as his forebears had done, but he also increasingly relied on them in another capacity: as highly trained warriors.

Although the Questmongers had not been staffed with this in mind, there were nonetheless some very able fighters among them. Kechkuna recruited more champions of this sort into the organization, thereby strengthening the diversity of their already very wide array of skills. Kechkuna is thus reckoned to have brought the Questmongers to encompass all of the functions that they carry today. (These functions are discussed in more detail in Section 3 of this appendix.)

Eskinaw, Kechkuna's son and successor, codified and named the specific positions in the Questmongers that his father had laid the groundwork for, and he broadened the Questmongers' scope still further, as he was the first to send them on missions outside of Argonis. He also established more rigorous requirements for admittance to the Questmongers, while at the same time delegating a greater spectrum of responsibility to the leader of the organization, who was known as the Questkeeper.

In the first century of the Latter Epoch, Eskinaw's descendant, Hennasog, colloquially known as Darkroot the Keen, was the first to allow Wood-Gnomes to join the Questmongers. Hennasog's great-grandson, Semmoquaw, advanced this trend even more by appointing a non-Ingan to the office of Questkeeper and permitting even more kinds of Narthanna to join the group. During his reign, there were quite a few Wood-Gnomes, a number of Leprechauns and several Timber-Elves who were admitted to the Questmongers. Today, in LE 717, during the reign of Assartanu (more commonly known as Thornoak), the Questmongers are actually led by a Leprechaun, Fergus O'Brannadon. The organization looks quite different than it did when it was founded by Nachoonateg, but it still serves the same core function, which is faithfully serving the Konaskwa of Argonis.

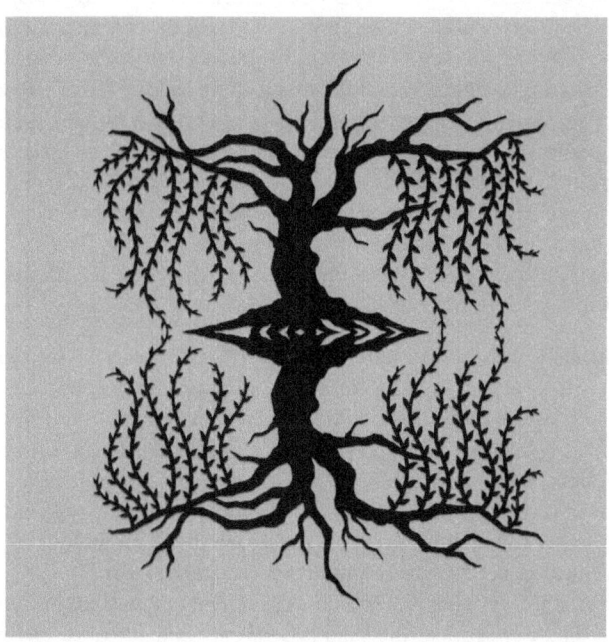

2 – Notable Quests of the Questmongers

The following list of quests is in chronological order, and the name of each quest is followed by parentheses containing the name of the reigning Konaskwa who commissioned it. (A chronology of these Konaskwas can be found in Section 7 of this appendix.)

The Search for the Spear of the Silver Pashakway (Nachoonateg) – Nachoonateg had discovered an ancient riddle about this legendary spear, which belonged to a warrior of the early Apex of Archaea named Quessitoc, and commissioned the Questmongers to go find it. They located both the spear and Quessitoc's skeleton in a cave in the Balgorra Hills in northeast Argonis. Inside the cave was a strange tree next to a pool, and the Questmongers adopted this tree and its reflection as the secret symbol of their organization. (NB: A fuller account of this quest can be found above in Section 1 of this appendix.)

The Search for the Mystic's Kenga (Nachoonateg) – Nachoonateg had heard of a wandering mystic named Uknashewatta, who lived in the early centuries of the Apex of Archaea and was said to have written some of the greatest secrets of his knowledge of the Haedra on a kenga, a large slab of bark. It was unknown where the mystic had placed this kenga, but some stories connected it with the Taggawasha Uplands. Determined to locate it, Nachoonateg sent the Questmongers to the Taggawasha Uplands to inquire of Ingans who dwelt there about the matter.

Many leads proved fruitless, but eventually the Questmongers found an old, lore-steeped Ingan hermit, who took them to an area where the mystic was thought to have roamed. After several weeks of searching this area, they located a cave system behind a waterfall. Far back in these caves, they found a kenga and a statuette of an Ingan. They brought these artifacts to Nachoonateg, and he turned them over for analysis to scholars at the Taquenarium, the library beneath Strongbranch Citadel. The statuette was of the reigning Konaskwa during the period the mystic lived, and the kenga contained poetry, undoubtedly written by the mystic or one closely associated with him, since it featured many of his trademark sayings. As for great secrets, none could be found there save a stanza about the spirits of the Teraska River imparting some marvelous knowledge to the author. However, this knowledge was not presented in the poem and was said to be only attainable through many days without food and only drinking water from the Teraska. Though many devout Ingans have attempted to follow this recommended procedure since the kenga was found, none have received any revelations of note.

The Quannamet Cabal (Bangurasa) – A number of guild leaders in the Quannamet (a district of Anganor) were doing favors for various ministers of Bangurasa. Ultimately, they were seeking to replace him as Konaskwa with one of his minsters with whom they had strong ties, for they could use such a person as a puppet ruler. Bangurasa thought something of this sort might be going on, but he didn't want to openly accuse either his ministers or the guild leaders, lest the matter should go amiss or reflect badly on him. In order to acquire proof of what was really transpiring, he commissioned the Questmongers to infiltrate the guilds in the Quannamet and expose any plots that might be afoot.

Though it took them a number of months to accomplish this task, the Questmongers eventually obtained evidence of the guild leaders' treachery. The cabal was exposed, and many of the guild leaders were removed from office, as were a number of Bangurasa's ministers, and the primary culprits in the cabal were executed.

The Malgennaquin Insurrection (Yenkasona) – Certain Ingans living in the Malgennaquin Thickets in southwestern Argonis grew greatly displeased with Yenkasona, who was Konaskwa at the time. Consequently, they decided to declare themselves independent of his rule. They imagined that they would be safe from any attacks he might make with his soldiers, for the terrain surrounding their camps was quite unfavorable to such an endeavor.

In response to this rebellion, Yenkasona sent the Questmongers to enter the camps in the Malgennaquin Thickets and pretend to assist in the insurrection, all the while gaining as much information about the rebels as they could. The Questmongers accomplished this objective and then brought news of their findings back to Yenkasona, who had them devise the most effective strategy for him to capture the secessionists with his soldiers. Following their advice, he moved several battalions into the Malgennaquin Thickets.

Since the Questmongers still had spies in the rebel camps, they used them to help convince the rebel leaders to attack the Konaskwa's soldiers in a particular way and at particular locations, although this advice was purposely tainted, as it was designed to lead the secessionists into a trap. All according to the Questmongers' plan, the trap sprung, and the rebel leaders were captured, as were the majority of their followers.

The Terror of Lake Seggatuc (Kechkuna) – Since the close of the Apex of Archaea, there had been an ashaska, a taboo of sorts, upon approaching Lake Seggatuc, which is in the Taggawasha Uplands of southern Argonis. However, the oracles at Hadoga Taquenassa received a revelation from the machaswa that prompted them to lift this ashaska during Kechkuna's reign. They encouraged local groups of Ingans to settle next to the lake, as they claimed it was a gift to them from Masku, the River Princess. Several months after these groups set up villages there, their leaders reported to the oracles that some of their comrades had been slain by a monster living in the lake. The oracles insisted that the monster was a foe of Masku and needed to be destroyed. They then sent word of the matter to Kechkuna, who dispatched the Questmongers to go slay the creature.

The Questmongers spent a number of days camped by the shores of the lake, waiting for the monster to appear. At last it surfaced near them, and they were able to kill it, though it was an exceedingly difficult fight. When the Questmongers dragged the monster's body onto the bank, they saw that it was like a huge eel with long, serrated teeth, and they realized it was one of the fabled creatures called nakayataswe, the 'lake-writhers.' It was thought that the last of these creatures had gone extinct many hundreds of years ago, but, since the Ingans had abandoned Lake Seggatuc for quite some time, apparently the nakayataswe had survived there, though none were ever seen again, so the one killed by the Questmongers may well have been the last of them.

The Smugglers of the Iron Highway (Eskinaw) – Long ago, Dwarves built the Iron Highway, which lies some distance south of Argonis and runs from the Byram interior all the way to its coast. The Dwarves had for some time used it as a route to transport resources and products from inland Byram to the shores of the Indurian Deeps, where they could load them aboard their ships and sell them abroad. However, some of the Dwarven merchants involved in this operation would take their goods down the Perinac River to Argonis rather than across the sea. But there were steep tariffs placed on transporting these goods into Argonis, since the Dwarves would make a large profit selling them. However, Eskinaw, the Konaskwa at the time, noticed that there was more of the Dwarves' merchandise in his kingdom than there ought to have been based on how much he had received from tariffs. Concluding that smugglers were at work, he asked the Questmongers to investigate the situation.

The Questmongers were unable to catch anyone smuggling goods in at any of the gates of Argonis, so they had to look farther afield for answers. Dwarven merchants customarily brought their merchandise into Argonis in wains, and these wains were brought down the Perinac on barges from a landing some distance to the east of Argonis' northeastern corner. The wains were brought to this point via a road that ran through Toldrennon Wood, the forest to the east of Argonis. This road eventually ran into the Iron Highway, so the Questmongers decided to track the route of these wains all the way back to their origin, which was several hundred miles down the Iron Highway, at the spot where they were first laden with merchandise.

At the camps where the wagons were first loaded up, the Questmongers spied some Dwarves hiding their merchandise in ingeniously crafted secret compartments in the wains. The wains with these compartments had a distinctive design, so the Questmongers returned to Argonis and shared what they had learned with guards at the kingdom's gates. Armed with this knowledge, the sentries were able to apprehend a good number of the smugglers, and the rest, recognizing that the soldiers were privy to their schemes, ceased further attempts at smuggling.

The Race for the Brittle Bark Antidote (Pattaruc) – During Pattaruc's reign, many of the inhabitants of Anganor were afflicted by a horrible disease known as wengastu-ghura, the Brittle Bark Plague, which made their skin stiff and caused it to break out in painful boils. In many cases, this disease proved fatal. Pattaruc sent the Questmongers to the Stony Wilds to consult medicine men deep in the Elder Forest about where they could find a remedy for this plague. Some of these medicine men spoke of a plant called kenjowara that might serve to cure the victims of the plague and keep it from spreading further. However, it was only known to grow in the Haunted Thickets, which lie to the north of Blackbough Woods.

The Questmongers went through many, many miles of dangerous territory, battling hostile tribes and beasts of the forests and crossing the treacherous Arkanian Mountains, before they came at last to the Haunted Thickets and located this plant. They collected as much kenjowara as they could and returned to Anganor.

Extensive cultivation of kenjowara was begun immediately, and it was administered to as many victims of the Brittle Bark Plague as possible. It proved remarkably effective, and in time, the plague was halted and many of those suffering from it were restored to good health. Since that time, each household in Anganor has hung strands of kenjowara near its door, and there are patches of it kept in Taskula North, just in case the plague ever strikes again.

The Timekeepers of Lakarnia (Hennasog) – Hennasog received some Elven explorers from Huldion at his court, and they told him of the fantastic flora and fauna of the Eldritch Isles (also known as Lakarnia), for they had heard tales of such things when they were in Pollona, the region of Byram to the north of the Elder Forest. As Hennasog was a devotee of Hanidosha, the Forest Queen, and had something of an obsession with ornithology, he ordered a select group of Questmongers to sail to the Eldritch Isles and find the most extraordinary birds they could, so they could bring them back to his court.

The Questmongers assigned to this task first sailed north to Pollona, then hired some guides with the funds Hennasog had given them. With these guides, they sailed through the dangerous straits lying between Byram and the Bushbelt and eventually came to the island of Zinthros in the Eldritch Isles. They spent three years there, inquiring of the natives about local birds and then seeking them out in the wild.

From conversations with inhabitants of Zinthros, they learned that many of the birds in the Eldritch Isles were especially active at particular times of day. Since they knew that Hennasog had a special fascination with the Manus-Romelliad Calendar, which had been recently introduced to him, one of their guides, an Elf named Ardisco Ramenca, helped them select fourteen species of birds that were active at each of the fourteen times of day specified in the Manus-Romelliad Calendar.

Once they had captured or purchased several pairs of each of these birds and learned how to properly care for them, they brought them back to Hennasog. Beyond elated with the Questmongers' success, he dedicated a room in Strongbranch Citadel as an aviary for the breeding of these exotic birds.

The Reigen Scandal (Semmoquaw) – During the reign of Semmoquaw, Argonis was heavily involved in political squabbles with kingdoms surrounding the Indurian Deeps, the sea lying between Byram and Quarana. This was because Semmoquaw had signed a trade treaty known as the Pendellion Pact with the Goblins of Morga, a large island offshore from northwest Quarana. Many kingdoms had poor relations with Morga at the time and were displeased about the matter but not enough to retaliate against Argonis for being on friendly terms with Morga. However, the Dwarves of the kingdom of Reigen in southwest Quarana were furious about the situation, since they were trying to best the Goblins in trade agreements with merchants from Huldion, and Argonis' treaty was tampering with that. However, Reigen had already made several treaties of its own with Argonis and couldn't openly attack any ships bearing goods from there without severe repercussions from the Indurian Rimlands Port Authorities, the organization that had mediated these treaties. Thus, the Tharlog of Reigen (Tharlog is a Dwarven term for 'ruler'), whose name was Eratuk Dengrinet Urmgessen – or simply Urmgessen – hired some mercenaries to intercept Morga-bound ships from Argonis and steal all their goods, so as to dissuade them from further ventures of that sort.

Semmoquaw heard reports of these mercenary attacks and suspected Reigen's involvement, but he needed proof of it in order to bring censure on Reigen from the Indurian Rimlands Port Authorities. Thus, he sent the Questmongers to sail to Reigen in disguise and see if they could find links between the mercenaries and Urmgessen. In what is considered to be the greatest Questmongers' adventure abroad to date, the Questmongers managed to sneak into the Tharlog's summer estate in the port of Gessel, a place known as Mindestallen. There they discovered and made off with some documents signed by his own hand that contained information about Argonis' shipping schedules and instructions for subsequent attacks by the mercenaries.

The Questmongers brought these documents to the Indurian Rimlands Port Authorities' headquarters, which were in the kingdom of Waldonia at the time (the territory that formerly belonged to Waldonia today straddles both the Dwarven kingdom of Reigen and the Trollish kingdom of Karna). With these papers serving as primary evidence, Reigen's misdeeds were exposed, and the kingdom had severe sanctions placed upon it by the Indurian Rimlands Port Authorities. This act, of course, had devastating effects on Reigen's trade with merchants from Huldion. However, Argonis was now able to carry out trade with Morga unhindered.

The Lost Treasure of Lannendau (Margwalu) – Margwalu had borrowed a fair sum of money from the Indurian Rimlands Port Authorities, an organization that mediated trade and various treaties in the lands near the Indurian Deeps, the ocean between Byram and Quarana. He had used this money primarily to fund renovations in Strongbranch Citadel and Anganor. However, much to his dismay, the Indurian Rimlands Port Authorities demanded that they be paid back sooner than was originally agreed. Margwalu had heard stories from a Dwarven bard, whom he had recently entertained, of a Dwarven treasure from the late Apex of Archaea that was supposed to have been hidden somewhere in the kingdom of Lannendau, which lay some distance to the south of Argonis. Thus, Margwalu called upon the Questmongers to see if they could go find this treasure so that he might use it to pay his debt.

The Questmongers traveled to Lannendau and gathered all the information about this treasure they could find. From their research, they pieced together what they thought had happened. A Dwarven colony had erected some structures in Lannendau but was attacked by local Gnomes. The colonists hid their treasure, since they were fleeing in haste, but they assumed they would be able to return someday and retrieve it. However, it seems they never had.

Through further investigations, the Questmongers linked the treasure to an abandoned watchtower in the marshes of Lannendau, which they subsequently visited. After excavating at this watchtower, they located a number of secret chambers beneath it where a large amount of treasure was stored. They sent word to Margwalu, and he dispatched porters to help the Questmongers bring the treasure back to Argonis. Margwalu then had enough to pay back the Indurian Rimlands Port Authorities and a fair amount besides, most of which he stored in vaults beneath Strongbranch Citadel.

The Midnight Marauder of Seruga (Tengwaru) – The Ogres living in the Pastures of Seruga noticed that some of the animals from their herds were disappearing. Upon more detailed investigation, they realized the animals were vanishing during the nighttime. Attempts to set more comprehensive watches were of no avail in exposing the culprit, so they brought the matter to Tengwaru. He consulted the Questmongers and asked them to see if they could discover who or what was taking the animals.

The Questmongers stayed among the herds for a full week, day and night, but were unable to apprehend the thief. However, after questioning the Ogres, they learned that the area where they were grazing their herds was one that they had not used before. Also, they noticed many large, flat stones in the area, and upon lifting a particular one, they found that it led to a burrow. However, they thought it unwise to enter it, since a foul creature or persons might be lurking in it. They deemed it better to fight whatever it was above ground rather than in its (or their) own territory, for they now suspected that the animals were not being dragged off, but were actually being taken into a den or burrow in the midst of the herd.

After making this discovery, the Questmongers told the Ogres to purposely keep their animals in the same area. A few of the Questmongers stayed on the outside of the herds, while the rest of them stayed among the animals. In the middle of the night, the Questmongers noticed a peculiar odor and also saw that the animals in the center of the herd seemed to be entering a trance of sorts. Suddenly, the stone they had investigated earlier lifted up and a large, sleek, black and furry creature exited the burrow. The creature had vicious claws and used them to cut open the belly of one of the Ogre's animals, which did not cry out, due to the odor that was effectively tranquilizing it. The Questmongers, while holding their noses with one hand in order to keep their senses from being dulled, fought and killed the creature that had just emerged from the tunnel.

They examined the creature's body thoroughly and, after conducting some research, surmised that it was a tyengachuc that had roamed far from its original habitat. The tyengachuc was an animal that Ingan tribes deep in the Stony Wilds told stories of, although sightings of it were extremely rare, so clear characteristics of it were difficult to come by. Nonetheless, the descriptions that did exist in these legends matched the specimen the Questmongers had slain reasonably well.

Thanks to the Questmongers' killing of the tyengachuc, the Ogres' animals ceased disappearing, and the incident forged stronger relations between the Ogres and the Konaskwa.

3 – Positions and Placement in the Questmongers

In this section, there is a list with descriptions of the four positions within the Questmongers, as well as an explanation of how individuals are placed in those positions after being admitted to the organization.

Following are the four positions (though it must be clarified that none of these positions bore their current names when they were first introduced), arranged in the order in which they appeared in the historical activities of the Questmongers:

1) Questkeeper – There is only one Questkeeper, and he is the leader of the Questmongers, the direct liaison with the Konaskwa and the chief organizer of all Questmongers activity. He is appointed to his position by the Konaskwa. However, one must always fulfill another role in the Questmongers before being appointed as a Questkeeper in order to establish rapport and familiarity with the organization and its workings.

2) Questseeker – Questseekers are primarily gatherers of information. Early on, they mostly collected lore, but later, their activity encompassed much more than that. Nowadays, Questseekers must be masters of espionage and disguise and are regularly assigned to infiltrate either places or organizations that are difficult to access. Oftentimes, they are stationed throughout the kingdom to procure the intelligence that Questmasons subsequently analyze.

3) Questmason – Questmasons analyze intelligence that has been gathered by Questseekers and then orchestrate plans, usually of an extremely complex nature, to deal with various problematic situations. It is necessary for the Questmasons to confer regularly with the Questseekers so that they are apprised of as much information as possible, which will ultimately assist them in coming up with more effective plans. They are also in frequent contact with the Questkeeper, so he can implement the plans they have created, oftentimes adding touches of his own. Due to the Questmasons' organizational and analytic abilities, they often act as direct assistants to the Questkeeper, sometimes fulfilling administrative roles.

4) Questguard – Questguards are highly skilled fighters and frequently have some training in acrobatics and hand-to-hand combat. They are expected to be proficient in as many weapons as possible but are encouraged to hone their skills to a greater degree with whichever weapon(s) they are the most comfortable. Since the Questguards possess a substantial level of athletic ability and can thus generally run faster than other Questmongers, they often have a secondary function as messengers or scouts.

If a Barada wishes to join the Questmongers, he must go to the Questmongers' Den (also referred to simply as the Den) and apply (only males are allowed to do so), although he will not be admitted into the Den at that time. Rather, a Questmonger will meet with him in a room set aside for interviews on the third floor of the Gnarly Stump Tavern. The Questmonger will take down his information and then set up an appointment for his abilities to be assessed at a site in Taskula North, an area north of Strongbranch Citadel. As soon as this process is initiated, the Barada is referred to as an Okwesna, which means 'inquirer.'

Since Questmongers are expected to have at least some ability in each of the three positions of Questseeker, Questmason and Questguard, the candidate will be given tests for each of these roles. Generally, candidates score much higher in one role than the other two, although there are exceptions, as in the case of extremely gifted individuals who excel in all three. If a particular candidate's performance is deemed to be high enough overall and in each area, he will be considered for the role corresponding to the trial in which he scored the highest.

However, before the candidate is admitted to the Questmongers, he must meet with the current Questkeeper for an interview, which is held in Taskula North. The Questkeeper is aided in this process by a panel of Questseekers, since they are the most skilled at detecting any character deficiencies or deceptions. If the candidate passes muster, he is then put on a period of probation for three months, in which he is referred to as a Kantokwe, a word meaning 'applicant.' The Questmongers make thorough inquiries into his past and current activities during this time.

If all is clear and no questionable elements are revealed, then the candidate has a final interview with the Konaskwa himself at Strongbranch Citadel. Afterward, the Konaskwa and the Questkeeper confer about the candidate, and if they are in agreement that he should be accepted, he is permitted to move into the dormitories at the Den where he will begin more extensive training in all areas, but particularly in tasks related to the position to which he has been assigned. At this time, he receives the title of Questling.

For a period of time (it varies from Barada to Barada, although it is usually on the order of several months), he is not permitted to actually participate in any quests. However, when he demonstrates sufficient competency and prowess in his position and has acquired some familiarity with the Questmongers, he is allowed to join quests and receives the rank of a full Questmonger, which is officially bestowed by the Konaskwa in a ceremony at Strongbranch Citadel.

However, it should be noted that Questmongers may not always reside at the Den, as they may be staying in an area to which they have been dispatched for a mission or they may maintain a residence elsewhere in the city of Anganor (which they may only visit or live at part of the time) in order to better facilitate covert activities or gathering of information.

Also, Questmongers are sometimes sent out in a group known as a Questpod to temporarily reside somewhere other than the Den. Such a group consists of one Questseeker, one Questmason and one Questguard. In any given Questpod, the Questmason functions somewhat like the Questkeeper of the group (in addition to fulfilling his role as a Questmason), while the Questseeker is the one who selects the specific location where they will be staying in order to maintain the highest level of secrecy. He also must devise many precautions and develop a protocol for the group to ensure that its activities remain covert. The Questguard is the one generally designated to bring periodic reports of the group's activity back to the Den. Questpods are dispatched as miniature extensions of the Questmongers to carry out missions of a smaller scale or ones requiring fewer agents. Sometimes, they dwell as close to the Den as within the walls of Anganor and other times as far away as in a foreign kingdom. However, Questlings are never sent out with a Questpod, since they lack the extensive experience that is required to make such an operation successful.

4 – Famous Questmongers

Following is a list, accompanied by descriptions and arranged in chronological order, of some of the most renowned Questmongers. The name of each is given, followed by three additional pieces of information in parentheses, the first being his Narthaya, the second being the Konaskwa's reign (or Konaskwas' reigns) during which he served and the third being his position in the Questmongers. (Although the four positions used in the Questmongers today were not named as such before the reign of Eskinaw, whichever of the four positions that is most closely analogous to the given roles fulfilled by respective individuals before his reign is given in their respective descriptions.) After this, a brief account is given of the cause for each Questmonger's fame. (NB: For more information about some of the quests mentioned in this section, see Section 2 above, and for a chronological list of Konaskwas who reigned during the operation of the Questmongers, see Section 7 of this appendix.)

Moskamash the Finder (Ingan; Nachoonateg and Bangurasa; Questkeeper) –
Moskamash was selected by Nachoonateg to be the leader of the very first mission of the
Questmongers, which was the Search for the Spear of the Silver Pashakway. It was he who
actually stumbled upon the cave where the spear was hidden, as he was wandering alone in
the moonlight while the others were resting at their camp in the Balgorra Hills. He served
as the leader of the Questmongers for many decades and was able to guide them to find
a fair number of artifacts, which, of course, is how he garnered his moniker, 'the Finder.'

Tehassu the Gregarious (Ingan; Bangurasa; Questseeker) – Tehassu was the chief
operator in infiltrating the Quannamet Cabal. He was known for being extremely friendly
and had extraordinary interpersonal skills, which he used to collect information in an
unassuming way. In quests after the Quannamet Cabal, he used disguises to achieve his
objectives and was the first Questmonger to do so.

Gechnawot the Architect (Ingan; Yenkasona; Questmason) – Gechnawot led the
Questmongers during the Malgennaquin Insurrection and was the chief strategist in that
endeavor. He earned his moniker based on his brilliant plans in that affair. His marvelous
planning ability was put to use in further quests as well. He was also known for always
traveling about with a pet meeka (a little creature that looks rather like a mushroom)
named Yanakuk.

Mankasec of the Mighty Arm (Ingan; Kechkuna and Eskinaw; Questguard) –
Mankasec actually lost one of his arms in a battle before joining the Questmongers, but
he was such an amazing fighter that he was actually appointed to be a Questguard. It was
said that he fought better than a Barada with four arms, and he was a master of all kinds
of weapons, although his favorite was his spear, Kettichoc. Mankasec was the one who
actually dealt the final blow to the Terror of Lake Seggatuc. He is widely deemed to be the
greatest Questguard of all time.

Karongwa the Drunken Denna (Ingan; Pattaruc and Ornaquesta; Questguard) –
Karongwa was a denna by profession. ('Denna' is a technical term in Asla'gu for a fighter,
but the word encompasses an entire way of living, not just one's vocation.) However, he
was said to have fought most magnificently whenever he had had a fair amount of tapusa.
He proved to be one of the Questmongers' most valuable assets during their journey to the
Haunted Thickets in the Race for the Brittle Bark Antidote.

Okanate the Earless – (Ingan; Lammaquot; Questmason) – Although Okanate did
actually have ears, he was deaf, and that was how he received his moniker. In fact, he was
the only deaf Barada to have ever served as a Questmonger. He was exceedingly observant,
having honed his other senses to make up for his lack of hearing, and had a powerfully
analytic mind. Consequently, he was often selected to engineer the Questmongers' most
complicated plans. Generally, he communicated his ideas to the other Questmongers by
writing or drawing them on bark or by using a system of hand signs that he taught to some
of them. Renowned for thinking unconventionally, he often came up with very surprising,
even outlandish, solutions to problems the Questmongers were facing, and often his most

outlandish plans were the most effective ones. For this reason, he is considered to be the greatest Questmason of all time.

Driggo the Astute (Wood-Gnome; Hennasog; Questseeker) – Driggo was the very first non-Ingan Questmonger, and he was part of the group selected to go to the Eldritch Isles on the quest of the Timekeepers of Lakarnia. This was partially because there were some Gnomish populations in the Eldritch Isles, and Hennasog thought the natives might take to the Questmongers more kindly if there were a Gnome among their ranks. While in Lakarnia, Driggo proved extremely useful, since he was a master conversationalist and was able to extract more information from the natives than were any other members of his party. These abilities also served him well in quests in Argonis.

Kendaroc the White (Ingan; Passenot and Tennawashu; Questkeeper) – Kendaroc was an albino Ingan, the only albino of any Narthaya to ever serve in the Questmongers as a matter of fact, and he was promoted to the position of Questkeeper during the period when Trolls from western Quarana were attacking the seaboard of the Elder Forest. He organized numerous raids on the ravaging Trolls, and many attribute the Trolls' subsequent cessation of attacks on the Elder Forest to the great success of Kendaroc's maneuvers. Kendaroc also led the Questmongers on a number of expeditions inland during the reign of Tennawashu, where they sought out cultural treasures, both material and immaterial, to bring back to his court. In addition to all this, he found much favor with the Konaskwas he served and was greatly loved by all those under his leadership.

Sando the Strategist (Wood-Gnome; Semmoquaw; Questkeeper) – Sando was the first non-Ingan Questkeeper (leader of the Questmongers). Semmoquaw had actually chosen him for the position because he showed rare talent in many regards and had served as a Questmason, a Questguard and a Questseeker before being promoted to the office of Questkeeper. He performed extremely well in all these roles and is widely considered to be the single greatest Questmonger of all time due to his versatility, although he is not necessarily regarded as the greatest Questkeeper. Also, Sando was the one who actually organized the mission to Gessel during the Reigen Scandal, which is how he earned his nickname, 'The Strategist.'

Pallorinoth and Falledrinon the Bamboozlers (Timber-Elves; Semmoquaw, Menniget and Karmatu; Questmasons) – Pallorinoth and Falledrinon were identical twin brothers, and they used this to their advantage early on when they served as Questseekers, since it allowed them to use their physical indistinguishability to bamboozle the Barada they were spying on. However, their greatest fame came from their subsequent roles as Questmasons. During much of the reign of Menniget, they served in this capacity, and it was they who designed the plan to catch the otterloo poachers that were troubling the Emerald Run during the reign of Karmatu.

Amargeen the Tall (Leprechaun; Margwalu; Questseeker) – Amargeen, whose full name was Amargeen McCrasnick, was exceedingly tall for a Leprechaun (hence, his moniker). He was extraordinarily perceptive and highly adept at questioning and getting information out of Barada without them being aware that he was doing it. In fact, it was he who learned the location of the Lost Treasure of Lannendau. Also, Amargeen was a master of disguise and proved amazingly effective during a number of missions while employing false personas. He is thus widely regarded as the greatest Questseeker of all time.

Nart the Thrasher (Ogre; Tengwaru; Questguard) – Nart was one of the few Ogres to have ever joined the Questmongers to date. He was exceptionally strong and quite pugnacious and was a pivotal member in many quests involving a need for physical confrontation, especially when the odds were numerically against the Questmongers. However, his greatest renown came from delivering the death blow to the Midnight Marauder of Seruga.

Shennakam the Whirlwind (Ingan; Tengwaru and Assartanu; Questguard) – Shennakam was renowned for using a spinescourge (a thorny vine whip) amazingly well, which is how he received his nickname, 'the Whirlwind.' Often, he would rush to the forefront of battles, exercising his brilliant maneuvers and slaying many a foe. He is regarded as the greatest Questguard of the Latter Epoch. However, due to a battle injury, he retired from the Questmongers and currently lives in the Ikona, where he runs a bakery called the Oldster's Oven, for he is now somewhat aged. Due to his prior associations, he always grants discounts on his wares to former and current Questmongers.

5 – Rooms in the Questmongers' Den

The following is a list, accompanied by brief descriptions, of the most important rooms/ areas in the Questmongers' Den, which is housed in a nawakona, a stump building in the Taskula, a district of Anganor. That particular nawakona is known as Weggimnawa, which means 'gnarly stump.' This is whence came the name 'the Gnarly Stump Tavern,' which is the establishment directly below the Den. The front door of the Questmongers' Den is actually on the second floor of Weggimnawa and is accessed by passing through the Gnarly Stump Tavern proper and going up a set of stairs to the second-floor hallway; the door to the Den stands in that hallway.

The Quest Hall – The Quest Hall is the main entry hall of the Questmonger's Den and is always guarded by at least two Questmongers. It is on the second floor of Weggimnawa. Although the room has several functions, it primarily serves as the Questmongers' lounge area, so it is filled with couches and chairs and has a large fireplace, as well as east-facing windows overlooking the Taskula. The Quest Hall also contains a number of important artifacts, including the log of the Questmongers' adventures under the current Questkeeper, which is kept on a table against the north wall. The only way out of the Quest Hall besides the main door (which leads to the second-floor hallway of the Gnarly Stump Tavern) is a door into a hallway known as the Lower Spoke.

The Lower Spoke – The Lower Spoke is a hallway on the second floor of Weggimnawa that runs from its edge to its center. It is entered from the Quest Hall and has a staircase that runs up to the Parley Attic, from which the majority of the Questmongers' Den can be accessed. A secret door in the side of the Lower Spoke leads down to Parunga's Postern.

The Parley Attic – The Parley Attic is a large room at the center of the third floor of Weggimnawa. It is commonly used for debriefing of the Questmongers by the Questkeeper before they embark on a mission and is also used for many group discussions and planning sessions. The Parley Attic is at the top of the staircase leading up from the Lower Spoke, and there is a ladder running up from it to the Hatchnook. Also, it has eight doors, three of which lead to the Dormitories (one to the Dormitory of the Questseekers, one to the Dormitory of the Questmasons and the third to the Dormitory of the Questguards). One of the doors out of the Parley Attic leads to the Commons Ambry, one to the Guisery, one to the Sparring Loft, one to the Okaragwan's Cell and the Alcove of the Annals and another to the Suppery and the Provender Post.

The Hatchnook – The Hatchnook is a small room on the fourth floor of Weggimnawa. It is accessed via a ladder leading up from the Parley Attic and has a spiral staircase running up to the Upper Spoke. It also has several secret compartments in its walls for the storing of artifacts and other important items. These compartments are actually big enough that Questmongers could hide in them if the Den were ever invaded.

The Upper Spoke – The Upper Spoke is a hallway running from the center of Weggimnawa to the Questkeeper's Office. It is on the fifth floor of Weggimnawa and is accessed via a spiral staircase leading up from the Hatchnook.

The Questkeeper's Office – The Questkeeper's Office is where the Questkeeper does much of his work in planning, leading and organizing the activity of the Questmongers. It is adjacent to his sleeping quarters. This room is also where confidential discussions and interviews are held. Located on the fifth floor of Weggimnawa at the east end of the Upper Spoke, it has a window looking out to the east over the Taskula. The office contains an antique writing desk imparted by Lammaquot, the Konaskwa at the close of the Bridging of the Tides, to Parunga, the Questkeeper at the time. The cause for this bestowal was Parunga's long and faithful service, which included his conception and management of the construction of Parunga's Postern, a secret tunnel used to aid the Questmongers in their missions.

Dormitory of the Questseekers – The Dormitory of the Questseekers consists of a hallway connected to a number of sleeping chambers, as well as a washroom. It is the personal quarters of the Questseekers and is on the third floor of Weggimnawa, connected to the Parley Attic via a door at the end of the dormitory hallway. Also, it contains a special storage area both for miscellany and for various articles used in espionage, such as stationary and simple costumes that are used more frequently than those found in the Guisery.

Dormitory of the Questmasons – The Dormitory of the Questmasons consists of a hallway connected to a number of sleeping chambers, as well as a washroom. It is the personal quarters of the Questmasons and is on the third floor of Weggimnawa, connected to the Parley Attic via a door at the end of the dormitory hallway. Also, it contains a special storage area both for miscellany and for maps and books that are used more frequently than those found in the Okaragwan's Cell.

Dormitory of the Questguards – The Dormitory of the Questguards consists of a hallway connected to a number of sleeping chambers, as well as a washroom. It is the personal quarters of the Questguards and is on the third floor of Weggimnawa, connected to the Parley Attic via a door at the end of the dormitory hallway. Also, it contains a special storage area both for miscellany and for weapons and armor that are used more frequently than those found in the Sparring Loft.

The Commons Ambry – The Commons Ambry is a storage area for all kinds of miscellany, including artifacts, food, clothing and anything else the Questmongers may not want cluttering up other areas. Notably, it contains three jail cells for prisoners if the Questmongers ever want to interrogate persons at the Den, and it has janitorial supplies that are used to keep the Den clean and tidy. The Commons Ambry is on the third floor of Weggimnawa and is accessed via a door from the Parley Attic.

The Guisery – The Guisery is a room containing a great many costumes and an assortment of makeup, all of which are primarily used to assist the Questseekers in donning disguises to carry out their missions (although it must be noted that all the Questmongers must employ disguises on occasions). Consequently, it is most frequented by the Questseekers, who are also wont to discuss many of their findings there around a large, round table. The Guisery is on the fourth floor of Weggimnawa and is accessed via stairs coming up from a door leading out of the Parley Attic.

The Sparring Loft – The Sparring Loft is a large hall for practicing various types of combat. A wide assortment of weaponry and armor is stored there to assist in this endeavor. The hall is on the fourth floor of Weggimnawa and is accessed via a door in the Parley Attic, beyond which lies a set of stairs leading up to the Sparring Loft. It serves as the principal gathering spot for the Questguards and contains several couches for them to rest on between their exercises.

The Okaragwan's Cell – The Okaragwan's Cell is a small library housing a number of works to aid the Questmongers in research for their quests. (Okaragwan means 'researcher' or 'avid reader' in Asla'gu.) Its materials include books, maps, pamphlets, scrolls and more. Since the Questmasons are the ones who most often utilize the resources in this library (especially when consulting plans previously employed by the Questmongers), they frequently gather there to share and refine their ideas. The Okaragwan's Cell is on the fourth floor of Weggimnawa and is reached via a staircase running up to it from a door out of the Parley Attic. At the back of the Okaragwan's Cell is an area known as the Alcove of the Annals.

The Alcove of the Annals – The Alcove of the Annals is the room where the records of the Questmongers' adventures are stored. Each Questkeeper records the adventures that occur while he is in office in a tome known as a Questlog. Usually the Questkeeper makes his initial notes on quests in the Questkeeper's Office and then transfers them to his Questlog, which rests on a table in the Quest Hall. When he is succeeded by another Questkeeper, a new Questlog is begun, and the old one is placed in the Alcove of the Annals, which is on the fourth floor of Weggimnawa. One must pass through the Okaragwan's Cell to get to the Alcove of the Annals, and the Okaragwan's Cell is reached by a set of stairs coming up from a door leading out of the Parley Attic.

The Suppery – The Suppery is both the Questmongers' dining room and kitchen and is located on the fourth floor of Weggimnawa. It has a long table, an oven and a fireplace for the preparing of food and another table, surrounded by a number of chairs, for the consuming of it. At the back of the Suppery is the Provender Post, where all the Questmongers' foodstuffs are kept, and the Suppery itself is accessed via a staircase coming up from a door leading out of the Parley Attic.

The Provender Post – The Provender Post is a pantry for the Questmongers' foodstuffs. It is on the fourth floor of Weggimnawa and is at the back of the Suppery, which is itself accessed via a staircase coming up from a door leading out of the Parley Attic.

Parunga's Postern – Parunga's Postern is a secret tunnel running from beneath Weggimnawa over to Kandican's Courtyard. It was conceived and its construction overseen by a Questkeeper named Parunga, who was operative during the reign of Lammaquot. The need for it arose because the Questmongers were conducting missions that required very high levels of secrecy, and they had to be able to come and go from the Questmongers' Den without being seen. Parunga's Postern is accessed via a ladder running down from a secret door in the side of the Lower Spoke. It runs generally east to west, and the Malinoc Cut runs off from it to the northeast and exits on the north side of Malinoc Hill. At the west end of Parunga's Postern, there is another ladder going up to a storage room off of Kandican's Courtyard. The whole length of the tunnel is lit by pachacuri, a bioluminescent moss cultivated by the Wennatoga. Also, both Parunga's Postern and the Malinoc Cut are used as running tracks by the Questmongers, especially by those who act as messengers, that they might retain high levels of both endurance and speed.

Kandican's Courtyard – Kandican's Courtyard is the structure where Parunga's Postern exits. It is a courtyard in a building called Kandican's Emporium, which is in the western area of the Taskula. When Parunga's Postern was built, there was an Ingan named Kandican who owned a business known as Kandican's Emporium. The Questmongers requested to have their secret tunnel exit in a storage room adjacent to his courtyard and offered to make him an honorary Questmonger in exchange for this favor. Kandican agreed to this deal, and since that time, every proprietor of Kandican's Emporium has been an honorary Questmonger. (The store still goes by the same name, even though Kandican himself is long gone, since there is such a substantial tradition behind the place.) The store operates as a regular business but simultaneously acts as a front for the Questmongers' secret exit.

The Malinoc Cut – The Malinoc Cut is a secret tunnel leading from Parunga's Postern to the north side of Malinoc Hill. It runs to the northeast from roughly the midway point of Parunga's Postern, diving under the Honnamec River and then skirting through some of the roots of Strongbranch Citadel before reaching the far side of Malinoc Hill, where it exits behind a root running down the hillside. The Malinoc Cut was made during the reign of Passenot so that the Questmongers (and particularly the Questkeeper) could reach Malinoc Hill and speak with the Konaskwa without having to pass through the gates leading from the Taskula to the Sentinels' Strand. In this way, they could keep their meetings with the Konaskwa more secretive.

6 – Artifacts Housed in the Questmongers' Den

Here the reader will find a list of various artifacts kept in the Questmongers' Den. They are arranged chronologically according to when they were obtained; the name of the corresponding Konaskwa during each instance of acquisition is given in parentheses after the name of each artifact. This is followed by a brief description of the item.

Spear of the Silver Pashakway (Nachoonateg) – This spear belonged to the Wennatogan warrior Quessitoc, who lived in the early Apex of Archaea. After it was acquired by the Questmongers, it was housed in Strongbranch Citadel for many centuries, but it was eventually gifted to them by Semmoquaw after their completion of the quest known as the Reigen Scandal. It is currently displayed above the fireplace mantle in the Questkeeper's Office.

Kettichoc (Kechkuna) – Kettichoc means 'Sudden Storm' in Asla'gu. This was the spear that Mankasec of the Mighty Arm used to kill the Terror of Lake Seggatuc. It is mounted above a weapons rack in the Sparring Loft, for it is considered to be the greatest artifact associated with the Questguards.

Kenjowara Pendant (Pattaruc) – After the Questmongers completed the Race for the Brittle Bark Antidote, Pattaruc awarded them a golden pendant shaped like the plant that acted as the cure for the Brittle Bark Plague. This Kenjowara Pendant hangs over the round table in the Guisery, the gathering area of the Questseekers, since they played a pivotal role in discovering the whereabouts of the kenjowara plants in the wild.

The Amber Eyes of Zinthros (Hennasog) – These are orbs acquired by the Questmongers while they were in the Eldritch Isles looking for the Timekeepers of Lakarnia. They heard the natives speaking of orbs they referred to as 'amber eyes' that were believed to have secret, magical powers. The Questmongers learned that these artifacts were distributed throughout the island of Zinthros and subsequently found several at an abandoned temple. Half of them went to Hennasog, and the other half are currently stored on some shelves in the Quest Hall.

The Reigen Papers (Semmoquaw) – During the Reigen Scandal, the Questmongers found a set of extremely important documents in the city of Gessel in Reigen, and they used these documents to expose Reigen's subversive attacks against Argonis. These papers, referred to as the Reigen Papers by the Barada of Argonis, were gifted to the

Questmongers by Semmoquaw after they served their purpose. They are now housed in a glass case in the Okaragwan's Cell, for they are considered to be the greatest artifact associated with the Questmasons.

Horn of the Tashigway Bird (Menniget) – While Menniget was Konaskwa, he grew very ill, so he sent the Questmongers to find an isle called Tashigway that was spoken of in legends of the coastal Ingans of the Elder Forest. It was reputed to contain glowing flowers called henhenna that could be used to make a healing elixir, which he thought would almost certainly cure him.

Although the Questmongers never did find this isle, while they were at sea searching for it, they were attacked by a strange, winged creature with a long, shiny horn. They fought and defeated this creature, then took its horn. They named the creature the Tashigway Bird, for they thought it to be a guardian of that sacred island. They had never heard stories of anything even resembling that creature nor has one like it ever been seen since.

When the Questmongers returned from their voyage, Menniget was in much better health, and after they told him of their adventures, he was persuaded that the Tashigway Bird had actually cast a curse upon him, causing his illness. He believed that the Questmongers' killing of the creature had set him free from the curse, so he instructed them to keep the Tashigway Bird's horn in the Questmongers' Den as a trophy of their victory. It is currently mounted above the desk in the Questkeeper's Office. This desk, incidentally, was a gift from the Konaskwa, Lammaquot, who bestowed it upon Parunga, the Questkeeper at the time, as a token of gratitude for his faithful and excellent service.

Chests from the Lost Treasure of Lannendau (Margwalu) – Since Margwalu had more than enough to pay his debts with the Lost Treasure of Lannendau, he gifted several chests of it to the Questmongers, and they have kept them in the Questmongers' Den as a trophy of their success. Occasionally, if they want to fund a special celebration of their own, they draw from these chests, but there is still plenty for many centuries to come. A few of the chests are housed in the Quest Hall, while others are stored in the Commons Ambry.

Hide of the Midnight Marauder of Seruga (Tengwaru) – After the Questmongers killed the creature that was taking the Ogres' animals from the Pastures of Seruga, they skinned it and made its hide into a rug, which now rests in front of the fireplace in the Quest Hall.

7 – Chronological List of Konaskwas During the Operation of the Questmongers

Nachoonateg – reigned BT 792 to BT 885

Bangurasa – reigned BT 885 to BT 941

Yenkasona – reigned BT 941 to BT 983

Kechkuna – reigned BT 983 to BT 1070

Eskinaw – reigned BT 1070 to BT 1170

Pattaruc – reigned BT 1170 to BT 1216

Ornaquesta – reigned BT 1216 to BT 1256

Lammaquot – reigned BT 1256 to LE 8

Hennasog – reigned LE 8 to LE 103

Passenot – reigned LE 103 to LE 138

Tennawashu – reigned LE 138 to LE 270

Semmoquaw – reigned LE 270 to LE 363

Menniget – reigned LE 363 to LE 406

Karmatu – reigned LE 406 to LE 468

Margwalu – reigned LE 468 to LE 513

Agwassu – reigned LE 513 to LE 546

Tengwaru – reigned LE 546 to LE 645

Assartanu – reigned LE 645 to present (LE 717)

APPENDIX 5

Associations of the Sacred Quinary

The Sacred Quinary are at the heart of the Taquenar, and as the Taquenar encompasses all of Wennatogan thought and life as well as the workings of the larger world, the Wennatoga associate numerous entities in Orona with the jurisdiction or symbolic repertoire of specific members of the Sacred Quinary. A few of these are given in the table provided below, but there are many more of this sort that are not listed here. For example, each member of the Sacred Quinary has a particular flower associated with him or her and a specific bird as well (e.g., the kendarill, a bird, and the sigwalu, a flower, are associated with Palquanoga).

However, it is imperative to note here that the Wennatoga distinguish between ritual and non-ritual usage of these symbols or entities. Ritual usage or association is referred to as 'tawenka,' and non-ritual usage is called 'kenkacha.' To illustrate the difference between these two, let us suppose that a Wennatogan Ingan owns a pitcher made of gold. If the pitcher is tawenka, it has a sacred usage associated with Tagwan, the Sun Prince, since gold is regarded as his material. However, if the pitcher is kenkacha, no such association is present. Oftentimes the difference between which entities are tawenka and which are kenkacha is indicated by subtle clues to which the Wennatoga are uniquely privy.

[For concise definitions of the terms 'the Sacred Quinary,' 'the Taquenar' and 'Wennatoga,' see Appendix 1.]

ASSOCIATIONS OF THE SACRED QUINARY						
		Members of the Sacred Quinary				
		Masku	*Tagwan*	*Hanidosha*	*Yaggawat*	*Palquanoga*
Associations	*Epithet*	The River Princess	The Sun Prince	The Forest Queen	The Hill King	The Sky Lord
	Season or Time	Spring	Summer	Autumn	Winter	Timelessness
	Direction or Location	East	North	West	South	Center
	Period of Life	Childhood	Adolescence	Adulthood	Old Age	Birth, Death
	Material	Silver	Gold	Bronze	Iron	Wood
	Element	Water	Light	Animals, Plants	Stone	Energy, Barada

343

Pronunciation Guide and Index

This final appendix is included for those readers who would like to delve deeper into the lore of Orona, especially its linguistic landscape. Accordingly, it contains an alphabetical listing of all the Oronic entities, along with their proper pronunciations, which appear in the text of this book in the main story and in the appendices. Each entry is immediately followed by a page number reference, set within square brackets, which usually marks either the location of the term's first appearance in the text or the instance in which it is most clearly explained.

Due to its conciseness and suitability for accurately representing various phonemes, the IPA (International Phonetic Alphabet) system of phonetic transcription has been chosen to represent the pronunciation of persons, places, things and events used throughout this volume. Several tables of correspondence between IPA symbols and phonemes in the English language precede the listing of Oronic entities mentioned in this book. There is also a small list identifying grammatical abbreviations that are used in this appendix. Please note that items are generally listed with the singular form as the primary entry unless the plural form is more prevalent in the text, with the exception of the various Narthanna and a few miscellaneous items, which are all listed in the plural. If the plural is irregular, it will often have its own entry, as in the case of the Daigan word 'Narthanna'.

NB: Words or parts of words which are of English origin are not generally provided with IPA representation, as their pronunciation can be readily deduced without it.

NB: A few terms which may seem to be rather mundane are included in this index because they are used in this book in a technical Oronic sense.

Consonants

b – book, mob

c – hearts, vats

d – dog, mad

f – fire, laugh

g – gold, flag

h – hill, hand

j – yard, yore

k – castle, lake

l – loss, call

m – mark, ram

n – nail, barn

p – pond, tap

r – row, bar

s – soft, pass

t – tale, rat

v – vale, have

w – world, always

x – as in Scottish loch or German Bach

z – maze, trays,

θ – throw, bath

ð – although, father

ṭ – better, little

ʃ – shore, ash

ŋ – ring, anger

t͡ʃ – chimney, latch

d͡ʒ – jar, age

ʒ – treasure, barrage

ʔ – glottal stop as in uh(ʔ)oh

Vowels

ɑː – father, cot

ɛ – let, head

iː – feed, leaf

oʊ – show, mole

uː – rude, too

æ – sat, shack

ə – agree, suppose

ɪ – lid, pin

ɔː – fall, law

ʊ – should, good

ʌ – duck, sun

aɪ – hive, pile

eɪ – pay, race

aʊ – now, loud

ɔɪ – toy, coin

ᵊ – mutton, sudden

Vowels Followed by 'R' Sounds

ɑr – far, carpet

ɛər – bear, where

ɪər – fear, cheer

ɔər – bore, oar

ɝ – burn, work

' – This symbol precedes the syllable which is most strongly stressed. (e.g., delectable: dɪ'lɛktəbəl)

Abbreviations

Sing. – singular

Pl. – plural

Adj. – adjective

Masc. – masculine

Fem. – feminine

Disamb. – disambiguation

Acrynon [39] – 'ækrɪnɑːn

Action Step Fergus [106] – 'fɝɡəs

Agleri [286] – ə'glɛəriː

Agleri, Plains of [286] – ə'glɛəriː

Agwassu [133] – ə'gwɑːsuː

Ag-Wiwsut-Jubbu [320] – ɔːg 'wɪwsuːt 'd͡ʒuːbuː

Agzareeb [89] – 'ɔːgzəriːb

Akannuwet [254] – ɑː'kɑːnuːwɛt

Akantasakwe [121] – əkɑːntə'sɑːkweɪ

Akwarna [126] – ə'kwɑrnə

Akwursa [xii] – ə'kwɝsə

Alareth [297] – 'ælərɛθ

Alcove of the Annals, The [338]

Altar of Dust, The [193]

Amargeen McCrasnick [335] – 'æmɝgiːn mək'kræsnɪk

Amargeen the Tall [335] – 'æmɝgiːn

Amber Eyes of Zinthros [340] – 'zɪnθroʊs

Amethyst Angujap, The [304] – 'æŋgud͡ʒæp

Amulet of the Akwarna [126] – ə'kwɑrnə

Ancestral Ward, The [310]

Anganor [286] – 'æŋgənɔr

Annuchoku [315] – ænuː't͡ʃoʊkuː

Apex of Archaea, The [296] – ɑr'keɪə

Aradath (adj. Aradathian) [286] – 'ɛərədɑːθ (ɛərə'dɑːθiːən)

Aradathian (disamb., Barada) [286] – ɛərə'dɑːθiːən

Aradis Kingblade [xi] – 'ɛərədɪs

Aragest [286] – 'ɛərəgɛst

Archaea [296] – ɑr'keɪə

Arctelius [274] – ɑrk'tɛliːəs

Ardisco Ramenca [329] – ɑr'diːskoʊ rə'mɛŋkə

Ar-ghan-is [203] – ɑr'gɑːniːs

Argonis [286] – ɑr'gɑːnɪs

Arkanian Mountains [293] – ɑr'keɪniːən

Ashaska [286] – ə'ʃɑːskə

Ashworthy [101]

Askaleeka Soup [66] – æskə'liːkə

Asla'gu (adj. Asla'gu) [286] – ɑːs'lɔːʔguː

Asquamot [286] – 'æskwəmɑːt

Assartanu [204] – æsɑr'tɑːnuː

Autumn Pavilion, The [118]

Avenue of the Konaskwas [7] – koʊ'næskwəz

Ayonashka [52] – ɑːjoʊ'nɑːʃkə

Azlangorash [42] – ɑːz'lɑːŋgɔərɑːʃ

Bajjarun [303] – 'bɑːd͡ʒərʊn

Balgorra Hills [288] – bɔːl'gɔərə

Banaka Gate [63] – bə'nɑːkə

Banaka, The [313] – bə'nɑːkə

Bandugong, Wullunga [303] – wuː'luːŋgə 'bænduÉ¡ɑːŋ

Bangurasa [324] – bɑːŋguː'rɑːsə

Bannacheg [264] – 'bænət͡ʃeg

Bannagum [73] 'bænəgʌm

Bannymagracket [286] –
'bæniːməgrækᵊt

Barada (pl. Barada; adj. Baradic) [286] –
bəˈrɑːdə (bəˈrɑːdɪk)

Barolla (pl. Barolli) [286] – bəˈroʊlə
(bəˈroʊliː)

Bellin [297] – 'bɛlɪn

Benga (pl. Bengwa) [314] – 'bɛŋgə
('bɛŋgwə)

Bennio Lorenzari [305] – 'bɛniːoʊ
lɔərɛnˈcɑriː

Berker Massadar Bodvassar [xv] –
'bɝkɚ 'mæsədɑr 'boʊdvɑːsᵊr

Bernalla Elmensill [23] – bɝˈnɔːlə
'ɛlmᵊnsɪl

Bezgaron [89] – 'bɛzgərɑːn

Billowtwig [46]

Bippledrops [286] – 'bɪpᵊldrɑːps

Blackbough Woods [286]

Blackwings (sing. Blackwing; adj.
Blackwing) [286]

Blue Moon, The [190]

Blunderbob [287] – 'blʌndɚbɑːb

Bodvassar, Berker Massadar [xv] –
'bɝkɚ 'mæsədɑr 'boʊdvɑːsᵊr

Boffin [96] – 'bɑːfɪn

Boss [xiv]

Bratbangles [287] – 'brætbæŋgᵊlz

Breena NicOrrikin [46] – 'briːnə
nɪkˈɔərɪkɪn

Briar Gate, The [xiii]

Bricklebick [91] – 'brɪkᵊlbɪk

Bridging of the Tides, The [296]

Brightbeam [287]

Brightbole [22]

Bright Marda [5] – 'mɑrdə

Brines of Ferassi [39] – fɛˈrɑːsiː

Brittle Bark Plague [328]

Brooding Marshlands, The [193]

Bungarung [304] – 'bʌŋgərʌŋ

Bushbelt, The [287]

Byram [287] – 'baɪrəm

Callamor Pendellion [302] – 'kæləmɔər
pɛnˈdɛliːɑːn

Call of Marda [299] – 'mɑrdə

Cape Loresso (disamb., geographical
feature) [290] – lɔərˈɛsoʊ

Cape Loresso (disamb., region) [290] –
lɔərˈɛsoʊ

Capering Kendarill, The [309] –
'kɛndərɪl

Captain Felding Starwash [xii] – 'fɛldɪŋ

Captain Fragezi [xii] – frəˈgɛzi

Captain Tandarron [xiii] – tænˈdarən

Caskman's Ward, The [316] –
'kæskmənz

Central Market Ward, The [312]

Chalguna (pl. Chalgunas) [61] –
tʃɔːlˈguːnə (tʃɔːlˈguːnəz)

Chanuta (pl. Chanutwa) [314] – tʃəˈnuːtə
(tʃəˈnuːtwə)

Charka [xiv] – 'tʃɑrkə

Chasakara [224] – 'tʃɑːsəkarə

Chasm of Erynos, The [293] – 'ɛərɪnɑːs

Chelashu [185] – tʃɛˈlɑːʃuː

Chenagwan [314] – tʃɛˈnægwɑːn

Chennaselga [149] – tʃɛnəˈsɛlgə

Chests from the Lost Treasure of
Lannendau [341] – 'lænᵊndaʊ

Enkipag's Corner [313] – 'ɛŋkɪpæɡz

Ennadug [320] – 'ɛnədʌɡ

Ennadug's Span [320] – 'ɛnədʌɡz

Eoreth [288] – 'eɪərɛθ

Eoreth's Lament [299] – 'eɪərɛθs

Eoreth's Tale [299] – 'eɪərɛθs

Eratuk Dengrinet Urmgessen [329] – 'ɛərətʌk 'dɛŋɡrɪnɛt 'ɝmɡɛsᵊn

Erdion [288] – 'ɛərdiːɑːn

Erynos Divide, The [293] – 'ɛərɪnɑːs

Eskagwan [311] – ɛs'kæɡwɑːn

Eskagwan-Naskanu Gate [74] – ɛs'kæɡwɑːn nɑːs'kɑːnuː

Eskagwan, The [311] – ɛs'kæɡwɑːn

Eskinaw [325] – 'ɛskɪnɔː

Estereth [289] – 'ɛstərɛθ

Fallbury [xiii] – 'fɔːlbɝiː

Falledrinon the Bamboozler [335] – fæ'lɛdrɪnɑːn

Fall-Elves [xiii]

Fall of Yaruzadar [296] – jə'ruːzədar

Farga (sing. Farga; adj. Fargese) [288] – 'fɑrɡə (far'ɡiːz)

Farren, The [288] – 'farᵊn

Felding Starwash, Captain [xii] – 'fɛldɪŋ

Feldryn [288] – 'fɛldrɪn

Fell Alliance, The [288]

Felling of the Sacred Sampanogwa, The [62] – sæmpə'noʊɡwə

Fenrost [288] – 'fɛnrɑːst

Ferassi, Brines of [39] – fɛ'rɑːsiː

Ferenos [297] – 'feərɛnɑːs

Fergus O'Brannadon [26] – 'fɝɡəs oʊ 'brænədən

Fergus the Fearless [26] – see 'Fergus O'Brannadon'

Field-Gnomes [39]

Fiery Fortress, The [193]

Five Fabled Lands, The [288]

Fivefold Vision, The [193]

Flowering Mound, The [193]

Fontskals, The [161] – 'fɑːntskɔːlz

Forebounder [289]

Forest Queen, The [118]

Forgotten Days, The [295]

Fragezi, Captain [xii] – frə'ɡɛzi

Galadin Greycloak [274] – 'ɡælədɪn

Galrim [297] – 'ɡɔːlrɪm

Gamdakgan [302] – 'ɡæmdɑːkɡæn

Gamundi [304] – ɡə'muːndi

Ganassa [133] – ɡə'nɑːsə

Gandahnwa [309] – ɡɑːn'dɑːhᵊnwə

Gannoget [207] – 'ɡænoʊɡɛt

Gardeners' Quarter, The [152]

Garden of Hanidosha [118] – hɑːniː'doʊʃə

Garden of Masku [118] – 'mɑːskuː

Garden of Palquanoga [118] – pɔːlkwə'noʊɡə

Garden of Tagwan [118] – 'tæɡwɑːn

Garden of Yaggawat [118] – 'jæɡəwɑːt

Garlen [203] – 'ɡarlɛn

Garlenwood [286] – 'ɡarlɛnwʊd

Garwanna [303] – ɡar'wɑːnə

Gassawot [264] – 'ɡæsəwɑːt

Gates of Iron, The [275]

Gechnawot the Architect [334] – 'ɡɛtʃnəwɑːt

Gennucha [315] – gɛˈnuːtʃə

Gessel [330] – ˈgɛsᵊl

Gharnobac, The [316] – ˈgɑrnoʊbæk

Girion Ringmark [xi] – ˈgɪərɪːən

Gnarly Stump Tavern, The [336]

Gnomeling [28] – ˈnoʊmlɪŋ

Gnomes (adj. Gnomish) [289]

Goblins (adj. Goblin) [289]

Goldquiver, Lodgemaster [xiii]

Gornok [88] – ˈgɔərnaːk

Gorondil [xii] – gəˈraːndiːl

Grandmother Shenkanet [312] – ˈʃɛŋkənɛt

Grath [295] – ˈgræθ

Great Adversity, The [128]

Greater Taskula, The [319] – tæsˈkuːlə

Greenwall, The [289]

Gren [xv] – ˈgrɛn

Greycloak, Galadin [274] – ˈgælədɪn

Gronk, Boss [xvi] – ˈgraːŋk

Groves of Silent Reverie, The [51]

Guardians' Quarter, The [116]

Guisery, The [338] – ˈgaɪzəriː

Gunnapeg [303] – ˈgʊnəpɛg

Hadarnagari [42] – hædɑrnəˈgari:

Hadathi (pl. Hadathi) [289] – həˈdaːθiː

Hadoga Taquenassa [197] – həˈdoʊgə taːkwɛˈnaːsə

Haedra, The (adj. Haedran) [289] – ˈheɪdrə (ˈheɪdrən)

Hakona (pl. Hakonas) [149] – haːˈkoʊnə (haːˈkoʊnəz)

Hakwandasha [61] – haːkwaːnˈdaːʃə

Hala-hanarwa [134] – ˈhɔːlə həˈnɑrwə

Halengasec Lane [317] – hɔːˈlɛŋgəsɛk

Hall of Cascades, The [185]

Hamarnia Pendellion [302] – həˈmɑrniːə pɛnˈdɛliːaːn

Hamtari [89] – hæmˈtɑri:

Hamtaric [88] – hæmˈtɑrɪk

Hanidosha [118] – haːniːˈdoʊʃə

Harasa [297] – həˈraːsə

Harlin Halehand [xii] – ˈhɑrlɪn ˈheɪlhænd

Harnabrig [xv] – ˈhɑrnəbrɪg

Hatchnook, The [337]

Haunted Thickets, The [328]

Hayarwassa [195] – haːjarˈwaːsə

Heggawan Tessikaw [320] – ˈhɛgəwaːn ˈtɛsɪkɔː

Henge of the Sampanogwa, The [62] – sæmpəˈnoʊgwə

Henhenna [341] – hɛnˈhɛnə

Hennasog [329] – ˈhɛnəsɔːg

Hentachog [315] – ˈhɛntətʃɔːg

Hide of the Midnight Marauder of Seruga [341] – sɛəˈruːgə

Higher Lore [129]

High Gurrajan [303] – ˈgʊrədʒæn

Hill King, The [118]

Hill of Ten Thousand Streams, The [246]

Hoarstaff [18] – ˈhɔərstæf

Hoggawesh Road [7] – ˈhɔːgəwɛʃ

Honnamec River [197] – ˈhaːnəmɛk

Honnamec Valley [197] – ˈhaːnəmɛk

Horn of the Tashigway Bird [341] – ˈtæʃɪgweɪ

Hour of Rayalta [299] – raɪˈjɔːltə

Huldion (adj. Huldionite) [289] – ˈhʊldiːɑːn (ˈhʊldiːənaɪt)

Huldionite (disamb., Barada) [289] – ˈhʊldiːənaɪt

Huldionization [289] – hʊldiːənɪˈzeɪʃən

Hundareth [96] – ˈhʌndərɛθ

Ikona, The [312] – iːˈkoʊnə

Ikona-Sagwan Gate [7] – iːˈkoʊnə ˈsægwaːn

Ildurion [297] – ɪlˈdɝiːɑːn

Indurian Deeps, The [289] – ɪnˈdɝiːən

Indurian Rimlands Port Authorities, The [329] – ɪnˈdɝiːən

Ingans (sing. Ingan; adj. Ingan) [289] – ˈɪŋᵊnz (ˈɪŋᵊn)

Innaket [312] – ˈɪnəkɛt

Innaket-Awaktu [313] – ˈɪnəkɛt əˈwaːktuː

Innaket-Shapers [313] – ˈɪnəkɛt

Iron Highway, The [327]

Iswa Hanahoma [51] – ˈiːswə haːnəˈhoʊmə

Iyontarka [88] – ɪjoʊnˈtarkə

Janura [126] – d͡ʒəˈnɝə

Jassa (pl. Jassa) [289] – ˈd͡ʒæsə

Jassuna [289] – d͡ʒəˈsuːnə

Jecko [102] – ˈd͡ʒɛkoʊ

Jewelcakes [290]

Jibkanagga Fever [304] – ˈd͡ʒɪbkənægə

Jiffaloo Timtale [xii] – ˈd͡ʒɪfəluː ˈtɪmteɪl

Journey of Marda [299] – ˈmardə

Jumankurra [302] – d͡ʒumənˈkʊrə

Jurdis [298] – ˈd͡ʒɝdɪs

Kachu [317] – ˈkaːt͡ʃuː

Kahonasi [310] – kaːhoʊˈnaːsiː

Kalathar [221] – ˈkæləθar

Kamonasoc [61] – kəˈmoʊnəsaːk

Kanapacha [224] – kaːnəˈpaːt͡ʃə

Kanassoka [249] – kaːnaːˈsokə

Kanassoka Iwe [249] – kaːnaːˈsokə ˈiːweɪ

Kandahoga [212] – kændəˈhoʊgə

Kandican [339] – ˈkændɪkᵊn

Kandican's Courtyard [339] – ˈkændɪkᵊnz

Kandican's Emporium [339] – ˈkændɪkᵊnz

Kandossa Chanaqua [311] – kænˈdoʊsə t͡ʃəˈnaːkwə

Kannaset Lake Byway [44] – ˈkænəsɛt

Kantarec [292] – ˈkæntərɛk

Kantasosh [235] – ˈkæntəsaːʃ

Kantokwe [332] – kænˈtoʊkweɪ

Kapaqua [168] – kəˈpaːkwə

Karmatu [342] – karˈmaːtuː

Karna [330] – ˈkarnə

Karongwa the Drunken Denna [334] – kəˈrɔːŋgwə ðə ˈdrʌŋkᵊn ˈdɛnə

Kaslannaquet [6] – kaːsˈlaːnəkwɛt

Kassimaw Forest [197] – ˈkæsɪmɔː

Kayusanot [315] – kaːˈjuːsənaːt

Kayusanot Hentachog [315] – kaːˈjuːsənaːt ˈhɛntət͡ʃɔːg

Kazamar [290] – ˈkaːzəmar

Kechkuna [324] – kɛt͡ʃˈkuːnə

Kelwyn Faircrest [58] – ˈkɛlwɪn

Kemmeraw House, The [312] – ˈkɛmɛrɔː

Kendarill [290] – ˈkɛndərɪl

Makwaru, Prince [18] – məˈkwɑruː

Malatar [133] – ˈmælətɑr

Maldis [298] – ˈmɔːldɪs

Malgennaquin Insurrection, The (disamb., event) [334] – mɔːlˈɡenəkwɪn

Malgennaquin Insurrection, The (disamb., quest) [327] – mɔːlˈɡenəkwɪn

Malgennaquin Thickets [324] – mɔːlˈɡenəkwɪn

Malinoc Cut, The [339] – ˈmælɪnɑːk

Malinoc Hill [321] – ˈmælɪnɑːk

Mallengar [304] – ˈmæleŋɡar

Mamgaburra [290] – mæmɡəˈbʊrə

Manfellow (pl. Manfellows) [290] – see 'Menfolk'

Manfilth [169]

Mankasec of the Mighty Arm [334] – ˈmæŋkəsek

Mankawotchee [312] – mæŋkəˈwɑːt͡ʃiː

Mannetoc [199] – ˈmænetɑːk

Mannewug's Weald [197] – ˈmænəwʌɡz

Manniog [207] – ˈmæniːɔːɡ

Mannish [291] – see 'Menfolk'

Manusian Empire, The [295] – məˈnuːʒən

Manusians (adj. Manusian) [273] – məˈnuːʒənz (məˈnuːʒən)

Manus-Romella, The Empire of (adj. Manus-Romelliad) [295] – ˈmɑːnuːs roʊˈmelə (ˈmɑːnuːs roʊˈmeliːæd)

Manus-Romelliad Calendar [295] – ˈmɑːnuːs roʊˈmeliːæd

Manus-Romelliad Empire [295] – ˈmɑːnuːs roʊˈmeliːæd

Marda [290] – ˈmɑrdə

Marda's Farewell [299] – ˈmɑrdəz

Marda's Feast [299] – ˈmɑrdəz

Marda's Glory [299] – ˈmɑrdəz

Marda's Passing [299] – ˈmɑrdəz

Mardelac Forest [291] – ˈmɑrdˤlæk

Margwalu [133] – marˈɡwɔːlu

Marlassi Coast, The (disamb., geographical feature) [291] – marˈlæsiː

Marlassi Coast, The (disamb., region) [291] – marˈlæsiː

Marnu Senkawa [151] – ˈmɑrnuː senˈkɑːwə

Masku [118] – ˈmɑːskuː

Massanoc Street [7] – ˈmæsənɑːk

Masterfarmer [xiv]

Masters of the Seasons, The [291]

Master Warden of the Bounds [43]

McDasher's Mirth [291] – mˤkˈdæʃɝz

Meditation Shelter, The [317]

Medrinos Pendellion [302] – ˈmedrɪnɑːs penˈdeliːɑːn

Meeka [334] – ˈmiːkə

Mellora Kingblade [157] – meˈlɔərə

Memories of Mentasqua, The [309] – menˈtæskwə

Mendalas [291] – menˈdɔːləs

Menfolk (masc. sing. Manfellow; masc. pl. Manfellows; fem. sing. Maena; fem. pl. Maenas; adj. Mannish) [291] – (ˈmeɪnə; ˈmeɪnəz; ˈmænɪʃ)

Menniget [341] – ˈmenɪɡet

Mentasqua [291] – menˈtæskwə

Meridot, The [228] – ˈmeərɪdɑːt

Meskwasha Street [7] – mesˈkwɑːʃə

Miccasaw Brakes [46] – ˈmɪkəsɔː

Middings, The [297] – ˈmɪdɪŋs

Midnight Marauder of Seruga, The (disamb., creature) [336] – sɛəˈruːgə

Midnight Marauder of Seruga, The (disamb., quest) [330] – sɛəˈruːgə

Mindestallen [330] – ˈmɪndɛstɔːlᵊn

Ministry of Correspondence [105]

Mists of Old, The [295]

Moieties of Orona, The [291] – ˈmɔɪətiːz

Mokwet [317] – ˈmoʊkwɛt

Moonhound [xii]

Moonhound Moor [xii]

Mordie [58] – ˈmɔərdiː

Morga [329] – ˈmɔərgə

Morningstem [65]

Moskamash the Finder [334] – ˈmɑːskəmæʃ

Motillids [174] – moʊˈtɪlɪdz

Munnateg [149] – ˈmʌnəteɪg

Munnig Alley [312] – ˈmʌnɪg

Munnig Alley Register, The [312] – ˈmʌnɪg

Murnia [289] – ˈmɝniːə

Murrugan [304] – ˈmʊrʊgæn

Nachaga (pl. Nachagwa) [206] – nəˈtʃɔːgə (nəˈtʃɔːgwə)

Nachagwa, The [197] – nəˈtʃɔːgwə

Nachakep Yengwe [320] – ˈnaːtʃəkɛp ˈjɛŋgwɛ

Nachoonateg the Dreamer [322] – nəˈtʃuːnətɛg

Nagello [xi] – nəˈgɛloʊ

Nagota [134] – nəˈgoʊt̪ə

Na'ikeyana [115] – nɑːʔiːkɛˈjaːnə

Nakayataswe [327] – nəkɑːjəˈtaːsweɪ

Nannaqued Tree, The [324] – ˈnænəkwɛd

Naqua Senkawa, The [291] – ˈnaːkwə sɛnˈkaːwə

Nardis [298] – ˈnardɪs

Nart the Thrasher [336] – ˈnart

Narthanna (sing. Narthaya) [291] – narˈθaːnə (narˈθaːjə)

Narthaya (pl. Narthanna) [291] – narˈθaːjə (narˈθaːnə)

Naskanu Gate [63] – nɑːsˈkaːnuː

Naskanu, The [316] – nɑːsˈkaːnuː

Naskwanoc [134] – nɑːsˈkwaːnaːk

Nawakona (pl. Nawakonwa) [310] – nɑːwaːˈkoʊnə (nɑːwaːˈkoʊnwə)

Neathmarda (pl. Neathmarda) [291] – ˈniːθmardə

Neldon Broadbuckle [73] – ˈnɛldᵊn

Nennasakwa [311] – nɛnəˈsaːkwə

Nine Lasses of Mellany Mountain, The [286] – ˈmɛləniː

Nippi-Nappa [291] – ˈnɪpiː ˈnaːpə

Noggaset [192] – ˈnɔːgəsɛt

Northern Moiety of Orona, The [291] – ˈmɔɪəti əv ɔəˈroʊnə

Ogres (adj. Ogric) [291] – (ˈoʊgrɪk)

Okanate the Earless [334] – oʊkəˈnaːteɪ

Okaragwan [338] – oʊˈkarəgwaːn

Okaragwan's Cell, The [338] – oʊˈkarəgwaːnz

Okwalu (pl. Owkalwu) [307] – oʊˈkwɔːluː (oʊˈkwɔːlwuː)

Okwesna [332] – oʊˈkwɛsnə

Oldster's Oven, The [336]

Onohalga [100] – oʊnoʊˈhɔːlgə

Ontara (pl. Ontara) [291] – oʊnˈtarə

Ornaquesta [342] – ɔərnəˈkwɛstə

Orona (adj. Oronic) [291] – ɔəˈroʊnə (ɔəˈroʊnɪk)

Orowan [134] – ˈɔəroʊwɑːn

Osachi [22] – oʊˈsaːʧiː

Osguna [310] – ɑːsˈguːnə

Otterloo [292] – ˈɑːʧɚluː

Outhedge, The [292]

Paanu Assagwa [169] – ˈpɑːnuː əˈsɔːgwə

Pachacuri [68] – ˈpaːʧəkʌriː

Pacha Tokwasi [317] – ˈpaːʧə toʊkˈwaːsiː

Padarellig [99] – pædəˈrɛlɪg

Palace of Eoreth [299] – ˈeɪərɛθ

Palaces of the Seasons, The [254]

Pallorinoth and Falledrinon the Bamboozlers [335] – pəˈlɔərɪnɑːθ ændfæˈlɛdrɪnɑːn

Pallorinoth the Bamboozler [335] – pəˈlɔərɪnɑːθ

Palquanoga [126] – pɔːlkwəˈnoʊgə

Pannanook [311] – ˈpænənʊk

Pannanook Tapusaries, The [310] – ˈpænənʊk təˈpuːsəriːz

Parley Attic, The [337]

Parunga [339] – pəˈrʌŋgə

Parunga's Postern [339] – pəˈrʌŋgəz ˈpoʊstɚn

Pashakway [322] – ˈpæʃəkweɪ

Paskasha [115] – paːsˈkaːʃə

Passagwon [263] – ˈpæsəgwaːn

Passenot [342] – ˈpæsɛnaːt

Pastures of Seruga, The [292] – sɛəˈruːgə

Pattaruc [328] – ˈpæʈərʌk

Pavilion of the Ages, The [119]

Payagwannah [311] – paːjəˈgwaːnəh

Pelarond [297] – ˈpɛləraːnd

Peleus Chula [xv] – ˈpɛliːjəs ˈʧuːlə

Pemmidac Hall [319] – ˈpɛmɪdæk

Pendellion, Callamor [302] – ˈkæləmɔər penˈdɛliːaːn

Pendellion, Hamarnia [302] – həˈmarniːə penˈdɛliːaːn

Pendellion, Medrinos [302] – ˈmɛdrɪnaːs penˈdɛliːaːn

Pendellion Pact, The [304] – penˈdɛliːaːn

Pennosqua [177] – pɛˈnaːskwə

Perinac River [292] – ˈpɛərɪnæk

Pesgawa [146] – pɛsˈgaːwə

Peskanneh [313] – pɛsˈkaːnɛ

Peskanneh's Pool [313] – pɛsˈkaːnɛz

Pessanagwa [121] – pɛsəˈnɔːgwə

Pine-Elves [287]

Plains of Agleri [286] – əˈglɛəriː

Plaza of the Eskagwan [311] – ɛsˈkægwaːn

Plaza of the Ikona [312] – iːˈkoʊnə

Plaza of the Naskanu [316] – naːsˈkaːnuː

Plaza of the Quannamet [318] – ˈkwaːnəmɛt

Plaza of the Sagwan [317] – ˈsægwaːn

Ploughman's Shanty, The [292]

Pollona (adj. Pollonan) [292] – pəˈloʊnə (pəˈloʊnən)

Rumbadinny (pl. Rumbadinnies) [37] –
ˈrʌmbədɪni: (ˈrʌmbədɪniːz)

Rylish NicOrrikin [46] – ˈraɪlɪʃ
nɪkˈɔːrɪkɪn

Sabakwani's Girdle [292] –
ˈsɑːbəkwɑːniːz

Sacred Quinary, The [118] – ˈkwaɪnəri:

Sagwan Gate [63] – ˈsægwɑːn

Sagwan, The [317] – ˈsægwɑːn

Sakwessa [149] – səˈkwɛsə

Salarna [296] – səˈlɑrnə

Salnagok [293] – ˈsælnəgɑːk

Samayanta [270] – sɑːməˈjɑːntə

Sampanog (pl. Sampanogwa) [308] –
ˈsæmpənɔːg (sæmpəˈnoʊgwə)

Sanagwa [137] – səˈnɔːgwə

Sanctuary of the Sacred Quinary, The
[118] – ˈkwaɪnəri:

Sanctuary of the Seasons, The [151]

Sandorio Lorenzari [305] –
sænˈdoʊriːoʊ lɔərɛnˈcari:

Sando the Strategist [335] – ˈsændoʊ

Sannadosh, The [128] – ˈsænədɑːʃ

Sannasok [186] – ˈsænəsɑːk

Sannekway [312] – ˈsænɛkweɪ

San'ua [315] – sænˈʔuːə

San'ua Annuchoku [315] – sænˈʔuːə
ænuˈt͡ʃoʊkuː

Saquot [264] – ˈseɪkwɑːt

Saranek [47] – ˈsɛərənɛk

Sardolia, The [293] – sɑrˈdoʊliːə

Sarganath [293] – ˈsɑrgənæθ

Sarranil [101] – ˈsɑrənɪl

Sassanog Enclave, The [199] – ˈsæsənɔːg

Sayings of the Sages, The [293]

Sayuga, The [310] – saɪˈjuːgə

Scepter of Eoreth [299] – ˈeɪərɛθ

Search for the Mystic's Kenga, The
[326] – ˈkɛŋgə

Search for the Spear of the Silver
Pashakway, The [326] – ˈpæʃəkweɪ

Seggatuc, Lake [327] – ˈsɛgətʌk

Semmoquaw [293] – ˈsɛmoʊkwɔː

Sengara [127] – sɛŋˈgɑrə

Sengwa Senkawa, The [254] – ˈsɛŋgwə
sɛnˈkɑːwə

Sennec [293] – ˈsɛnɛk

Senniquet [190] – ˈsɛnɪkwɛt

Sennuraga [323] – sɛnuːˈrɔːgə

Sentinels' Strand, The [320]

Serona [297] – sɛəˈroʊnə

Seruga, The Pastures of [292] –
sɛəˈruːgə

Shadowed Garlens, The [254] – ˈgɑrlɛnz

Shalkanu Ataqua [207] – ʃælˈkɑːnuː
əˈtɑːkwə

Shallamec [262] – ˈʃæləmɛk

Shammaquen, The Waters of [254] –
ˈʃæməkwɛn

Shamrock Lake [293]

Shenkanet [312] – ˈʃɛŋkənɛt

Shennakam the Whirlwind [336] –
ˈʃɛnəkæm

Shillelagh McDasher [xiii] – ʃɪˈleɪli:
mᵊkˈdæʃɚ

Shonnagwet (pl. Shonnagwets) [149] –
ˈʃɑːnəgwɛt (ˈʃɑːnəgwɛc)

Shonataquenna [129] – ʃoʊnətəˈkwɛnə

Shore-Elves [293]

Tapagwenna [309] – tɑːpəˈgwɛnə

Tapusa [293] – təˈpuːsə

Tapusaries (sing. Tapusary) [310] – təˈpuːsəriːz (təˈpuːsəriː)

Taquenar [294] – ˈtɑːkwɛnɑr

Taquenarium, The [223] – tɑːkwɛˈnɑriːəm

Tarnadin [273] – ˈtɑrnədɪn

Tarnadin, The [273] – ˈtɑrnədɪn

Tarwyn [xi] – ˈtɑrwɪn

Tashigway [341] – ˈtæʃɪgweɪ

Tashigway Bird, The [341] – ˈtæʃɪgweɪ

Tashkala [166] – tɑːʃˈkɔːlə

Taskula-Eskagwan Gate [65] – tæsˈkuːlə ɛsˈkægwɑːn

Taskula North [319] – tæsˈkuːlə

Taskula, The [308] – tæsˈkuːlə

Tasquenash [303] – ˈtæskwɛnæʃ

Tassaru [289] – təˈsɑru:

Tawenka [343] – tɑːˈwɛŋkə

Tawmpah [303] – ˈtɑːmpə

Tehassu the Gregarious [334] – tɛˈhɑːsuː

Telnara (pl. Telnari; adj. Telnaric) [294] – tɛlˈnɑrə (tɛlˈnɑriː; tɛlˈnɑrɪk)

Telnari (sing. Telnara; adj. Telnaric) [294] – tɛlˈnɑriː (tɛlˈnɑrə; tɛlˈnɑrɪk)

Telyon [219] – ˈtɛljɑːn

Tekkinog's Stump [318] – ˈtɛkɪnɔːgz

Tengawwa [311] – tɛŋˈgɑːwə

Tengwaru [133] – tɛŋˈgwɑruː

Tennawashu [342] – tɛnəˈwɑːʃuː

Teraska River [294] – təˈræskə

Teric Kingblade [266] – ˈtɛərɪk

Terror of Lake Seggatuc, The (disamb., creature) [334] – ˈsɛgətʌk

Terror of Lake Seggatuc, The (disamb., quest) [327] – ˈsɛgətʌk

Teskagwe [174] – tɛsˈkɔːgweɪ

Tessikaw, The [320] – ˈtɛsɪkɔː

Thalma-thernanna [287] – ˈθɔːlmə θɛərˈnɑːnə

Tharlog [329] – ˈθɑrlɔːg

Thornberry Thicket [xiii]

Thornoak, King [xi]

Tijkarot [89] – ˈtɪd͡ʒkərɑːt

Timber-Elves [10]

Timekeepers of Lakarnia, The [329] – ləˈkɑrniːə

Tokenowga [212] – toʊkɛˈnaʊgə

Tokenowga Stew [212] – toʊkɛˈnaʊgə

Toldrennon Wood [328] – ˈtoʊldrɛnᵊn

Tongapin Swath, The [28] – ˈtɑːŋgəpɪn

Tonquit (pl.) Tonquit [163] – ˈtɑːŋkwɪt (ˈtɑːŋkwɪt)

Toonbargi [303] – ˈtuːnbɑrgiː

Torfields, The [xii] – ˈtɔərfiːldz

Torrent of Tapusa, The [309] – təˈpuːsə

Torrent, The [309]

Tortrunk [66] – ˈtɔərtrʌnk

Touch of the Haedra, The [225] – ˈheɪdrə

Tower of Tangarosh [xvi] – ˈtæŋgərɑːʃ

Traveler's Table, The [71]

Treefellow (pl. Treefellows) [294] – see 'Treefolk'

Treefolk (masc. sing. Treefellow; masc. pl. Treefellows; fem. sing. Treemaena; fem. pl. Treemaenas; adj. Treeish) [294] – (ˈtriːmeɪnə; ˈtriːmeɪnəz)

Yasna-Innaket [312] – ˈjɑːsnə ˈɪnəkɛt

Yassator [304] – ˈjæsətɔər

Yawandis [298] – jəˈwɑːndɪs

Years of the Middings [297] – ˈmɪdɪŋs

Years of Yore, The [295]

Yenkasona [324] – jɛŋkəˈsoʊnə

Yenkawash [316] – ˈjɛŋkəwɑːʃ

Yennapuc [200] – ˈjɛnəpʌk

Yetis (sing. Yeti; adj. Yeti) [294]

Yongaban [302] – ˈjɑːŋgəbæn

Yonnachot, The [314] – ˈjɑːnətʃɑːt

Zinthros [329] – ˈzɪnθroʊs

Jarrett Skaddisson

Jarrett Skaddisson is a native of the Midwestern US, an accomplished musician and composer and an avid linguist, philosopher, author, researcher, mountain climber, spelunker and tea enthusiast. He lived in the Orient for several years as a child and has traveled to more than 30 countries for mission work, performance tours and good, old-fashioned adventures. His favorite pastimes are reading, writing, making music, learning languages, eating exotic foods, doing improv comedy, impressions and engaging in a wide variety of shenanigans. He lives with his wife Michelle, to whom he has been married for more than ten years, and their son, Fritz, who is an exceedingly happy, curious and energetic toddler. Jarrett can be contacted via email at jarrettskaddisson@gmail.com or through his Facebook page, facebook.com/TheKingblade Chronicles. He also has a website, thekingbladechronicles.com, which features concept art for the series, along with other material not found in the books, and you can follow him on Twitter at @AradisKingblade and on Instagram at @thekingbladechronicles.